Where Courage Began

Velma's Story

G.L. Gooding

Copyright © 2021 G. L. Gooding.

All rights reserved. No part of this book may be reproduced, stored, or transmitted by any means—whether auditory, graphic, mechanical, or electronic—without written permission of the author, except in the case of brief excerpts used in critical articles and reviews. Unauthorized reproduction of any part of this work is illegal and is punishable by law.

This is a work of fiction. All of the characters, names, incidents, organizations, and dialogue in this novel are either the products of the author's imagination or are used fictitiously.

Library of Congress Control Number: 2020921596

Paperback isbn: 978-1-7340228-4-1
Ebook isbn: 978-1-7340228-5-8

Because of the dynamic nature of the Internet, any web addresses or links contained in this book may have changed since publication and may no longer be valid. The views expressed in this work are solely those of the author and do not necessarily reflect the views of the publisher, and the publisher hereby disclaims any responsibility for them.

First Edition

10 9 8 7 6 5 4 3 2 1

TABLE OF CONTENTS

Preface 1
Prologue 3
Chapter 1: Cold Beginnings 5
Chapter 2: Five Long Miles 26
Chapter 3: Traumatic Transition 49
Chapter 4: Woodward 69
Chapter 5: Mystery Solved 86
Chapter 6: The Good Life? 103
Chapter 7: Turning Point 121
Chapter 8: A First 139
Chapter 9: Shocking Change 157
Chapter 10: Unwelcomed Advances 187
Chapter 11: Relatives and Romance 205
Chapter 12: Negotiations 232
Chapter 13: An Uneasy Alliance 249
Chapter 14: Changing Times Changing Minds .. 257
Chapter 15: Turn Again 285
Chapter 16: More Signs of Hard Times 308
Acknowledgments 329

*To the two women who inspired my writing:
My wife Sarah, who has endured and encouraged me, while giving me honest feedback, and my late mother Velma, who nurtured my creativity, taught me persistence, and instilled in me the joy of life.*

"Courage doesn't always roar. Sometimes courage is the little voice at the end of the day that says I'll try again tomorrow."
– Mary Anne Radmacher

PREFACE

This novel is loosely based on my mother, Velma Gooding's life that spanned 102 plus years. The idea to write a book on her life came many years ago when she first shared the dramatic memory of her father's death. Though very young when he died at 33 on their rural Iowa farm, she remembered the event in vivid detail, as if it had happened yesterday.

This tragic story moved me. It also helped me realize how different life was just a hundred years ago. There I sat with someone who had lived from horsepower to nuclear power, from birds in the sky to humans on the moon, the silence of no technology to the endless distractions of it today.

So, during each visit, I made it a point to probe her memory for more stories. She never let me down, for her mind remained clear and sharp until the day she died. Only now do I fully appreciate how uncommon that ability. It was a gift.

After reading *The Greatest Generation* by Tom Brokaw, it struck me how little Americans alive today really know about living a hard life. Mother's experiences, unassumingly told to me, were certainly not unique. They typified the physical and emotional hardships endured with incredible resilience, self-reliance, and grace.

Sadly, I kept her stories in my head, not on paper. If I had written them down, this book would have become a biography. Instead, I used her stories as the framework for a historical novel that explores the world surrounding her 102 years. In this way, I seek to honor my mother and the others of her time.

Mom would hate all this fuss, suggesting I'd made her sound bigger than life, a superwoman with a walker. But when someone lives as long, cares at much, gives so freely, and keeps family connected with a passion like she did, well, it's hard to avoid being called remarkable. She *was* bigger than life because of the way she lived it.

Garry Gooding
January 9, 2019

PROLOGUE

Living on a farm with chickens and cattle, Velma saw death frequently without paying much attention. Animals were regularly slaughtered while people occasionally died from accidents or illness. She could recall playing at the first funeral she attended while the adults cried.

Velma was born January 9, 1916 near a rural Iowa town far from a war yet to take an American soldier's life and before influenza began killing millions. If that nearby town could be called isolated, the farm her parents worked might as well have been on the moon.

While the war to end all wars was being fought and the global epidemic began, Velma lived her first years in blissful ignorance. By three, she was helping her mother by feeding chickens, washing dishes, and tending the garden. She actually enjoyed these chores. Other aspects of home life, however, were not so good.

Her parents' marriage alienated both families – his Catholic, hers Protestant. If not for having a contract to work family land, the two would have started off living in abject poverty. Reconciliation, though only partially achieved, was long in coming. As a result, they were shunned. So were their children. In a place and time where family was critical to survival, this branch of the family was left on their own.

The Steele's, living far from war and sickness, escaped those tragedies, but lived another. They were left to endure the hardships of rural Iowa life on their own. The life of a farmer was backbreaking, dangerous, and fickle. The lives of wives, mothers, and daughters on a farm were just as difficult and challenging.

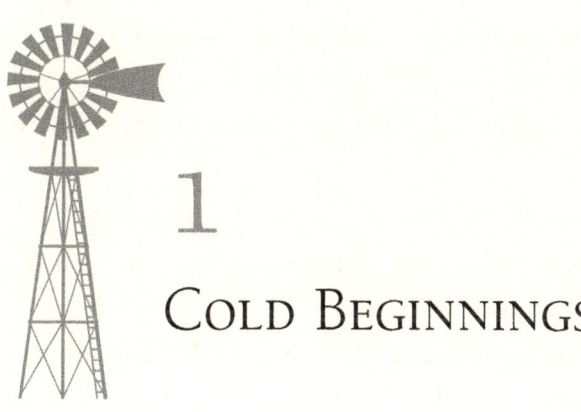

1
Cold Beginnings

Velma was always cold. She was born that way. Her chill this February night, however, did not come as the result of the blizzard raging outside that seeped through every crack in the ancient farmhouse. No, this feeling came from what she saw across the room.

An isinglass stove, the only source of heat, glowed a dull red beside her. She and her older sister, Wilma, sat in woolen nightgowns watching their toddler and infant brothers, Eugene and Edward. Before rushing out into the storm, saying something about getting help, their mother had ordered then to mind the boys, the fire, and stay inside. They had been obeying those instructions faithfully for over two hours.

From where she sat, Velma could look directly into the living room. There a single coal-oil lamp placed at the head of the couch illuminated her father's face. At first, she wondered why he was sleeping there, not watching the boys so she could go back to bed. Then she realized something was wrong. Papa must be sick.

"Why can't we go in to see Daddy?" she asked Wilma.

Wilma hissed. "Mama said to stay here."

"But he looks awful sick," Velma implored. "Shouldn't we be..."

Wilma cut her off, "No! We're supposed to stay here."

"Okay," Velma replied, just as Eugene started to whimper. She turned her attention to the two-year-old wedged between the cradle holding Edward and the wall. It took only a minute of soothing whispers to stop her brother's fussing. Soon he joined his brother in sleep again.

Going back to her chair, Velma once again glanced in the living room. She immediately saw there was something different about Papa. It took a minute before she recognized what it was.

"I think Papa's dead." Unaware, she had said this aloud, her voice cracking.

The concept of death was not new to either of the girls being raised on a farm. It was, more or less, a daily occurrence dulling their reaction while expanding their education. Neither had seen a dead person, however. Now it appeared the first would be their father.

"What?" Wilma cried out. She quickly glanced into the living room, then just as quickly looked away. "Why, why do you say that?"

"Well, Papa's not breathin' no more. See for yourself."

Wilma wouldn't look. "Don't say that. It's probably the light," Wilma suggested.

"I hope you're right," Velma said. "But shouldn't we go see?"

Wilma shook her head. "No, absolutely not. Remember Mama's orders."

"But what if Mama doesn't come back?"

"She will," Wilma said emphatically.

"Where do you think she went anyway?"

"For help, stupid." Wilma's sarcasm was lost on her little sister. "She was going for help, to get Papa help."

"Well, now it's too late." Velma's own words suddenly struck home. Her stomach tightened and her heart raced.

Wilma's sharp reply was edged with irony. "Stop looking in there. Let him be!"

Her strong voice caused Eugene to stir again. This drew the girls' attention away from all the terrible possibilities. After a few moments of restless whimpering, however, he went to sleep again.

"I want Mama. Mama needs to get back here now," Velma said insistently. Then, in the next moment, dread filled her voice. "You don't suppose she's dead too?"

"What? Oh no, no," Wilma hissed out as her body began to shake.

"But she's been gone so long."

Wilma gave her little sister a horrified look, then her face calmed just a little as she said, "Remember, she took Nelly, and that horse knows the way home."

"But look how hard it is snowing now." Velma pointed to the window, shivering at the sight. "I think she's lost or..."

"Or at the neighbor's by now," Wilma insisted.

"I hope you're right," the newly turned five-year-old replied with growing anxiety.

Wilma gave her sister a brave smile. "Of course I am. She'll be here any time."

Then the room fell silent again. Though Velma tried, she could not stop looking at her Papa and praying to see his chest heave. She turned to see if Wilma was peeking as well but found her softly crying.

Suddenly, Velma was overwhelmed with feelings previously unknown to her. When older, she would describe this jumble as a combination of fear, grief, loss, and abandonment. The result was a stream of her own tears that she could not seem to stop.

Desperate to avoid these powerful thoughts, Velma racked her brain for reminders of better times. She often did this when faced with bad or painful things. What was happening now, however, went far beyond anything she'd ever tried to escape before. Alas, the first vision that came to her was of another bitter cold day.

It was winter a year earlier. The sisters had just emerged from the warmth of Mama's church service into a wind so cold and strong it nearly tore their coats off. Velma could see herself saying hello and smiling at the people she passed who paid her no mind. Still she kept trying.

As her mother lifted her onto the wagon rather roughly, she had shouted over the wind, "Don't them people like me?"

Her mother glanced quickly over at the congregants leaving the church as she replied sternly from the corner of her mouth, "Never you mind girl. Don't be impertinent."

"Yes, Mama."

"Now git under those blankets and be quick about it."

The girls did just that, settling in the back and glad for the layers insulating them from winter's harshness. Climbing aboard, wearing only a shawl against the bitter wind, Mother snapped the reigns and guided the horse away from her family church.

The farm was not far distant, though it had seemed otherwise to Velma that frigid day. Heading up the rock-hard track to the farmhouse, her mother had stopped the wagon near the barn. She shouted for the two children to head inside, an order they didn't need any encouragement to obey.

When they were halfway to the house, the back-porch door flew open and their father emerged. He passed them wordlessly, rushing to help with the horse. Velma followed her sister at a run across what she thought, at the time, was a great distance.

Through the screen, over the porch, and into the kitchen, slamming the heavy door behind them, they headed immediately for the warmth of the isinglass stove. In the nearby cradle Eugene was trying unsuccessfully to climb out. The smell of a dirty diaper mingled with that of burnt coffee.

Their parents soon entered the house, accompanied by a gust of wind. Papa was saying, "I expected as much. I don't know why you keep goin', Mother." Velma had learned early on that when her Papa referred to Mama as "Mother," he was not happy.

"I've told you why," Mama replied with a scowl.

"Well, if they ain't shown any signs of comin' round by now, it ain't going to happen no matter how many services you attend or how much prayin' you do."

"At least, I'm tryin'," she said sharply.

"So did I for a long time," Papa countered. "I finally saw the writin' on the wall and let it go."

"Well, I haven't asked you to start tryin' again, so don't ask me to stop."

Papa moved to the kitchen table, picked up his pipe, and lit it before speaking again. "You got a point, Mother. Will you at least agree to stay home on Sundays when the weather's this bad?"

Mama laughed without humor. "This is winter in Iowa, William. The weather's always bad."

Their father did not reply, just sat down, puffing on his pipe, and picked up his paper. A moment later, he said from behind a wall of words, "Baby's dirty."

Sundays were the only time Papa was around much. Otherwise, he was in the fields, in the barn, or in the pens working as long as there was light. His moods were dictated by those of his wife or the state of the farm. On this Sunday, it looked to Velma like it would be best not to press for his attention.

Velma watched Mama change the baby, then start supper. Though their Sunday meals were meager by local standards, the little girl thought they were feasts. The clanging of pots and pans was music to her ears, and the familiar smells had quickly taken root in her memory, never to be dislodged.

While Wilma began peeling potatoes, Velma, at a little under four years of age, headed for her assignment, dish duty. She had proven to be an incredibly quick and willing learner. As a result, her mother had been slowly integrating her into kitchen chores. She was careful to limit what her littlest daughter handled, however.

Mama poured hot water from a kettle on the stove over the silverware and smaller, sturdy items like crocks, spatulas and the like. Velma pulled a chair to the sink and climbed up, looking forward to putting her hands into the warm water. Then she carefully washed and dried each item before climbing down.

While Velma was at the sink, Mama put a roast in the oven and set pots to boil for potatoes and beans. Soon the smell of dough for biscuits mingled with the aroma of roasting meat. "Can I cut out the rolls, Mama?" she asked eagerly.

"Let me check the job you did with the dishes first." A moment later, her mother turned back with a nod. "Okay but be very careful with that glass."

As she sank the glass in the dough, plopped the round disk out of the glass, and put it on the flowered tray, Papa put down the paper and went to the icebox. He pulled out a brown bottle, removed the top, and returned to his seat. Velma turned up her nose at the smell when he took a long swig. Her mother just glared.

Though no angry words were exchanged on the subject, this did nothing to improve the mood in the room. From that moment until dinner was served, there was little talk, mostly kitchen clatter and Eugene's whining. Velma tried to break the uncomfortable silence with small talk on several occasions, but neither Mama nor Papa were much interested.

The sudden rattling of a window jarred Velma back to the present. Papa still lay unmoving on the couch. Mama had not returned. Wilma was up, covering Eugene with an old quilt as the room grew colder. In silence, her sister passed by and sat again, looking prim and proper like Mama taught them. She still didn't look into the living room.

Velma could tell the storm was getting worse from how deep the cold penetrated into the room. Reflexively, she glanced at the nearly empty log-holder sitting near the back door. If Mama didn't come soon, someone would have to fetch more wood. She shivered at the thought.

This triggered the return of those strange feelings that had assaulted her earlier. Once again, tears began to trickle down her cheeks. When Wilma saw this, she could not restrain herself and started sobbing. This had Velma attempting another escape into a happier past.

This time, what emerged was the image of dawn on the first day of the last harvest season. Voices from below woke her in near darkness. Quickly out of bed and dressed, she'd crept downstairs to find the kitchen filled with young men. They sat at the giant kitchen table while being served great platters of food by her very pregnant mother. The tiny woman flitted around the room like a bee in a hive.

The smell of bacon, eggs, and coffee filled the air. Papa and the others ate voraciously while talking in hushed tones about the workday ahead. Now fully awake, Velma took a platter from her mother. She received a rare smile in return.

Shortly after the men had headed to the fields, Wilma came down dressed for school with just enough time to eat before leaving. As the older girl slammed out the back door, mother and Velma turned to face the breakfast dishes. The fact that Wilma often found a way to avoid chores like these made her sister a bit angry.

Wilma's noisy exit brought a wail from upstairs. Mama headed in that direction, waddling more than walking. On the way to the stairs, she spoke to Velma for the first time that day. "There's some toast and jam left. Get a glass of milk and eat."

"Yes, Mama."

Velma went to the icebox to find the pitcher nearly empty. Papa milked the cow in darkness every morning, so there was usually plenty to drink or churn. That day, however, the men and her sister had nearly consumed it all. Finding only a small glass left, she sat at the table and slathered two pieces of cold toast with butter. The nearly empty jam jar yielded just enough for a thin layer on each slice.

With Mama still upstairs, she finished quickly, grabbed the egg basket, and headed out to feed the chickens. Though the day would be warm, there was still a chill in the morning air. So, she made short work of spreading the feed and collecting the eggs. Back inside, she started clearing the table.

Just then, her mother returned carrying Eugene above her swollen belly. Velma couldn't know that brother Edward's arrival would coincide with the end of harvest. She could see, however, that Mama was already exhausted, and the day had just begun. Working a bit faster, Velma asked, "Is Gene better today, Mama?"

"Not sure," her mother said flatly. She took a seat at the table, unbuttoned her blouse, and started nursing the boy. "I'll be there to help ya in a minute."

After the hectic start to the day, Velma appreciated the near silence as she and her mother finished the dishes. A now-contented Eugene dozed quietly in the hand-me-down cradle all the kids had used. No sooner was the cleanup finished, however, than preparations began for feeding lunch to the same ravenous crew.

Mama efficiently put three freshly-dressed chickens in the oven and started mixing biscuit dough. Meanwhile, Velma started setting the table, then saw the basket of eggs resting on a side table. "Did you see all the eggs, Mama?"

"Yes, dear. And we'll need every one of them afor the day's done."

Velma glance at her mother expecting to see a frown but saw what could almost have been a smile. Such a look was a rarity for either of her parents. At her young age, Velma didn't understand their dourness, but had accepted that was just the way they were.

"Now, Velma, this is the first harvest you've been old enough to help with. All those men will be back too soon for my likin', but we'd be sunk without 'em."

"Yes, Mama," Velma replied, though she wasn't sure what her Mama meant.

"When they arrive, keep an eye on your brother. If he behaves, I'll expect you to help serve some like you did this mornin'."

"Yes, Mama."

"That's a good girl," her mother said, turning to the hot stove while wiping perspiration from her brow. It was going to be an unusually hot September day.

Velma soaked up what she considered to be a compliment as she continued placing flatware for twelve on the table. Next, she put the plates and glasses around carefully. A few weeks earlier, while hurrying, she had broken a plate, earning a harsh rebuke. Even at a cautious pace, however, she finished with time to spare.

Lunch went off well, and, after the men had left, mother and daughter immediately began to clean up and prepare for a supper to be served around sunset. Wilma returned from school in time to help. While setting the table, peeling potatoes, and watching Eugene, she shared what had been taught that day.

Soon, an exhausted crew straggled in silently, ate heartily, and left exhausted. Some went to their own homes. The transient hired hands headed for cots in the washhouse. It would be a short night's rest before another grueling day in the fields.

While Wilma and Velma helped their mother clean up and prepare for the next morning, Papa sat at the table sipping a cold cup of coffee. He startled his daughters when he suddenly spoke. "We made good progress today, better than last year."

"Glad to hear it." Mama's words were brighter than her exhausted tone.

Papa didn't seem to notice. Instead, he looked at Velma and, to her surprise, gave her a warm smile. "It must be because of our new little helper here, Alice."

Her mother wore no smile but agreed. "Yes, she surely pulled her load, William."

Wilma spoke up in a hurt tone. "If I didn't have school, I'd have helped more."

"Quiet, child," her mother said sharply. "Don't you have homework?"

Wilma gave Velma a venomous look as she replied, "Yes, Mama."

"Then say good night and get too it." Mama's famous hard look had the older sister on the move without another word. "Now, where were we, William?"

Velma seldom heard her parent's call each other by their Christian names. They used them during their occasional arguments or infrequent pleasant conversations like they were having that evening. Most of the time, their exchanges didn't extend beyond a few impersonal words.

"At this rate, we may finish a day early if the weather holds. The help we hired is good, not a slacker among 'um," William said proudly. "Hate to cut them a day short on wages though, but they hopefully can make it up at their next stop."

"Well, with the state of farmin' these days, I'm not sure that will be possible," Alice suggested.

Velma saw her Papa nod. "I have to say that my Pa was smart not to let me buy that other twenty acres back in '17, though at the time, I thought he was just bein' plain stupid. Everythin' we grew was going for top dollar what with the war."

"Sure can't say that no more."

"That's for sure," Papa agreed. "Half our relatives are mortgaged to the hilt right now. If prices don't improve, they'll face foreclosure."

"That's a sad fact," Alice said, then added, "but at least they don't have to pay for hired help like we do."

"That's not much of a trade-off for lost profit."

Alice snorted, "Still, we shouldn't have to be payin' anybody." Velma saw her father's brow furrow, but he said nothing. Then her mother went on in a less harsh tone. "My folks are as much to blame as yours."

"They'd all say we were the ones to blame," Papa said flatly. "But no use cryin' over spilt milk." He changed the subject. "The corn crop is looking good. I expect an increase in yield. If the market holds, we'll enjoy a comfortable winter."

"That's a big if, isn't it?" his wife retorted. "Every day for months futures have been goin' down."

"Well, they seem to have stabilized, Alice," Papa said encouragingly. "I expect with the increase in the crop, we'll clear enough to rest easy, at least for this year. I'm already considerin' changes for next year."

"Like what?"

"I'm not sure. Maybe cut down on the corn and try soybeans. That seems to be an up-and-coming cash crop."

"Well, we'll have the whole winter to consider that," Alice said as she put bread in the oven for the next day's breakfast. Turning back to William, she asked for reassurance. "So, you really think we'll have no problem meetin' the rent?"

"Nope. The folks won't be able to threaten us with eviction this year."

Though she didn't understand the word eviction, Velma knew the meaning of threaten, and it made her anxious. When she saw her mother calmly sit down saying, "Oh, that is good news," she relaxed.

William shrugged. "It is if the old coot doesn't raise the rent. After all, with the market off so much and so many of the other farmers over-planted..." He let the thought drop.

"But you have a deal," Alice said hotly.

William gave her a wary look. "That went out the window when we got married, Alice." Velma saw her mother stiffen as Papa quickly went on. "That's not your fault. I said they'd come around, but they haven't and, most likely, won't."

"Plenty of blame to go around, Will." Velma had never heard her mother call her father Will before.

"And with this here farm depression, everybody's scramblin'," Papa added.

Mama got up and circled the table, putting a hand on her husband's shoulder. "True, Will. These last three years have been hard on all farmers. I kinda lost sight of that. But, it's good to hear we'll get by. Then again, we always have."

Her husband patted her hand. "I'm sure we will even with another mouth to feed." He glanced toward her swollen belly. "It won't be long now."

"Corn may not be the last thing harvested this month," Alice said, flirting with a smile. "Another pair of hands someday to help us survive on our own."

"True," William said with a slight frown. A moment later his face brightened. "It's encouraging to see some of the cousins are reachin' out. Someday, I expect we'll have some of our families back, at least the next generation."

"I'm more doubtful of that than you these days," Alice said with a sigh.

William patted her hand again. "Well, we won't be waitin' around for that day and that's the truth. There's too much to be done." His tired face held a brief smile before he stood and stretched. "Now if we can just make it up to bed."

Then Velma's parents did something she couldn't recall seeing before. They hugged and kissed each other's cheek. As they parted, Velma saw the two briefly look at each other with a contented expression. The moment passed quickly, however.

As William headed upstairs, Alice said, "No one works harder than you."

"Except you," he said, stopping with one foot on the bottom stair. "And you carryin' another little one. I don't know how you do it."

Alice shrugged. "Because I have too. It's you I worry about though."

"What's to worry about, woman?" William said as he headed up.

Alice turned to Velma, a worried look lingering. "It's been a big day, girl, with another one to come. So, to bed with ya."

Velma didn't need to be told twice as she hurried upstairs wearing a smile.

She was flung harshly out of her mind's eye and back to the present when the kitchen door flew open. The figure that stumbled in was nearly unrecognizable.

"Mama," both girls yelled, rushing to her.

A thick layer of snow obliterated the black of their mother's coat. From under an ice-crusted scarf encasing her head, two black holes stared back at them. Ice hung from her brows and nose. Bare red hands began to fumble for buttons, then stopped as she collapsed.

The girls guided the nearly frozen figure to one of the chairs by the stove. Then while Wilma ladled a glass of water from a bucket, Velma helped unbutton her mother's coat. Unable to hold the cup of water in her shaking hands, Wilma held it to her lips.

After several sips, her first attempt at speaking failed. After more water, however she managed to say, "No help. No one would come out in this blizzard."

Suddenly, their mother tried to stand. "I, I must check on..." Her words faded as she looked into the living room, then slowly sank back down.

"Papa's dead, Mama." It was Velma who said the words. "No one could have helped."

"How long?"

Velma had no sense of time so turned to Wilma who looked like she was about to cry again. Instead, she managed to say, "Not long after you left, Mama."

Their mother's head dropped, and her body began to shake.

Assuming it was from the cold, the girls started to get her coat off again, but she pushed them away. "Leave me be." Her raspy reply surprised them.

The girls stepped back and huddled together in the growing cold in the kitchen and waited. After a short while, their mother stopped shaking and looked up. "Come help me now girls. As they hurried over, she shared, "I went to the two closest places, your Papa's brother and father."

"And they wouldn't come?" Wilma asked again incredulously. Their mother nodded.

"But didn't you tell them..."

Wilma's follow-up question was interrupted sharply. "Of course, I told them, but..." She did not finish, instead changing her tone to say, "Just as well, now. They will be here sometime after the storm is gone and..." Once again, she halted.

Alice started to peel off her scarf and coat as the snow began to melt and pool at her feet. As the three struggled, steam began to rise from the wet, stinking wool. Their mother hardly noticed, while the girls were focused on their mother.

"How are the boys?" Alice suddenly asked in a husky voice, straining to see them around her daughters. "Were they any trouble?"

Velma started to answer, but Wilma piped up first "Well, Eugene fussed and cried a bit, but *I* finally got him to sleep."

"And Edward never made a peep," Velma added. "Doesn't smell either, at least not the last time I checked."

In spite of the night's horror, Alice forced a weak smile at hearing this and relaxed a bit. "That's good." Then she gazed toward the living room, tensing.

Suddenly Wilma spoke with urgency, "Mama, I ain't, I mean haven't been to the outhouse since before you left. I'm about to burst."

"Me too," echoed Velma.

Their mother gave them both an exasperated look. "Well, I guess that's what I get for telling you two not to move. Now there's no way to get to the outhouse in this storm. You'd surely be blown away or get lost."

"Lost?" Wilma asked in confusion. "But it's only across the yard."

"Far enough away to get good and lost in this blizzard." After another moment she said, "You got chamber pots upstairs. Get to it. And bring 'em down when you're done. We'll put 'em out on the porch."

The girls raced up stairs, eager for relief. A few minutes later they were back with the covered pots in hand. Alice glanced toward the kitchen door and the two headed that way. When opened, snow blew in like an unwanted guest. The room turned ice cold in the seconds it took to complete the task.

Stepping back in faster than they had gone out, both girls began to shiver. Their mother shook her head. "You could have put on your coats first, you know." Letting the subject drop, she glanced toward the living room again. "That lamp is runnin' low. Wilma, go get it while I fetch the oil."

Wilma didn't move.

"Come on girl, get goin'."

"But, but Papa's in there and..." The older girl's voice choked off.

Alice gave her oldest a disappointed look. "He's dead, and dead people don't bite."

Velma was surprised to hear this. She remembered scary tales about ghosts and goblins she'd heard last Halloween. It gave her a moment's comfort to hear Mama say that. Then she remembered her Papa and looked in at him lying peacefully on the couch.

Wilma still didn't move, so Velma did. "I'll do it, Mama." She moved off quickly and picked up the lantern.

As she turned, the weak light illuminated her father's face. Velma thought his skin looked like chalk. Stepping away, her foot caught in something. At her feet was a blanket spread the length of the couch. It had not been there earlier. She thought her mother must have put it there while she and Wilma were upstairs.

Quickly regaining her balance without dropping the lantern, Velma returned to the kitchen to find Wilma softly crying. Whether this was due to Papa being dead or because she'd disappointed Mama was beyond Velma's comprehension. Her mother just ignored the tears.

"Thank you, child," Alice said absently while setting to the task of refilling the lamp. Once it was burning brightly again, she returned it to the living room, pausing for only a moment to stare at her late husband.

Returning to the kitchen, their mother finally noted the cold and glanced at the stove no longer glowing red. Wordlessly, she went to the wood bucket, finding it next to empty. With a sigh, she put the remnants of wood on top of the glowing embers in the stove. When the fire took hold, Alice moved to retrieve her coat.

Realizing what her mother was going to do, Velma quickly crossed to the coatrack and began putting on her overcoat, scarf, and gloves, and said, "I'll help, Mama."

"No, child," her mother said firmly.

"But I help do it all the time."

"Not in weather like this. It's too bad out there," Alice said, then, with a sigh, pulled on her soaking coat.

"Can I at least help?" Velma pleaded.

Alice relented with a compromise. "You can stand on the porch and bring in the logs when I hand them to you."

"Okay, Mama." Velma turned to Wilma. "Come on, Sis."

Moments later, they were out the kitchen door while Wilma lingered. Even with all they had on, the cold and snow that blew across the porch was shocking. Velma held the screen door open and watched her mother disappear into a white haze as soon as she reached the bottom step. The snow peppered Velma's face until her mother returned with two logs.

"Use one of these to prop this door open," she said, tossing both at Velma's feet before disappearing again.

Doing as she was told, Velma leaned the first piece against the door, then headed for the kitchen. There Wilma stood, coatless, and took the second log. It was clear to Velma that her sister regretted not wearing her coat.

By the time she got back to the porch entrance, her mother was back with two more logs. As Velma carried them one at a time to Wilma, she noticed snow was already drifting against the wall of the house. This time when the door opened, Wilma had on her coat and gloves.

Not able to keep pace with her mother, a pile of logs accumulated near the door. The next time the two arrived simultaneously, Alice instructed Velma, "Take one more, then stay inside. I'll put some more here for later and be right behind ya."

Velma was perspiring by the time the job was done. In contrast, her fingers had gone numb inside the worn gloves. Entering the kitchen, she put the log in the bin saying to Wilma, "I'm to stay inside now."

"What about Mama?" Wilma asked with concern.

"She's going to pile more logs on the porch, then be in soon."

"Thank God."

Velma collapsed in a chair as they waited and listened to their mother bring load after load of wood to the porch. Then, while her younger sister continued to rest, Wilma started to make cocoa with milk she'd been warming.

When their mother finally came inside, she fell in the chair next to Velma. Eagerly she accepted a mug of chocolate while giving Wilma an approving nod. The three then sat at the table sipping in silence. Soon the girls put their heads down on the table and began to doze off.

Edward's fussing prevented Alice from succumbing to sleep as well. She struggled to her feet and, with a deep sigh, headed to his cradle. Laboriously picking up the infant, she made a quick assessment, then quietly said, "Wilma, your brother needs changin'."

"Aw, Ma," Wilma started, but Alice's look stopped her. "Okay, Mama."

As the older sister trudged upstairs with the baby, Alice quickly glanced at Eugene who continued to sleep contentedly next to the isinglass stove. Turning to Velma, she said urgently, "We've got somethin' else to do and it needs doin' now." Then she gazed toward her dead husband.

Without further delay, she quickly pushed the kitchen chairs and then the table to the wall. Then Alice headed into the living room while explaining to Velma, "When I call for your help, I expect you to come quick like, you hear?"

"Yes, Mama."

Alice leaned down to her husband, whispered something, and kissed his cheek. Then, in quick succession she stepped behind his head, leaned over the sofa, grabbed William under the arms, and slid his stiffening body onto the waiting blanket.

Velma watched mesmerized as her Mother tossed the sides of the blanket up around her father. For a brief moment, she saw his face still looking more asleep than dead. Then he disappeared under the blanket.

Fort the first time, Velma noticed ropes hidden under the blanket. Alice fastened them around both the blanket and body and tied sturdy knots. Then Alice whispered urgently without looking up, "Come here now, child."

Velma crossed quickly to her mother's side. Alice went to the head of the blanket and grabbed the loop of rope at that end. She began pulling until the body was turned toward the kitchen. Then Alice whispered again, "Grab this rope with me and pull hard."

The body moved with surprising ease over the worn living room rug and onto the faded, non-descript linoleum of the kitchen. At the back door, they stopped to put on their overcoats, gloves, and scarfs once more. They were just moving back to the body when Wilma came into the room carrying Edward.

"Mama, what are you doing?" Wilma's shout woke both the baby and Eugene.

Alice gave her oldest an angry look. "Never you mind, missy. Just take care of those babies you just woke and leave the rest to me and your sister." With that, she opened the door, then turned back to Velma. "Grab hold and pull."

Through a momentary ease in the storm, Alice, with minimal help from Velma, struggled to place the late William Devon Steele near the woodpile. Then, the two wrestled with a tarp from atop the cords of wood to cover the body. As her mother weighted down the corners of the canvas with wood, Velma hurried inside. Her mother didn't return for a long time.

When Alice finally entered the kitchen, the boys' crying greeted her. Wilma sat on the couch where her Father had been, matching her brothers' tears. Mama ignored them. Instead, she joined an exhausted Velma who lay propped against the wall near the freshly stoked stove. Soon the two were asleep.

Velma awoke to a dull gray sky still choked with blowing snow. Alice had moved the table and chairs back in place and was stoking the isinglass stove yet again. Rubbing her eyes, Velma saw a sad look on her mother's face as she asked in a whisper, "What would you like for breakfast, child?"

2

Five Long Miles

The storm ended the next day, but no one came. Having no other choice, life on the Steele farm went on more or less as usual in the still bitter cold. Each morning, Alice waded through knee-deep snow to the barn where she spread hay in the corral among the dozen head of cattle that stood in a quagmire.

Velma, following the trail Alice had made, fed the chickens and collected eggs. Wilma stayed home from school and watched the boys. During the day, the family stayed in the kitchen, never far from the isinglass stove. At night, they dashed upstairs to bed through the cold house. Everyone avoided the living room, while only Alice went near the woodpile.

For three nights, everyone slept together in the big bedroom. Edward had the cradle, while Eugene slept on an old loveseat at the foot of the bed. The girls shared Mama and Papa's bed. Velma cried herself to sleep to the scent of her father. She cried again when she woke to see his denim overalls hanging behind the door.

Alice went through those initial days as if in a trance, only broken occasionally by fits of temper. Velma never saw her cry again. One night as the little girl drifted off, however, she felt Mama's body shake uncontrollably for a long time.

Truth be known, there was no time for grieving, at least during the day. If the boys didn't need tending, there were plenty of other chores to divert attention from their loss. What tears there might have been were converted to sweat or lost out to total exhaustion.

On the fourth day, a warm front moved through. The snow soon melted into rivulets, then small streams that turned everything into oozing mud It became even more effortful getting from the house to the barn or outhouse than in the snow. On one occasion, Alice had to extricate the girls from the quicksand like muck.

By day five, Velma was thinking they were the only people who had survived the blizzard. Then at midday, she saw a wagon drawn by two huge draft horses slogging its way along the main road. The wagon turned into the track that led to the farmhouse. As it got closer, Velma recognized some of the Steele clan.

It was Papa's father and two of his brothers. They stopped between the house and barn and climbed down. Alice never left the porch. She stood guard at the threshold, while the girls peeked out from behind her skirt.

"Where is he?" her father-in-law asked in a harsh voice that frightened Velma. Alice said nothing, just pointed toward the woodpile.

Waving the young men over, the three waded through the ooze to the canvas-covered body. Papa's father pulled back the tarp, then stood aside. Without delay or comment, the two young men each took an end of the blanket and, with some difficulty, carried it to the wagon. Once loaded, the three climbed back aboard.

"We'll let you know when the funeral mass will be, if you have any interest," her father-in-law said flatly, then urged the horses into motion.

"So kind of you, Mr. Steele!" Alice yelled in a tone dripping with venom, "Especially since it was likely that you caused William's death." None of those on the wagon looked back as the wagon made its slow retreat.

Alice and her daughters watched them disappear from the porch as a chill wind whipped around them. They sighed as one, then went back inside. After lunch, the girls were sent to the root cellar to gather vegetables for dinner, while Alice fed Eugene and nursed Edward. Nothing was said about the visit again.

The next morning, Wilma returned to school, leaving Velma alone to help her mother with all the chores. There was no more time to be a little girl playing with dolls, napping, or looking through well-worn picture books. Those early days all seemed filled with gray skies and dark sadness.

If it hadn't been for a compassionate Steele cousin, who risked being ostracized, Alice and the children would have missed Papa's funeral. As it was, the five sat alone in a back row of the parish church, shunned by nearly everyone. Their wagon brought up the rear of the precession to the graveyard.

At the cemetery, Alice cradled Edward while the girls each held Eugene's hands. They stood alone as the coffin was lowered into the nearly frozen ground. Ceremonial shovels of dirt marked the end of the service. When everyone else had gone, Alice moved to the graveside reluctantly in tow with her children.

During the silence that followed, Velma's eyes scanned the rolling countryside still dotted with snow. She saw gray clouds gathering in the west and felt a cold breeze on her face. Pulling Eugene closer, Velma looked up at her mother, who remained motionless for what seemed to her a very long time.

Finally, in a whisper, her mother said something Velma would never forget. "I don't know why God is challenging us, but we'll face whatever comes because our faith is strong."

Then, as the gravediggers went to work, Alice led them back to the wagon. By the time they reached the farm, the breeze had become a strong winter wind and smelled of snow. Velma shivered at the thought of another blizzard. Still, she knew there would always be plenty of chores to help keep her warm.

The next few weeks became a monotonous and backbreaking routine. If it was possible, Alice's demeanor grew ever harsher. As winter made its laboriously slow trek toward spring, Alice's girls watched as their mother withdraw more and more.

On the day the crocus broke through the still frosty ground, the reason for Alice's behavior came more into focus. That morning, the same wagon brought Alice's father-in-law, this time alone. He never got off the wagon. Mama told her daughters to stay on the porch and went out to meet him.

The girls watched as the man spoke and mother listened in stony silence. Within a few minutes the wagon pulled away and Alice slowly returned to the house saying nothing. She went to the stove and poured a cup of coffee. Then she sat at the table for a long time in silence. The girls took seats as well and waited.

The coffee was long gone when Alice sighed deeply, but still said nothing. Instead, she slowly stood and proceeded to change and feed Edward. Lying the sleeping infant back in his cradle, Alice finally spoke, "I need to share somethin' with ya girls." They said nothing. "We're gonna be movin' away from here soon, and..."

Wilma interrupted in a frightened voice, "Why Mama?"

"Because your father's family owns this land and is takin' it back," she replied in a matter-of-fact tone.

Wilma blurted out, "Where?"

"I don't know yet, Wilma," Alice said flatly. "We have until the end of spring to find a place, no longer."

Velma had no sense of the seasons yet, so asked, "When is that, Mama?"

"After Wilma gets out of school, another few months."

Then with a sigh, Alice gave them more bad news. "Most of this stuff will be stayin' here." No sooner was this out than Wilma began to cry. As Eugene joined in without understanding, Alice went on, "Until we have a place, we'll go on as usual. The chores won't stop simply because we're leavin'."

"How will you find another place, Mama?" Velma asked.

Her mother shrugged. "I don't know, child. But I'll start lookin' right away."

In mid-April, twenty members of the Steele clan, led by Alice's hateful father-in-law, arrived to start planting. They literally took over the property during the day, showing no respect for Alice or the children. While the crops went in, most of the livestock went out as back pay for rent. They were clearly trying to drive Alice out, and it worked.

At dawn the next day, Alice loaded the family and a basket of food into the wagon and headed out. After dropping Wilma at school, she continued on to the nearest town, Woodward, which was five miles from the farm. Velma had never been to town. Hearing this wonderful news, she suddenly recalled an earlier attempt she had made on her own.

It had been two summers earlier that Alice had left for town in the wagon to get provisions. She had refused her youngest daughter's plea to go along. Instead, Mama had ordered her to stay and help Wilma look after the then-infant Eugene, while Papa did repairs to the barn.

A short time later, when her father was distracted, Velma took off alone through the lingering cloud of dust left behind by their wagon. She ran as fast and as long as she could but couldn't catch her mother. Exhausted from the effort, Velma sat down at the edge of the road and started playing with dandelions.

Though the road had little traffic, a wagon happened by, headed back in the direction of the farm. Seeing the child, the driver stopped. He turned out to be a cousin from the Steele side of the family. After introductions, the boy asked what she was doing. She didn't understand why the young man laughed at the idea of walking to town.

The cousin told her to climb aboard and drove the quarter mile back to the farm's entrance. She got off there and scurried up the track toward the farmhouse. As the wagon moved off, Velma saw her father heading her way, looking more than a little angry. For days it hurt a bit for Velma to sit, a lesson hard-learned.

Two years later and Velma was finally heading to town, filled with excitement. Woodward was small as towns went, near Des

Moines, and still rather behind the times. Its business district was only three blocks long and two wide. When they arrived, Velma was still awestruck, especially when she saw her first automobile. It was stuck in the muddy street and being pulled out by a horse.

Alice stopped at one end of town close to the wood plank sidewalks and gingerly unloaded everyone. Then leaning down to Velma, she said sternly, "I can't afford any misbehavin' today. I'm puttin' *you* in charge of the boys. I just fed Edward, so he should be fine. Eugene won't be so easy. You understand?"

"Yes, Mama," she said anxiously.

Alice nodded. "Good. Now follow me."

Alice entered the first store, carrying Edward. Velma followed dragging a disagreeable Eugene behind. The little girl stopped and stared wide-eyed at the wonderous sights, while her mother marched purposefully up to the counter.

The L-shaped barrier ran along a good portion of one wall, which was lined with merchandise. The short portion of the counter faced a seating area in the front window of the store. There several men sat smoking or chewing, deep in conversation.

A spittoon, showing clear signs of poor marksmanship, sat nearby. Glaring at the men, Alice pushed it aside with her foot while clearing her throat. In response, a few of these squatters moved aside while two men offered their chairs.

Alice nodded curtly but didn't take a seat. Rather, she sat Eugene in one and waved Velma to the other. "Keep an eye on him," her mother said, then turned back to the counter with Edward still on her hip. There was no one there, so she tapped the service bell and waited patiently.

A moment later, a young woman approached from the back of the store, smiling warmly. "Sorry to keep you waiting, ma'am.

Welcome to the Woodward Mercantile; I'm Annie Shaw, your friendly service clerk. How may I help you?"

Alice gave the clerk an equally warm smile. "My name is Alice Steele, and I'd like to know if it would be alright for me to leave my children here for a short time. Velma there is a very responsible girl for her age, and, as you can see, Eugene is a little gentleman."

Annie looked doubtful. "Well, ah, I don't know, ma'am. You see I'm not the owner, and they're away at present."

"Oh, please," Alice pleaded. "You see, I'm recently widowed and need to find work and a place to live."

This earned a sympathetic look from the girl. "How awful. I'm so sorry." The clerk looked more closely at Velma and then to the momentarily angelic Eugene. "Well, perhaps..."

Alice jumped at this opening. "Oh, that is so kind. And if there is any problem, you can send them away. Velma will find me."

"Well, I guess it will be okay, but don't be gone long," Annie said, wearing an anxious expression.

Alice nodded. "Oh, I can't be long. We have a hard five miles back to the farm on bad roads."

"Very well then," the clerk concluded with a nod.

Alice quickly stepped to Velma. "I'm countin' on you, girl." She handed Edward to his sister, drawing a choking sound from the clerk.

"I didn't even see your baby. You intend to leave him as well?" the girl asked, more distressed than ever.

Alice gave her a pathetic look. "But how can I talk to people about work with a baby in my arms? You must understand that."

The clerk shook her head but said nothing, so Alice turned once more to Velma. "I'll be goin' down one side of the street to the end, three blocks is all. Then I'll cross the street and work my way back and be as quick as I can."

"Yes, Mama," Velma said hesitantly, while looking to her brothers.

Alice checked Edward's diaper quickly as she said, "I fed him on the wagon. You know how that will have him sleeping for hours. And he's not wet or stinky right now." She put a cloth bag next to Velma. "But I'll leave this just in case." The clerk couldn't know that the little girl had never changed a diaper.

With that, Alice was out the door, leaving Velma and the clerk nervously staring at each other. Velma smiled reassuringly even as Eugene began squirming to get down. Reaching over with her free hand, Velma yanked him back roughly while speaking to the clerk, "Hello. I'm Velma Steele. Don't worry. He won't be no bother."

No reply came as Annie continued to look uneasy. So, Velma kept talking.

"I ain't ever been to a town before. It sure is big and exciting."

This made the young lady laugh. "I guess for a girl your size and age, it would seem that way." Then her face darkened. "I am so sorry about your Daddy."

Suddenly, Velma's chest tightened, and she found herself on the verge of tears. It had been days since she'd last cried about Papa, distracted by all that was happening. Now the reality of his being gone came back with a vengeance. She felt the loss deeply and feared not knowing what was to come even more.

Seeing the reaction and taking pity, Annie reached into a bin on the counter and pulled something out. She moved to Velma and Eugene, handing each a piece of hard candy. "I won't tell your mother about this if you don't tell my boss."

Velma didn't know the word boss but nodded agreement anyway as she took the gift. "Thank you, ma'am."

"You're welcome. Now I have to get to work." The clerk moved back behind the counter as two women entered the mercantile. Before turning to help the ladies, she added, "And do keep your brothers quiet if you can."

Just behind the two women, a group of men in overalls came through the door talking and laughing loudly. Their arrival startled all three children, causing Eugene to whimper and Edward to cry. Annie gave Velma a *"what have I done"* look while putting a finger to her lips in an attempt to silence the men.

For a long moment, Velma felt everyone's gaze on her. Then without thinking, she smiled broadly and asked, "Won't one of you come sit with me and my brothers? They'll quiet right down if you do." She didn't know that for sure, but it was all she could think to say at that moment.

When Alice got back to the mercantile, she was surprised to find a crowd gathered around her children. Velma stood in the middle as a matronly woman sat holding Edward in her arms. A grizzled old farmer in dirty overalls held Eugene, who was happily chewing on his piece of hard candy.

Not noticing her mother's arrival, Velma chattered away. "Then Papa spanked my bottom for running off like that. I couldn't sit down for a long time."

The group laughed genuinely as the five-year old returned to chewing her own candy.

Pushing her way through the audience, Alice stepped up to the counter where the young clerk stood and addressed her apologetically, "I'm so sorry for..."

Annie held up a hand, stopping her. "Nothing to be sorry about, Mrs. Steele. Your little girl there has not only taken good care of her brothers, but she's entertained my customers while I filled their orders."

One of the women standing nearby added, "And it's a lot more pleasant to have candy-eating kids in this corner rather than cigarette-smoking, chaw-spitting fellas." This brought a laugh from the women present while the men just stared.

"Well, I thank you for keeping an eye on them," Alice said humbly. "We'll be on our way."

A large man standing next to the clerk spoke up. "Not a problem, madam." His smile had the clerk relaxing. "According to Annie here, you'll be moving to Woodward."

Alice frowned. "That depends on me findin' work. I had no luck today."

"Sorry to hear that," the man said. "I'm Henry Hanks, owner of the Woodward Mercantile and..." He paused. "And gentlemen's social club."

This brought laughter from everyone. Then Mr. Henry continued. "Tell you what. Write down your name and what you can do, and leave it here? I'll post it on our board over there. If anyone inquires, I'll save the information for your next visit. How does that sound?"

"Oh, that's most kind of you," Alice said warmly but without a smile.

Annie reached under the counter and grabbed a piece of paper. "Here, madam."

Velma watched as her mother slowly and meticulously wrote down her name and a long list, then handed the paper back to Annie. Briefly glancing at the list, the clerk handed it to Mr. Hanks. "This woman does it all."

After scrutinizing the items covering the page, Henry said, "Annie's right. This is a long list. But how good are you at all of these?"

"Well, I don't mean to brag, sir, but I have won prizes at the county fair for my cookin', bakin', and sewin'," Alice said. "They didn't have contests for doin' laundry and ironin' or I'd a won them too." A murmur of laughter from the room was cut short by Alice's hard look.

Henry reviewed the list again. "Well, there are a whole lot of lazy folk in this town that would love to have someone else to do their chores. Too bad most don't have the money. Times are getting tough, especially for farm folk."

"That *is* too bad," Alice said then added, "but, if I could find some regular work, I could pick up extra from the few who can pay. Besides Velma here," she said, nodded toward her daughter. "I have another girl in school. They'll be helpin' me."

Henry handed the list back to Annie. "Tack that on the board please." Smiling at Alice, he said, "You and your family would be a welcomed addition to Woodward."

Instead of a smile, Alice looked glum. "That is if I can find a place to live that I can afford."

"Oh," was all Henry could muster. Then he called to his clerk, who was halfway across the store. "Annie, bring that back here." When she did, he added a note. "Now it's truly ready to put up."

"What did ya add?" Alice asked in confusion.

"Just a note about seeking rooms for a family of five."

Alice nodded. "I'd plain forgot that."

At that moment, the woman standing near Velma, holding Edward, wrinkled her nose. "Seems someone's getting' a bit ripe."

Alice quickly took the baby from her and headed for the door. "Much obliged, ma'am, and thanks again, Mr. Hanks and Miss Annie, for all your kindness. We'll be seeing you again soon. I pray that note works."

"God willin'," came from someone in the gathered crowd.

Once outside, Alice changed her youngest, then started the long drive home. The day was chilly but clear, making it a pleasant ride. A mile or so out of the town, Alice pulled off the road on a piece of high, dry ground. There she opened her basket of food, and they ate huddled under a blanket as a cold wind came up.

Velma was surprised that her mother didn't seem to be in a hurry to get back to the farm. They lingered on the high ground until Eugene began to fuss and tried to escape into a nearby muddy field. Once back on the road, Alice let the horse set its own pace until finally urging her along toward the school to pick up Wilma.

Velma regaled her sister with the day's events in Woodward the rest of the way home. Wilma didn't seem interested, but that didn't stop her sister. She went on and on about the town, the people she'd met, their kindness, and all the wonders inside the mercantile.

"And they gave me and Eugene not one but two pieces of hard candy."

This was more than Wilma could take. "I know all about that stuff. I've been there *several* times. And I'm sure I'd have gotten three pieces if I'd come."

"Jealousy doesn't become ya, Wilma," Mama declared. As Wilma fell silent, the two girls stuck out their tongues at each other.

They were forced to wait at the entrance to the farm as a long line of Steele relatives exited from a long day of planting. Other than a surreptitious smile or nod, there was no acknowledgment of their presence at all. Mama's stoic expression never changed.

There was still enough daylight on this mid-April day to finish the evening chores. While Alice fed the horse, cattle, and hogs, Wilma and Velma shared in brushing Nelly. Then, before heading in, they all took turns in the outhouse.

Once inside for the night, Alice went to the icebox for food to cook but found the men had nearly emptied it. It was too late to kill and pluck a chicken. So, they had to settle for potatoes, turnips, and carrots from the root cellar. Alice simmered these with stock and remnants of what once had been a roast chicken.

The next day, Alice gave her former father-in-law a piece of her mind about the food when the man arrived to oversee more planting. Though he said nothing in response, one of the cousins left a short time later and returned in a few hours with a basket of food and a fresh block of ice. Velma thought this was kind, but her mother's expression said otherwise.

Thankfully, the plowing and planting was completed over the next few days. Once again, an air of tranquility returned to the farm as Alice and Velma filled the day with endless chores. The two worked well together, which gave Velma a degree of joy.

A few days after the planting crew left, a large, unfamiliar wagon came up the track to the house. In the back was a crate, which filled the entire bed. Two men jumped down as Alice went to greet them. After a brief conversation, the wagon was pulled to the entrance of the barn and a ramp angled up to the crates.

Velma watched forlornly as their two hogs were loaded, a difficult task. Then the men gave Alice some money and rolled away, taking another piece of their former life with them. Then their mother returned to the house, saying nothing. When Wilma came home and learned what had happened, she cried.

The next Saturday, Alice harnessed the horse again. After loading a basket of food, she settled the old cradle that had been used for all four children in the back for Edward. Then everyone else climbed aboard and they headed off.

Repeating the routine of the previous trip, Alice parked near the mercantile. As she entered with the family, the familiar group of men in the corner promptly stood and moved away. Annie the clerk was not at the counter. Instead, a large, well-dressed, middle-aged woman greeted her warmly. "Good morning, madam. How may I help you?"

"Is Mr. Hanks around?" Alice asked.

The woman's smile faded a bit. "He's busy at the moment. I'm his wife. What is it you need?"

Alice hesitated, then replied, "I, well, your husband was kind enough to put up a notice for me. My name's Steele, Alice Steele." She glanced toward the wall where the notice had been posted. It was gone.

"Oh, yes. I heard about you and, ah, your children." Mrs. Hanks' warm expression had waned.

Seeing this look, Alice apologized. "I'm sorry if our last visit caused any trouble. It won't happen again. You see, I have my two girls to take care of the boys this time, and we won't impose. I was just wondering if the note got any response."

"Nonsense," the booming voice of Mr. Hanks came from behind his wife as he walked up. "I see you've met my Tessa."

Alice nodded tentatively, generating a chuckle from the man. "Don't let her put you off. She tends to do that to people at first. In no time, she'll be treating you like family."

"Not likely," Tessa said tersely, then turned on her heels. "I'll leave this matter to you then."

"Thanks, dear," Henry said, giving Alice a smile. He reached under the counter and came out with a pile of papers. "Your post drew a lot of interest as you can see." He handed over the stack. "Take a seat," he said, nodding to the now vacant chairs, "and have a gander at all those."

"Thank you," Alice said, beginning to move to the chairs then stopping. "What about the children?"

"Oh, that's right." Henry smile grew larger. "I see you have a new one in tow."

"Yes. She's my oldest, Wilma," Alice said with an encouraging nod in her direction. "Say, hello to Mr. Hanks, girl."

"How do you do, Mr. Hanks?" the girl said, offering a weak curtsy.

Henry chuckled. "Yet another polite child. You do have pleasant children."

"Except Eugene when he's upset," Wilma said reflexively, drawing one of Mama's famous glares.

"He wouldn't be a boy otherwise," Henry said. Then he looked to Velma. "The usual?"

She nodded and soon Wilma, Eugene, and she were sucking on a hard candy. "Now don't let Mrs. Hanks know I gave those to you. She's a miser."

"What's a my-sir?" Velma asked.

"Someone who doesn't give out free candy. Let's leave it at that." Then addressing Alice, he shared, "I divided those slips into a jobs pile and a rent pile."

"That wasn't necessary, but thanks." Then her expression turned dour.

Henry rubbed his chin. "Is there something wrong?"

"Don't know yet. I'm just getting started."

"Then I'll leave you to it." He turned and saw the small cluster of men the Steeles had displaced. "Hey, quit looking so put out, gentlemen. Come with me. I got a wagon to unload. If you help, there will be a cold soda in it for you."

The men's frowns disappeared as they headed for the back. Watching them leave, Velma asked, "What's a cold soda, Mama?"

"Something you don't need and won't have for a long while I expect," Alice replied curtly, as she waded through the papers. "Now take Eugene outside with that candy and don't let him get it all over his clothes."

"What about me, Mama?" Wilma asked.

"You stay with me and tend to Edward," she replied. "I don't want him fussin' and botherin' the mercantile's customers."

Velma and her brother walked along Main Street amid the weekend hustle and bustle. The sidewalk and street were filled with people, horses, and horseless carriages. It was a struggle keeping Eugene out from under passing wagon wheels. A half-hour later, they returned to find Alice talking with Mr. Hanks.

Wilma and Edward were nowhere to be seen. Not wanting to interrupt the conversation, Velma put Eugene in a chair and sat beside him. She didn't know how long it had been since breakfast, but her stomach suddenly began to growl. She hoped her mother would finish soon as she listened with some interest to what they were saying.

"I don't exactly see what the problem is, Mrs. Steele," Henry was saying. "I would think this would be good news."

Her mother gave him a frustrated look. "First, some of the work takes money to get started, cookin' and bakin' for example. So, I probably shouldn't have put them on the list."

"I can't argue with that. Have you put those aside?" Henry asked.

Alice held up a pile. "These are the ones requesting cookin' or bakin'. As you can see, there looks like a lot of folk willin' to buy a little but not many to buy a lot." She lay them down on the counter.

"That is a quandary. What else?"

As her mother began sorting through the remaining sheets, Velma lost interest and got off the chair. "Come on Eugene."

She dragged him through the store, looking for their sister and brother. There were plenty of people wandering the aisles, but none was Wilma carrying Edward. Velma headed for a curtained doorway. Stepping through tentatively with Eugene in hand, she entered a storage room. There she found Wilma, Tessa, and Annie busily entertaining the baby.

After a brief time, Tessa struggled up quickly as if remembering something important. "Look at the time. And poor Henry is out on the floor alone. Come on Annie, let's get back to work"

It turned out that Tessa's idea of helping was to drag her husband upstairs for lunch. As they left, Mr. Hanks said, "I'll be back shortly, Alice, and we can make those stops."

Tessa gave Henry a confused look but didn't slow down. As they disappeared, Annie laughed. "Mrs. Hanks does like a good meal."

"Speaking of which, I need to feed my young'uns." Alice turned to find her four all within easy reach. Heading for the door, she asked Annie, "What about you?"

"Oh, I'll get something at the drugstore down the street when the Hanks return. Feel free to eat in the front here if you like."

Alice hesitated. "You don't think that Mrs. Hanks would mind?"

"Shucks, no." Seeing a doubtful look on Mrs. Steele's face, she reassured her. "Trust me. Their kids are grown and gone, so they are a bit lonely. They would have insisted you eat inside if they were here."

Accepting the invitation, the Steeles were sitting in the familiar chairs when the Hanks returned. "Well, make yourself at home," Tessa said curtly.

When Alice saw her smile, however, she relaxed. "I know it looks like we're becomin' squatters like the men, but I promise we'll be out of here soon. And I don't mean just for today but for good."

"No rush on our account," Henry protested. "Now, can you and the girls handle the boys, while Alice and I go check out some places to live?"

"I'd appreciate that." Alice smiled weakly, expecting pushback from Tessa.

Instead, Mrs. Hanks stepped up and took Edward from his mother. "Just don't dilly-dally," Tessa said, giving the baby a squeeze that produced a tiny burp.

Henry nodded and headed for the front door, waving a piece of paper. "Tessa said these three places are likely to be the best. They are all within a few blocks of here."

"I'll walk with you if you're heading toward the drugstore," Annie offered.

"We sure are." Henry held the door open and bowed as the ladies passed by.

It was mid-afternoon and the boys played contentedly, Edward in his cradle on the floor and Eugene in the chair he'd staked a claim on. The flow of customers had been steady with many stopping to gaze at the children. The hustle and bustle seemed to mesmerize the girls, while the boys were soon sleeping through it all.

Velma, having drifted off, was jerked awake by the sound of her mother and Mr. Hanks' return. They rushed in, chattering cheerfully. It was clear to the little girl that something good had happened. Mother had a spring in her step, and the usual dour expression was gone.

"What is it, Mama?" Velma's eager voice woke Wilma.

Alice found a spare seat and took a deep breath. "Well, I found a place for us to live."

"A place to live?" Wilma asked incredulously.

Alice patted her daughter's knee. "Yes, dear. We have to move. Remember?"

"Oh, yes," her eldest replied woefully. "When?"

"We can move in two weeks."

Velma clapped her hands excitedly, while an even deeper frown crossed Wilma's face. "What's wrong with you, girl?" Alice asked testily.

"My school isn't out until June, Mama."

"Oh, is that all," Alice said casually. "Don't worry, child. I'll get you into school here as soon as we move in."

"Oh, Mama," Wilma wailed and headed out the door.

Velma started to go after her, but Mother said sternly, "Leave her. She'll get over it. She needs to start dealin' with things instead of always runnin' away."

"Yes, Mama."

Alice's expression softened. "And she's missin' the rest of the news."

"There's more?"

"Yes, dear. Thanks to Mr. Hanks, I got the place at a discount."

"What is a dish-count?" Velma asked.

While Tessa and Henry chuckled, Alice patiently explained. "The word is discount, and it means we don't have to pay the full rent in cash. In return for providin' some services, we get the place for less."

Though she still didn't understand, Velma smiled anyway and asked, "Is there anything else?"

"Oh, yes, indeed," Alice said glancing outside. Wilma was sitting on the wooden sidewalk with her feet in the street, quietly crying. With a sigh, she continued. "You remember the pigs I sold?" Velma nodded. "Well, that money will help pay the rent for a while."

"Then what?"

Alice shrugged. "Well, I do have a little more set aside, and I'll have enough work to get us by long before that runs out."

"I'll help, Mama. What can I do?"

"Oh, I'm sure we'll find something for you to do. After all, you won't have to do farm chores anymore, well, except for taking care of the chickens and old Nelly."

"We get to keep Nelly?"

Alice looked back at Henry. "Thanks to Mr. Hanks. He's going to let us use one of the stalls in the barn behind this place."

Tessa gave her husband a disapproving look. "Oh, really?"

"She's going to pay us for the space and hay," Henry said defensively.

"With what?"

Alice answered for him. "With eggs and baked goods."

"Baked goods?" Tessa asked incredulously.

"Yes. I'll be giving you pies at a discount each week to sell or eat. Biscuits and bread too if you like." Alice gave Tessa a hard look. "It's a good deal for us both."

Henry agreed. "Yes, it is. And if all goes well, we'll be selling even more if Alice is as good a baker as she claims."

"It's not a claim, it's a fact," Alice said firmly.

"Is there anything else?" Velma inadvertently ended the uncomfortableness as she sought more good news.

"Well, besides the money for the hogs, we get a quarter of the meat. Added to what is left in the smokehouse back at the farm, we'll get by for a good while if we're frugal."

Henry added rather sheepishly, "I offered to store the meat in our cooler in return for additional baked goods."

Tessa stroked her large stomach absentmindedly as she said, "Well, seeing as you seem to have this all worked out, I'll just wait to sample the products."

"Mama?" Velma asked timidly. "Will you tell me about our new home?"

Alice patted her little girl's hand. "Better yet, I'll show you and your sister the place. It's right down this same side of the street." Then she gave the Hanks and Annie a pleading look. "That is, if somebody will keep an eye on the boys."

Taking the cue, Annie spoke up, "I'll do it."

"We'll *all* be happy to," Tessa added genuinely. "Just don't be too long. I don't do diaper-changing anymore."

Tessa waited until Alice and Velma were out the door to ask, "Why are you taking that woman and her family under your wing, Henry?"

"Oh, I don't know. Maybe because they are suffering so. Maybe it's because I can see through Alice's hard exterior to a good soul fighting for her four little ones. She's fighting rather than begging, and I admire that."

"Sounds a bit like your mother," Tessa suggested.

Henry thought on that a minute. "You're probably right. Plus..." He hesitated.

"Plus what?"

"Well, I was just remembering when I was struggling to get started. If it hadn't been for old man Jenkins seeing through my bravado and mentoring me..."

Tessa stopped him, "I understand now."

"Plus, those darn kids can steal a heart."

"Indeed."

3
Traumatic Transition

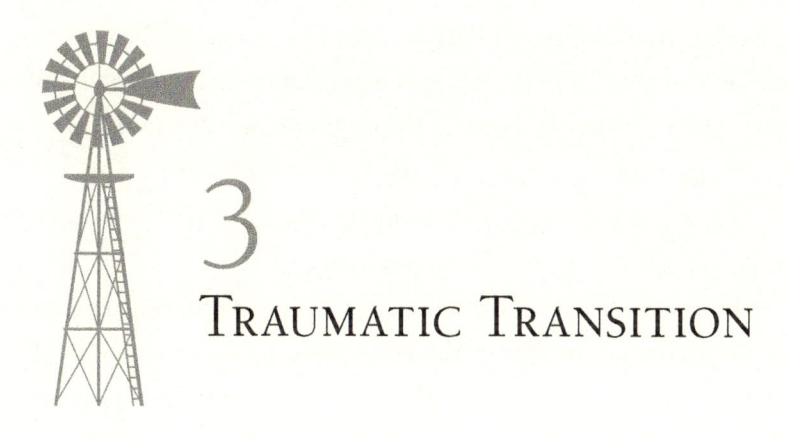

Much of the trip back to the farm that night was in darkness. The boys were soon lulled to sleep by the jerking motion of the buckboard. Wilma sat by her mother, sullen and silent. It was hard for Velma to understand her sister's mood, especially after seeing their new home. To her it was like moving to a new planet.

It turned out the apartment was at the end of the second block down from the mercantile. As they approached the last building, Alice veered off the wooden sidewalk and headed to the back. Once there, she stopped and pointed to a stairway leading up.

After the girls gave the exterior of the place the once-over, Wilma immediately started to complain, "Look at all those stairs." She was right. The apartment was two flights above the Grimminger Hardware store.

"It will be good exercise since we won't be runnin' around all that land at the farm anymore," Alice said, motioning them to get moving.

At the top of the stairs, they found a large porch. "We'll make good use of this," Alice said, moving quickly through the front door. "And this living room is as big as the one at the farm."

"Where's the dining room?" Wilma asked sourly.

"There is none, but you'll soon see the large kitchen in the back. There's plenty of room to eat there."

Alice reached over and turned a switch, illuminating a single light bulb in the middle of the room. Both girls squealed with delight. "Woodward just got electricity this year. So, no more smelly lanterns," Alice said with pride. "There is a bulb and plug in each room."

"We don't have anything to plug in, Mama," Wilma chided, as her negative attitude returned.

Ignoring this exchange, Velma rushed to one of two windows in the room overlooking the porch. "Come see, Sis. You can see over the tops of buildings all the way to the cornfields from here."

"Just dandy," the unmoved Wilma replied.

Unfazed, Velma turned and dashed to the stove by the wall across from the windows. "Look at this. It's not as pretty as the one in the kitchen at the farm, but it works, right, Mama?"

"Indeed. It's called a Franklin stove," Alice answered with assurance. "Now let's get moving."

The three filed down a long hall, passing the bedrooms before reaching the door to the kitchen. "Are there only three bedrooms?" Wilma asked in shock.

"Yes," Alice replied, giving her oldest a warning stare.

Missing this look, Wilma blurted out, "Five of us in those three tiny bedrooms?"

"The last one's big," Velma pointed out.

"And that's the room I'm giving the two of you." Alice's positive tone was still accompanied by a harsh look at Wilma. "I'll be between all you children."

"Oh, thank you, Mama," Velma said while her sister just grunted. "We'll have such fun fixing it up."

"Oh, yes. I'm *sure* it will be just great fun," Wilma said, then finally noticed her mother's expression and quickly added, "The kitchen is nice and big."

With a nod, Alice went on with the tour. "Yes, it is as big as the front room. Behind that wall," she pointed across the room, "is the landlord's apartment. He, his wife, and son live there. See there, the stove has two big ovens for my baking."

Wilma gave her a puzzled look. "Seems like more than you'll need for that."

"Not if I'm bakin' things to sell. I do have to make a livin' if we are to survive."

Wilma opened her mouth to say something but then thought better of it. After searching for an alternative, she finally said, "Well there is plenty of room, and the windows make it a bright space."

"And look at the storage." Alice sounded almost excited. "That pantry in the corner is huge with all those shelves. Plus, the table's big enough for us to use for meals *and* rollin' out dough. You two are good at that. And look, we have a sink with a pump to bring up water. No hauling buckets up those stairs."

Velma ran over, trying to reach the pump handle without success, while Wilma continued to rain on her mother's parade. "Does that mean there is a bathroom?"

"No," Alice snapped. "The facilities are across the alley. The landlord's family has indoor facilities now, so we will have it all to ourselves. Plus, it is attached to a space that used to be a Chinese laundry. I hope to use it for laundry customers."

"You plan on taking in laundry too?" Wilma sounded shocked.

"No, *we* plan on takin' it in," Alice shot back.

"Ugh."

Trying once again to overcome Wilma's pessimism, Alice said, "And the school is only a few blocks up the street."

"Oh, how nice," Wilma replied ironically.

Velma started to add another positive note, "And it will be so nice being in Woodward with..." when her mother interrupted angrily.

"That's right, Wilma. You will be able to help more in the morning before headin' to school and be home quicker to lend a hand. That will be helpful." Not giving Wilma time to respond, Alice moved off down the hall, adding sharply, "Now it's time to get back to the farm and start packing."

Dark had arrived well before the Steeles reached the farm that night. The boys had gone to sleep shortly after leaving Woodward, lulled to sleep by the jerking motion of the buckboard. The girls rode next to their mother, Wilma sullen and silent, while Velma couldn't understand why she acted that way given their exciting new home.

Arriving at the farm, Alice jostled the girls awake. "Help me get the boys inside and into bed. We've got church tomorrow." In a silent caravan, the family entered the dark farmhouse.

Unable to sleep, Velma watched out her bedroom window as her mother put Nelly in the barn. On her way back to the house, Velma could see her mother walking with a spring in her step.

The next morning, as she had faithfully done as long as Velma could remember, Alice got the family dressed and headed off to the Methodist church. The day had dawned sunny and mild, with a gentle tailwind pushing them along as if to celebrate their recent good fortune.

At the church, Alice and the children were again greeted coolly. The Skinners continued to be as unforgiving as the Steele clan now praying over at the Catholic church. Even the minister, perhaps fearing reprisal from a majority of his congregation, was unwelcoming. For once, however, Alice seemed totally unaffected.

When the children were back in the wagon after the service, the girls watched their mother go over to her parents. Velma couldn't remember ever seeing the three talk. It was a short conversation devoid of emotion. Turning from her own mother and father as well as the past, Alice returned to the wagon wearing a triumphant expression.

The gentle wind that had escorted them to church was now blowing briskly in their faces, heavy with humidity. The once sunny sky was now filled with billowy clouds fighting for space. Some were trimmed in shades of gray. Seeing this, Alice urged Nelly into a trot.

Arriving home, their mother jumped down quickly and began to unhook the horse while barking instructions. "Velma, get the chickens fed and collect the eggs. Wilma, get the boys settled inside."

When the girls moved more slowly than Alice desired, she barked again, "Get a move on, you two. There's a storm comin'." In response, Wilma and Velma looked up into what looked to them like the farthest thing from bad weather. They shrugged at each other but got moving anyway.

As Velma emerged from the chicken coop, she saw her mother fastening the barn door, giving it an extra look to ensure it was secure. Heading to the house, the two converged halfway there. "How many?" Alice asked.

"Not a lot," Velma said frowning. "Not like usual."

"They sense a storm comin'." Alice nodded to the west, and Velma's eyes followed her mother's gaze. She saw the once white clouds were now somewhere between ash grey and black, boiling rapidly up toward the heavens. "We need to secure the house. It won't be long now."

"But what about Sunday dinner?" Velma protested.

They reached the porch door as Alice shook her head. "All in good time. The house comes first."

Velma wasn't exactly sure what her mother meant but sensed she was more than a little worried. They hurried inside and made rounds through the house. They closed it up tightly except for the windows on the east side. "Why aren't we closing those, Mama?" Velma asked.

"Just in case," was all her mother said. "Now let's just watch the storm move in, shall we?" Her matter-of-fact tone, if intended to ease the girls' concern, was only partially successful.

So, she tried a different tact. "Well, if you don't like bein' lazy, let's see what we're gonna have to move into Woodward out in the root cellar and smokehouse. We can grab somethin' to have after the storm passes."

With that, she led them out into a sudden sultry calm. The entrance to the root cellar was just past the end of the screened porch to the left. Throwing open the wooden doors revealed a half-dozen dirt steps leading into darkness.

"Hand me that lantern, Wilma," Alice ordered as she pulled a box of wooden matches from her apron. In a few moments, light from the kerosene lamp illuminated the entrance. She handed the lantern back to Wilma. "Get goin', girl."

Inside the cellar, plank shelves resting on dirt columns circled the room on three sides. Burlap bags, some nearly empty, others brimming, covered the dirt floor. The upper shelves were stocked with glass jars filled with fruits and vegetables. In addition, braids of onions and corn hung from the rafters.

"This is a wagonload alone," Alice said distractedly. "We'll take most of this with us our next trip to town and leave it in Mr. Hanks' barn until we make the final move. Now let's take some potatoes and a jar of those beans for supper."

They closed the cellar but kept the lantern with them. After putting the potatoes and jar of beans on the porch, the three headed for the smoke house. It was a small, whitewashed building nestled among a scattering of large oak trees some twenty yards or so from the east side of the house. A metal clothesline stretched between the buildings.

Reaching the smokehouse, they looked to the west again. The sky had grown more ominous, as an anemic wind replaced the stillness. There were the first faint sounds of thunder in the distance.

With sudden urgency, Alice pulled the smokehouse door open and stuck the lantern into the darkness. A smell somewhere between a long-dead fire and slow-roasted meat greeted them. The space was more than half empty. Still, there were several hams, slabs of bacon, and racks of dried beef and plump brown chickens from which to choose.

"Let's grab a chicken and head back," their mother said, stepping aside for Velma to do the honors, "The hams are the only things that will be left to take with us to Woodward."

They quickly made their way back to the house as a stronger wind finally took hold. Thunder, much closer now, rolled as they reached the back porch. The girls had been through some bad storms before in their short lives, so they weren't overly frightened as they went in to help prepare supper.

No sooner were they inside, however, when a sudden gust rattled windows and caused the entire house to groan. Stopping the preparations, the three went to the kitchen window over the sink, which faced north. From there they saw a distinct line in the sky dividing sundrenched blue from a mass of thick blackness

As the wind steadily increased, they moved to the living room where there was a west-facing window. The view was breathtaking. Storm clouds billowed ever higher as the blackness stretched from horizon to horizon. This sky was laced with lightning and punctuated by cannon-like thunder. Then, as they watched, the sky began to turn a putrid green.

"Let's head for the root cellar girls," Alice said, sweeping them back toward the kitchen. "Grab the boys and the lantern and leave the rest."

Within less than a minute, they were out the back door. In that brief time, however, the intense storm was already bearing down on the farm. Crossing the porch, a flash of lightning streaked a sky now dark as night. Acting like a prologue, the lightning and thunder brought a sudden squall that was gone as fast as it had come.

Alice struggled to finally get the cellar doors open in the intense wind. She headed down the steps first with the lantern that she'd had the foresight to leave lit. Wilma followed with Edward, while Velma shooed Eugene down the steps a moment later. At the top of the stairs, Velma paused to take one last look at the sky and froze.

From the bottom of a greenish cloudbank, flat as a tabletop turned upside down, snaked something she had only heard about—a tornado. In seconds, the funnel broadened and dipped to the ground just beyond the row of fir trees bordering the open farmyard. It was only a few yards away.

Velma watched, half terrified, half mesmerized, as branches were ripped off like matchsticks. In a flash, the tornado advanced into the open yard, seemingly headed right for her. At that moment, Alice reached up and yanked her inside, slamming the wooden doors shut. Only then did Velma hear the sound.

Sliding a metal bar in place to hold the door shut, Alice staggered down the steps yelling something that the girls couldn't hear. They did understand their mother's hand gestures, however, and moved quickly back into a far corner.

By then, Eugene was wailing, unheard in the deafening noise of the tornado. To Velma, it seemed eerily like the tornado's roar was coming out of the boy's mouth. The root cellar door started rattling violently, as if someone were trying desperately to join them.

Then came a cacophony of sounds, ripping, cracking, pounding, breaking, screeching, howling, so loud that Alice and the girls had to cover their ears. At the same moment, all the air in the cellar was sucked out, taking their breath with it.

Just as quickly, the air returned, and the incredible roar suddenly dropped, as if smothered by a pillow. The sound of thunder and pounding rain returned, only to quickly fade as if being sucked along by the tornado. As everyone sighed with relief, Wilma drew everyone's attention to Edward. He had slept through the whole ordeal.

Alice rose slowly and moved to the doors. "I'll take a look, make sure it's safe."

She slid the iron bar aside and attempted to open the doors. They wouldn't budge. She tried again without success. After testing each door individually, she said calmly, "Girls, put the boys down and come over here."

There was barely room for the three of them on the narrow dirt stairway as their mother instructed them. "Wilma, when I tell you, pull down on this handle while Velma and I push here." The girls nodded. "Okay, now!"

After several attempts, they managed to get one door open wide enough for Velma to squeeze through. Once outside, she couldn't believe her eyes. "Mama, oh, Mama," was all she could say.

"No time to waste, child," came Alice's muffled voice from inside the cellar. "What's holding the doors down?"

Velma examined the debris preventing their escape. A large tree limb was wedged between the house, which still stood, and the cellar doors. "It's a big limb Mama, and it's stuck to the house."

After a pause, Alice replied, "Go to the chicken coop and find the axe I left there. Bring it back and start hackin' away at the door."

"But Mama," the child began, but her mother interrupted sharply.

"But what?"

"It's gone."

"What's gone?"

Velma looked behind her again. "The coop and..." She hesitated, trying to comprehend what she saw. "And the barn."

"What do you mean, gone?"

Velma began to cry. "Oh, poor Nelly, poor Nelly."

"We still need to get out of here, Velma." Alice's voice was calm again. "Can you see the chopping block? Is it still there?"

Glancing in the direction of the coop again, she saw the stump. "Yes, Mama. And the hatchet is still there."

"Get it and use it to hit the door."

Weaving her way through the debris, she quickly reached the place where the fenced-in chicken yard and coop had been. It took her several tries to finally remove the hatchet from the blood-stained stump and carry it with some difficulty back to the cellar door.

Without delay, Velma swung it, as well as she could, chopping at the edge of the door that she had crawled out. After great effort and much time, one board finally gave way, allowing the rail-thin Alice to escape. Using a thick branch for leverage, mother and daughter managed to shift the large limb enough to free everyone.

Then they paused to assess the damage. It could have been much worse. The back porch was gone and the siding above the root cellar damaged, but a circuit of the house showed it to be otherwise unscathed. Entering through the front door, Alice left Wilma with the boys in the living room while she and Velma went back outside.

First, they moved to what was left of the barn. As happens with tornados, it had serendipitously spared the wagon sitting right next to it. Velma started to cry at the sight, remembering their horse. She stopped suddenly, however, when Nelly trotted up from behind a large pile of debris.

"Mama, look. How did Nelly get out of the barn alive?" Velma asked in astonishment.

Alice replied flatly, "'Cause I never put her in there. I let her run free in the back pasture figurin' she'd know how to avoid the storm."

That was the only happy news concerning the barn, which was totally destroyed. Though the coop was gone, many of the chickens were roaming the yard pecking away. The outhouse, corncrib, washhouse and smokehouse seemed intact. That only left the interior of the farmhouse to inspect.

The two returned there to find Wilma cleaning up glass from a broken window in the kitchen. "We have plenty of scrap wood now to cover that," Alice said, then asked, "where are the boys?"

"Edward's over there." Wilma nodded to his cradle. "I put Eugene in the pantry with *my* dolly that you gave him. I didn't want him stepping on the glass."

Alice frowned. "With the door closed? He's probably getting into everything." She headed to the pantry quickly and threw open the door. Her prediction proved accurate. The toddler was covered head to toe in flour.

With all that had just happened, Velma expected her mother to be angry. Instead, Alice started to laugh. Picking up Eugene, she gave him a big kiss. Looking back at the girls, they saw her face was now a powdery white as well. The sight got the girls laughing. It took a while for everyone to calm down before starting the inspection.

When they finished, Alice pronounced that, except for the kitchen window, all the others had survived. There did not seem to be any roof leaks either. She concluded with, "This place ought to hold up long enough for us to leave it behind."

There was little that could be done outside with so much debris from destroyed buildings and the ground being a muddy mess. After slogging to and from the outhouse, they ate their supper in near silence.

Sunset that night was breathtaking, all pinks, purples, and golds weaving through an azure blue sky. The girls watched the stars slowly emerge and the moon rise as they babbled on about the storm until their mother sent them to bed. That night, Velma had a nightmare about being chased around the farm by a tornado.

The next morning broke much like the day before, sunny and cool. With some trepidation, Wilma headed off to school. Wandering through the debris, Velma found eggs lain in the strangest places—between the spokes of an old wagon wheel, in a metal pot, and yet another in a straw hat that had blown in from another farm.

As Velma brought in her dozen or so finds, she saw a familiar wagon coming up the lane. When her grandfather pulled past, he ignored the little girl. Stopping a few yards farther on, the old man surveyed the destruction and shook his head.

Alice came around the corner from the front and fixed him with a scowl. "Sorry we're not out of here yet." Velma didn't think her mother sounded sorry at all. "But as you can see, we had a little storm here yesterday. Nice of you to come check on us though."

Mr. Steele scowled back, then his face slackened, and he sighed. "Everyone made it here, I take it."

"Like you care," Alice snarled. "Your only interest is in the property. Well, you can see you'll have some work to do when we're gone."

Her father-in-law scanned the devastation again. "'Fraid so. Don't forget you need to be gone by the end of next month."

"Oh, we'll be gone long before then," Alice said, raising her chin defiantly.

The man started to speak, paused, then started again. "You do that. The family will be back to start on a new barn soon as we bury young Willard."

Hearing this, Velma froze. Willard was the cousin who had given her the ride back to the farm two years earlier when she'd set out walking to town. He had risked stopping by a few times after that, being one of the few who treated them like family. Now he was dead like her Papa.

"What happened?" Alice's voice had gone from harsh to grief-stricken.

Her father-in-law didn't reply, just snapped the reins and left. As the wagon moved off, Velma burst into tears, burying her face in Mother's apron. "Oh, Mama. Willard, Willard's..."

"There, there child." Alice patted the little girl's head, then pushed her away saying stoically, "Time to get breakfast started."

Velma couldn't understand. Didn't her mother care that they had lost one of the few family members that liked them? She could be so mean sometimes. The little girl spent the rest of the day mourning the cousin that had made her laugh. Meanwhile, her mother went about the business of packing to leave.

Days later, Alice left in the wagon for a brief time without saying why. The day after that mystery trip, everyone dressed in their church clothes even though it was a Wednesday. After loading everyone on the wagon, they headed off and arrived at Papa's church, where a crowd had gathered. It was cousin Willard's funeral.

Respectfully, Alice slipped into the church, carrying Edward, with Velma at her side. She had left a fussy Eugene in the wagon with Wilma. There was an open casket at the altar with a line of mourners shuffling by. Alice did not go forward, choosing to remain in the back pew where they'd sat in February for Papa's service.

After the funeral, Alice sought out Willard's parents, pulling a reluctant Velma along. Her mother's soft and gentle expressions of sympathy were received warmly. Willard's father even took the time to explain what had happened to their son.

Apparently, Willard was attempting to release some of his animals just as the tornado struck the farm. Instead of destroying the barn, however, Willard had been swept away. His body was found a quarter mile away in a freshly planted field. Velma joined her mother in a tearful goodbye to the grief-stricken couple.

Alice headed directly home from the church, choosing not to go to the cemetery. Back at the farm, mother and daughters worked all afternoon to construct a makeshift enclosure for the chickens from remnants of the destroyed barn. They salvaged enough chicken wire to cordon off a small space to keep the vermin out.

Then Alice went inside and continued sorting items that were hers to take when they moved. The girls did the same. The majority of the day was spent in a sad silence. For once, it was Velma who did the soft sobbing. She would miss Willard.

Late the next morning, the family was off to Woodward. The wagon was loaded with children, foodstuffs from the remains of the root cellar, and other personal belongings from the house. They only stayed in town long enough to unload everything into Hanks' barn and eat their lunch at the mercantile.

Of course, the bulk of the conversation at the store was about the tornado. The Woodward folk, being north of the storm's worst damage, listened about the latest example of a hostile Iowa spring. The locals described the events in the usual matter-of-fact style. Even among that group, Alice was more stoic than most.

As they loaded up for the return to the farm, the count of those killed in the storm had risen to over twenty. The worst instance was at a church northwest of Woodward and directly west of the Steele farm. The tornado hit the church in the middle of a service. Ten had died and dozens more were badly injured.

The ride home was a long, glum five miles. When they arrived back at the farm, however, Alice was surprised to see much of the yard clear of debris. Several wagons were loaded to the brim and heading out to the main road as they drove up.

There was no exchange between the men and Alice as they passed by. She didn't thank them either, which made Velma sad. Entering the house, their mother put them immediately to work packing again. It was obvious she was anxious to leave the farm once and for all, and soon.

They made another trip to town on the next Saturday. This load consisted of clothes and the few pieces of furniture that belonged to William and Alice. As they had done on their last visit, the stay was short. In spite of an offer to eat with the Hanks, Alice had them heading back in the early afternoon.

As the family headed to church the next day, Alice addressed the girls, "I talked to our new landlord yesterday. He said if we wanted to move in early, we could. So, tomorrow we load up the rest of the food and take it to town. Then one more trip and we'll be done."

Velma greeted this news with a gleeful giggle, while Wilma wore an angry look and said nothing. So, Mama addressed her older daughter directly, "Wilma, we are movin', so get used to the idea."

Wilma remained silent, though her expression had turned to a pout. Unmoved, Alice shared more of what was coming. "The Monday after we are settled in the apartment, I will enroll you at your new school to complete the year. It will be up to you to make new friends, your choice."

"Can I go see the school, Mama?" Velma asked, receiving a hateful look from her sister.

Alice thought on this for a minute. "I don't see why not. You'll be going there in the fall."

"Mama, it's my school now!" Wilma cried.

Alice's mouth turned up at the edges. "Well, I'm glad to hear that. And you'll be in *your* new school within a week."

"And Velma can't go," Wilma demanded.

Alice shook her head. "I already said she could. So, let that be the end of it."

The rest of the morning, Wilma sulked in the wagon and while sitting in the pew. She didn't speak again until they returned home. "What's for supper, Mama?"

"Whatever you want, child," Alice said. "Go pick out your favorites from what's left in the pantry and grab what you want from the smokehouse." This suggestion was greeted with a frown. "What's the matter?" Alice asked.

"Ah, well, I'm not feeling so good, Mama," Wilma replied.

Alice frowned. "Kinda sudden. Why just a second ago, you were askin' what's for supper. So, if you're not feelin' well, how can you be hungry?"

"Oh, ah, it's a headache not my tummy," Wilma said, giving mother her best forlorn face.

Alice turned to Velma. "Well then, little one," She said with a warm smile. "It looks like we'll be eatin' your favorites tonight."

"Oh, thank you, Mama," Velma said clapping her hands. "Fried chicken with *smashed* potatoes, yum."

Alice nodded. "I'll take care of the chicken, and you get some potatoes and a jar of corn. Then I'll whip up some biscuits, and gravy too."

"It will be like my birthday all over again," Velma said, heading to the pantry.

Alice turned to Wilma. "Set the table, then you can go lay down in your room until dinner."

"But, Mama," Wilma started to protest.

Alice stopped her with the dreaded stare. "If you don't get movin', you'll stay up there the rest of the day."

"Yes, Mama," her oldest said angrily.

As she stomped to the silverware drawer, Alice headed for the new chicken coop. By the evening, calm had returned inside the house. The same could not be said for the weather outside. Again, clouds gathered in the west. This time the approaching storm seemed less severe, not requiring a trip to the root cellar. Still, plenty of thunder, lightning, and rain arrived just as darkness fell.

In spite of the trauma associated with the recent tornado, Velma still liked storms, found them exciting. Her favorite place to watch from was the window on the stair landing. That's where she stood that night, marveling at the display.

She looked out into the cluster of great oaks surrounding the smokehouse, barely visible through the torrent. This storm moved much more slowly than the last, putting on a spectacular light show for the little girl. Then suddenly, a streak of lightning snaked out, hitting one of the nearby oaks. Steam and smoke rose as a large branch fell to the ground.

"Mama, come see!" Velma yelled loudly.

Moments later, Alice arrived wearing a concerned expression. "What is it, child?"

"Look."

The two of them gazed out at the still smoldering limb as more lightning and thunder filled the sky. "Oh, my. Did you see that?"

"Yes, Mama," Velma said excitedly. "I was watching just like we are now when..."

At that moment, another flash nearly blinded them. This time the thunder came in unison with the light, rattling the house like an earthquake. Mesmerized, Velma watched, as what looked like a fireball rolled down the metal clothesline toward the smokehouse. When it arrived, the small white building exploded.

As Velma cried out, Alice headed downstairs and out the front door. From the window, Velma could hardly see her mother, nearly invisible in the deluge as she ran toward the burning building. Pausing for only a moment as the pounding rain began to extinguish the flames, Alice headed back to the house, that was illuminated by more flashes.

Velma raced to the front door, arriving as her mother burst inside gasping for air. Water already was puddling at her feet. "If that ball had come this way, the house would have gone," she said, then rushed upstairs. Returning shortly in dry clothes, her hair wrapped in a towel, Alice gathered everyone in the living room until the storm slowly ended.

With nothing salvageable from the smokehouse, one trip to Woodward had been eliminated. That was the only good thing to come from the lightning strike. Alice focused on leaving the farm behind just as soon as she could. For the next few days, she and the girls worked so hard that they fell asleep before their heads hit the pillow.

It was not in Alice's nature to leave anything undone. So, once their last possessions were on the front porch waiting to be loaded, she began cleaning the house from top to bottom. More than once, she mumbled to the girls how she wasn't about to give the Steeles any reason to complain. And she didn't.

4
Woodward

It was near midnight on April 29, 1921 when Alice and the children pulled into Woodward from the farm one last time. It had been a slow and difficult pull for Nelly with the wagon filled to overflowing. Stopping outside the mercantile, Alice got down and rapped on the locked door, which woke Velma.

After several attempts, a light came on inside, followed by the sound of a latch being opened. Henry Hanks stood there in a long nightshirt, a surprised expression on his face. "We had another incident at the farm a few days ago," Alice explained. "Lost the last of our meat in the smokehouse. So, we decided to move early."

"An incident?" Henry asked in alarm. "What kind of incident? Did someone do something to you or your children?"

She shook her head. "No. It was just good old Mother Nature again. I'll explain tomorrow. I wanted to know if we could just put the wagon in your barn overnight. We're all pretty much done in, and it looks like more rain."

"Of course. I'll throw on some clothes and meet you round back." The door closed as Alice wearily climbed back on the wagon and urged Nelly into reluctant motion. Once turned around in the street, they headed for the alley.

Reaching the barn, they found the doors open and the hastily dressed Henry holding a lantern illuminating the way. Once the wagon was pulled inside, he helped Alice and a sleepy-eyed Velma down, then moved to unhitch Nelly. "I'll get the horse settled. You go now."

"Thank you so much, Mr. Hanks," Alice said in a hoarse whisper. She shook Wilma awake and helped her down. "We're here, we're home. Grab those blankets and let's go."

Collecting the boys, Alice led them down the alley to the apartment two blocks away. As thunder rumbled on the horizon, they made the trip up the switchback stairs to the rear deck. For the exhausted Velma, it was like climbing a mountain. Once inside, they went to bed without undressing.

None of them heard the new storm pass by only a short time later. Out of habit, Alice was up before dawn the next morning, a Saturday. She left the rest of the family sleeping and headed back to the Hanks' barn. Thankfully, he had left the side door unlocked, so she stepped inside, then opened the larger doors as quietly as the heavy hinges would allow.

She had nearly gotten Nelly harnessed, when a shadow from the glow of a lantern fell across the opening. It was Mr. Hanks carrying two mugs of coffee awkwardly in his free hand. "I figured you'd be up at an ungodly hour. Come get this."

"All hours are God's hours, Mr. Hanks," Alice retorted while gladly taking the mug. "Thank you, for the coffee and this." She made a sweeping motion toward the wagon. "And for all you and your wife's kindness, and..."

Alice fought the urge to cry but saw Henry had noticed. Stepping forward, he took an arm and guided the suddenly fragile woman to a nearby bale of hay. Smiling, he said, "Don't wear yourself out being grateful, Alice. Just sit down here for a while. There's no rush to deal with all this."

"But we have to..." She started but Henry interrupted.

"No, you don't. First things first." He sat down next to her. "We'll finish our coffee while you tell me about this latest encounter with Mother Nature."

"Oh, it weren't nothin'," she protested weakly.

Henry shook his head. "Let me be the judge of that. Then when you've finished, we'll have breakfast in the house. I'll send Tessa to get your kids when we're ready to eat."

Lacking the energy to argue, Alice nodded. "Now I owe you two for yet another kindness."

"Pay that back by telling me what happened," Henry said firmly.

A few minutes later, she had finished the story, and they headed inside for a refill. Tessa greeted her with a hug that made Alice a bit uneasy. Then, while she watched for one of the few times in her adult life, someone else started breakfast.

When everything was ready except the eggs, Tessa left them and headed down the alley to roust the Steele children. While Alice and Henry waited, they nibbled on toast and bacon. It was some time before the bleary-eyed girls arrived. Tessa managed to carry Eugene under one arm with Edward in the other.

Alice made her daughters clean the dishes after breakfast in spite of Tessa's objections. While the girls handled that chore, their mother headed back to the barn. Henry followed.

Seeing the makeshift cages barely holding in two dozen or so chickens, Henry suggested, "Why not put those in this spare stall. We have plenty as you can see. I can reuse that chicken wire to pen them in for now."

Though she wanted to say no, Alice could find no good reason. "Alright, but I'll pay rent for the space."

Henry burst out laughing. "You must have quite a ledger in that head of yours, Alice. You're the most beholdin' person I've ever met."

"Don't like to owe nobody," she said, not sensing the humor in Henry's voice.

"Have it your way." He tacked the wire along the front of the stall. As he finished, a thought came to him. "You can pay me in eggs for the space and feed. They can stay here, and we'll sell the eggs you don't need in the mercantile. If it turns out we make money, I'll build a bigger coop and add more chickens."

Alice gave this some thought, then nodded. "How many eggs?"

"I don't know. You tell me."

She did a quick calculation. "If you buy a couple dozen more right now to replace the ones we lost in the storm, I reckon we could start with a couple dozen a week."

"That's not many," Henry said disappointedly. Then he brightened. "But if you can give them to me on the weekend, that should appeal to a lot of my customers."

Alice pondered the idea. "I guess we can give that a try. But if my baking business gets going, I may have to pay you in cash instead of eggs."

"Or build a bigger coop," Henry said with a laugh, then added, "We can set that price when the time comes. Let's shake on it."

That done, Alice asked, "Do you know where I could find a good supplier of milk and butter?"

Henry nodded. "We have several, but I think Two-Timer would be your best bet."

"Who?" she asked while closing the gate on the stall, penning in the chickens.

"The man's name is Thomas Thomas, if you can believe it. So, everyone calls him by the nickname, Two-Timer, or Double T," Henry explained with a smile. "He has a big dairy farm out west of town and supplies much of the town. You can't miss his wagon. It's painted white with *'Thomas Dairy, Udderly the best'* on the side in red."

Even Alice had to smile at the image. "Sounds like a character."

"Indeed," Henry said, then added, "But he's reliable and the prices are fair. He delivers our milk here Mondays, Wednesdays, and Fridays early."

"What's early?"

Henry thought for a minute. "Oh, around six."

"I'll be here before that if you're willing to introduce me," Alice said hopefully.

"Well, sure, but a little later in the morning if you don't mind."

"Guess so, but I don't want to waste no time."

"Why am I not surprised?" Henry said, chuckling, then turned serious. "You got any cash?"

Alice moved to the wagon and climbed aboard. "Some."

"Good, 'cause Two-Timer will want a deposit."

Alice frowned as she picked up the reins. "How much?"

"How much milk you plan on needing?"

She pondered this for a minute. "How much do you think you can get for, say, one of my apple pies if you sold them?"

"A whole pie?"

"Yup."

It was Henry's turn to think. Then he shared his calculation. "Well, if you sold them to me at say fifty cents each, I could sell them for a buck. If they are any good, that is." He said this with a smile.

Alice wasn't smiling. Her mind was racing. "I never had to calculate what it cost me to make a pie. I'll have to think on that. Then we can negotiate."

"Fine by me, but remember you have to consider what's in season," Henry said, stepping out of the way.

Alice gave him a half smile this time. "I got a ton of canned apples, pears, peaches, and more. Plus, strawberries will be comin' in soon. So, I can get by for a while."

"That's great," Henry said, happy at the thought. "While you're at it, figure in other things—bread, rolls, and the like. We can talk about all this next week."

Alice clicked her tongue and Nelly moved out onto the alley, which was still showing signs of the storm from the night before. "We'll do that. And thank you again."

Henry waved her away. As he dodged puddles on the way back to the mercantile, Alice shouted over her shoulder, "Send the girls home when they've done the job proper."

"Will do."

Their first week in Woodward was crammed with activity, making it pass in a blur. The rest of that first Saturday, the girls and their mother made trip after long trip up and down the stairs as they emptied the wagon. Then they traveled to and from the barn, bringing the items stored there temporarily from earlier trips.

That evening, they began to set up the apartment, filling it the best they could with their limited belongings. There were no closets or wardrobes in any room. Alice and the girls neatly folded their clothing in corners temporarily until storage could be found. Two large cabinets that covered a wall in the kitchen managed to hold the contents of the root cellar.

Even though it was a full, hard day, it was nothing compared to the last weeks at the farm. Their biggest problem was keeping Eugene out of the boxes and away from the stairs. He tested them all frequently, while Edward thankfully just ate and slept.

Visiting the barn the next morning, Velma heard Mama ask Mrs. Hanks whether there was a Methodist church in town. Tessa chuckled, "Land's a Goshen, Alice. What Iowa town doesn't have one? We're members. Service is at ten. We'll come by and pick you up today and introduce you around. Nice folks there."

"Much obliged, Mrs. Hanks."

"Don't you think it's time you started calling me and Henry by our Christian names?" Tessa said with a smile. "You'll hurt my feelings if you don't."

"If you insist," Alice said shyly.

Tessa teased her. "Then try it out, won't you?"

"Yes, Tessa."

Mrs. Hanks reached out and took Alice's hand. "My really good friends call me Tess." Alice nodded and smiled but didn't say anything.

So, Tessa showed Alice and Velma how to get in the barn to feed the chickens and gather the eggs each morning. The trip had obviously affected the egg production, but there was plenty for a good breakfast. By 9:45 the next day, the family was waiting on the curb, gazing at a steeple less than two blocks away.

Henry and Tessa arrived promptly, and the little group made their way to services on a bright and warm morning. As promised, the Steele clan were happily welcomed by nearly everyone. Reverend Jones was especially attentive, promising to make a visit later in the week.

While talking to the pastor after the service, however, a couple approached them, wearing less than friendly expressions. Seeing them approach, Alice pulled Edward closer to her breast. The man immediately began speaking in a rude tone. "You've got your nerve. My wife here is a Skinner by birth."

Pastor Jones stepped in awkwardly. "Please, Mr. Brown, this isn't..."

Interrupting, the man addressed the reverend. "Do you know about this woman? She abandoned her family to marry a Catholic. He's dead now and, well, his wife is paying the price for her..."

"Stop, Edgar." It was Pastor Jones' turn to interrupt vehemently. "If there is a price, that is between God and Mrs. Steele. I think this is a subject best left to them." Then the reverend turned back to Alice and said warmly, "We look forward to seeing you next Sunday. Sunday school starts at 9:00."

Nodding silently, Alice turned and, with the girls close behind, joined the Hanks on the street where they stood with Eugene in tow. "What was that all about?" Henry asked.

"They're relatives of mine and don't seem to appreciate me attending *their* church." Alice took Eugene's hand and headed off down the street.

The others quickly fell in behind her as Henry responded, "Edgar and Edith Brown try the patience of Reverend Jones, the congregation, and God regularly. So, I wouldn't pay them any mind."

"What were they upset about anyway?" Tessa asked innocently.

Alice stopped and turned to face the Hanks. "My husband was Catholic."

After a brief pause in which Tessa and Henry exchanged looks, they both chuckled. Seeing Alice's annoyed look, Henry managed to get out, "Is that all? Heck, you'd think people would be over such things. After all, this is the 20th century."

"And I'll tell you a secret, Alice." Tessa said, moving closer to her new friend. "I used to be one of those Catholic heathens." She winked. "And my punishment for converting was marrying Henry here."

He gave the women a look of mock indignation. "Punishment? Well, I never."

Both women laughed as Tessa retook her husband's arm. "Now see what I've done. The poor man's feelings are hurt."

"Oh, Tess," Alice said, trying to regain her composure. "You are a hoot."

Tessa gave her a little bow as their little gaggle moved off again. "I'll take that as a compliment." After a pause, she added, "Join us for Sunday dinner, won't you?"

The group halted in front of Grimminger Hardware while Alice considered. "Oh, we have a lot of organizing yet to do before tomorrow."

"All the more reason to join us and eliminate cooking from your list," Henry countered.

"Don't worry, Alice," Tessa added with a mischievous smile. "I promise not to cook for you every day."

Alice slowly nodded. "We'll come if you promise to join us next time."

"Well, I guess so," Tessa said getting an eager smile of agreement from her husband. "Say, it sounds like the start of a new tradition."

Then Henry asked excitedly, "Will you make a pie for this afternoon?"

"Two," Alice said, smiling back.

"Deal," the Hanks said in unison. The couple headed toward their own home as Tessa said in parting, "Come on over about three."

Nodding again, Alice offered, "I'll bring a jar of my best pickles too, if you like them that is."

"Are you kidding?" Tessa replied as they continued along the sidewalk. "Henry would eat the whole thing if I let him."

The Steeles watched the Hanks continue chattering away at each other pleasantly. Before the Hanks were out of sight, Alice turned to her brood. "Upstairs with you all and into work clothes. We can get some work in before heading over for supper."

By Monday, the apartment looked like the Steeles had been living there for quite some time. Everything was in its place. Getting to sleep was hard for them all with the town noises that continued into the late evening. Still, they had gotten more rest over the first few days in Woodward than the weeks leading up to the move.

Alice left Velma with the boys after breakfast and headed off early to school with a reluctant Wilma. The younger daughter reminded her mother, "You promised to take me to see the school too."

"And I will, but not this morning. I need to get Wilma enrolled today."

There were only a few weeks left before summer vacation, thus making this an awkward situation for a child who tended toward the dramatic. Alice was insistent, however, saying the sooner this was over the better.

While meeting and taking care of the paperwork for Wilma, Alice asked the teacher when would be a good time to bring Velma back for a visit. The woman seemed less than enthused but suggested that if they came back right after school that day, she could show them both around. Promising to be back, Alice headed home.

The accuracy of Alice's earlier theory regarding Wilma's rapid adjustment seemed doubtful as soon as Wilma got back from school that afternoon, somber-faced and silent. Mama and Velma considered even this a small victory, however, given what the girl's reaction could have been.

Instead of pushing the matter at that moment, Alice told Wilma to watch the boys and took Velma to school, where the little girl was awed by the school's size and ignored the teacher's continued lack of enthusiasm as she rushed them through the tour, giving one-word answers to questions. The reason why became clear in the end when she announced this was her last year at the school.

Back home, Alice said to Wilma apologetically, "I am sorry that you are having to deal with a less than enthusiastic teacher."

"She was awful to me," Wilma said woefully. "I don't want to go back."

This comment was greeted with a frown. "I said unenthusiastic, not mean. Anyway, you don't have a choice, but it's only for four more weeks." The sympathy was gone from Alice's voice.

"But, Mama." The scowl this earned brought her to a halt.

"Do you have homework?"

"Yes," came the weak reply.

"Then get to it while we get dinner ready," Alice said sternly. Then she headed to the kitchen with Velma at her heels. Wilma brought up the rear, mumbling something as she turned into the bedroom. Mama chose to ignore her.

The next morning, Wilma said nothing but headed off to school willingly. By midweek, she was talking again and not about missing her old school friends. On Friday, she arrived home with two girls in tow. They didn't stay long, as there were chores to do, but this was a clear sign that she was moving on.

After taking Wilma to school that first Monday, Alice went to meet Mr. Smith with Henry and ordered four gallons of milk and twice as much butter, to be delivered on Wednesday. She purchased flour, sugar, and spices at the mercantile, where Mr. Hanks insisted, she set up a line of credit. He also ordered her first dozen pies.

Then she placed an ad in the Woodward Enterprise weekly newspaper offering baking, cleaning, sewing, and ironing. Laundry would wait until she talked to her landlord about using the washhouse. The paper also offered a printing service, so she ordered flyers saying the same thing as the advertisement.

While Alice was roaming the town, Velma spent that morning watching her brothers. Eugene quickly grew bored wandering the apartment and being told no. Fearful the toddler might escape her watchful eye and fall from the outside deck, Velma left Edward asleep in his cradle and headed downstairs with Eugene.

The two made several trips around the block before heading up repeatedly to check on the baby. Velma was soon exhausted, while Eugene craved more. They were making yet another circuit when mother returned and relieved her daughter.

After a lunch of leftovers from dinner at the Hanks, Alice went downstairs to the hardware stores and, with most of her remaining cash, purchased a large icebox. While it was being carried upstairs, she arranged for weekly deliveries of ice starting that very evening. All this had been accomplished before Wilma arrived home from school the first day.

The milk and butter arrived at six-sharp on Wednesday morning. After putting it in the icebox, Alice was off to collect the fliers she'd ordered. These were distributed door-to-door before noon. The plan was to return the next day to collect orders and assignments.

That afternoon, while Velma managed the boys, Alice launched the new family business. Even though it was a stiflingly hot day, a dozen pies, made from the canned fruit they had brought, were ready for delivery by the time Wilma got back home.

Alice carefully loaded them in two crates Mr. Hanks had provided, cleverly redesigned for the purpose. Then she called for the girls. "Take these to the mercantile and be careful not to drop them."

"But what about my homework?"

"Time for that later, missy. Now git."

Wilma grumbled all the way down the stairs and along the alley. Velma, on the other hand, was delighted to leave the boys behind for a while. Mrs. Hanks answered her back door and squealed with delight. "Henry, come see what just arrived. Henry!"

When he appeared and took a look, Velma saw him licking his lips. So had Mrs. Hanks. "These are for us to sell, Mr. Hanks, not for you to eat." Before he could launch a protest, his wife giggled. "Don't worry, dear. You'll get one."

"One?"

"One slice!"

"Oh well," Henry said resignedly, then brightened. "Tell your mama that the sign Annie made about the pies is already working. She has two sales pending, three if you count the one for me, I mean us."

"Wow," Velma said while Wilma just nodded.

"Pay the girls, Henry and let them get back home."

"Let me go get the money. We need to do this right." Leaving the kitchen, he was only gone a minute before returning with cash in one hand and a ledger in the other. After giving the cash to Wilma, he started to make an entry in the ledger then stopped. "What's your mother calling her business?"

"Ah, I don't know." Wilma stuttered, then turned to Velma. "Do you?"

She shook her head, then asked, "You want we should run and ask?"

"No, that's alright. I'll get the name the next time I see her." He closed the book, then reached out to the girls. "And here's something for your labor."

Tessa had emptied all the pies from the carrier and was returning them to Wilma and Velma as Henry gave each a piece of hard candy. "Henry. Alice won't like you spoiling them like that."

"You just don't want me giving away our profit, dear." Mr. Hanks said, winking at Velma. Then he handed her another piece. "This one's for Gene."

"Thank you, Mr. Hanks," the girls said as one, then headed out the door.

Back at the apartment, the girls gave their mother the money. Alice took it with a smile, "My, my, our first sale." After counting the cash, she added, "I guess the wholesale price has already gone up."

The girls didn't understand, and Alice didn't explain. Instead, she put the money in a mason jar on top of the new icebox. "Let's hope they sell."

Velma replied excitedly. "They are, Mama. Annie sold two already."

"And Mr. and Mrs. Hanks bought the first one. So, three are gone."

"That's encouraging." Alice said while her expression turned serious. "At that rate we'll earn back the money I've spent so far in a few months just from the pies."

"That's wonderful, Mama," Wilma said, apparently not noticing her mother's look.

Alice produced a cookie sheet of dough-floppy while saying, "That is a good start but won't be enough to cover all our expenses." She held the tray out to the girls. Velma grabbed some, but Wilma was distracted by what her Mother was saying. "There is the rent for starters. We'll need to sell more pies to cover that."

"Oh," Wilma said, suddenly looking concerned as she finally attacked the tray of treats. "But you'll be baking more than pies."

Alice brushed a crumb from the seven-year old's' face. "Yes and doing other work as well. So, don't fret child. We'll make do, and we'll do it on our own."

"Yes, Mama," Wilma said uncertainly. "Hey, leave some for me," she yelled at her little sister whose mouth was filled to the brim.

A muffled "Sorry" came from Velma who stepped back from the tray, making room for Wilma to finish off the last of the crisp cinnamon and sugar treats.

Alice turned back to a kitchen filled with the tools of her pie-making trade. "Now, Velma, come help me clean up, and Wilma, you get to your homework."

While the little girl filled the sink with water from the pump, her mother added more from the kettle simmering on the stove. The result was a warm bath for the bowls, pie pans, and drip sheets. As Velma finished the first bowl, Alice quickly snatched up, dried, and put it back to work again.

"What are you making now, Mama?" Velma asked with a sigh.

"Cookies," was Alice's matter-of-fact reply.

Velma was not sure she should ask but did anyway, "For us?"

Alice shrugged. "I expect you will get a few, but I'm making most of these to sell. Mr. Hanks may want to sell a few along with the pies. Tomorrow I do bread."

Velma said nothing more and returned to her chore. Just then Edward began to cry in his cradle that was tucked in a corner of the kitchen. "So soon?" Alice said frustratedly as she put down her hand mixer. Unbuttoning her blouse, she headed his way.

Lifting the baby, Alice first confirmed which end was in need of attention. While moving to a chair and helping Edward find her breast, she shouted, "Wilma, get me some more wood for the kitchen stove."

"Ah, Mama," came her typical response. "I just got started on my homework."

"Plenty of time for that. I need the wood if you want dinner tonight."

There was no further argument, and in a few minutes, Wilma entered from the long hall with an armload of wood. "Is this enough?" she asked hopefully.

"One more load should do it."

With a "harrumph," the girl stomped out of the room as Velma smiled and kept washing. After returning with the second load, Wilma attempted a hasty retreat but didn't quite make it. "Is Eugene still sleeping?"

"I, ah, yes, I think so, Mama."

Alice frowned. "You don't sound too sure. Go check on him and, if he's awake, bring him in here. You can do your homework on the end of the table."

Velma saw her sister's look of displeasure, then turn on her heels and head down the hall. Within seconds she was back wearing a happier expression. "He's still sleeping."

"Get busy then and keep a closer eye on the boy. He'll be into somethin' when he does wake up if you don't. And I'll want your help with dinner soon."

The evening meal consisted of a stew, again made from leftovers, with dumplings added. The girls and Eugene each got a cookie for dessert, while several dozen others were packed for delivery. Then Eugene got a bath in the sink. After struggling with the obstinate boy, Alice told the girls her next purchase would be a washtub for them all.

There was still light clinging to the western horizon when the children were tucked in and Alice closed their doors. Velma fell asleep to the sound of her mother still moving about in the kitchen. She woke to the same sound the next morning.

The girls found everything was organized for more baking, with the first batches in the oven and bread rising in loaf pans. "Is baking all you'll be doing now, Mama?" Wilma asked.

Alice shook her head as she cracked eggs in a skillet for breakfast. "No, child. I'll be doin' this until I get other work. Then I'll just bake once durin' the week and once on the weekend." Noticing the crock of butter was already getting low, she sighed. "Glad I don't have to churn all the butter I've been a usin' anymore."

5
Mystery Solved

In fact, all Alice did during the month was bake. For some reason, there had been no rush to hire her for any of the other services she'd advertised. A couple of local restaurants had ordered bread and pies in limited quantities, however, and she cleaned two houses once each but had not been called back. That was all.

In response, Alice approached her landlord, Mr. Grimminger, and got his approval to use the washhouse for laundry. Then she printed new flyers including laundry service. Within the week she had walked the town again distributing them.

She expected laundry, along with ironing, to be popular choices, especially with the heat of summer coming. When she got no takers, Alice sought Henry's council. "A lot of people seemed interested in me doin' laundry when you put that noticed on your board months back, but I got no responses."

"That does seem odd," he replied scratching his head. "Let me do some checking around and see what I can find out."

"Thank you, Henry."

"You're welcome." Noting her worried look, he asked, "You doing alright?"

Alice put on a brave front. "Oh, my bakin's quite popular, but not popular enough to cover all the bills."

"What if I ordered more of your wares? They are selling like hot cakes," Henry offered.

"To do more, I'd need a bigger kitchen with more stoves, and I can't afford that. Besides, I can hardly stand the heat up there with the days getting' hotter."

"Well then, I'll see what I can find out and let you know."

"Thanks again."

It was an angry Henry that greeted Alice two days later. "Just the woman I wanted to see. I was about to head over to your place." Then he paused. "Say, where's my little Velma this morning?"

"She's tendin' the chickens. Since you bought those new layers, it takes her longer."

"Sorry about that."

"Oh, don't be. I need them."

"So does the mercantile," Henry added, then gazed at the basket Alice was carrying and got distracted. "Cookies?" he implored.

"As a matter of fact, yes." She folded back the red and white checkered cloth revealing her bounty. "In addition to sugar and oatmeal, I added molasses."

Henry clapped his hands together. "Are all those for me, I mean the store?"

"Afraid not, Henry," Alice said apologetically. "A dozen are for Clarke's Café and the other for..."

"I know, Delmonico's," Henry said with mock disdain. "I wanted you all to myself, you know."

"Just double what you pay me and that could be arranged."

Henry laughed. "Since I eat half of what you deliver, I don't think Tess would go for that."

Then, noticing Alice's dress was already drenched through, though it was still early morning, he turned serious again. "You look exhausted."

"Not really, just hot."

Henry was doubtful that was true. "That reminds me of why I wanted to talk to you, why I'm so ... well, I can't say what I'm really feeling in the presence of a lady."

"What is it, Henry?"

"I said I'd check into the mystery of why so many people said they were interested in your services back in April but then didn't use them." Henry became more animated as he spoke. "Well, the reason is Edith and Edgar Brown. They've been talking to anyone who would listen, badmouthing you and your husband."

Alice remained uncommonly calm. "I'm not surprised. I've never told you about that."

"I've only heard what the people poisoned by the Browns have said," Henry offered.

Alice shook her head. "I guess I better get my side in then."

"Not now, I got shipments to get unloaded, and I know you're always busy," Henry said with a knowing smile. "Why don't you and the children come for dinner tonight? You can tell your story, and we can figure out how to deal with this."

After a moment's consideration, Alice nodded. "Thanks for the invitation. I'll bring dessert."

"And a loaf of your seeded bread?" Once again, a childish look of anticipation crossed the rotund man's face.

"Sorry, Henry," she said, seeing his expression fall. "All I have is a plain loaf."

His smile returned. "I'll, I mean *we'll* take it. See you at six."

When the Steeles arrived at the back door that night, they were greeted not only by the Hanks but also by Pastor Jones and his wife. "Hello, Mrs. Steele. I've been wanting to make a pastoral visit for weeks, but, frankly, you're hard to catch. I believe you've met Grace."

Alice smiled weakly and extended a hand as she stepped inside with Edward in her other arm. "Yes. Nice to see you again." Then she nodded to Wilma. "You know my children?"

"Yes. Hello, Wilma, Velma, and Eugene." Grace reached out and tickled Edward under his chin, causing him to smile. "I think this is my first up close encounter with Edward, however. He is adorable." This comment had the girls giggling.

"Give the saver to Mrs. Hanks, Wilma." As her oldest did so, Alice continued, "Can't say you aren't right about my being busy, Reverend."

"Please, call me Alan," he suggested, his smile broadening.

Alice blushed a bit. "I'm not sure I can do that. My Ma would frown on such forwardness."

The pastor nodded. "Have it your way, but I like to escape the reverend label once in a while. And this is one of those occasions."

"Some days I'd like him to escape permanently," Grace added with a smile.

The reverend chuckled and patted his wife's hand. Then turning to Mrs. Steele again, he asked, "May I call you Alice though?"

Blushing again, Alice nodded, then turned to Velma. "Now give Mrs. Hanks the bread, dear." Hearing her cordial tone, Velma decided it was especially nice being with her mother around other people.

The dinner was a feast, from Velma's perspective. Then the children were sent to the other room with the boys while the adults talked over coffee. What they were saying caught her interest. So, while Wilma did homework and the boys dozed, she listened.

"I think we know the core of the issue," Henry started. "You married a Catholic man and that didn't go over well with either family."

"That's right."

"Well, I won't go into the version of what happened that's being spread by the Browns, but suffice it to say, it paints you both in a pretty bad light."

"That sounds like a Skinner. We tend to hold grudges and find forgivin' difficult. Sorry, reverend."

"Nothing to be sorry for, Alice. We all struggle with that skill from time to time," Pastor Jones replied. "I come from a family like that too."

"As do I," Tessa added.

"But this is Alice's story tonight," Henry reminded them.

"Right," Grace agreed. "So, let's hear it."

"Well, I don't like to talk much."

"Just give it your best effort," Tessa encouraged.

With a hesitant nod, Alice began. "I was what you might call an angelic child. I don't mean no disrespect when I say that.

I just mean, I was a good girl, the one always doin' the right things, at least in my parent's eyes. That is sayin' somethin' as I'm one of eleven."

"That's a big family," Grace said with awe. "Where in line were you?"

"I got, or had, three older brothers. One of them is dead, and one older sister. Then came me. Four more girls and two more boys. We were all raised on a farm, like most folk around here. It belonged to my grandfather until he died.

"Anyway, I dropped outta school after eighth grade to help around the place. I had a knack for cookin' so spent most of my time in the kitchen learnin' from my ma."

"Thank God," Henry interjected, generating nods and laughter around the table.

"Now, let me cut to the chase," Alice said, fidgeting in her seat. "It was the cookin' that started it all. When I was around sixteen, I entered my baked goods at the annual flea market and bazaar in Granger. By the next year, I was winnin' every category I entered. My reputation started attractin' attention, includin' from young men.

"The summer I turned eighteen, my husband to be, *William Devon Steele*, stopped by my stall." She'd said his name reverently. "I sold extra pies, breads, and the like there to make spendin' money. He was a handsome rogue and quite a flirt. Wore a jaunty hat suited to his personality. I must say I was smitten.

"That was until I learned he was the ne'er-do-well of the Steele clan. Oh, he was a hard worker, farmed the 80 acres his family owned and where I lived after we married. But he was also a hard partier and drinker. Now my family abhorred drink, as do I. So after learning that, I would have nothin' to do with him.

"I guess that was what attracted him to me, my unwillingness to give him the time of day. Not that we had much chance to see each other. Our farms were miles apart."

"So how did you end up married?" Tess asked impatiently.

"Well, the next summer, he came to my stall every day. When I finally told him why I'd have nothin' to do with him, he said he'd change his ways and change my mind. During the week of the fair, he did both.

"Next time I saw him, he showed up at our place. His farm was about ten miles away as the crow flies. So, he had to go far out of his way to find me. I was flattered. Anyway, Papa shooed him off right quick, but not before he and I jawed for a bit.

"It seemed after that, every time I went to Granger over the course of the year, the closest place to get supplies, he'd be there." She gave the group a wry smile. "I can't imagine how he managed that. Bein' older, I often went alone. So we got to know each other pretty well during those times.

"When the rumor reached my Pa's ears that I'd been sparkin' with Will Steele, well, things got pretty bad quick like. He forbade me to see him and made sure one of my kin went to town with me from now on. Ma was on his side too, so I felt put upon. At eighteen and deeply in love, you can kind of guess where this is goin'."

"Let me guess," Tess said. "You eloped."

Alice nodded. "Will and I were so in love and so naïve that we were sure things would blow over in a few months and we'd be welcomed back by both families. Though we were both church goers, neither of us realized the level of hatred between we Methodies and the papists.

"Even if our folks might have let us back in, the relatives wouldn't. In fact, many stopped associatin' with our parents just because of us. Can you believe it?"

"Yes," Reverend Jones replied for the group as the others nodded.

"Well, we didn't mind at first. The one good thing was that Will's Pa didn't take the farm back. Instead, he started charging us rent, and a high one at that. Still, with our hard work, we managed."

Grace interrupted with a question. "Didn't the arrival of children make a difference?"

Alice laughed hollowly. "Not in the least, may have made things worse. I had a miscarriage a year after we married. No family came to help us. Two years in, I had a stillbirth. Still, no family came or went to the burial. After Wilma was born, we took her to see both sets of parents. They wouldn't answer the door. That's when Will gave up on the Steeles. I was more stubborn and kept goin' to my family's church every Sunday.

"Sadly, in the year prior to Will's untimely death, a few of the cousins on both sides had begun to reach out. They did so secretively, however, to avoid bein' punished in some way by the others who are still in the majority." After a pause she asked, "Do you want to know something funny?"

The group nodded. "I'd never met the Browns, as far as I recollect, until that first Sunday at your church, Reverend Jones."

"Really?"

"Yup. But I bet they claim they know all about Will and me, what happened and all."

"Well, their story doesn't sound much like yours," Henry answered angrily. "The people I talked to were told you had to get married, that you did this to spite your parents, and that Will was a drunk and beat you, causing the babies to be lost."

"Well, the part about spite might contain some truth," Alice said, dropping her eyes, then quickly looking up defiantly. "The rest is hogwash. William had a beer at home once in a while, which I didn't like. But he never got drunk. There was no time for that with all it took to keep the farm goin'.

"As for beatin's, he never hit me, though he spanked the girls a time or two when they deserved it." She glanced at Velma when she said this, then went on. "Our home may have lacked a bit in the way of outward affection, but there was no cruelty. Hard work for sure, but nothin' else."

As she concluded, Alice sat back, obviously drained of words and overcome by emotion. "Can I have some water, please?"

"Sure, honey," Tessa said, grabbing the pitcher and leaning over to refill Alice's glass. "Thank you for sharing all that. There was a lot of pain in your story."

"No more than others have had, I'm sure," Alice replied unpretentiously.

"Now that we know what's what, *what* are we going to do about it?" Henry said, his anger simmering just below the surface.

At that point, Velma began to nod off as the hour grew later. The adults continued on for quite some time strategizing. The little girl drifted in and out, missing most of the remaining conversation.

What seemed like hours later, the Steele family headed home, carrying food packed by Tessa. Velma couldn't tell what her mother was feeling, either relief or anxiety. Whatever her mood, no one said anything during the short walk. While the children went straight to bed, Alice headed for the kitchen and started baking.

The next day was Sunday, and after morning chores, they all put on their good clothes. Once again, they joined the Hanks in front of the hardware store. This day, Alice was carrying a large basket that smelled of cinnamon and had Henry drooling. She told him he'd just have to wait, as they headed off to church.

At the end of the service before the benediction, Pastor Jones stepped down from the pulpit. He stood on the steps of the alter in silence, scanning the gathering. He remained that way so long that the congregation became a bit uncomfortable.

At last, he began speaking calmly. "As Christians, we are taught to live by the Ten Commandments. Alas, it would appear that some of us have forgotten at least one of them, the one about not bearing false witness. To me, this commandment means more than being honest. It means not doing harm to others with our words.

"Now I have come to know that one among us, one new to our town, one trying to put down roots through hard, honest work, is suffering because of a few who spread false witness. Further, those who have done so have also forgotten another lesson from Jesus, the one about forgiveness and casting of the first stone."

Pastor Jones paused, scanning the sanctuary. As he spoke again, his eyes were on Edith and Edgar Brown. "Well, I must have failed in my ministry, as those lessons have obviously eluded some among us. Only God can forgive you, and I pray those who have strayed from that particular commandment will seek it.

"Now, following the benediction, please join me in fellowship hall for refreshment." His gaze went to Alice. "Rumor has it there will be some marvelous cinnamon rolls there that I am already coveting."

This broke the tension and brought soft laughter to the sanctuary as Pastor Jones concluded, "And now, may the Lord bless and keep you; the Lord make his face to shine upon you, and be gracious unto you; the Lord lift up his countenance upon you, and give you peace, now and forever more. Amen."

The fellowship hall crowd was initially subdued. Reverend Jones stood with Alice and the children as congregants approached to acknowledge his sermon and closing remarks. He would introduce the family, then direct them to partake of Alice's delicious rolls, one of the many skills she was offering the community.

When the Steeles and Hanks headed home, it was unclear what the long-term impact of that morning's events might have. Many of the congregation, starting with the Browns, had not attended the social hour. Pastor Jones addressed this with Alice, telling her not to read too much into that but, rather, to wait and see.

It proved a long wait. Undaunted, Alice expanded her baking trade and cleaned out the washhouse in anticipation of future laundry trade. Thankfully, Mr. Grimminger's agreement to a three-month trial would begin only when she had customers.

When not baking, Alice made the rounds of businesses and neighborhoods with another layer of flyers. Less than a week after the pastor's speech, she got her first laundry customer. It wasn't as a result of the reverend's impassioned appeal, however. It came from Delmonico's, the fanciest restaurant in town. Soon, the café also started sending their linens her way.

The first non-business laundry customer came after church the next Sunday. Agnes Warren, a church member, asked Alice what she charged for laundry and ironing. The price was acceptable, and arrangements made for a weekly pickup starting that next Monday.

Agnes and her husband, Carl, lived just a long block from the church. They had two children, a boy, Freddie, and a daughter, Katie. The little girl turned out to be just a few months older than Velma.

Early the next day, Alice hitched up Nelly, while Velma fed the chickens and collected eggs. While Wilma watched the boys before school, Alice and Velma drove the few blocks to the Warren place. Velma had never seen such a fancy home.

A white picket fence framed a yard filled with great oaks and elms. At the center of the lot stood a monolithic three-story Victorian mansion. The roof was covered with gingerbread gables painted a dark green. Each window frame bore the same color, contrasting starkly with the bright-white clapboard siding.

Mother and daughter made their way up the brick sidewalk to an ornate glass and wood front entrance and knocked tentatively. In a few moments, Mrs. Warren opened the door. "I thought I heard a knock." With a smile, she pointed to a button beside the door. "We have one of those newfangled doorbells now."

"Oh," Alice said sheepishly. "I'll remember that next time. Or should we come to a different entrance, Mrs. Warren?"

A little girl peeked out from behind her mother's billowing dress as Mrs. Warren said, "Oh, do call me Agnes." She reached down and pulled the child to her side. "And, this is my little Katie. Say hello, dear."

"Hello," came the shy response as she stared at Velma.

"Hi, my name's Velma," she said firmly, displaying a big smile.

"That will do, child," Alice said sharply.

Mrs. Warren clucked, "Oh, that's fine, Mrs. Steele. I know Katie here was so excited to finally meet the girl she's been curious about at church these last weeks."

"Well, Velma tends to be a bit too easily excited," Alice replied. "I regret our schedule hasn't made it possible for her to attend Sunday school as yet."

Alice let Velma step forward as she asked Katie, "How old are you?"

"Five," the blonde replied with a shy smile.

"Me, too," Velma said, beaming. "Will you be going to school this fall?"

"Yes. You too?"

Velma nodded enthusiastically. "I can't wait." She noticed Katie didn't seem quite as eager. "We'll have so much fun together. I hope the teacher is smart."

This brought a laugh from Mrs. Warren, who then asked, "Can you and your daughter come in for a minute? I have coffee brewed." Agnes stepped aside to allow them to pass.

Alice shook her head. "I'm afraid we can't stay. My older daughter, Wilma, is watchin' my boys."

Agnes colored. "Oh, of course. You sure have your hands full."

"Some days for sure," Alice said humbly, "but I got the girls to help."

Mrs. Warren frowned. "That doesn't leave much time for little girls to play."

"No," Alice said flatly, in a tone aimed at ending the subject. "So, if I can get your laundry and ironin'."

"Of course. It's right here." Agnes stooped and picked up two canvas bags filled to the brim. "I divided it into wash and fold and wash and iron. Most of the ironing is for my husband. He wears a lot of dress shirts for his job at the bank. He's the president, you see," Agnes said without braggadocio.

Alice took the bags. "Any sheets?" Agnes nodded. "You want them ironed?"

"No, folded will be fine."

"All right now then." Alice hoisted the bags and headed down the path. "Come along, Velma. "

Agnes stopped the two as they moved away. "When do you want your money?"

"I'll do a count and calculate that before I return them on Wednesday. Then you can see my work." Agnes nodded approvingly. "Where shall I return it?"

After a moment, Mrs. Warren said with a smile, "Bring it to the kitchen side, then you'll be closer to the coffee. There's a doorbell at that entrance as well."

Alice did not comment, just hefted the bags down the front steps before pausing. "If I find something to mend, do you want me just to do it?"

"Yes, that would be fine." Agnes gently pushed her daughter forward. "See your new friend to the gate, Katie." Then she made another appeal to Alice. "Please bring Velma and the boys back when you return. We'll have that coffee, and the children can play even if it's only for a short time."

Velma looked to her mother hopefully but was disappointed to hear her say, "I'm not sure there will be time for that, but I'll give it some consideration. Good day."

Wednesday found Nelly hauling everyone but Wilma back to the Warren home. Agnes and Katie happily greeted them at the side-kitchen door. "Won't you come in, Alice?" Agnes asked hopefully.

"I suppose so. I need to go over the bill with you after you check out my work."

"There's little doubt your work will be far better than mine." Agnes chuckled. "I'm embarrassed to admit that."

"No need, Mrs. —Agnes. You did it out of necessity. I'm doin' it to make a livin'."

After unloading the laundry and ironing, Agnes gave it a quick, approving once over, and the women sat to review the laundry bill over coffee. While Alice held Edward, the girls headed off with Eugene tagging along.

"You mind your brother doesn't get into trouble," Alice admonished.

"Yes, Mama," Velma said happily, as she and Katie disappeared.

Agnes gave Alice a sympathetic look, "I know you and your girls have little free time."

"None more like it."

"I'm sure. Anyway, I have found our brief time today as a pleasant break from my more mundane duties. Please try to fit this time each week. It will do us both good, and my Katie adores your Velma."

"I will do my best, Agnes. Thank you for the invitation." Alice took a last sip, then stood. "Now we must get going."

"Of course. Oh, let me get your money." As Agnes got up, she called to her daughter. "Katie, Mrs. Steele and Velma need to leave."

"Yes, Mother," a small voice came from somewhere nearby, followed by the sound of footsteps. The two girls arrived with Eugene trailing behind just as Agnes returned with her purse in hand. "Here you are."

"Can we set up a regular schedule?" Alice asked, moving to the door with Velma hanging back by Katie.

"Yes, we should."

"How about I pick up and drop off each Wednesday? That way we take care of everything all at once."

"Fine by me."

"Good, Agnes." Alice waved Velma over and the two exited.

"Coffee again next week?"

Alice nodded as she climbed on the wagon. "Thank you." The wagon pulled away with the little girls smiling and waving at each other until they were out of sight.

Shortly, Grace Jones started joining Alice at the Warren house on Wednesdays. She also brought a few items to be laundered and ironed each week. In spite of her busy schedule, Alice managed to spare an hour each week. Everyone but Tessa was happy with the arrangement. When she heard about the coffee clutch, she lamented not being able to escape the mercantile.

As the new school year approached, however, Alice announced, "After next week, I can't come any more with both Wilma and Velma off to school."

"But the boys are welcome here," Agnes protested.

"Yes, but I will have a heavier workload without the girls' help."

This news set Tessa to thinking, and she made a suggestion to Henry. "Why don't we have a get together with Alice, the Reverend and Grace, and the Warrens, plus all the kids on Sunday?"

"Do you mean this Sunday or every Sunday?" Henry asked with some trepidation.

Tessa hesitated. "Ah, I hadn't gotten that far. What do you suggest besides not doing it at all?"

"Are you kidding, miss out on one of Alice's pastries?" Her husband was smiling broadly. "I'm in." Then he added, "Just not every weekend. We'd run out of things to say."

"Okay. I'll run it by the others and see if there is any interest."

Thus, deep friendships between the four families, especially the wives and children, began that summer. Velma and Katie had already bonded, while Wilma and Freddie, being in the same grade, established a positive, though fragile at times, connection. The women, different in so many ways, became remarkably close, which would prove valuable in many unexpected ways.

Most importantly, the Warrens were the first of many families that began to use the many services Alice offered. By the end of that summer, though they didn't have much to spare, Alice worried a little less about making ends meet.

As for the girls, they too had prospered. In the remaining weeks of the school year, Wilma adjusted well, excelled academically, and made several new girlfriends. Her melancholy over the move had rapidly waned.

Besides Katie, Velma quickly made friends with those at Sunday school once she was able to attend regularly. Among them was Pastor Jones' daughter, Charity, who was three years older. In time, the three girls would play together most Sundays during the families' rotating bi-weekly suppers.

By fall, Alice and the girls had more than adjusted to life in Woodward. They had established a cottage industry and cemented many positive relationships with local businesses and people in the community. Most valuable of all, however, was the new extended family, one that cared for and about them, that they had gained.

6

THE GOOD LIFE?

A new world opened for Velma that first September in Woodward when school started. On an unusually cool morning, she dressed in darkness, having slept little, and attacked her chores. Back at the apartment, she helped her mother tend to the boys and prepare for the day's baking before literally running out the door.

She had walked around the impressive brick school building and nearby wooden gymnasium whenever she got the chance during the summer. Given the grandeur of these buildings, she was sure the place was chock full of learnin'. Now she arrived in a rush, just as a man dressed in a suit was unlocking the door.

Seeing her arrive out of breath, he gave her a smile and said, "My, my, we are eager, aren't we?"

Velma didn't understand who the "we" was, so said, "Oh, *I* am excited to start school. This is my first day ever."

The man chuckled. "I'd never have guessed. What's your name, my dear?"

"Velma Steele, sir."

"Well, hello, Miss Steele. My name is Mr. Dickinson. I'm the principal."

With a crisp curtsy, Velma replied, "Pleased to meet you, sir."

"Likewise, Miss Steele," the man said, stepping aside to let her pass. "Now it's just the two of us here. So, why don't you take a seat on that bench until the festivities begin."

"Festiv'ties?" she tried to repeat, not understanding.

Mr. Dickinson chuckled again, "That just means when the school day starts."

"Oh," Velma said with a nod, as she took a seat.

The principal headed off toward a door, saying, "Now if you need anything in the meantime, just come get me in here. And have a good first day, Miss Steele."

With a nod, she watched him disappear. For what seemed like forever, the five-year-old fidgeted on the hard bench. Then two women came through the door and stared at the early arrival.

"Ah, our first victim," the matronly one of the pair said with a cackle.

Velma's mouth fell open, suddenly frightened, until the other young woman said, "Don't scare the poor thing to death on the first day, Martha." Addressing Velma directly, she added, "You'll love it here, if you like to learn that is."

"Oh, yes," she blurted out.

"That's what we like to hear, right Martha?" the younger woman asked.

Martha just nodded while heading to the door that Mr. Dickinson had entered. "My name is Miss Fletcher," the young lady said to Velma. "I'm sure we'll see each other again soon."

"I'd like that."

"Good," Miss Fletcher said, then headed off swiftly toward the same door. A moment later, the door closed, and silence returned.

It wasn't long, however, before other students began to arrive, Freddie and Katie Warren among them.

"Over here, Katie!"

Her friend hurried to her side. "I just knew I'd find you here already."

"I can't wait. Can you?" Velma asked breathlessly.

"Well, I guess not, but don't you find it a little scary?"

Velma was surprised at the question. "Why, no."

Just then Wilma arrived with some of her new friends. Velma waved, but her sister just turned her back and started talking to Freddie. Velma frowned. "What's the matter with her?"

"Who?" Katie asked, not having seen what happened Velma shrugged, "Never mind. Look at all the kids coming in. I didn't know there were enough kids in town to fill this place."

"That's because a lot of the kids come from farms around here and from Granger and other small towns that don't have a school."

"Granger?"

"It's down the road from here maybe ten miles on the way to Des Moines."

Velma only vaguely recalled hearing those names and had never been to either as far as she could recall. "I'd like to go there, to both places someday."

"You sure haven't been around much, girl," Katie mocked.

"And I suppose you have?" Velma replied in a miffed tone.

Katie said ruefully, "I didn't mean to hurt your feelings. We'll go to both places together someday."

Then the two fell silent just watching the large central hall grow more crowded and much noisier. Finally, a bell rang. Mr. Dickinson, along with a group of women, emerged through the now-familiar door. He led them to the large, main stairway and held his arms up for silence. This took a while.

After a brief and cheery welcome, he went over some of the general rules of behavior outside the classroom, then concluded by stating, "Those of you returning to school here this year should follow your teacher from last year to their new classrooms right now. You new students or transfers, please remain here."

A brief period of chaos ensued as the majority of the students headed off shouting, laughing, and, in a few cases moaning. Among them were Freddie and Wilma. It was a relief to both girls that they would not have to spend every day in class with either of them.

Velma and Katie watched in awe and excitement as each room begin to suck-up its portion of the crowd. As the process wound down, the girls suddenly saw that Miss Fletcher had remained next to the principal.

When the sound ebbed with the echoes of doors slamming shut, Mr. Dickinson spoke to the thirty or so students standing in total silence. "Now, the rest of you will be joining Miss Fletcher. This will be her first year here at Woodward Elementary, and we were lucky she chose to join us."

Not knowing exactly how to react, there were only a few murmurs from the assembled. While smiling at Miss Fletcher, Velma whispered to Katie. "I like her already."

"So, without delay," Mr. Dickinson said enthusiastically, "please follow Miss Fletcher to her very special, first-floor classroom and prepare to learn."

Young voices echoed loudly off the walls. The excited chatter continued, even when Miss Fletcher moved to the desk at the front of the room. Clearing her throat, she said, "Children, settle down, please." Velma, Katie, and the rest of the first-graders quickly complied, but the others ignored the timid request.

"Children." This time, Miss Fletcher's voice rose an octave. "Face forward and be quiet." The noise fell some but did not stop completely until she shouted, "Now!"

That did the trick. After an uncomfortably long silence, Miss Fletcher spoke calmly again. "That will not happen again, students. Do you understand?" She scanned the room. "Do you eighth-graders understand?"

Velma snuck a peek behind her seeing the back rows nodding in silence. She turned back as Miss Fletcher continued, "Good. Now stand and let's start the day with the pledge of allegiance. For some of you this will be new, but we do this every day."

When they finished, she told them to take their seats, which they now did in silence. "Well done. Now, let's get started, shall we? You are my very first class since I completed training." This drew a variety of reactions ranging from sighs to snickers.

"What kind of training?" A female voice in the rear asked.

Miss Fletcher frowned. "We will raise our hand to ask or answer a question. Understood?" There were nods throughout the room. "Good. Now who asked that?"

A hand went-up tentatively. Velma turned to see an embarrassed older girl she didn't know with her hand in the air.

"We also stand when called upon." The girl rose slowly as her face turned red. "And you are?"

"Lillian Larson, ma'am."

"Well, Miss Larson, I just graduated with a teaching certificate from Illinois State Normal School. You may be seated."

Then she addressed everyone again. "Does anyone know where that is?"

A boy started to speak but abruptly stopped, then raised his hand. When Miss Fletcher nodded toward him, he stood. "It's east of here." He was seated again before his words were out.

"And what is your name?' Miss Fletcher asked in a friendly tone.

The boy stood again. "Jacob Hite, Miss Fletcher." Then down he went.

The young teacher could not stifle a chuckle. "Well, thank you, Mr. Hite, not only for giving the class its first geography lesson, but also for demonstrating the proper classroom etiquette so well."

Titters rippled through the room before silence returned. Then another hand went up. "Yes," Miss Fletcher said.

A tall, olive-skinned girl with raven black hair stood. "My name is Maria Barber, and my question is why aren't I in a class with those who are my age?" When she finished, the girl sat down gracefully.

"Good question, Maria," Miss Fletcher said while smiling. "Woodward Elementary has been planning to move away from the small-school model where everyone was in one classroom because of necessity. With this building able to handle more students, we will be moving to separate classes divided by age next year."

Velma's hand went up, and Miss Fletcher nodded. "So, does that..." she started, then remembered. "Oh, my name is Velma Steele, and I want to know if that means you won't be our teacher all the time."

"I'm afraid so," Miss Fletcher said, sounding genuinely disappointed. "But I, and all the teachers, will always be available to help if you need it."

"Thank you, Miss Fletcher," Velma said disappointedly as she sat down.

"Are there any other questions?" When there were none, Miss Fletcher turned to the blackboard and wrote her name. Under this, she wrote the words *"Class Rules"*. "Those able to write, take your slates and copy these rules down. Don't worry if you can't write yet. We will all be working on that skill, either to learn it or improve in it. Now, you'll be expected to memorize these rules."

There was an audible groan. "Don't worry. The list is not going to be long, but it will be subject to additions, if necessary. Let's not make that necessary, shall we?" Without waiting for a reply, she recited each rule while writing it on the board.

Velma could read a bit. Her mother often wrote words and basic sentences on a slate back on the farm. She also read to the girls from the Bible regularly and challenged Velma to read from a worn child's book on occasion. So, she could tell that Miss Fletcher's rules were simple, common sense.

Before recess, Velma had memorized nearly all the rules. Once outside, she and Katie practiced what they had learned with other students from their classroom. Except for Nancy Brown, the youngest from the hostile family at church, everyone else got along well.

Back inside, Velma and the other first-graders found books placed where they had been sitting before recess. There were an alphabet, penmanship, phonics, and math books for everyone in her row. A quick glance around showed Velma that different grade levels had different books.

The rest of the morning, Miss Fletcher had everyone take up each book, explore it, and try to use it. She went from desk to desk asking questions, challenging everyone to demonstrate their current capabilities in each subject.

It took less than half a day for Velma to recognize that her teacher loved what she was doing. Miss Fletcher's enthusiasm was infectious. She made every subject special. Her patience seemed unending, and her ability to praise and encourage made even the slowest student feel worthy.

For much of the last hour of the school day, Miss Fletcher worked at her desk. Each student filled this quiet time focused on tasks the teacher had given them while making her rounds. Velma and Katie practiced writing the alphabet in cursive. The older boy next to Velma was trying to do simple addition problems.

Just as the first day came to a close, Miss Fletcher put small slips of paper in a top hat and sat it on the edge of her desk. Then she called for the class to put their books away so they could participate in one last exercise.

"Though we will be doing group study appropriate to different grade levels each day, I am also going to form teams for the school year. Each day these teams, made up of students regardless of age, will work together on different skills through shared projects and one-on-one sharing."

A hand went up in the back. When Miss Fletcher acknowledged the student, an older boy stood wearing a pained expression and said, "I'm Billy Franks, Miss Fletcher. Are you saying I'll be on a team with first-graders?"

"That very well could happen."

"But why?"

Miss Fletcher smiled. "Firstly, because they are part of the class. Secondly, because we all can learn something from each other no matter our ages. So, everyone on a team will be helping me to help you." Billy didn't seem to like the answer but said thank you anyway and took his seat.

Velma's hand went up again. "Yes, Velma?"

"Are you doing this just because us little ones don't know nothing?"

Miss Fletcher couldn't contain a chuckle, "First, Velma, you say 'I don't know anything,' not 'nothing.' And you do know more than you think. I truly believe that we all can learn something from each other."

Disbelieving, Velma asked, "Like what? I mean from me that is."

Hardly hesitating, the teacher replied, "Well, like living on a farm or how to bake. I know you help your mother with her baking."

"Yes, ma'am."

"And do you know that arithmetic is an important part of baking?" Miss Fletcher asked the entire class rather than Velma. She got a mixed response. "Well, you'll all learn more about that during this year together."

"Thank you, Miss Fletcher," Velma said, as she took her seat.

"Any other questions?" There were none. "Very well, we'll start with the first row and work our way to the back of the room." She waved to Velma's row, and they came forward to pull one slip from the hat.

Each student took their turn reaching in the hat, pulled a slip, and handed it to Miss Fletcher before returning to their seat. Each time, the teacher leaned over and wrote something down on a sheet of paper. The entire process was completed with time to spare before the three o'clock bell.

Miss Fletcher studied the paper in front of her intently for a long time, as the students waited in anxious silence. Then she stood before them again. "I think we have just enough time for the rest of this exercise if you follow my directions without delay. Can you do that?" Nods and excited murmurs rippled through the room.

"Good," Miss Fletcher said. "Now, first, all the girls join me up here and bring your books with you as fast and as quietly as you can." Once this was accomplished, she instructed the boys to do the same, except directing them to the rear of the room.

Everyone complied admirably. "Wonderful job everyone," Miss Fletcher said, then held up the paper in her hand. "Now, as I call names, you will move forward to the first empty row. There will be eight teams. Let's get started, shall we?" She didn't wait for a reply but read the first name.

Over the next few minutes, girls and boys scurried around the room to join their new teammates. Velma ended up on team three while Katie was on number eight. Disappointment over being separated faded quickly as Velma looked at the mix of kids seated with her. The only person she knew at all was Nancy Brown.

"Well done, everyone," Miss Fletcher said. "First thing tomorrow, you will pick a name for your team."

"But what..." A tall older girl stopped suddenly and put her hand up slowly. "Sorry Miss Fletcher."

"That's alright, Miss Ballard. Everyone will need to practice that."

"Thank you. I was just wondering that since we're on teams, will there be competition between the groups?"

"Yes," she said as the bell rang. "More on that tomorrow. Now we end the day by making sure everything is neatly stacked on your desks. Then you will stand still and silent behind your seat until I release you. And when I do, you will walk out, no running."

"Yes, Miss Fletcher," the class said in unison as they rose.

"Thank you for a great first day, everyone. You are dismissed."

Though happy chatter broke out, the students left in an orderly fashion. Velma was nearly out the door before remembering her sweater and headed back into the room. As she did, the girl saw Miss Fletcher leaning over her desk, looking quite unwell.

"Teacher," Velma said loudly, causing Miss Fletcher to jerk upright. "Oh, I am so sorry, Miss Fletcher. I didn't mean to frighten you. It's just you don't look so good."

"Oh, I'm fine, dear," the teacher said, while forcing a smile. "Miss Steele isn't it?"

"Yes, Miss..." Velma said, then remembered and put up a hand.

This sight made Miss Fletcher laugh. "I can see I need to work on the hand-up rule in more detail. Now what brings you back here?"

"I left my sweater." Velma pointed toward her new seat in the third row.

"Come get it then." Miss Fletcher waved the girl forward as she dropped into her chair with an exhausted sigh. "We'll be assigning cubbies and hooks tomorrow, so you'll have a place for that."

"Goodie," Velma said gleefully, dashing up to grab the sweater and then sprinting for the door."

"No running," her teacher reminded.

Velma switched to a walk instantly. "Yes, Miss Fletcher." Then, just as she reached the door of the room, she said over her shoulder, "I love school."

That evening, Velma rattled on and on about her teacher, while Wilma remained silent. Velma figured her sister's teacher wasn't nearly as much fun as Miss Fletcher. Finally, Wilma said her teacher was *just* fine, though her tone wasn't very convincing.

On the second day, team three became Team Lincoln. Miss Fletcher did not restrict what a group could select but retained veto power. Then she gave the class only the morning recess to make a choice. The debate in team three was between their final choice and Washington, which was ultimately taken by team five.

There were six members of Team Lincoln. Velma was the only first-grader. Nancy was a fourth-grader. There were two fifth-graders, a boy named Charles, and a girl named Barbara. Audrey was a seventh-grader, and the last of the team was an eighth-grade, teenaged boy named Daniel.

This random collection of classmates soon proved to be a good mix as far as Velma was concerned. By the end of the first week, each member was either helping or being helped. Miss Fletcher put Daniel and Velma with Audrey to work on reading and spelling. Audrey became the teacher while Velma and Daniel learned.

Each team member filled a different role—Velma the energizer, Daniel the protector, Charlie the clown, Barbara the taskmaster, Audrey the peacemaker, and Nancy the rule keeper. In addition, all had strengths in different subjects. Velma was amazed at how well Miss Fletcher's old hat had worked to create such a compatible group.

The team felt they had a good chance of winning the competition, which ran the entire year. It would cover all subjects, plus much more. Miss Fletcher would keep score and be the final judge the following May.

At this point, a girl from Team America raised the question Velma wanted to ask. "What do we get when we win?"

"I didn't see a hand," Miss Fletcher admonished gently.

A hand went up and the teacher waved the girl to her feet. "Penelope Martin, Miss Fletcher. And sorry." After a pause she started to ask again, "What will we get when..."

Daniel interrupted, "*If* you win, you mean." This brought laughter across the room.

"Mr. Waters, that was rude," Miss Fletcher snapped.

Daniel colored. "Ah, yes Miss Fletcher. Sorry, Miss Fletcher."

"That reminds me, Daniel. Behavior is an example of another thing I'll be judging during the year," the young teacher said sternly. "Following the class rules, being polite, and being respectful will be an important part of the competition.

This worried Velma a bit because of Nancy Brown being in her group. She recalled the interaction with the fourth-grader's parents at church. Though Nancy seemed to quickly bond with the other members of Team Lincoln, Velma had gotten a very cold shoulder. There was not a lot of respect in her behavior.

"Now, back to Miss Martin's question." Miss Fletcher's pleasant expression was back. "First, any team scoring above 80% will receive a certificate of merit suitable for framing. The third-place team will receive a book to read over the summer."

This met with a mixed reaction, but Miss Fletcher didn't seem to notice. "Second place will receive a book, plus a map of the world for their wall at home." After a pause, she concluded, "and the first-place team will receive the book, the map, *and* their names on the wall of scholars."

The young teacher stepped over to the wall and pulled down a sheet to display a lovely wooden sign underneath reading *'Woodward Elementary School Scholarship Team.* Below that was written the present school year, 1921-22. "Your team and each individual's name will be placed here for all to see in years to come,"

The room buzzed with excitement. "Oh, I almost forgot." Miss Fletcher added, "If all the teams score at least 80%, there will be a party on the last day of school." She let the students get away with a brief, but raucous, cheer.

After that, each school day flew by for Velma as every subject came to life for her. Under the guidance of the freckle-faced young teacher, everyone in Team Lincoln was consistently striving to do their best. On Friday, Miss Fletcher put the team rankings on the board for that week but never gave cumulative scores. This kept motivation and morale high.

Wilma and Velma welcomed their time at school and dreaded the final bell. It marked the end of school and the beginning of their workday. They would race home, knowing Mother would have heard the bell just blocks away. Friends that hurried along trying to visit with them were soon left in front of the hardware store.

A rigidly adhered to routine had quickly been put in place. Save for Sunday, each day started with Alice delivering baked goods, while the girls prepared for school and watched the boys. Once the girls left, Alice headed for the washhouse with both boys and started on the day's laundry and ironing.

As soon as the girls got home from school, Alice headed off to clean houses on that day's schedule. While she was gone, Wilma tended to the boys and got a head start on her homework. Velma went to collect additional eggs from the expanding brood and pick up the order for the next day's baked goods from Mrs. Hanks.

Once the eggs were in the icebox, Velma took over watching the boys while washing any dishes left in the sink. Wilma went to the washhouse where she filled hampers with dry laundry off the lines and lugged them upstairs. Then, in the living room, the girls sorted and folded items into stacks for each customer. Anything found that needed mending was put aside for Alice's attention.

Neither girl was allowed to iron without close supervision, however, and was limited to the napkins and tablecloths for the restaurants. So, after the folding was complete, the girls tried to do homework. This was always challenging with Eugene and Edward needing almost constant attention.

Most afternoons around five, Alice came trudging up the stairs and fell exhausted onto the couch. Velma would bring her a glass of water, while Wilma went over the status of the afternoon's activities. After everyone got a second wind, they all moved to the kitchen.

Everyone pitched in so the meal was ready quickly and consumed in the same manner. Eugene now ate on his own at the table, while Edward, sitting in a highchair, was spoon-fed by his mother. Any talk dealt exclusively with school, business, and chores. After doing dishes, they moved to the living room.

There was no money for a newfangled electric iron, so Alice used an old flatiron heated on the living room Franklin stove. During the hot summer when it wasn't too windy or raining, the ironing was done on the shaded deck at sunset. While Alice ironed, the girls watched the boys and finished homework.

By nine o'clock, the boys were in bed with the girls not far behind. Before she turned in, Alice would set up the kitchen for the next morning's baking that started at four a.m. By five, the girls would awake to the aroma of pies, breads, rolls, or cookies in the oven, marking the start of another exhausting day.

Saturday mornings began the same way, but as their mother put it, there was no school to *interfere* with chores. Wilma took responsibility for the boys on Saturday mornings, while Velma helped her mother deliver baked goods. Once back at the apartment, they would have breakfast.

Often carrying an unfinished piece of toast with her, Velma ran to the barn to feed the chickens and collect eggs. Once that chore was complete, she helped her mother deliver laundry and ironing, gather the next orders, and collect payments. During these rounds, Velma got to hold the tin cash box.

Not yet noon, the three did new laundry and hung it to dry. After a quick meal, it was time for the weekly apartment cleaning. The kitchen got a very thorough going over. Then it was homework, folding, ironing, and mending, which waited until Monday for delivery. With no pickups on Sunday, the Steele family did their own laundry on Mondays like all but their customers did. Supper and bed soon followed.

Sunday was the only day that afforded any recreation for the Steele family. They slept in until dawn, ate a generous and, for them, leisurely breakfast before Velma headed for the barn to tend to the chickens and collect eggs. Since the mercantile was closed on Sundays, all the eggs came home with her.

Once the eggs were stowed, Velma hurriedly dressed for church while Wilma waited impatiently. The two girls then hurried off to Sunday school. An hour later, Alice joined the Hanks on their way to church.

Regardless of whose turn it was to host Sunday supper every other week, Alice baked bread and dessert for that day's meal. Not wasting any ingredients or time on those Sundays, Alice made tray after tray of hardtack to be sold at the mercantile at ten cents a bag. She made a nickel on each.

Since Alice provided the bread and pies on most Sundays, she didn't have to prepare anything else for those shared feasts. One out of four times, however, she replaced pie and bread making with meal prep for the group. Either way, the only time during the week she had to rest was from mid-afternoon until bedtime.

The fall of 1921 turned out to be cool and wet. With the weather change, laundry was regularly hung inside the washhouse or on lines stretched across the living room. Meanwhile, the daily pie menu now included pumpkin and mincemeat. Cinnamon rolls, breads, and hardtack remained part of her regular offerings.

Meeting the growing demand for baked goods was complicated by Alice's expanding laundry and house-cleaning business. In turn, some of this new workload meant more chores for Wilma and Velma. Alice clearly understood this unpleasant fact but saw no other option if they were going to make ends meet.

The toddler Eugene and now fifteen-month-old Edward added to the challenge. Eugene was not the three-year old Velma was when it came to helping. His effort with the chickens ended quickly when he pelted the birds with their feed and threw eggs at the town mongrels. He also failed at dishwashing, being too slow and too careless.

Meanwhile, Edward was making up for all the time he'd spent sleeping during his first year. So, with the girls at school, Alice was forced to spend the majority of the time watching the boys. This redoubled the pressure on her and the girls when school got out each day.

Making rounds had also become more difficult as the weather grew steadily worse. Recognizing this was just a hint of the winter to come, Alice bought a cover for the wagon, with money she really couldn't spare, to protect her cargo and family.

Each day, it became harder for the girls to rise in the morning or stay awake each evening. They were suffering, but while Wilma complained, Velma worried. Her mother was struggling mightily to keep up, and this was showing in the sickly pallor that grew more ominous each day. Still, what could a little girl do?

It was just a week before Thanksgiving when the girls were jolted awake by the sound of breaking crockery. They jumped out of bed and headed for the hallway. Light from the kitchen lit their way.

At the entrance, Wilma came to an abrupt halt, causing Velma to crash into her. Still half asleep, the two stared in horror at their mother lying on the kitchen floor. Pieces of broken pottery and spilled flour spread in all directions. Their mother wasn't moving.

7
Turning Point

As Velma stepped past her sister, Wilma shouted, "Stop! You'll get cut. Let's get our shoes on first."

The two rushed back to their room and returned in moments in their unlaced boots. By that time, Alice had begun to stir while groaning. As Wilma knelt beside her, Velma grabbed a broom from the corner and swept the glass away quickly.

While Wilma wailed and Alice moaned, the little sister went to the sink and dampened a cloth. Gently moving her sister aside, Velma placed the rag carefully on Alice's brow. "Mama, can you hear me? What should we do?"

Getting no response, she tried again. "Where does it hurt, Mama?" Her mother had asked the same thing of her once when she was sick.

"I, ah, give me..." Alice attempted to get to her knees without success. "Help me up, girls," Alice finally managed, but this attempt also failed as she slid back to the floor and fell unconscious again.

"What are we going to do?" Wilma asked in a panic.

Velma thought for a moment, then rose quickly. She rushed to the bedroom and brought her blanket back. Handing it to Wilma, she said, "Put this on her. I'm going for help."

The little girl rushed toward the front door. Passing the boys room, she saw Eugene stirring but didn't stop. Throwing her coat on over a nightgown, Velma went through the door, careful to make sure it latched tightly. Then she was down the stairs and running down the alley as fast as her five-year-old legs would go.

In less than a minute, she was at the Hanks' back door, pounding away and shouting for help. It seemed much longer than it actually must have taken for Mr. Hanks to open the door.

"What is it, Velma? What's wrong?"

Velma threw herself into Henry's arms. "It's Mama. She's fallen and can't get up." Envisioning her father dead on the couch, she added, "I think she's dying."

Henry turned and yelled, "Tessa, get up. Alice needs help." Mr. Hanks stepped back inside and grabbed a coat, as his wife came groggily into the kitchen.

"What did you say? Something's happened to Alice?"

Velma nodded, her eyes wide with fear. "Yes, Mrs. Hanks. She's real sick."

"Tess, go get Doc Joseph and bring him to the Steele place as fast as you can," Henry said, as he stepped outside and hustled Velma back along the alley.

When they arrived, Wilma was sitting in the living room couch crying hysterically. "Mama?" was all Velma could manage, as her sister shook her head. Fearing the worse, the little girl led Mr. Hanks to the kitchen.

They arrived to find Alice pulling weakly at the oven door handle mumbling something about cookies burning. She looked up pleadingly. "They need to come..." Her voice faded as she slipped to the floor again.

Henry moved Velma aside and, after finding the stove was not on, knelt next to Alice. In one quick motion, he swept her up and carried her toward the hall. "Which is her room?"

"Huh?" Velma said.

"Her bedroom, girl," Henry shouted.

"The middle one."

The large man dashed into the room, then gently put Alice down on her crisply made bed as Velma hit the switch. In the dim light, her mother's skin looked just like her Papa's had that day in February. She started crying and left the room.

To Velma, it seemed like hours later when Mrs. Hanks arrived with a young man the little girl had never met. It turned out to be Dr. Joseph. He went directly to Alice's room and stayed there for a long time. When he came out, followed by the Hanks, all three faces were drawn.

"What I gave Mrs. Steele will have her sleeping for hours," the doctor said, closing his medical bag. "I found nothing life threatening, no flu, consumption, or the like. From what you just told me, I'd guess she's exhausted. It's amazing she held up this long given the load she's carrying."

Henry's brow was deeply furrowed. "The problem is she can't afford not to be working. She barely makes ends meet as it is."

"Well, she's going to need a new plan," Dr. Joseph said emphatically. "Otherwise, she'll likely follow her late husband to the grave. Then what will happen to these girls?"

"She has two boys as well," Tessa said.

"My God," the doctor said, then added, "All the more reason to make some big changes."

"I'll talk to her about it tomorrow," Henry said.

Tessa moved to comfort the girls. "I'll stay the night, dear."

"You do that." Henry led Dr. Joseph to the door. "I think the girls better stay home tomorrow. It's a Friday, so they won't miss much."

"Oh, I can't miss school," Velma protested.

"Don't be silly," Tessa said, stroking the little girl's head. "You'll catch up quickly. You're smart."

Velma shook her head. "You don't understand. We have a contest and..."

"Nonsense, girl," Henry said from the doorway. "Taking care of your mother is more important than any old contest."

Velma didn't agree but said no more. Instead, she stood and gave Tessa a hug. "Let's get to bed," Velma said to Wilma as she headed down the hall.

Still sniffling, Wilma got up and followed. When Velma turned in at their mother's room, her sister kept going. Velma found Alice sleeping deeply. This filled her with relief. Velma kissed her mother's cheek, then headed for her own bed. "She's sleeping soundly," Velma said to Wilma, who was already under her covers. There was no reply.

In spite of the efforts of the Hanks and Dr. Joseph to stop her, Alice was back in her kitchen the next Monday. Though not doing the laundry, she supervised Wilma and Velma in doing that work. As a recognition of her poor health, Alice allowed Mr. Hanks to deliver the completed laundry. He did not bring any back.

The girls stayed home from school until after the holiday, caring for their brothers and mother, as much as she would allow. The Sunday supper group and church families brought meals to the Steeles every night until the Sunday after Thanksgiving.

Miss Fletcher sent home lessons for Velma with Katie every afternoon. Wilma's teacher did the same. On the Friday after Thanksgiving, Miss Fletcher came to visit. She assured Velma that her absence was not counting against Team Lincoln. In fact, she announced that Velma's team had come in first that week.

At that end of the first Sunday supper after Thanksgiving, Henry Hanks cleared his throat, drawing everyone's attention, including Velma's. "Alice, I know you won't like hearing this, but you cannot continue at the pace you are going. If you do, another incident like just happened is inevitable."

"I agree," said Reverend Jones.

Alice just glared, though the usual intensity of her look was gone.

Tessa patted her friend's hand. "Henry's right, Alice." She turned to Agnes. "Tell her, Aggie."

Agnes hesitated, then plunged in, "I'm afraid it's true."

Alice remained silent.

To fill the void, Pastor Jones' wife Grace said, "We don't mean to gang up on you, dear, and we know this is not news to you."

"But what to do about the situation is what we really want to focus on," Carl Warren, Agnes's husband, added.

Alice snorted a half-laugh, half-snarl. "What to do? If you're suggesting charity, I'll have none of it. I'll die first."

"At the rate you're going, that is likely to happen," Henry fired back in a harsh tone Velma had never heard from him. "Then what becomes of your four children? Do you have family to take them in?" He didn't wait for a reply. "Do you want them in an orphanage?"

Alice turned silent again. So, Mrs. Hanks spoke to her calmly, "We know you are a proud woman."

"And pride goes before a fall," the pastor added, receiving a hard look from Alice in return.

Grace took over for her husband. "We know you want, no, you *expect* to stand on your own as you always have, but right now that is not realistic. We're not here to give you charity. We're here to give you help until the time when your health returns and you get a bit more established."

"What kind of help?" Alice asked warily.

Henry took the question. "First, to help put a plan together for getting from today until that glorious day Grace just alluded to."

"Then we can implement the parts of the plan we can help with," added Pastor Jones.

"And what if I say no?"

"Then you are a fool, the worst kind," Henry snapped. "You're a selfish fool. Look at your children." He paused, and, when Alice just stared at him, he barked, "Look at them, Alice!"

Velma watched her mother slowly scan the room filled with children. When her eyes returned to Henry, he continued. "Now, before you turn down the plan, don't you think we ought to put one together first?" He ended with a smile.

Alice offered a weak smile of her own. "I guess that would be reasonable. But I'm not promising anything."

"We wouldn't expect anything less," Henry said with a chuckle. "Now, where shall we start?"

It took all her friends and another visit from Dr. Joseph to convince Alice to take the week after Thanksgiving off. While she rested, her friends took care of the boys in shifts so the girls could return to school.

Since most of the people that Alice had as laundry and house-cleaning clients were members of the Methodist church, they were aware early on about the situation. All were more than understanding. They accepted a break in her services, while continuing to provide meals during the week.

The restaurant clients were understanding as well but had needs that had to be met. So, the collective group of Agnes, Grace, and Tessa, along with the girls, took care of tablecloths and napkins to keep these customers happy. In doing the work, they also gained an even greater appreciation of the challenges facing Alice.

Of course, there was no baking done that week. Henry was surprised by how upset his customers were about this. It was clear to him that Alice had no risk of losing that business no matter how long her recovery took.

At the next shared Sunday supper, the adults had their heads together again. The first order of business was Alice's condition. "I am fit as a fiddle."

"Do you agree, ladies?" Henry asked.

Agnes spoke first. "More importantly, what does Dr. Joseph say?"

Tessa replied, "Last time, I talked to him, he said she was making progress but had a long way to go. Right, Alice?"

Alice glared at her friend. "He just wants to make more money, money I don't have."

"Stop changing the subject," Tessa said coolly. "Personally, I'd say you're much better, but nowhere near going back to all you were doing before the breakdown."

"Especially the laundry," Grace said with a half-smile before adding, "and I speak from firsthand experience."

Agnes nodded, "I agree. Now that I know how much she and the girls are dealing with, I feel awful having sent my laundry to her every week."

"But I need the money to pay the bills," Alice protested.

"And therein lies the rub," Carl Warren said. "You need all you do to make ends meet, but in doing so, you face the likelihood of a similar incident, or worse."

"And don't forget the boys," Tessa added.

"That's a good summary of my predicament," Alice said sourly. "Now all I need is to double my prices or double my help. You all did some fine work on my behalf. Any interest in hiring on? I can promise you plenty of hard work and no pay."

Everyone laughed at this except Henry who stayed focused on the problem. "Alice, can you tell us what part of your income comes from each of your businesses?"

"My ledger is at the apartment. It has all my records of income and expenses." This evening they were eating at the Hanks', so she turned to her daughter. "Wilma, run home and get the ledger book on the shelf in the pantry cabinet." Wilma frowned. "Get goin', girl."

Without enthusiasm, Wilma headed out into the late afternoon of early December 1921. The adults waited in silent contemplation with another cup of coffee and cookies, the first Alice had baked since her breakdown. Wilma was back in a few minutes, exchanging the heavy book for a cookie of her own.

"Thank you, dear," Alice said while opening the ledger. She looked up, asking, "What do you want to know?"

"Well, I hope you don't think I'm prying, Alice, but do you have any money put aside?" Henry asked apologetically.

Alice frowned. "Well, yes. I was raised to save for a rainy day." Her lips curled up. "This has been more like a right great flood."

"Indeed," Grace said, patting Alice's knee.

Alice looked at a page toward the back of the ledger. "If I hadn't bought that cover for the wagon, I'd-a been in better shape. Over the last few months, I've been able to put a little, very little, aside each week. So, right now I have this much." She turned the book toward the others and pointed.

"My, that's an impressive sum for someone in your circumstances," Henry said, "but, of course, in order to do that, you practically killed yourself."

"And you and yours must do without much of the time," Agnes added.

Alice smiled again. "That's true except, of course, for the leftovers everyone sends home with us on Sundays. You think I don't realize what you're doin', don't you?" Then she lowered her eyes. "We make that last half a week, don't we, Velma?"

Her daughter, who had been listening from the shadows, stepped forward. "Yes, Mama," she said with pride and added, "She can do magic with whatever we take home. The meat and veggie pies are yummy."

There were nods all around as Henry said, "Sounds like a meal we should try one of these Sundays."

"So, let's deal with your expenses," Carl requested. Alice turned a page and sat back. The group ran down a list, starting with rent, electricity, food, supplies for baking and laundry, wood, ice, feed for the chickens and horse, and incidental expenses. The last item on the list was planned savings.

"Based on this, your savings will cover you for a month or more," Carl pointed out.

Alice nodded. "And that month has already started without any income for the last week and more. And if I don't get back at it, my customers will be gone."

"That brings us to the source of that income," Henry said.

"I've never looked at it that way," Alice then explained, "I just put my flyers out and took on whatever came my way. That was especially true in the beginning when I was so desperate."

"Well, that is no longer a problem, correct?" Pastor Jones asked and Alice nodded uncertainly.

Henry picked up the analysis. "Let's take a few minutes to determine what percentage of your earnings come from each source."

"We should also figure how much time Alice spends to earn a dollar baking, cleaning, ironing, and laundering," Carl proposed.

"Alice and the girls," Tessa reminded.

"Right," Henry said. "Pass me another cookie, will you?"

The group worked together as the last light faded. Even though she didn't understand it all, Velma got a good lesson in addition and subtraction while watching. Once the calculation was completed, the discussion turned to what the figures meant.

Carl spoke first. "Well, it's clear to me that you work the longest and the hardest doing laundry and ironing. At what you charge, your earnings per hour of work is the lowest of the three categories too. Baking is long on hours but reasonably easy for you."

"Except in the heat of summer," Tessa added.

"Right," Carl acknowledged, then continued, "You make a pretty good return on the baking. House cleaning is difficult for me to assess."

"I think the house cleaning can work for Alice if she sets up a sliding scale for her services," Agnes suggested. "Right now, you charge a flat rate regardless of the house's size or work performed. I'm ashamed to say the Warren family has been taking advantage of you, Alice."

"Don't be silly, Agnes. Apparently, I'm the one taking advantage of me."

Though not intended to be funny, Alice's comment brought a hail of laughter to the Hanks' kitchen and woke a couple of sleeping children in the living room. Once the group recovered, Henry suggested that everyone sleep on what they'd learned and meet at Alice's place tomorrow night with suggestions.

Everyone nodded. "And I'll have a mess of my pot pies ready for dinner, if the men left enough of tonight's meal that is," Alice said with her usual stoic expression.

Then they called it a night, exchanging optimistic comments as they headed home. This attitude carried over into the next night's gathering. As they enjoyed Alice's pot pies, something the Hanks requested to sell at the mercantile, they presented a variety of ideas for dealing with her quandary.

In the end, Alice agreed to focus her attention on baking and house-cleaning, while restricting the laundry and ironing business to the restaurants for the time being. In spite of her protests, her women friends would continue taking morning shifts caring for the boys so Alice could increase her baking production.

Henry arranged for the restaurants to pick up their baked goods at the mercantile. They also would drop off and pick up their linens at the same time. Velma continued tending the chickens and Nelly. A sign went up at the mercantile offering a wagon and horse for hire, creating a potential new source of income for the Steeles.

If successful, this plan would give Alice the chance to recover physically. Mentally, however, was another story. A gap would remain, albeit a small one, between income and expenses. Plus, she felt guilty at all her friends were doing. To her, this felt like charity, and she didn't know how she could ever pick up what they were doing without again jeopardizing her health.

The day before Christmas Eve, a Friday, the Warren family held a holiday dinner for the four families. The purpose ostensibly was to celebrate Christmas. The ulterior motive, however, was to check on how Alice and her family were faring financially, physically, and emotionally since implementing the new plans three weeks earlier.

It was an unusually mild evening as the Steeles arrived. Agnes greeted an Alice who seemed a new woman. She almost looked relaxed, a characteristic Agnes had never seen. "Why Alice, you look positively radiant."

"Don't be silly, Agnes. No one has ever accused me of being radiant."

"Well, now they have." Mrs. Warren stepped aside and waved the five Steeles inside. "Merry Christmas all."

Freddie and Katie came running in from the kitchen, nibbling something. "Merry Christmas," the two echoed each other.

"My mom made sugar cookies," Freddie said, then added, "They're not as good as your mom's but the icing is tasty."

Agnes laughed. "Thanks a lot, dear. Now everyone, give me your coats. Did you leave any cocoa for the others, children?"

Freddie nodded. "You said we had to, Ma."

"I know, but since when has that stopped you?" Agnes asked with a smile. "Take Wilma and Velma, oh, and little Eugene to the kitchen and give them a mug."

"Come on," Katie called out as she hurried away with the others close behind.

Carl Warren, his arms full of wood, dodged the gaggle of giggling children in the hallway. Doing a full turn, the man managed to retain his grip. Approaching the ladies, he said with a laugh, "Somebody should have warned me there were four tiny tornadoes on the lose."

Alice responded by putting down a squirming Edward and calling after her girls, "Wilma, Velma, come get Edward."

A moment later, Velma appeared, grabbed her brother's hand and took off again for the kitchen as Alice gave instructions. "No cocoa for him, just a cookie."

Turning back to the adults, she explained, "He'll make a mess with the cocoa, and the cookie will be more than enough sugar to keep him up all night."

"So, now there are five little whirlwinds assaulting our kitchen," Carl said, displaying a mock frown.

"Don't forget Edward," Agnes pointed out.

As if in agreement, Edward pointed where his sister and brother had just disappeared and said, "Dah."

"Dah?" Carl repeated in confusion.

Alice chuckled. "That's about all he can say so far. It's that word and his gestures that tell me what he wants." Then to Edward she said, "No, Edward. I'm not letting you loose in the Warren's kitchen."

As they all laughed, the doorbell rang. "You get the door dear, and I'll handle the fire," Carl suggested while moving toward the fireplace. Alice took a seat, trying to control her disappointed youngest."

Agnes opened the door to find the Hanks and Jones had arrived together along with a suddenly cold wind. "Merry Christmas everyone. Come on in."

The first part of the evening was filled with eating, drinking, and cheery conversation. After desserts of sugar cookies and apple cider, everyone moved to the living room. They sat around for an hour singing carols as Agnes and Grace took turns playing on an upright piano in the corner.

After Reverend Jones did a dramatic reading of *A Visit from St. Nickolas*, the older children were told that they could stay the night as an early Christmas present. It took almost an hour to get them calmed down and heading upstairs. The girls settled in Katie's room, while Freddie gladly headed to his own bed alone. Eugene and Edward were already passed out on the Warren's living room couch.

Several false starts and some parental admonishments later, the children finally gave in to sleep, all, that is, except Velma. She was still too excited. Leaving the others snug beneath layers of bedding, the almost six-year-old went to sit at the top of the stairs and listened to the quiet conversation coming from the living room.

"I think they have finally passed out," Carl Warren said with a sigh. "Where were we?"

"Alice was saying that she was well enough to take over caring for the boys," Tessa said. "The rest of us ladies aren't quite so sure."

"I'm telling you, I'm up to the task especially with my present workload. Without the laundry, I feel like I'm a woman of leisure."

Grace chuckled then said, "If you call your workload a life of leisure, I'm living in heaven on earth."

"We can't forget about the girls," Agnes added. "With you taking over the boys until they get home from school, you all will be back to double duty in the afternoons."

"Not without laundry. When we get back to doing that, what you say will be true." Alice said with resignation.

"What about a compromise?" Henry asked.

"What do you suggest?" Alice prodded hopefully.

"Ah, well," Henry started, but came up with nothing, and so fell silent.

Reverend Jones said firmly, "You ladies can cut back on the days you are there. If you took over Fridays, would that be easier than other weekdays?"

"I think so," Velma heard her mother say, then add, "And we'd all be well rested on Monday. So, we could try that."

"That's a good start," Mr. Warren said. "What else?"

There was a long pause where the only sound was a ticking clock. Then Tessa spoke excitedly, "You bake bread, rolls, and a first set of pies before any of us get there to tend the boys. Then, when the girls leave and we watch the boys, you do more baking, more pies, cookies, and whatever else you have dough for."

"That's right," Alice said. "What are you gettin' at?"

"I was wondering why you don't just walk the boys down to the mercantile when you bring your first batches, giving them some fresh air, and then do the second batches at our place. I've got a big oven and..." Velma heard a chuckle. "I could learn a thing or two about baking."

"Good idea," Agnes seconded the idea.

After a pause, Alice disagreed. "No way I can manage my baked goods and the boys."

"Then I'll come and escort you," Henry said.

"Or me, or Annie," Tessa added enthusiastically. "After all, most of your baked goods are for the mercantile."

"Oh, I couldn't expect that," Alice protested. "I thought part of this plan was to ease you all out of takin' care of us Steeles."

The room was silent for a moment. Then Henry had an answer. "Look, consider us doing the deliveries in lieu of you charging us for it."

"But what about the boys?"

Tessa responded to this quickly, "We have plenty of room and some extra hands. Besides Henry and me, Annie will more than likely love the opportunity to practice."

"Practice?" came a surprised response from several at the table.

Tessa giggled again. "Our little newlywed is in the family way."

"Mrs. Anderson is on the nest?" Grace asked excitedly.

"Yes. She just told me yesterday," Tess explained. "She's going to tell her husband Christmas morning."

"What a blessed gift," Grace chortled.

"And free too," Henry laughed.

"Since when are children free?" Carl countered. "We all know how much they cost us."

"In our pocketbooks and in our hearts," Grace replied.

"Amen. This is turning out to be quite a Christmas for a lot of folks." Reverend Jones' words were greeted with joyous chatter.

As Velma yawned, she heard Henry say, "So, we'll give the baking at the mercantile a try, agreed?" Everyone affirmed the idea. "Good. Now, Alice, how are you doing money-wise?"

"Well, I had to use up a good chunk of my savings the first couple of weeks what with the doctor bill and a lot less comin' in. But once things got organized, we're doin' better. With Nelly and the wagon starting to bring in a little, I'm quite hopeful. And thank you, Henry, for managing that for me."

"Not me," Henry corrected. "Thank Tess. Besides, we get a piece of the profit at your insistence."

Alice shrugged. "Just crumbs."

"Enough for the time it takes," Tess said. "Now, let's move on, shall we?"

Carl did just that. "What more would it take going forward, keeping in mind your health and the health of your girls?"

"Well, there is no margin for error in budgetin', and I still can't include things like clothes, which the children need badly. You see how they are all growin'," Alice said with a sigh, then added, "If I just had all the laundry business back…"

"We know that was the straw that broke the camel's back for you," Henry pointed out vehemently.

"I know, but you asked what it would take."

"How about sewing?" Agnes suddenly interjected. "Don't you make a lot of your own clothes?"

"Well, yes, when I have the time and the material."

"And though they are not fancy, they are clearly well made." Agnes' voice rose with enthusiasm. "So, you can take clothing orders, not just mending services."

"It would be great for our business too if we sold the material and you made the dresses." Tessa's delighted voice joined the chorus.

Velma heard excited agreement all around. "And you could control the schedule for such things more than any of your other jobs," Carl contributed.

"But when and where would I do it?" Alice asked plaintively. "There's no good space for such work at the apartment."

After a brief pause, Henry answered Alice with a question of his own, "How does the Woodward Mercantile, Bakery, and Dress Shop sound to you?"

"What?" Velma heard the women ask in unison.

"It just seems like destiny," Henry said. "We have the spare bedrooms what with the kids gone."

"Oh, I couldn't possibly..." Alice started but didn't get to finish.

"Nonsense," Tess interrupted. "Henry's right. We should at least give it a try."

"Well, there is still the question of money to buy the material, needles, thread, and a decent machine to do the work. I had to leave the machine at the farm."

"I have a machine," Grace said excitedly. "It was my mother's and is a little dated but has all the fancy features. It's in great shape since, I'm ashamed to say, I don't sew. You can use it, at least until you can afford a better one of your own."

"That is more than generous, Grace," Alice choked out.

"It will be a pleasure to see Mother's machine in use again," Grace replied, then added, "You can make me, make all of us something in return for our help, in your free time, of course."

Everyone laughed heartily at this until Agnes shushed them. "Hold it down or we'll wake the children."

When silence returned, Henry said, "Let's figure out how we make all this happen."

As the adults dug into the minutia, Velma's eyes grew heavy. She rose slowly and went to join the other girls. Passing a window, Velma looked out to see big flakes of snow hitting the panes. It was going to be a white Christmas after all: a positive, hopeful end to a year filled with tragedy, challenge, and adventure.

8
A First

Christmas 1921 was a transformational moment for the Woodward Steeles. God had blessed them with a circle of friends that enabled them to survive the tragedies of the recent past. And the community had, slowly at first but ultimately with vigor, supported the trades Alice Steele brought to town.

Thankfully for Alice all her businesses required little in the way of public relations. In many ways, it was her girls that earned the town's affection. They were the face of the Steele family, while Alice was the tireless machine of production.

The sisters were both excellent students, models of studiousness, dedication, and commitment. Their teachers appreciated how hard the two worked at school and home, respecting their work ethic greatly. In class, the two were quick to help other students and enthusiastically participate in activities.

Making deliveries with her mother rain or shine during this first year had introduced Velma to many in the town. Most were amazed at how willing and able the little girl was, thinking her older than her years. More often than not, she delivered a smile along with the laundry or baked goods.

In spite of having little free time, Velma had become a fixture at the mercantile during the year, delivering eggs, baked goods, and good cheer every day. Annie, the clerk, had embraced her like a younger sister, while Tessa and Henry had become surrogate grandparents to all the Steele children.

In spite of their heavy workload at home, the Steele girls interacted regularly with their peers thanks to school. The buildup to the end of the calendar year gave Velma and Wilma the chance to shine in the holiday programs their respective classrooms put together.

Each team in Miss Fletcher's room created their own piece for the event held on the Friday before the Christmas break, the same day as the party at the Warrens'. Together, Team Lincoln demonstrated ways to say Merry Christmas or the like from around the world, then sang Jingle Bells and Silent Night.

The holiday week was a whirlwind of activity for the whole family. Christmas fell on a Sunday in 1921, so school was out the following week. This proved to be a blessing and a curse for Velma and Wilma.

That week, Alice redoubled her baking to meet the holiday demand. That meant extra items to be delivered and a few to be enjoyed by the family. In addition, the girls either watched the boys or helped Alice clean houses. Most of these cleanings were one-time scheduled a few days before Christmas and New Year's.

In-between, the girls managed to spend holiday time with friends, playing and enjoying the trappings of the seasons, including candlelit trees, glorious meals, sweets of all kinds, and gifts. Katie gave Velma a small stuffed doll, while she got an embroidered handkerchief from the mercantile in return. They also exchanged handmade cards.

There was no tree or decorations in the Steele apartment, but there were glorious presents. Somehow, in spite of all she did every day, their mother had managed to make each girl a new dress. The boys got new clothes too, shirts and pants that fit the rapidly growing pair. Mother got breakfast made by her girls.

After a New Year's Eve and day filled with banging pans, more food, and hours of play, Velma and Wilma dragged themselves out of bed unenthusiastically that Monday morning. They soon perked up as they left for school under a cold threatening sky, however, thanks to the new dresses they were wearing.

The transition back into school life was easy for Velma. Miss Fletcher saw to that. Adjusting to the morning dash through bitter cold and inclement weather to feed chickens and gather eggs was more difficult. Now, however, the end of each school day promised a more pleasant evening of chores than only weeks earlier.

When the bell rang that first day back, the girls raced home. Wilma went to the washhouse to deal with the limited laundry, while Velma went upstairs to clean the kitchen and do dishes. Then she joined Wilma, who had already put the previous day's table linens in bags. Together they hung that day's restaurant wash on the lines.

Grabbing the bags, the girls headed for the mercantile. There they found their mother putting a batch of hot oatmeal cookies on a rack. Annie held a subdued Eugene at the kitchen table. Seeing their mother looking healthy and in high spirits seemed to say that this new arrangement might just work.

"Right on time, girls," was Alice's pleasant greeting. "Let me finish putting these on the rack to cool, then we can deal with that laundry."

"I'll get the chickens taken care of while you're doing that," Velma said, heading for the door.

"No need, dear," Mrs. Hanks said as she entered the kitchen with Edward in her arms. "Eugene and I went out awhile back and took care of that."

Velma was shocked. "And he didn't bust any eggs or hurt the hens?"

"No, none of that. He actually seemed to enjoy working with me right, Eugene?"

"Ya, ya, good time with *Te.*" The fact that the boy said something to the group was almost as amazing to Velma as hearing that he had actually been helpful.

Tess chuckled while putting Edward down near his brother. "You can get back to the store now, Annie," she said, puffing from the exertion. Then to Alice she added, "and your boy here is nice and clean."

"Oh, you didn't need to do that, but thank you," Alice said, showing what passed for a smile.

"Just give me a cookie and we'll call it even,"

This turned Alice's smile to a laugh. "They're too hot to handle right now. *And* you can have just one. All these are sold already."

While deftly ladling the fragrant disks from the cookie sheet to the mesh rack, Alice issued orders to the girls. "You get started on the ironin', Wilma, and be careful with that new appliance. We're payin' the Hanks for that on time, and I'd like to pay it off before it gets busted."

"Yes, Mama."

"And you, Miss Velma, take the boys upstairs so they're out from underfoot."

"Yes, Mama." Velma moved slowly to gather her brothers. Taking care of them was probably her least favorite chore, since watching them demanded her full attention.

"Don't forget you promised an extra set of meat pies for tomorrow." Tessa's words wiped any remnants of a smile from Alice's face. "They've been big sellers," Mrs. Hanks added.

"I plain forgot. Thanks." Alice turned to see a sink full of the pots and pans she would need to make the pies. "Tess, I need to go home and get the meat and vegetables I was plannin' on usin'."

"Nonsense, sweetie," Mrs. Hanks replied. "I've got leftover chicken and steak you can use in our cooler and plenty of potatoes, onions, mushrooms, and the like."

"Well, I'll only use your stuff if I can pay ya for it."

Mrs. Hanks laughed, as she snatched a cookie from the rack and popped it in her mouth. "Oh, that's hot."

"Told ya." Alice's smile was back.

After devouring the cookie, Tess addressed Alice's proposition. "Just take a nickel off each and we'll call it even.'

"How about another cookie instead?"

"I thought all the others were sold," Tessa said incredulously.

Alice smiled. "That was my way of keeping you out of them. But that changed with your offer. Have another."

"Make it two more and we've got a deal."

That first full week of 1922 set in motion a pattern of life for the Steeles and their new friends that would endure for years filled with joy and sorrow shared by all. The year past had seen Alice and her children lose a father, blood relatives, and hope.

The new year began with a better family and renewed hope for the future. And there was no better symbol of this new reality than celebrating a birthday. So, on the afternoon of the 9th, Velma arrived in the Hanks' kitchen after school, where all their new friends waited to give her the first real birthday party Velma ever had.

"Surprise!" the crowd shouted as lights came on in the Hanks' darkened kitchen. She stopped dead in the doorway, nearly dropping the basket of clean restaurant laundry she carried.

"Come on, birthday girl," Wilma said, giving her a push from behind. "It's cold out here."

Looking around the room, she saw all the familiar faces that she had come to know so well since moving to Woodward. Out front, were some of her new friends from school and adults she assumed were their parents. Behind them were the Hanks, Warren, and Jones families. Annie Anderson and her husband were there too. At the very back, almost hidden, was Miss Fletcher. Her being there was very special.

Overwhelmed, Velma opened her mouth to speak but nothing came out. "Look everyone. My sister is speechless." That had everyone laughing.

"Come on now, grab a plate," Tessa said. "It is a school night. Right, Miss Fletcher?"

All eyes turned to the attractive young, freckle-faced teacher who blushed deeply. "Never mind that," Henry stepped in to rescue her. "We've got plenty of time."

"Can you guess what your mother fixed for you, Miss Velma?" Annie asked.

Velma suddenly got her voice back. "I don't need to guess."

"If you have a nose you know," Reverend Jones broke in. "It's my favorite."

"Mine too," Velma cried. "Fried chicken!"

"And all the trimmings," Tess added, then waved to the plates again. "Come on now. Don't be shy. There's plenty. But save room for dessert."

Soon the room was abuzz with chatter. Those not filling their plates came over to Velma. Her friends giggled and the adults offered hugs. By the time everyone was served, every seat in the room was taken and some had moved into the store.

Alice served the birthday girl and sat beside her, then whispered, "There is a real surprise for dessert."

"One of your pies?" Velma asked excitedly.

Alice actually laughed. "Now that wouldn't be much of a surprise, would it?"

After a moment's reflection, Velma smiled back, "Well, it would be if I got to eat it."

"Very funny, dearie," Alice said with another laugh. "How are the potatoes?"

"Nice and creamy."

Alice nodded toward Eugene. "He helped."

"No!"

"Yup. Fortunately, we had enough left after he finished coating himself from head to toe," Alice explained, her smile never leaving. "He was so proud but couldn't understand why everyone in the kitchen at the time was laughing so hard."

"That must have been a sight."

"Indeed. Now eat up so we can get to the presents."

"Presents?" Velma said in shock.

"Yup."

After gulping down two helpings, Velma patiently waited for others to finish. Once the table was cleared, Velma sat as some of her guests came forward with wrapped packages. Not everyone had brought one, but that didn't matter to her. There were more presents at one time than she had ever seen before.

The presents ranged from homemade art by Eugene to a beautiful new Sunday-go-to-meeting dress from her mother. As she swirled around the room holding it up, she overheard her mother whisper to Wilma, "I got one in the works for you too."

There was a pad and pencil from Miss Fletcher, socks from Wilma, a Bible from the Jones, and her own bank account from the Warrens with five whole dollars in it. Katie and the other friends from school chipped in for a pair of warm gloves. Annie's gift was a lovely necklace. The Hanks had two gifts: the new wool coat she'd been eyeing in the mercantile and a matching scarf. She was now set for winter.

Velma could not believe the bounty that lay before here. By the time everything was opened, she broke down and cried with joy, thanking everyone repeatedly between sniffles. Then it was time for dessert.

Mr. Hanks held back the curtain that led into the store, as a glow in the doorway turned into a very large cake. It must have had five layers and was ablaze with six large candles. It was held by Tessa with Agnes and Grace guarding against disaster.

As the three entered the kitchen, everyone began to sing. It was a raucous, off-key rendition, but it seemed like a choir to the little girl. At the end, everyone gave a cheer that melted into laughter and more happy conversation.

"Come now, Velma. Make a wish and blow them out," Tessa ordered.

Velma stood and took a good look at the cake, a white mountain with lettering that read *Happy 6th Birthday Velma* in her favorite color, violet. After a brief pause to generate a wish, she closed her eyes and blew. When she opened them again, the candles were out, and everyone was hurrahing again.

"What did you wish?" Wilma asked.

"Oh, no," Miss Fletcher warned. "It won't come true if you tell anyone."

Velma nodded. "I won't."

"Go ahead, Agnes. Cut it," Tess directed.

"I'd be delighted," she said, picking up the knife and then pausing. "Isn't there ice cream too?"

"Oh, I almost forgot," Henry said, rushing off to the cooler inside the store. In a minute, he was back holding a large container covered in frost. "I'll scoop."

"I'll help," Grace said, moving to Mr. Hanks' side.

"The first piece goes to the birthday girl," Agnes said, cutting a thick slice. "I hope you saved room."

"I sure did," Velma said and followed up by asking, "Who baked this?"

"Not me," her mother said with a smile.

"We did," Grace shouted from across the room.

Velma glanced around the room. "Who is we?"

"Tess, Grace, and me," Agnes said. "Right here in this kitchen. We had some coaching, mind you."

"But I didn't touch anything," Alice confirmed.

"It looks delicious," Annie said while others agreed.

An anxious look suddenly crossed Agnes's face. "Looks can be deceiving. It's the taste that counts. So..." She said no more, just slid the plate in front of Velma.

Inside the white frosting were alternating layers of dark chocolate and vanilla cream. While everyone waited anxiously, especially the three novice pastry chefs, Velma took a bite. It was ambrosia and she said so. "This is the bestest cake I have ever had, ever."

"Yay!" The three women cried out as one.

"Well, don't just stand there," Carl Warren said. "I want a piece of the bestest cake ever."

With that everyone started talking at once and pushing forward to get a slice. While Velma watched the happy chaos, her mother brought over a big bowl of vanilla ice cream to complete her dessert. "Is it really that good?"

"Yes, Ma. The best." Then, thinking this might hurt her mother's feelings, she added, "But I haven't had much cake before."

"Don't worry, dear. They used my recipe to make it," Alice said, squeezing her daughter's shoulder. "Would you like cake every birthday from now on?"

Velma nodded. "That would suit me just fine."

"Consider it done."

"Oh, Mama. I am so happy tonight. I wish it would never end."

"Was that your wish?" Velma shook her head, looking a bit embarrassed. "What's the matter, girl?"

Velma looked around, then leaned into her mother and whispered, "I couldn't think of anything else I needed after all this."

"I can understand," Alice said, giving her another hug. "You'll get another chance next year."

It was a group of very happy and full guests that ventured out into a cold January night. Henry opened the front door so that everyone could "leave proper."

Leading the way out was Velma in her new coat, scarf, and gloves. Everything else was in a large mercantile bag slung over her shoulder. Even though the wind was biting, the Steeles moved along slowly, warmed by the company around them. Soon, they reached the hardware store.

"I'll bid adieu here," Miss Fletcher said. "I hope you can make it to school tomorrow after all the excitement."

"Oh, I will, Miss Fletcher," Velma said, then added. "And thank you for my present."

"I was joking, dear," she replied, pulling her coat up higher against another gust. "I'm more worried about me. I ate too much." This was said with a chuckle and a wave. "Good night all."

"Good night," the others said, returning the wave.

Then the Warrens headed off after Katie had given her best friend a last birthday hug. "See you at school."

The two families parted and the Steeles made their way to the back of the hardware store. "Who needs the outhouse?"

"I do," Wilma said.

"Me too," Velma chimed in.

"Let Velma go first."

Wilma flared. "Because it's her birthday?"

"Don't ruin the evening, girl." Alice flared back. "Just do as I say." After Velma ran off, Alice said, "Follow me."

The two took the boys up, tucked them in and were back just as Velma emerged from the privy. "You head up, brush your teeth, and I'll tuck you in in a minute."

"Yes, Mama."

In spite of her mother's instructions, Velma dawdled, not wanting the night to end. As a result, she was still at the kitchen pump when the others arrived. Her mother didn't scold, however. Instead, she escorted the new six-year-old to bed and tucked her in as promised.

Wilma came to bed, apparently over her little snit. "Happy birthday, Sis," she said, flipping off the light. "Good night, Mama."

"Good night, dear."

After Wilma had climbed in bed, Velma said, "Wasn't that the best birthday party ever?"

"Yeah, I guess so." Wilma's sounded low. "I haven't many to compare it with. Certainly not one of my own. Good night."

"Good night."

After lying in the dark for several minutes, Velma whispered, "Wilma, are you still awake?"

"Yeah. What is it?"

"I just wanted to say I'll make sure your next birthday party is even better than mine. I love you."

After a long pause, Velma heard a weak, "Thank you."

After New Year's 1922, the rest of the school year seemed to fly by for Velma. Besides learning the three 'R's', exposure to geography and history fascinated her. Science was a bit more challenging, made palatable by others on Team Lincoln. Nearly as valuable, however, was meeting other students of Woodard Elementary.

Initially, Velma spent her time adapting to town life, caring for her brothers, and supporting her mother's new businesses. The addition of school had her focusing on a whole new world of learning. Then Alice fell ill. So, it was not until after New Year's that she had time to notice the other children in her classroom.

Between recess and lunch breaks, Velma learned that not everyone came from a background similar to her own. Indeed, it was a varied group. Many lived in town, children of shop owners and the like. Many others also came from families not involved in farming.

She discovered the area was filled with mines and miners. It was becoming a major coal producer. Numerous mines had opened around the area in the last two decades, the latest just last year. With the steady wages and regular shifts, many of the young men from farms had taken jobs at the mines.

Besides farming and mining in the area, the Woodward Hospital for Epileptics and Feeble-Minded, located a half-mile north of town provided employment for a fair amount of the locals. Apparently, it was a grand building with beautiful grounds, though Velma had never seen it, and adults seldom mentioned the place.

Between farmers, miners, educators, and hospital workers, Woodward had a small but reasonably stable population. The same applied to surrounding towns, chief among them being Perry. It was apparently much larger than Woodward. Then there was Des Moines, the state capital, some twenty miles away as the crow flew. Only Miss Fletcher and a few of the older students had been there.

The school year culminated with Velma's team, Team Lincoln winning the very first-ever scholarship award. Since the whole class had achieved at least eighty percent on Miss Fletcher's grading system, she threw a party as promised. All the parents were invited.

Helping with the event were Agnes, Grace, Tessa, and Alice. It was during the party that the winners were announced. Miss Fletcher told all her students and parents that she was delighted, and a bit amazed at how much progress everyone had made during the year. All the children swelled with pride at hearing this.

With school now out, life got just a bit easier for the Steele girls. Their chores at home and in support of their mother's businesses did not ease, but they had more free time to spend with friends. The biggest challenge and source of conflict was over who got to be with their friends and who took care of the boys.

"It's up to you girls to work it out." Alice said firmly. "I've put together our weekly and daily work, including when the boys need tendin' by you."

"That should be easy, right, Wilma?" Velma asked expectantly.

"That depends."

"On what?" Velma asked incredulously.

Wilma gave her sister a superior look. "Well, that depends on when *I* need to be with *my* friends, silly."

"Right." Velma nodded. "Then we just check Mama's schedule and divide up the time."

"I suppose so." Wilma said tentatively. "But what if we both want the same times?"

"Oh."

"That's easy," Alice said. "You alternate. If one of you gets the first time, the other gets the next time."

Wilma protested vehemently, "But that's not fair!"

"How so?" Alice said with a raised brow.

"Well, I'm older and have more, ah, more important things to do with my friends than Velma."

"Oh, really," her mother said with a wry smile. "And just what would those things be?"

Wilma thought for a minute. "Well, ah, going exploring, or, ah, getting a head start on the next school year."

"How?"

"Ah, by reading, and talking about things."

"Sounds very important," Alice said patronizingly, "but I think we'll stick to my idea. That is, if you don't mind."

"Oh, Mother," Wilma said huffily and stomped off.

"And, if there is a conflict, Velma will get the first choice thanks to that little performance, dearie," Alice said to Wilma's back as she disappeared.

"Now, go talk to these friends that you want to spend time with," her mother said, then asked, "I know that means Katie, but who else? Ddo I know them?"

"Well, you met them at the school party, but I doubt you remember." Then her expression changed to one of concern. "Well, you do kinda know Nancy Brown."

"What?" Alice said with some heat. "You and her are friends?"

"Well, yes," Velma said, then attempted to mollify her mother. "But she's not like her parents at all. They don't know about us."

"Like I didn't until just now?" Alice asked rhetorically, wearing a hard look.

Embarrassed, Velma nodded. "Yes, Mama. Sorry, Mama."

"You should be, daughter," her mother said sharply. "How could you do that knowing what her parents tried to do to us?"

"But that's them, Mama," Velma pleaded. "And Nancy isn't like them at all. Oh, for the first few weeks, we was, I mean were, kinda mean to each other. Then one of our teammates set us straight. From then on, we got along just fine."

"And where did you plan on getting together over the summer without one of us finding out?"

"Well, we'd meet at the Warren's and the other girls."

Alice nodded in understanding, then frowned. "But isn't she near ten now? Why would she want to be around you and Katie?"

"Because she doesn't have a lot of other friends. That's because her parents aren't liked by nearly nobody."

"That's for sure."

Velma snickered nervously. "So, Katie and I are helping Nancy to be accepted."

After a long pause. "Very Christian of you both. Makes me feel more than a little ashamed."

"Oh, Mama. So we can see each other?"

Her mother's head shook slowly. "Best not, I'm afraid. If her parents found out, then learned I allowed it, well, you can imagine the stink they would raise."

"But what if I'm over at Katie's and Nancy shows up?"

"Then I would expect you to come home," Alice said regretfully. "I would expect you to explain why to Nancy. Feel free to blame me, so she knows it is not you and not about her, of course."

"Oh, Mama," Velma implored. "It's not fair."

"The world isn't fair, my dear," Alice said with a melancholy smile. "Now who are these other girls?"

Except for having to give up time with Nancy Brown, Velma's summer was the best of her life up to that time. She worked and played hard. Sleep came easily while waking was like pulling a boot from quicksand. In-between the days were a whirlwind of what, to a six-year-old, was endless adventure.

One highlight of the summer was the Fourth of July fireworks and ice cream social celebrated by the whole town. The main street was blocked off, a band made of the townspeople played, and free ice cream flowed until half the children in town were sick. The festivities concluded with more fireworks than Velma had ever seen.

The end of August was county fair season. No longer an amateur, Alice passed on traveling to Adel, a long trip just to win a bunch of blue ribbons. Many locals did make the trip, however, meaning Alice's business lagged just a bit. So, she informed Henry Hanks that she wouldn't be providing baked goods over the first weekend of the fair.

The next Friday morning, for the first time since Alice had been sick, the smell of baking bread, pies, and cinnamon rolls was missing. Instead, was the aroma of chicken frying. They found their mother forking chicken out onto a large platter. She had to smile at the wide-eyed looks the girls gave her.

"Well, don't just stand there. The Warrens are having a picnic on their front lawn this afternoon. I'll need your help to make some potato salad. Rumor has it that Mr. Warren will be churning ice cream."

That day turned out to be the second-best day of her life after her birthday. The picnic, in addition to all the usual delectable dishes, included chilled watermelon. After the meal, the children played hide-and-seek and Simon Says until dusk.

Then, the ice cream came out while the men put on a short but glorious fireworks display from 4th of July leftovers. At the end of the day, in the hot humid darkness, everyone took jars and collected fireflies until the mothers finally called the evening to a close, much to the displeasure of the children.

After lunch the next day, another hot one, Alice told the children to put on some older clothes. While they changed, she hitched up Nelly. With her four on the wagon, she swung by and picked up Katie and Wilma's best friend, Carla, and headed out of town.

She took them on a leisurely ride toward a town called Madrid that stood across the Des Moines river from Woodward. Once at the river, Alice parked the wagon under a large oak tree, and the children went wading and for a swim under a train trestle.

After drying out in the sun on a spit of sand, they headed back home sunburned and happy.

After putting Nelly away, the collective descended on the Hanks' kitchen to cries of mock protest from Tessa. "You're getting sand all over my floor. Who's going to clean that up?"

"I will," Alice said, with a relaxed and healthy grin, which made Velma smile too.

9
Shocking Change

A few weeks later, students returned to school carrying renewed anxiety. The system of assigning classes had been changed as Miss Fletcher had promised. This brought both good and bad news for Velma.

The first to arrive again, Velma exchanged greetings with Mr. Dickinson and then watched the arrival of teachers and students from the same bench. Velma slowly observed that there seemed to be fewer students waiting in the main hall. She pointed this out to Katie when she arrived. "Where is everybody?"

"What?"

"Look around."

Katie did, then acknowledged, "You're right. And I don't see Barbara or Daniel. And where's Sadie?"

"Well, Daniel moved on to high school, or at least I think he did," Velma said. "I don't have any idea where Barb went."

Katie shrugged, so Velma asked Nancy Brown who was standing nearby, "Do you know where Barb Schmidt is?"

"Moved to Fort Dodge," Nancy said flatly.

"Why?"

Nancy replied forlornly. "The bank foreclosed on their farm, and they had to move in with relatives over there."

"What's foreclosure?" Velma asked.

"When the bank takes away your property 'cause you can't pay the mortgage."

Velma frowned. "That's sad."

"Not as sad as you losing your farm 'cause your father died," Nancy said, then flinched at her lack of tact.

This comment had Velma recalling it had been a while since she had thought about her father. She suddenly missed Papa. "I guess you're right." Wanting to change the subject, she asked, "Do you know if Daniel went to high school?"

Nancy shook her head, then turned to an older girl Velma didn't know well. "Hey, do you know where Daniel is?"

"I think his family moved to Boone. My ma said he and his older brother went to work in one of the coal mines up there."

"Isn't he too young for that?" Nancy asked incredulously.

The girl smiled, saying, "He's a man now, turned sixteen in July." Just then the bell rang, sending them all off to class.

As it turned out, the combined class met in the familiar first-floor classroom from the year before. No sooner had Miss Fletcher reached her desk in the front, then Velma blurted out to her, "Is it true?" Realizing her error, she raised her hand, saying, "Sorry, Miss Fletcher."

"Apology accepted, Velma," the teacher said, while smiling warmly. Then she addressed the other students. "For those new to my class, we raise our hands and stand to ask questions. When you do that for the first time, you'll say who you are." Looking back to Velma, Miss Fletcher added, "Please demonstrate."

Velma blushed as she stood. "I'm Velma Steele and I'm asking if you know about Daniel Waters working in a mine up Boone way. I thought he'd be too young, but he's supposed to be sixteen now. Is that true?"

"Yes, he moved to Boone. I'm not sure about working in a mine." Miss Fletcher's expression had turned serious. "And he is now sixteen. You see, Daniel's family has moved a lot and he'd been unable to attend school regularly. That's why he was still in elementary school instead of high school last year. You may take your seat, Velma."

Then Miss Fletcher continued, "Let me just say to you all that times are difficult around here especially for the farmers. Many have had to make changes. Some have had to move away to find work in new and different jobs, including the mines.

"I am hopeful that things will settle down so we can all learn together for this whole year. I ask all of you students from last year to welcome our newcomers as many are dealing with some of those unpleasant changes."

Velma harkened back to the year before when she experienced what the few newcomers were going through that morning. She glanced at Katie and whispered, "Like you did for me."

"Now, if you look around, some of you are new to school, first-graders. Others have been here before, second-graders, and some are starting your third year. We've put you together because there were not enough of you to have a teacher for each grade."For some of you this will be familiar, especially if you went to a one-room schoolhouse. Raise your hand if you ever went to a one-room schoolhouse or the like?"

Over half the class, including Velma and Katie, raised their hand. "Well, for the rest of you, my class will be a lot less confusing as I'll just be covering three grades. And I will be putting learning teams together so you all can help me teach."

While most in the room didn't understand what Miss Fletcher was planning, Velma and Katie knew well what was coming. They would be on teams, hopefully together, competing for rewards in scholarship as well as other important skills. They gave each other knowing smiles across the aisle.

It turned out the bad news for Velma was that most of her previous classmates had moved to other rooms or plain moved away. Now in second grade, she, along with a dozen others, fell in the middle of the combined first, second, and third-graders. The good news was that Miss Fletcher was going to be her teacher again.

Velma and Katie did end up on the same team. That joy was short-lived, however. By Halloween, two of their team were gone. One girl's family moved to Indiana to run a family farm. Then a boy just didn't show up for school one day without explanation. Fears that more would have to leave left an ominous cloud hanging over the school.

Thankfully, through the end of the calendar year, things remained stable as the Christmas holidays approached. As in 1921, the Warrens invited the usual group of friends over for Christmas Eve dinner. The invite had gone out right after Thanksgiving, which had been celebrated at the Hanks'.

Then a little over a week before the party, Agnes informed Alice, "We may have to cancel. Katie and Frankie are down with something that looks like the flu."

Just mentioning the word flu made people nervous, conjuring up still-fresh memories of 1918's flu pandemic. Because of this, the group of friends fully understood why the event was in doubt.

Then just days before Christmas Eve, Agnes joyfully announced that the children had recovered, and the dinner would go on as scheduled. As if confirming this, first Freddie, then Katie, returned to school for the last few days before the holiday recess.

Christmas Eve fell on a Sunday, so the church put on a grand celebration that morning. It was a bright, sunny day, chilly but not bitter cold. The service ran long with favorite carols, Bible readings, and a cheery sermon by Reverend Jones. Toward the end, Agnes left heading home, it was assumed, to prepare for the evening's festivities.

Everyone arrived at the appointed hour, and the children had another wonderful time. They were disappointed when not allowed to spend the night again. It was only as everyone left that Velma noticed Mrs. Warren was not at the door to say goodbye.

Early on Christmas morning after opening there few presents, Velma headed to spend the day with Katie. Ringing the doorbell, she waited quite a while before Mr. Warren answered the door. "Hello, sir. I believe Katie s'pects me."

A bedraggled Carl Warren said, "I'm afraid she can't come out today. Her mother is not feeling well, and the children and I are taking care of her."

"Oh, I'm sorry, Mr. Warren," Velma said as she started to leave. "Tell her to get better, please. Oh, and tell Katie I'll check back tomorrow."

"I'll do that, Velma," Carl said with a tired wave. "And Merry Christmas."

Velma waved back and headed down the Warren's sidewalk just as Dr. Joseph hurried up the street and through the gate, accompanied by a worried-looking Freddie.

"Merry Christmas, Freddie," Velma said but received only a distracted nod from the boy. "Hope your mom feels better soon." Grabbing the swinging gate, she watched the two rush through the door, held open by an equally worried-looking Mr. Warren.

The sight frightened Velma, who rushed home and shared what had happened with her mother and Wilma. Alice told the girls to watch the boys and headed over to the Warren's to see if she could help.

When Alice returned over an hour later, Tessa Hanks was with her. Both wore somber looks. "What is it, Mama?" Velma asked. "Is Mrs. Warren going to be alright?"

"Can't say, dear. The doctor is still there."

"What does she have?" There was a tremor in Wilma's voice.

This time Mrs. Hanks answered. "It appears to be some kind of flu or the like."

"Is that bad?" Velma asked naively.

"It was certainly a bad thing a few years back," Tessa replied.

"Doc says this ain't the same kind as back then though, and he hasn't seen any widespread breakout," Alice added hopefully.

Mrs. Hanks dampened that hope. "Agnes has always had a fragile constitution though. She's been sickly all her life. She was lucky to avoid that nasty flu back in '18. This had been the longest stretch that I've known her to be healthy. Now this."

"So, what can we do?" Velma asked anxiously.

Wilma echoed her sister's sentiment, "Yes, how can we help?"

"Well, leavin' them be for now is a good start," Alice suggested.

After a pause to consider this, Velma piped up, "What about Katie and Freddie? Are they sick too?"

"Not at present," Tessa replied. "We don't dare move them out of the house, however, as they could come down with this and spread it to others."

"But Katie just got over being sick. Can she get it again?" Velma's voice conveyed her growing concern.

"Maybe, maybe not," her mother answered. "I don't know, and the doctor isn't takin' no chances."

"You two were around all those kids last night," Tessa pointed out.

Alice nodded. "Well, it's a good thing the girls have the rest of the week off. We'll just hunker down here and see what happens."

"Ah, Mama," Wilma's familiar whine returned. "That will ruin my time off."

Alice did not reply with her usual stern rebuke. This told Velma how worried her mother was. "I know, dear, but I need to keep an eye on all four of you so we can nip this in the bud if you start gettin' sick."

Then Alice turned to Mrs. Hanks. "You'll have to be the one to keep checkin' on the Warrens. We don't want to get any more exposure than we already have."

"But what about her?" Wilma asked, meaning Tessa.

"Not to worry, child. I didn't go inside at the Warrens' this afternoon. The doctor wouldn't let either of us in," Tessa explained.

"But you were at the party too," Wilma said incredulously. "Doesn't that mean you could..."

"Yes, dear," Mrs. Hanks interrupted. "But I'm a tough old bird with no children at home. I'll take care and, if I start catching something, I'll just shout messages through the door to the Warrens and you all." Her cheery delivery lacked conviction.

The girls nodded forlornly, then Velma through of something. "What about the eggs, baked goods, and the like?"

"We'll continue with business as usual unless things get worse," Alice said.

Tessa added, "You do all the baking this week at the mercantile. We'll keep it more or less off limits, especially for Annie and her new baby."

"Good idea. If this sickness spreads, well, we'll reconsider then. In the meantime, I'll have a bit more help in the kitchen from the two of you, as well as more time to catch up on my sewin'."

"Ah, Mama." This time the response came in unison from the sisters.

Tessa turned to go. "I'll check on the Warrens in the morning."

"Stop by here on the way," Alice requested. "I'll have somethin' for them."

"Will do. Let's hope this passes quickly," Mrs. Hanks said as she shut the front door behind her.

With a sigh, Alice turned to the girls. "Well, it is still Christmas Day, a time to celebrate the birth of our savior. So, let's get dinner started."

"But, Mama, how can we celebrate with what's going on?" Velma implored.

Alice gave both girls a comforting smile. "Because what's going on is, like always, in God's hands. We'll cook, sing carols, and pray for the Warren family. That's all we can do—pray and hope."

Ten days later, the same week as Velma's seventh birthday, everyone gathered at the Methodist church for Agnes Colfax Warren's funeral. She had gone steadily downhill, succumbing to pneumonia in a pattern reminiscent of the flu pandemic four years earlier. She was by far the youngest of the three people who died in this mild outbreak. She was twenty-eight years old.

To say Velma's birthday was vastly different than the previous year was a profound understatement. There was no party, no cake, and no friends in attendance. Last year's tears of joy were replaced by those of sadness and despair. Dinner at home, with gifts soon forgotten, marked the beginning of 1923.

Katie Warren was inconsolable, feeling responsible for giving the disease to her mother. No amount of assurance to the contrary could convince the little girl otherwise. She could not bear to be in the house and finally went to stay with an aunt in Perry for over a month. Returning, she relapsed and left again.

Freddie was in a stunned daze over these same months. He emerged from this depression angry and hostile. He would not mind his father, teacher, or anyone else. In desperation, Mr. Warren sent Freddie to live with his older brother, Irving, near Denison, Iowa, some eighty miles away. He'd attend school there.

Irv and his wife Dottie had two sons, one three and the other two years older than Freddie. Carl hoped this intact family, especially the presence of a mother figure would help. Irv's feedstore in Denison plus his small farm would offer plenty for the boys to do when not in classes. It seemed an ideal place for Freddie to recover.

Meanwhile, Velma also suffered greatly during this time. The loss of Mrs. Warren was compounded by the departure of her best friend. The rest of that school year, Velma spent in a fog. Her grades suffered and class participation waned. Thankfully, Miss Fletcher and her mother were most understanding.

When summer arrived, Katie returned and moved into a new home. Mr. Warren had sold the big house and bought a smaller place on the other side of town not far from the school. The new surroundings did little for Katie. What did pick up her spirits, however, was having Miss Fletcher rent a room in the house next door.

Katie's first stop after seeing the new place was the mercantile, where she found Velma babysitting the boys. "Hello. Remember me?" Katie said forlornly when her friend answered the door.

"Yippee!" Velma cried, awkwardly hugging her friend, squeezing Edward between them. "Are you back, really back?"

Katie managed a weak laugh. "I guess so. We'll see. I really don't..." She didn't finish as her expression darkened.

"Never mind that," Velma said enthusiastically. "You're here now and, oh darn."

"What?" Katie asked, suddenly concerned.

Velma laughed. "Oh, I just remembered. Today is Wilma's day to be with her friends."

"Where's your mother?" Katie asked.

"Back at the apartment baking away," Velma replied. "Can you stay here with me? You'll have to put up with the boys."

"I don't mind," Katie said blandly. "I'm just glad to see you and stay out of sight."

"Well, whatever you want," Velma said, not quite understanding what her friend meant. Then she remembered. "Say, have you been to your new place?"

"Yes." Katie sounded disinterested.

"I've walked by it several times but not gone in. It sure isn't like the old place. No picket fence or..." Velma stopped suddenly realizing this was not a subject Katie would want to discuss. "Anyway, it's good to know you and I will have the summer together again."

Katie suddenly perked up. "Oh, do you know who lives next door?"

"Unhuh." Velma broke into a broad smile.

"Miss Fletcher!" they yelled in unison, startling her brothers, who didn't care for the surprise and let the girls know it.

After calming them down, Velma turned back to Katie. "Have you seen her?"

"No. Daddy hasn't even met her yet. I heard someone say she took some time off and is traveling in the east. I think they said the trip was to see her parents."

"Well, will you let me go with you to surprise her when she gets back?"

"Sure."

Velma gave her friend another hug, this time free of siblings, "Thank you. She will be soooo glad to see you."

"And I'll be glad too. I went to school over in Perry, but it wasn't any fun without you and Miss Fletcher."

Velma glanced toward the curtain leading to the mercantile. "You haven't seen the Hanks or Annie yet, have you?" Katie shook her head. "Okay, just stay with the boys a minute and I'll get them."

Katie reached out and stopped her. "Ah, well, I don't know if I'm ready to..."

"Oh, come on Katie," Velma implored. "They'd be hurt if they knew you were here and didn't want to see them."

After a pause, Katie relented. "I'm not sure about this, but okay."

Disappearing through the curtain, Velma quickly returned with Tessa in tow. One look at Katie and the woman raced to pick her up and twirl her around. "Lord a mercy, darling. It is so good to see you. Welcome home."

Mrs. Hanks had no sooner put Katie down than Henry came into the room and repeated the act. "Bless my soul if you aren't a sight for sore eyes! And look how you've grown. We've sure missed you."

"Me too," Katie replied. Velma thought she might even have meant it.

Henry put her down and headed for the curtain. "I'll go relieve Annie, so she can introduce you to little Lizzy."

"The name's Elizabeth," Tessa corrected.

"She'll always be Lizzy to me," Henry said sweeping through the doorway.

Mrs. Hanks headed to the cooler and pulled out a plate of cookies. "Here, my dears. Some of Alice's cookies to celebrate the prodigal's return."

"Thank you, Mrs. Hanks," Katie said, her attitude on the upswing.

Velma took one and broke in in half for the boys. She'd learned how to avoid a tantrum from the greedy little beasts. Then she took her own. "Thanks, Mrs. H."

At that moment, Annie Anderson came through the curtain with the baby cooing in her arms. "Hello, Katie, and welcome home. Would you like to..."

"Oh, yes, Annie," Katie interrupted. "Can I hold her?"

"After you finish that, sweetie," Annie said, nodding to the treat in her hand.

After shoving what was left of the cookie in her mouth, Katie stepped up and took the baby. After staring at the infant for a moment, she looked up at Annie. "Oh, she is so precious. Mother would have..."

Katie stopped suddenly and choked back tears. She quickly handed the baby to Annie and slumped in a chair crying uncontrollably. Mrs. Hanks sat beside her, putting an arm around the sobbing girl's shoulders. "There, there, Katie. Let it all out."

"Oh, I feel bad, so resp..." Her sobs strangled the rest of the word.

"Oh, no, dear. You can't still feel responsible?" Henry asked gently.

Katie nodded as Velma said angrily, "It weren't your fault. God called her and she went to heaven. That's all. If you want to blame someone, it's him."

"Now don't blaspheme, Velma. There is no one to blame," Mrs. Hanks said. "Your momma was always sickly, Katie. You weren't the only one who got sick. Lots of folks did. It was nobody's fault."

"But I miss her so. She's the first thing I think about when I wake up and the last at night. I dream about her all the time." Katie buried her head in Mrs. Hanks' ample bosom. The boys began to cry too, then Lizzy joined the chorus.

Annie started back into the store, then stopped in the doorway. With a tear in her eye, she said, "I know how you feel, Katie. I lost my ma and a brother back in '18. It's been five years, and I still grieve for them. But life has a way of filling up and pushing the bad stuff down. Elizabeth here sure does a good job of that for me."

"Annie's right, Katie," Henry said firmly. "Now, why don't you and Velma have another cookie and get outside. It's a beautiful day. Go for a walk or find some of your old friends."

"Can't," Velma replied flatly. "I got to watch the boys."

"Nonsense," Henry said looking to Tessa. "We can handle them for a while, right?"

"Sure enough," Mrs. Hanks affirmed. "Now have another cookie."

It took several minutes for Katie to calm down. The treat helped. Then the girls were off, walking down Main Street hand in hand. The two made their way to the school only to find it locked. Then they headed for the Jones' house.

They found Charity sitting on the front porch steps looking bored. Her eyes lit up when she saw them, and she came at a run. "Oh, Katie! Oh, Katie!" was all she could manage before grabbing her very thin friend in a bear hug.

"Are you sick?" Charity blurted out, then caught herself. "Oh, sorry, Katie, it's just that..." She didn't finish.

"I know," Katie said with a sigh, then smiled weakly. "You should have seen me earlier. I'm a lot better now."

"Really?" Velma asked, unconvinced.

"Really."

Charity gave Katie's arm a tug. "Come on then. Mother was just making some lemonade, and I think we have some kinda cake left."

Heading inside, Mrs. Jones greeted Katie as everyone else had, with warm affection. Two pieces of cake and a tall glass of lemonade later, the three girls headed off for the Warren's new house. They arrived to find Mr. Warren looking for his daughter.

"There you are. And hello girls," he said, forcing a smile. "I've taken the rest of the day off, so we can pick up your brother at the train station in Perry. Your Uncle Irving was putting him on the train in Denison."

"I though you said he'd be spending the summer there," Katie said in a tone Velma couldn't identify.

"Well, that was the original plan. But according to your uncle, he seems better. And I want my family back together. It's been too lonely without you both here."

"Can Velma and Charity come?" Katie asked. Velma thought she sounded a bit desperate.

Mr. Warren shook his head. "Not today, dear." Then he had a thought. "But I can give them a ride back home in my new Model T."

Katie's disappointment was overwhelmed by the excitement of the other girls. "Can we?" Velma asked gleefully as Charity jumped up and down.

"If it's okay with Katie," her father replied.

Katie was less enthusiastic. "Yeah, sure."

"Then let's go." Mr. Warren led the way around to the side of the house where the shiny, dark-blue car sat.

Charity and Velma took off at a run. When Katie lagged behind, however, Velma turned back. "What's the matter?"

"I'm scared."

"Of riding in the car?"

Katie gave her friend an incredulous look. "No. Of seeing my brother."

"But why?"

The two paused at the side of the car as her father urged them on. "You and Charity ride in the back seat. The front's reserved for my little girl." Closing the passenger side door, he moved around to the driver's side.

In a whisper, Katie said, "I don't want to say. I just feel scared about it is all, and leave it at that."

Velma went to the only thing she could think of. "Because he thinks you killed your mother?"

Katie bristled. "Everyone's been saying it was not my fault. Why would you say that about my brother?"

"I just don't understand why you'd be scared I guess."

"Is everything alright?" Mr. Warren asked, seeing the look on Katie's face.

She nodded but said nothing. So, Velma spoke up saying, "I think all the excitement has tired her out. Maybe you could leave her with me at the mercantile. Then you and Freddie could pick her up on the way back."

He shook his head. "Thanks for the offer, but I already told Freddie we'd be coming together."

"And what did he say?" Katie asked anxiously.

After a pause, Mr. Warren said, "Well, he was excited of course." Velma wasn't sure Carl sounded like he meant it. "Now, are you ready to enjoy the ride?"

Charity practically shouted. "You bet. I can't wait for Mother and Father to see me." The other girls just nodded half-heartedly.

Charity was dropped off first. Her mother was impressed by the car and accepted an offer to take a spin after church the next Sunday. Reverend Jones was not at home so missed the excitement. Charity waved them off while Velma and Katie remained sullen. There demeanor apparently went unnoticed by Mr. Warren.

A minute later, the car halted in front of the mercantile. Cars had become much more common in Woodward over the last year, so they drew little attention. Before getting down, Velma made one more plea on Katie's behalf. "Are you sure Katie can't stay with me? We have a lot to catch up on."

"Sorry, Velma, but we have an important reunion of our own to attend." Mr. Warren put the car in gear. "You'll have all summer to catch up." Then he pulled off, giving her a jaunty wave while Katie just stared straight ahead.

Within a few weeks it became clear that Katie was right to be concerned. Freddie's return had not been what Mr. Warren had hoped it would be. The military academy had turned him into an outwardly disciplined and polite ten-year-old. Underneath the surface, however, he still carried deep-seated anger and hostility.

Freddie carried a chip on his shoulder for anyone who had an intact family. He regularly got into scrapes with boys of all ages. When it came to girls, he teased the older ones and bullied the younger. Even his sister and her close friends suffered. Try as he might, Mr. Warren seemed impotent to control his son.

Less than a month after the two Warren children returned, Mr. Warren arrived home to the sound of a heated argument coming from somewhere inside. As he headed for the kitchen, he heard Freddie's raised voice.

"It was your fault, and you know it," he screamed. "You should have been the one to die."

Stunned, Carl Warren came to a sudden stop in the hallway, listening in disbelief as Katie tried to respond, "But you were sick at the..."

Freddie interrupted, his voice rising, "You were the one that clung to her. She had no time for me. She even slept with you."

"In my room, not with me," Katie retorted. "And you were the one who got sick after me. She wasn't sick then."

"That does it." Freddie's voice was almost unrecognizable and broke Mr. Warren out of his stupor. As he took the last few steps to the kitchen, he heard Freddie growl, "Now you're trying to blame me. Get out! Get out!"

Mr. Warren arrived just as Freddie pushed his sister through the screen door and down the back steps. Once again Mr. Warren froze until he heard Katie cry out in pain. Crossing the room in two quick strides, he yelled at his son who stood just beyond the door, "Freddie!"

Whirling around, the boy's expression changed from anger to surprise, then something his father could not quite identify. "Oh, Dad. I'm so glad you're here. Katie just tripped and fell down the stairs. I didn't know what to do."

He pushed out the door and past his son without reply and went to his daughter lying at the foot of the stairs. She was cradling her arm and starting to cry. "Don't worry, Katie, I'll get you fixed right up. I see your arm is hurt." He touched it gingerly, generating a grimace, no more. "Are you hurt anywhere else?"

"I don't know, Daddy," she said with a sniff. "I didn't fall down, he pushed..."

"I know, honey," he said glaring up at Freddie. Then turning back, he conducted a brief check for other injuries.

"What happened?" A voice Carl didn't recognize came from behind him. Looking around, he saw a young woman wearing a concerned expression. Seeing his confusion, the woman added, "I'm Emily Fletcher, Katie's teacher. I live next door."

"Oh, right," Carl said, then struggled with whether to get up or stay with his daughter.

Miss Fletcher resolved the quandary for him as she knelt by his side. "I received a bit of first-aid training at school. Let me have a look."

"Thank you, Miss Fletcher," Carl Warren said as he stood and looked for his son. He was gone. "Katie, will you be alright with Miss Fletcher for a minute? I need to find your brother."

She just nodded as tears began to flow again. Misinterpreting the cause, Miss Fletcher tried to soothe her. "I know it hurts, dear, but we'll get you fixed right up."

Carl heard his daughter say, "Yes, Miss Fletcher," as he headed inside. Trying to avoid embarrassment, he called out in a controlled tone. "Freddie, where are you?"

There was no answer. He headed upstairs to the boy's room. It was empty. Turning to leave, he glanced out the window. There he saw Freddie turning the corner a block away onto Main Street at a run. Resisting the urge to chase him down, Carl headed back to Katie.

He arrived to find Miss Fletcher tying a sling around his daughter's right arm. She looked up to say, "I'm afraid her arm may be broken. We should get her to Dr. Joseph."

"Right," Carl said without questioning. "My car is right around the corner. I'll carry her."

"May I come with you?"

"Of course," Carl said, sweeping Katie into his arms, mindful to avoid her arm.

Minutes later, Carl drove up in front of Dr. Joseph's office. From the car, he could see a sign posted on the door. "Stay here with her please," he said to Miss Fletcher. "I need to read that sign." She just nodded.

Carl was quickly out of the car, reading the note, then tried the door. It was locked. Returning to the car, he said, "Dr. Joseph is out delivering a baby."

"Where?"

"He didn't say."

"And I saw the door is locked."

"I'm afraid so," Carl said as Katie moaned. He looked helplessly toward Miss Fletcher. "I don't know what to do."

He and Emily fell silent, thinking intensely. Then Miss Fletcher had an idea. "The best thing for her arm right now is ice for pain and to keep the swelling down."

"*And?*" Carl asked impatiently, then apologized. "I am so sorry. I'm just a little..."

"Upset," she interrupted, giving the man a forgiving smile. "I think we ought to head for the mercantile. They have ice, plus her best friend, Velma, and others she knows well are likely there."

"Good idea."

He started to get back in when she added, "Do you have a pen and paper? You could leave a note for Dr. Joseph telling him where to find us."

After a moment's thought, he reached in the back seat and grabbed his briefcase. In a minute he emerged with both. Scribbling a short paragraph, he hurried back and slid the note under the door. Back in the car, they headed for the mercantile.

"Take the alley," Emily suggested. "We'll go in the back where the cooler is."

"Another good idea," Carl said with an anxious smile.

A minute later, he was taking Katie from Miss Fletcher's arms. As he moved around the car toward the Hanks' backdoor, Emily rapped on it. Just as Carl arrived, Alice Steele threw it open, already wearing a worried look. "What happened?"

"She fell and hurt her arm," Carl replied. "Doc Joseph is out on a call, so we came here to get some ice and a place for her to rest easy."

After Alice gave Miss Fletcher a curious look, she nodded, "You came to the right place. There's a room upstairs with a bed she can have. I'll get that ice."

"And I'll alert the Hanks," Carl said.

"They're not here right now, but Annie will want to know."

As she held the curtain open, allowing Carl and Katie to pass through, Emily asked, "Where is Velma?"

"Don't know," Alice said, already digging ice out of the cooler. "She went off with friends. I would have thought that would have included Katie. Obviously not." When she came out with the ice, Miss Fletcher was gone.

After informing Annie, Emily headed toward the stairs just as Alice came from the kitchen with a bag of ice. "Here, you take this up. I got cookies in the oven."

"Okay." They parted as Emily hurried up the stairs. A quick glance around found the right room. A pale Katie lay on the bed in obvious pain. "Here's the ice. This should help."

"You do it, will you?" Carl asked Miss Fletcher.

"Of course." She spread a light blanket over the bump in Katie's arm and then ever so gently placed the bag on top.

Katie flinched but soon relaxed and gave her father and Miss Fletcher a reassuring smile. "That feels good. Thank you."

"Yes, thank you, Miss Fletcher," Carl said with genuine relief.

She gave him an unassuming nod. "It was nothing really."

"I would beg to differ, Miss Fletcher. I'd have been lost without your calm and wise advice."

"You flatter me too much, Mr. Warren."

"Daddy's name is Carl, Miss Fletcher," Katie whispered.

"I know, Miss Katie."

"Then why don't you call him that?"

"Because that would be presumptuous."

"What does pre, presume, what does that word mean?"

Emily couldn't help but laugh. "Let's just say it is not proper without invitation."

"Consider yourself invited," Carl said, suddenly looking embarrassed.

"I guess that would be alright seeing as we're neighbors," she said easily. "But only if you call me Emily."

"But not in the company of other students, right?" Carl suggested.

"Oh, of course." Emily said turning to Katie. "And I will always be Miss Fletcher to you, my dear."

"Yes, Miss Fletcher."

"Now, if you don't mind, I'd like a minute with my daughter alone."

"Of course." Miss Fletcher said, moving to the door. "I'll be back soon, that is if you want me to stay around."

"Oh, yes," Katie said imploringly. "I'd like that very much."

"Okay then. Try not to move that arm." With that, the young woman left the two Warrens alone.

Pulling over a chair, Carl gave his daughter a grave look. "Do you want to tell me what was going on before I found you at the bottom of the stairs?"

"A fight."

"I figured that much. What was it about?"

"Nothing."

"Katherine Elizabeth," Carl said sternly. "I heard part of it."

"Which part?"

"About you two blaming each other for your mother's death. Is that what this was about?"

"Partly," Katie said softly. "That's where we end up each time."

"Each time?" Carl asked in surprise.

"Yeah."

"How many times?"

"Lots."

"Has he ever hurt you before?"

She remained silent until prodded again. "Katie, has he hurt you before?"

"Not really," she said unconvincingly.

"One more time, Katie. What has he done to you?"

Instead of replying, she raised the hem of her dress a few inches with her good hand. This revealed a rather large bruise on her hip. Then she said in a matter-of-fact tone, "A kick. It's almost healed. Most of the other times they don't last, slaps and the like. This was the worst though."

"And why didn't you tell me?"

"Because I hoped he'd stop. For your sake, I didn't want him to have to go away again." Katie's voice trembled and she began to cry.

Carl stood and slid the chair back. "You rest now dear. Everything will be alright."

"I hope so, Daddy."

The arm was broken. Dr. Joseph set it with minimal pain thanks to the ice. Velma had arrived at the mercantile just in time to see the doctor wrap her friend's arm in bandages and put plaster on to form a cast. That evening, the Hanks entertained unexpected guests including Katie, Miss Fletcher, and Velma.

Alice and Wilma went home with the boys, while Carl scoured the town looking for Freddie without success. When he arrived back at the mercantile, he ate a few bits of leftovers, then headed home. Emily rode back with him, along with Velma who finagled the chance to stay overnight with Katie.

Days later Mr. Warren finally tracked down his son. Freddie had hitchhiked the dozen or so miles to Perry and knocked on his aunt's door, saying that he was there for a visit on summer break. Having cared for Katie previously, his father's sister, Pearl welcomed him with open arms until there came another knock at the door.

"Why, Carl, what brings my brother here in the middle of the week?"

"Hoping to find my wayward son," Warren said coolly.

Pearl gave him a surprised look, "But he said you knew he was here."

"Now I do."

The woman turned to look into the house. When she turned back, her face was filled with anger. "That little liar."

"And bully," Carl added.

"Bully?" she asked incredulously.

"That's a story for another time," Warren said, then asked, "Is he inside?"

Pearl nodded. "In the living room." She turned again saying, "Freddie, can you come here? You have a visitor."

"He just headed to the kitchen," came a male voice.

"Go get him will you, Edgar?"

"On my way."

Pearl turned back to her brother, "Where are my manners? Come in, Carl."

"I won't keep you and Edgar long."

"Long enough for me to tan his hide for you I hope," Pearl sounded serious.

"Oh, if that was all it took."

At that moment, Edgar came back in the living room with a confused look on his face. "He's gone."

Without a word, Carl rushed past Edgar and out the back door of the house. It was an early June evening with plenty of light left. Still, he did not see his son in any direction.

Rushing back inside, he spoke sharply to Edgar and Pearl. "Where might Freddie have gone?"

Both of them wore blank expressions, so Carl pressed them. "Has he made any friends or found places to hang out?"

"I, I don't know of any. I'm working all day," Edgar sputtered out.

Carl stepped closer to Pearl. "What about you?"

"Ah, he's been hanging out downtown; that's all I know."

Frustrated, Carl flew out the front door and climbed quickly into the car. His sister followed. "Can I come along?"

"Get in," Carl urged as he started the Model T.

Edgar and Pearl Perry lived on the east side of town just off Main. Carl turned onto the wide, tree-lined street past a collection of two-story Victorians. He traveled slowly as the two scanned for Freddie.

"If he was hightailing it, the boy could already be downtown," Pearl suggested.

Perry was just a larger version of Woodward with a longer main street. A block to the south was the train station, serving a spur of the Northwestern Line. Carl knew it came from Des Moines but didn't know where it went beyond Perry. The tracks marked the border of the town with farmland beyond. North of Main, the town ran four or five blocks.

"Where might he go down here?" Carl asked, barely containing his anger.

Pearl shrugged. "I have no clue. He's been out and about most days, just home for breakfast and back for dinner. We didn't want to press the boy after..." She let the obvious reason go unspoken.

"Pull over here," Pearl suddenly said.

Carl did so, stopping next to a group of young boys. With a warm smile, Pearl said, "Hello, Tommy, boys. We're looking for Freddie Warren. Do you know him?"

There were a few nods as Tommy replied in a less than pleasant tone, "Yeah, we've met."

"Well, he's my nephew, and this is his dad coming for a surprise visit."

"Gonna take him home with ya?" A voice from the group asked in a hopeful tone.

"If we can find him," Carl answered with a faux smile.

Pearl went on to explain, "He just left our house back on Maple." She gave a wave behind her, "Before my brother arrived. We think he headed this way."

"Yeah, he did," Tommy said.

Another youth added, "Saw us but crossed the street and kept goin'."

"Where?"

"Most likely the train station," Tommy replied. "That or the hotel."

"Maybe the pool hall," another boy added.

"Thanks," Carl said, switching off the Model T. "You guys want to make a buck?"

"Yeah, sure," came the collective reply.

"Help us find him. If you do, there will be a two-bits for each of you and a buck for the one who actually does the finding," Carl said adding, "Bring him to the car and wait if we're not back."

"You got it, mister," Tommy said, waving his friends into action.

"We'll check the hotel while you boys try the other places," Pearl suggested.

"Okay," Tommy said as the group headed across the nearly vacant street, spreading out as they went.

Carl gave his sister a jaundiced look. "You think he'd be at the hotel."

"No, but among the choices, it's the one where a lady can go and be comfortable while we wait. No reason we should traipse around town when you've hired a posse."

"Good thinking," Carl said and escorted Pearl to the hotel just east of the train station and switching yard.

Inside, they asked the desk clerk if he had seen Freddie. The answer was an unequivocal no. So, the two found seats in the front window near the hotel entrance from which they could see the Model T and waited. In a few minutes, the boy named Tommy came scurrying past. Carl jumped up and quickly stepped outside.

"Over here, Tommy!" Carl shouted.

The boy spun around and came his way. Breathlessly, he said, "We found him and you better hurry."

"Where? Why?" Carl sputtered out as Pearl joined him.

"He's about to hop a freight headed to Des Moines."

"What?" Carl cried. "Take me there!"

Pearl choked back her own anguished cry and waved them off. "I'll wait here."

Carl followed Tommy across the side street to and through the train station onto the platform. The boy continued on toward a switching yard full of box and coal cars. As they approached an engine that appeared to be preparing to leave, they saw a railroad man headed their way holding Freddie firmly by the collar.

"Let go of me," Freddie was saying belligerently.

The bull jerked him closer, "Oh, I'll let you go, boy, when we get to the jail."

Carl rushed over and addressed the railroader. "Thank you for finding my son, sir."

Freddie went limp at the sight of his father as Carl continued, "He was upset with me and ran off."

"Yeah, right," the bull said unsympathetically. "What I saw was him tryin' to climb in a box car. And I'm paid to keep folks off the trains."

"I appreciate that sir," Carl said in a most deferential tone. "But, as you can see, this was just a misunderstanding."

"No, can't say that I do."

Carl reached in his pocket and pulled out some bills. "Well, what would see your way clear to hand him over?"

The bull thought on this for a minute while maintaining a firm grip on Freddie. "Well, my bosses wouldn't like it if they..."

Carl peeled off a five-dollar bill as he interrupted. "Oh, they won't have to know."

"Well, I guess you could say I was just helpin' you find your boy."

"Right."

The bull took the five and let Freddie go. "Thank you, sir," Carl said taking his son by the arm and quickly leading him away.

"Here you go, Tommy." Carl handed him a dollar and a quarter as several of the other boys joined them outside the station.

"Thank you, sir," the boy said, then turned to his friends. "Soda's on me."

As the group of boys headed off, Carl addressed Freddie though clenched teeth, "Now for you, young man."

Back at Pearl and Edgar's, Carl filled them in on what had happened between Freddie and Katie. The Perrys displayed a mixture of shock, surprise, and anger. Freddie showed no emotion at all and said nothing.

"How is Katie doing?" Pearl asked. Before Carl could answer, she turned to Freddie. "That's something I would have expected you to ask, young man."

"Yeah, how is she?" the boy said halfheartedly.

"It will take weeks for the arm to heal," Carl answered. "I don't know how long it will take for her to get over what you did." He turned to Pearl and Edgar again. "That was not the first time he'd hurt her since coming home, you see."

"Oh, my God," Pearl croaked.

Then Edgar asked angrily, "What do you have to say for yourself?"

"Nothin'."

"Well, that won't do," Carl replied angrily. Freddie said nothing, just stared at the floor as silence filled the room.

Pearl finally broke the tension by asking her brother, "So, what are you going to do?"

"I'm not sure." There was anguish in Carl's voice.

"Take him back to the military academy," Edgar suggested flatly while glaring at his nephew.

After a pause, Carl asked his son, "Is that what I should do, or can you promise to behave for the rest of the summer?"

Without hesitation, Freddie snarled, "Probably not."

"Well, there's your answer," Edgar said, barely controlling his own anger.

"Can we stay the night so I can sleep on it?" Carl asked.

His sister patted his hand, "Of course, we've got the room."

"I think Freddie and I will be sharing one tonight," Carl said, looking at his son with distrust.

"Ah, Dad," Freddie managed but was ignored.

"Who's minding Katie?" Pearl asked with sudden concern.

"Her teacher, Miss Fletcher, and Velma are looking after her. I told the woman that I might not be back tonight."

Pearl patted her brother's knee. "This is not something you needed after the year you have had, Carl."

"It's not something any of us needed, except, apparently, Freddie."

The boy said nothing, just giving the adults a blank stare.

"Well, let's get something to eat and make an early night of it shall we?" Pearl said as she headed for the kitchen.

Carl sighed. "Good idea. It will be a long day tomorrow."

The next morning, Carl made two lengthy and expensive phone calls, first to his brother in Denison and then to Chicago. The very next day, Mr. Warren and his son took a train out of Des Moines headed east. Near Chicago, Carl enrolled the boy in a facility that specialized in handling troubled youth.

This new school provided tighter control as well as counseling services. It tore Carl apart to leave Freddie behind, but he saw little choice. His son showed no emotion as the two parted.

A dejected and depressed Carl Warren returned to Woodward to try and build a normal life again after losing half of his family. Katie was ambivalent about the absence of her brother. She spent nearly every waking hour of the summer with Velma, helping with Eugene and Edward, and learning to bake.

By the start of school, Katie outwardly seemed to be fully recovered from her physical and mental ordeals. Only Velma knew the truth of her friend's continued suffering. It had become Velma's full-time goal to help Katie truly mend. Soon, however, Velma's attention was diverted to a family crisis of her own.

10

Unwelcomed Advances

For the third year in a row, Velma and Katie happily were assigned to Miss Fletcher's classroom. It was like a tonic for both of them as they immersed themselves in their studies. With Katie living near the school and where Miss Fletcher resided, the girls spent as much time as possible at the Warren home, occasionally joined by the teacher.

Velma's new freedom came thanks to several factors. Katie often helped her friend with chores in return for the time they spent together. In addition, Alice was concentrating more on baking and sewing, with laundry and house cleaning limited to a select clientele. The Hanks and Annie Anderson also continued helping with the boys.

This opportunity for Allice to escape the most difficult drudgery was offset, however, by the increase in demand for the products she was providing. She struggled to keep up with the baking even with ovens at the apartment and at the Hanks' going nearly around the clock. At one point, Henry suggested opening a bakery in a vacant building next door, but Alice declined his offer to finance the project.

Wilma and Velma were both learning to sew under the demanding eye of their mother. In fact, Alice was also teaching Annie some of her techniques, while Tessa was becoming a skilled baker. The mercantile had, in fact, become a tiny factory of sorts.

Sadly, the family finally had to part with old Nelly who was not up to the livery work demanded of her. They found a kind farmer near town with plenty of pastureland for her to live out her days in the company of her kind. Velma and Wilma were able to visit her from time to time.

Utilizing the space the horse had occupied, Henry and Alice expanded the egg and chicken business. A new coop able to handle more hens was built inside the barn. Eugene, now five, assisted Velma with collecting and feeding the large flock. Alice and Henry supplied the local butcher with layers beyond their prime.

Things would have been idyllic for the tight circle of friends if not for the memories of the those no longer with them. While Katie continued mourning her mother, Mr. Warren agonized over the son he'd sent away. The two declined to attend the monthly group dinners, their absences a constant reminder of these tragedies.

That fall was warm and dry, perfect for harvesting a bumper crop. Ironically, this worked against the farmers as demand and prices fell again. By November, the cycle of farm foreclosures began again. This pattern was starting to impact the rest of the community as businesses began closing as well.

In spite of all this, Woodward tried to settle into an uncomfortable routine, like a pond returning to tranquility after being dramatically disturbed. Nowhere was this effort more visible than in Miss Fletcher's classroom. The young teacher took on the cause of raising the spirits of the community through the schoolchildren.

Emily volunteered to coordinate a weekend-long Woodward heritage pageant, complete with plays performed by the students. Her idea was to hold each play at different venues around the town, including the school, mercantile, and the bank. She solicited other teachers, friends, and even Mr. Warren to help stage the event.

"Mama's given me permission to work on the pageant tonight at your house, Katie." Velma could hardly contain her excitement.

Katie was less enthused. "Oh, yeah. Daddy and Miss Fletcher will be working on it *again* tonight. That's all they do anymore."

"Isn't that a good thing?" Velma asked incredulously.

Her friend shrugged. "I suppose so. It's just awkward what with Miss Fletcher being my teacher. I've heard some of the kids calling me teacher's pet."

"So what? I'd be proud to be called her pet. She's so nice, and plenty smart."

"Yeah. I know." Katie's expression remained dour. "I just wish she wasn't over so much. I don't get any time alone with Daddy."

Velma's smile faded. "But doesn't working on the pageant distract him from, thinking about, well, you know?"

Katie's face grew darker. "I don't think nothin' can do that."

"Anything."

"Right." Katie sighed. "See, I can't even stay focused on what I am learning in school."

"Don't be silly. You're doing just fine, better than me," Velma lied.

This made Katie smile weakly. "Nice try, Vel."

"Anyway, I'll be over right after dinner and my homework," Velma said, heading off down the street toward home. "I think Mama is baking some cookies for me to bring over."

Katie's face broke into a full grin. "Yum. I hope they are chocolate chip."

"Me too."

Arriving back at the Warren's just after five in the still-warm sunshine of the September afternoon, Velma joyfully held up the basket of cookies as Katie answered the door. "We got our wish."

Katie seemed distracted. "Huh? Oh, chocolate chip, right?"

"Right," Velma replied, then asked, "Is something wrong?"

"Oh, no. It's just, Miss Fletcher and Daddy have been working on the pageant skits for the last hour. He even left work early."

"Wow. He must really be excited about it." Velma's smile was not returned.

Just then laughter drifted out to the girls. "Yeah, right," Katie said flatly while holding the door open. "Let's get at those cookies."

The two passed through the foyer and into the dining room to find the table strewn with papers and books. Mr. Warren and Miss Fletcher's laughter was just fading as they arrived. "What's so funny?" Katie asked rather sharply.

"Oh, hello girls," Miss Fletcher said before explaining. "Your father just came up with a funny idea for a skit about the first wooden sidewalks."

"That's the one you students will do in front of the mercantile," Carl Warren added. Seeing the basket in Velma's hands, he added, "Please tell me those are some of your mother's famous cookies."

"Yes, sir." She put the basket in one of the few open places on the table. "Won't you have one?"

"Or two," he said, laughing again. "After you, Emily."

Miss Fletcher demurred. "Oh, I shouldn't." She quickly took one. "Yum."

"So, what do you want Vel and me to do?" Katie said curtly.

"What you were doing just a few minutes ago," her father said with a frown. "We need more bunting and streamers. And each of you can make your own poster announcing the event."

"We don't know what to say," Katie replied argumentatively.

Miss Fletcher handed over a sheet of paper. "It's like a newspaper article. You just make sure to tell people what, when, where, and why."

"But it's all over town."

"Right," her father said, then added, "Just list the locations."

"I don't think I can do that," Katie protested.

"Sure you can," Mr. Warren said frustratedly.

"He's right, Katie," Velma agreed.

Katie persisted. "But it's going to look, look stupid."

"Why do you say that?" Miss Fletcher asked.

After a pause, Katie answered. "Because we're just little kids. We can't draw and probably will spell everything wrong."

"But don't you see," Miss Fletcher replied, "That's just the point. This is a pageant for the town with you students taking the lead. What better way to publicize the event than for you to do it in your own way?"

"I think that's dumb," Katie said angrily.

"Katherine Elizabeth," Carl Warren said sternly. "You apologize to Miss Fletcher right now."

"That's not necessary, Carl," the teacher said while giving the little girl a forgiving smile. "If she doesn't want to do that, there are the streamers and bunting to make."

"Come on, Katie. Let's give it a try." Velma's cheerful tone eased the tension. "I have an idea for one."

"Good," Miss Fletcher said with a nod. "There are pens and the like on the kitchen table. Do try, Katie."

Without a word, Katie headed for the kitchen wearing an unenthusiastic expression. "I'll work on her, Miss Fletcher."

"Do that," Mr. Warren said, wearing his own look of displeasure.

As Velma headed after her friend, she heard Miss Fletcher say, "Don't be too hard on her, Carl. She just doesn't like having another woman in her house."

"You think that's it?"

Velma didn't hear the reply as she entered the kitchen to find Katie sitting at the table, arms folded in a defiant pose. "What is it, Katie?"

"I don't like it."

"What?"

"Her being here," Katie spit out. "I don't like her."

"Miss Fletcher?" Velma asked with a disbelieving chuckle. "But I thought you loved Miss Fletcher."

"Not anymore."

"Why?"

Katie said nothing for a moment, then sighed. "Never mind. You said something about an idea for a poster. Show me."

The day of the pageant arrived with a rush. It kicked off on Friday evening, October 12th, with a play at the school. It was a pantomime with a reading by Miss Fletcher covering the founding of Woodward. The plan was for events on Saturday and Sunday, to bring the story up to the present.

The big concern was the weather. Although the first night was indoors, the other two days involved outside events. Two other concerns were connected to weather—the state of the harvest and possible impact on attendance.

With a period of dry, warm weather, the harvest was nearly complete by the 12th. That day continued the trend. It was nearly eighty in the afternoon under cloudless skies. By the time the show went on at the school in front of a packed house, it was a comfortably mild 60 degrees.

"I'd say that was a successful start to the pageant, wouldn't you?" a smiling Emily asked the group who remained behind to clean up.

Alice chuckled. "Well, if the way they gobbled down my pastries is any indication, I'd have to agree."

"What about the play?" Wilma's question came with a pouty tone.

Her mother glared her way for a moment, then softened. "Why, it was very good, child. You made a real good sod buster's wife."

"A frontierswoman, Mama."

"Right."

Stacking up the last of the chairs, Henry changed the subject. "Did you notice how many folks from outside Woodward made the trip?"

"All I know is the school was packed," Tessa replied. "Oh, but I do recall seeing your sister and brother-in-law from Perry, Carl."

"It was nice of them to be here supporting our efforts." Mr. Warren said without a smile.

"Somethin' wrong with that?" Alice asked, after noting his demeanor.

Carl shrugged. "Not really. They just were asking after Freddie and..." He let the sentence drop.

Noticing his discomfort, Emily Fletcher directed a question to Velma and Katie. "Did you see Daniel Waters was here?"

"No," Velma said in surprise.

Katie nodded. "I thought I saw him, but he was gone by the time the play ended."

"He had to get back for his shift in the morning," Emily explained.

"So he is working in the coal mine over by Boone," Velma said with a touch of sadness.

"Yes, I'm afraid so," Emily replied, then added, "He said to say hello and that he missed school, especially Team Lincoln."

Katie and Velma gave each other a melancholy smile, then returned to clearing the last table. "That's too bad," Tessa said absently. "I also heard there were some folk here from over Granger way."

Alice's head jerked up at hearing this. "You know 'em?"

"No, but I overheard Edith Brown saying something about someone from over that way being in town."

"One of her relatives, maybe one of mine?" Alice continued to probe.

Tessa shook her head. "I don't think so. Mrs. Brown didn't sound happy about it."

"Well, I'm her relative and she sure isn't too happy about that either," Alice said with a wry smile. Then Alice turned to Velma. "Did Nancy Brown mention anything about relatives comin' over here?"

"No, Mama," Velma replied.

"Is this something to be concerned about?" Henry asked.

After a pause, Alice shrugged. "More a curiosity than a concern." Then she moved on. "Best now we get you all home for some rest. It's been an excitin' day."

"Indeed," Tessa said. "You go on home and we'll finish here." She said this to Mr. Warren as well as Alice. "We don't have children to calm down."

Alice didn't argue. "I'm sure Annie will want to get Elizabeth home as well. Surely Eugene and Edward have worn her out by now."

Just then Reverend and Mrs. Jones came into the room, "All the decorations are taken down outside and loaded in the back of your car, Carl," Pastor Jones said.

"Good timing, Alan," Mr. Warren replied. "I think we're through here."

Velma tugged on her mother's sleeve. "Remember, Mama, I'm staying with Katie tonight."

"And who's gettin' the eggs and feedin' the chickens in the mornin'?" Alice said with a mock frown.

"But Mama."

Her mother chuckled. "I'm just joshin' ya. Eugene will help me tomorrow."

"So will I," Tessa added. "We'll be baking up a storm at my place by seven and need all the eggs that brood can lay. Speaking of baking, how well did we do?"

"Made back the cost, plus a little for the kitty," Alice replied. Then she turned to Velma. "I expect you and your friend to be helpin' us before the sun's too high."

"Yes, Mama."

"Now get goin'. We got this covered." Henry waved the children and parents away.

"Out to my car, girls. You too, Emily," Carl Warren said, moving toward the door.

"Ah, Daddy," Katie said in a whisper as she gave him a hard look.

"I have to lock up here, Carl," Emily replied.

"I'll not have you walking home alone," Carl said sternly.

This generated laughter around the room. "This is Woodward, Carl," Reverend Jones spoke for the others.

"And I can see my place from the school," Emily chided. "So, I'll be fine."

"Alright," Carl said with a heavy shrug. "Come on Katie, Velma. Time to get you into bed."

The two girls quickly followed Mr. Warren out the door. Once out of sight, Tessa turned to Emily. "What's gotten into Katie Warren?"

"What do you mean?"

"She means her sullen attitude," Alice provided the explanation.

Grace Jones added, "Yes. She seemed to be coming around, getting back to the old, fun-loving Katie, or at least a reasonable facsimile, during the summer. Now..."

Henry interrupted. "Now she's walking around with a chip on her shoulder."

"Oh, I hope she's not headed the way of Freddie," Tessa said putting a hand to her mouth at the thought.

"Don't be silly, Tess," Emily said. "I agree she's slipped back a bit lately, but I'm sure it will soon pass."

"I hope you're right." Alice didn't sound convinced. Then with a shrug she added, "I need to get home to my brood and relieve Annie. Are we done here?"

"Yes," Emily said. "And thank you all for helping to make tonight so successful."

Henry helped the teacher put the last box away in the corner cabinet as he said, "Save the thanks until the whole weekend is over. We got a long way to go, starting with events down by the mercantile tomorrow evening." Stepping over to Tessa, he added, "I don't know why I let you talk me into this."

"Me?" his wife said in shock. "You're the one..."

She stopped when Henry broke out laughing. "I know dear. Now let's get going so Emily can lock up."

A few short blocks away, Carl Warren was rushing the girls to bed so fast that their heads were swimming. "What's the hurry, Daddy? It's not that late."

"It's past nine-thirty, my dear," Carl said firmly. "You two have been moving at a run for days and just had a very exciting night. You don't know it, but you're exhausted."

"Really?" Velma asked incredulously.

"Trust me," Mr. Warren said. "You two will be out before you know it." Herding them back toward bed, he said, "Besides, you have an early morning at the mercantile not to mention another play tomorrow, this one with lines."

"You're right, Mr. Warren," Velma nodded as she climbed into bed.

Katie joined her reluctantly. "I still don't see..."

Carl cut her off abruptly. "How about just doing what your Dad said?"

"Can we talk in bed?" Katie persisted.

Carl glanced out the window into the darkness, then relented a little. "I guess so. I'm not going to sit up here and listen, so I can't stop you." Then he had a thought. "Do you two *really* know your lines for tomorrow?"

"Yes," Katie said exasperatedly. "We only have a couple of lines each."

Velma corrected her. "Actually, you have three and I have four."

"Thanks," Katie said curtly.

Carl tucked the girls in, bringing the debate to an end. "Then practice them and remember who says what just before you deliver your lines."

"Good idea, Mr. Warren," Velma said compliantly.

"Yeah. Sure," was Katie's sarcastic reply.

The light went out and the door shut as Velma began to recite her lines. "I don't want to do that, Vel. Let's just talk about other stuff."

"Like what?"

"I don't know," Katie said grumpily. "Anything but the stupid old play."

Katie's choice of words surprised Velma. "But I thought you loved the plays."

"Never mind. Pick something else."

"Okay." Velma thought for a while. "You saw Daniel Waters?"

"Yes."

"What did he look like? Had he changed much?"

After a pause, Katie replied. "He looked tall and dirty."

"Dirty?"

"Like he came straight from a mine."

"That's sad."

"I know." Katie yawned dramatically then said, "Daddy was right. I'm suddenly sleepy."

"Me too. Good night, Katie."

"Good night, Vel," her friend said, rolling on her side facing the wall.

After a few minutes, Velma asked in a whisper. "You really don't think the plays are stupid, do you?" There was no reply. So, she rolled on her side and tried to fall asleep.

Being unsuccessful after several more minutes, Velma turned to Katie and listened to her steady breathing. This fact made her a bit angry. Her friend's comment about the play being stupid had her confused. Thoughts that would not let her sleep. Thoughts like what was wrong with Katie.

It was then that Velma heard muffled voices coming from downstairs. She was pretty sure one was Mr. Warren, but the other was indistinguishable at first. When she slipped out of bed and quietly opened the bedroom door, she was able to recognize the other voice. It was Miss Fletcher.

The conversation was coming from the porch. Miss Fletcher must have stopped on the way to her apartment. Velma wondered if the two might be talking about tomorrow's performance. Maybe they'd say something that might help her understand why Katie thought the play was stupid. She decided to find out.

"I am flattered, Carl, and can't deny I have feelings for you too." were the first words Velma could hear Miss Fletcher say clearly. "But it is far too soon for you, for us."

"I can understand you thinking that, Emily," Mr. Warren said in a strong whisper. "But there is no doubt in my mind and heart."

"You are just lonely, Carl," Emily protested. "You are still grieving, not only the loss of Agnes but Freddie's absence as well."

"True." Velma nearly missed his reply as it was delivered so softly.

"Right now, you must make Katie and yourself the priority," the teacher said, sounding like one. "I'll participate to the extent that is appropriate and not counterproductive. Please don't press the matter right now?"

"But when?" Carl said pleadingly.

"I think we will know if and when this is right and the time to move forward. I have come to love your daughter. She is so smart. Smart enough, I think to be suspicious of us. Plus, she is a beautiful, caring child whose heart is broken right now."

"Don't you think I know that?" The question came sharp-edged.

"Of course I do, Carl," Emily said soothingly. "You're just saying that because you know I am right."

There was a long pause, then, "Yes, I know that," came out as a croak.

"Then we're agreed," Emily said, standing, framed for Velma in the glass of the front door. "We will continue to see each other as circumstances dictate, but not as often or as closely as this pageant has created." Silence returned until she pressed him. "You do agree, don't you, Carl?"

A few beats later came what sounded to Velma like a very reluctant, "Yes, Emily."

"Good." Velma heard her say as her heels clicked on the front steps. "Now, let's focus on making tomorrow a special day for Woodward and the kids, especially Katie."

"Okay," Mr. Warren said. Then his tall shadow filled the glass of the front door before moving away. Velma sensed he was going down the steps toward Miss Fletcher as he went on. "But you must know, I am serious, and no amount of time will change that."

Velma peeked out the lower pane just as Mr. Warren attempted to kiss Miss Fletcher on the lips. Emily turned away but did not withdraw her cheek where Carl's lips lingered. Then the two parted abruptly. As Mr. Warren watched Emily leave, Velma scurried back upstairs, now fully understanding what was upsetting Katie.

Carl Warren woke the girls shortly before dawn. They were greeted by a cooler, but still sunny, day. After gulping down bowls of oatmeal and large glasses of milk, the girls hurried off to the mercantile, arriving just after the sun peaked over the horizon. They found the kitchen a beehive of activity.

Alice, Tessa, and Grace were busily baking. Annie gladly handed over care of the boys and Lizzy to the new arrivals. They were encouraged to take the youngsters out from underfoot. With the baby in a rickety, old baby carriage, Katie and Velma herded Eugene and the nearly three-year-old Edward to the one park in town.

While they took turns chasing after the boys, they practiced their lines for the play. Returning at noon, they found lunch waiting. Then, as the boys and Lizzy napped, the girls helped the adults arrange the mercantile inside and out for the festivities to come later that afternoon and evening.

Before they knew it, Velma and Katie were delivering their lines on the sidewalk outside the mercantile surrounded by a large audience filling the street. The humorous skit Mr. Warren and Miss Fletcher wrote had everyone laughing uproariously.

In no time at all the play was finished, and the crowd was enjoying the fruits of all the baking Alice and the others had done. Misters Hanks and Warren, along with Reverend Jones, dished out homemade ice cream. Even though the temperature outside hovered in the mid-fifties, the crowd inside the mercantile generated enough heat to make it seem like summer.

The women were trapped in the kitchen, replenishing the rapidly emptied trays of cookies, pies, and candies. The crowds began to thin well after sunset, leaving the organizers exhausted but happy.

"If this pageant gets any more successful, I don't think I can survive it." Henry said as he ate the last bowl of ice cream from the churn. "I must have scooped two hundred servings."

Carl Warren laughed. "Two hundred and one, you mean."

"I got coffee on in the kitchen," Alice said. "Why don't we all go sit down for a minute before we start the cleanup?"

"Sounds like a great idea," Grace Jones replied. "Come on dear, you need a wash-up first." Tugging the reverend toward the back of the store, she added, tongue in cheek, "It looks to me like you wore as much of the ice cream as you served."

"I'm a preacher, not a soda jerk," Alan protested.

"What's a soda jerk?" Velma asked as everyone headed to the kitchen.

"That's what some people call Wally, the guy behind the counter at the drugstore. I'm not sure why," the reverend shared.

"Well, head to the sink, preacher, before you touch anything else," Tessa said with a chuckle. "You too, Henry and Carl."

Soon everyone was gathered around the table sipping coffee and complaining about sore legs and arms. Then Carl glanced around asking, "Where's Em ... I mean Miss Fletcher?"

There was no response until Grace said, "The last I saw her she was mingling with the crowd, getting praised for the play and the event."

"Yeah, I saw her doing that too," Henry added as he stood. "I'll go look for her. She ought to be putting her feet up with the rest of us."

"For certain," Alice said, pouring another cup from the enameled coffee pot.

"I'm awful tired," Katie said suddenly. "Can Velma and I head back to your place, Mrs. Steele?"

"Oh, that's right," Alice said with a weak smile. "You're bunkin' in with Velma tonight. And Wilma's staying upstairs here with the boys."

Wilma shot her mother a displeased look. "Do I have to?"

"We've already discussed this, daughter. I'm not wakin' those two after all the sugar they've had tonight. Now git."

"Yes, Mama." She stood and trudged off toward the stairs as Katie and Velma headed for the back door.

Velma had wanted to wait and hear what Miss Fletcher thought of the day's events, especially the play, but knew that would not please her best friend. Katie didn't know what she had overheard the night before, and Velma was not about to tell her, knowing that would not help the situation. It was best to let sleeping dogs lie. She settled instead for upbeat small talk.

"You did great tonight, Katie," This produced only a disinterested grunt in reply. Undaunted, Velma continued, "How was I?"

"Fine, I guess."

"You guess?"

Katie's nod was lost in the darkness of the alley.

"Well, I thought it was the bestest thing I ever did, at least as an actress," Velma said emphatically. "I might just do that all the time when I grow up."

This comment finally pulled Katie out of her funk. "You think so? I'd sure like to do that too."

"That's good to hear." Velma slipped her arm through Katie's. "Maybe we could convince Miss Fletcher to..."

Katie suddenly pulled away. "I don't want to convince Miss Fletcher to do anything except leave me and my Daddy alone."

Velma cringed. "Okay, okay cranky puss. Let's get home and get some sleep so maybe you'll be in a better mood tomorrow."

"Sorry, Vel," Katie said, as they started to climb the stairs to the Steele apartment. "I'm sure I'll be fine tomorrow or at least when this pageant is over."

11

Relatives and Romance

Back at the mercantile, Emily Fletcher joined the others as the cleanup effort continued. "Where have you been?" Tessa asked casually.

"I got cornered by a few of the townsfolk," the teacher said as Grace poured her a cup of coffee. "They were asking if the pageant would become an annual event."

"I hope you said no," Henry blurted out. "This is way too much work for an old man like me."

"Well, I was noncommittal, if that makes you feel any better."

"I think this is a subject for the town council. If they want to do it, then they might fund the event and enlist a lot more help," Carl said.

Reverend Jones suggested, "We should probably focus on finishing this one before considering a repeat."

Alice mopped her brow as she agreed. "I'll second that. Let's see if we all survive through tomorrow. Meanwhile, we've got prep to do for that."

"Good point," Tessa said. "Let's get that done so we can get a few hours of sleep. Baking starts at seven."

After a collective sigh, Emily spoke again. "I don't know if I should tell you this now or not, but..." She hesitated.

"Tell me what?" Alice said warily.

"Well, your ma and pa are visiting the Browns."

"Are you sure?" Anxiety filled Alice's voice.

"Yes," Emily said, seeming to regret bringing up the subject. "Edith Brown told me. She was one of the ones who wanted the pageant to be an annual event."

Henry stepped to Alice's side, putting an arm around her. "How did Alice's folks get into the conversation?"

"She introduced me to them," Emily answered embarrassedly. "I was more than a little surprised."

"What did they say?" Alice asked in a rush.

"How do you do. That was it."

Reverend Jones joined the inquiry. "How did they seem?"

"What do you mean?"

"Did they seem upset, angry, what?" Alan clarified.

Before Emily could reply, Alice interjected sarcastically, "They always look angry and mean, especially when it come to me and my family."

"Well, they did look a bit dour," Emily confirmed.

"Did they or Edith say anything about the children?" Alice asked tentatively.

Emily nodded. "Yes, at least Edith did. She said everyone thought the play was fun and that Velma and Wilma did well."

"My Ma and Pa said that?"

This time the teacher frowned. "I can't honestly say who she was referring to when she said that." Seeing Alice's disappointed look, she added, "But your parents were right there and didn't disagree."

"I guess I'll have to settle for that," Alice said with a sigh, then asked, "Do you know if they're goin' a be here tomorrow?"

"I'm afraid not," Emily said apologetically.

"Nothin' to be sorry for, Miss Fletcher."

Grace Jones had a thought. "If they do stay, perhaps they'll be at church."

"Then I ain't goin'," Alice said sharply.

"You can't let them intimidate you, Alice." Reverend Jones argued.

Alice smiled. "It ain't that I'd be intimidated. I'm more afraid what I might say to them in God's house."

"We'll surround you, Alice," Tessa said.

"Like an army of Christian soldiers," Henry added.

Alice chuckled this time. "Marching off to war."

This had everyone laughing briefly before Carl Warren asked in all seriousness, "But why are they here?"

"Isn't it to visit family?" Grace Jones suggested.

"And enjoy the pageant," her husband added.

Carl chewed on this a minute, then asked, "Aren't they farmers? Isn't it harvest time?"

"Most farmers got their crops in early this year," Alice answered. "I know 'cause I was one and keep an eye on such things."

"Well, this isn't getting us anywhere," Henry broke in. "It's getting late. I suggest we get a good night's sleep and head to church tomorrow to hear Alan here preach up a storm."

"As long as that's the only storm we get," Tessa said with a smile. "Still got one more day of fun to pull off." Then she turned to Alice. "We'll see you in front of the hardware store at the usual time."

"Agreed."

With that, everyone rose and headed for their respective beds. At the door, Alice added. "I'm kind a curious to see how my ma and pa behave tomorra."

Alice and the others were disappointed. Neither the Browns nor Skinners attended the services. After making a few inquiries, Grace Jones shared that, "Apparently, they all went over to the Skinner farm right after the play last evening. There was some kind of celebration there."

The expression on Alice's face was one of recognition. "Oh, that would likely be the annual Skinner reunion. I haven't been to one of those since the year before William and I run off."

"Well, I have to say, I'm relieved we didn't have any kind of confrontation or scene," Tessa said with a sigh. "We best get ready for the big finale at the bank."

"I'm headed that way right now," Carl Warren said, glancing at his watch. "I imagine Emily is already there."

"She's Presbyterian, ain't she?" Alice asked innocently.

"Yup, and they get out earlier than we Methodists. Are you coming to help me, Katie?"

His daughter didn't move. "Ah, Velma and I need to practice some more for the play, Daddy. We'll come with the others, right, Vel?"

"Ah, I guess so."

"Very well, dear." Carl didn't sound pleased. "I'll see you all shortly."

"Come on everyone," Tessa addressed the others. "We got food and drink waiting in the cooler."

Everyone headed in different directions at a swift pace. As the Hanks and Steeles approached the front of the hardware store with Katie in tow, Henry shared, "Carl left his car behind the mercantile so I could bring everything over to the bank."

"He's trusting you with that new contraption?" Tessa asked mockingly.

"Careful dear. I'm thinking of buying one of those *contraptions*." His wife pushed away from him gently. "Seriously?"

"Yes," Henry said emphatically. "It is the way of the future."

"Oh, Lord," Tessa said with humor. "You in a car. I better warn the general population."

Everyone but Katie laughed at this exchange, as Alice guided her crew toward the apartment. "I'll get everyone changed in a jiffy and be over to help."

"Can Velma and I stay behind and practice our lines, Mrs. Steele?" Katie asked as the headed up the two flights.

"I'd a thought you two would have worn those lines out by now."

"We want to be perfect, Mrs. Steele. Right Vel?" Katie implored her friend.

Velma knew what this was really about, but just said, "Right, Mama."

"Okay then," Alice relented as she opened the apartment door. "But mind the time. Events kick off promptly at one." With a deep sigh she added, "This will all be over by three and we can get back to normal."

As if punctuating the culmination of the pageant, a cold wind came up, blowing autumn leaves off the trees as attendees headed home. With all the friends pitching in, along with others from the community, the bank lobby was restored in no time.

"Sunday supper is at our place at five," Grace Jones said.

Henry patted his belly. "I'm not sure I have room for anything more."

Tessa broke into a laugh. "You, not have room? That will be the day."

As others joined in the chiding, Grace turned to Carl and Katie. "Won't you join us to celebrate the success of the pageant?" Then, to Miss Fletcher she added, "You too, Emily."

The teacher saw Katie stiffen and replied quickly, "Oh, thank you, Mrs. Jones, but I have a lot of preparations to deal with for school tomorrow. I'm afraid that has suffered with all the work on the pageant."

"But you have to eat," Carl blurted out, then seeing his daughter's expression, added, "Ah, well, we all do."

Henry, missing the dynamics of the moment completely, laughed heartily. "Count on the bank president for such profound thoughts."

"Daddy, I'm not feeling well," Katie said with a moan. "I think I ate too many sweets."

"Oh, poor child," Tessa said. "Why don't you come over to the mercantile with me. I've got something that will fix that right up."

"I'd rather just go home and lie down, please."

"I guess we'll have to take a pass on supper," Carl said, putting a hand on Katie's forehead. "Maybe some other time. I'll just drive these leftovers and such to your place, then head home."

"No need," Tessa said, shaking her head. "There isn't that much, and we've got plenty of hands. Get Katie home to bed."

"Can I go with Katie?" Velma asked.

Alice snorted. "Didn't you hear what the girl said, child? She's not feelin' well. The last thing she needs is you hangin' around. Besides, if she's got somethin', I don't want you catchin' it and missin' school."

"Yes, Mama."

"Now, we better get to the mercantile and see if Annie has survived your brothers." Alice grabbed a tray of uneaten cookies and headed off, saying, "I have dessert for tonight right here if you all can stand any more of these."

"I can," Henry replied gleefully.

"See what I mean? He's a bottomless pit." His wife chortled as she grabbed a bag filled with tablecloths and bunting.

"Come on, Miss Fletcher," Carl said, reaching for her arm. "I can give you a ride."

"Oh, I should stay and help."

"Nonsense," Grace said. "We've got plenty of arms for this. Get home and start on that schoolwork. If you get done by five or even a little later, come on over."

"I'll do that, Mrs. Jones," Emily said weakly. Then she turned to Carl. "Thanks for your offer as well, Mr. Warren, but I think I will walk."

Carl started to protest, but Miss Fletcher cut him off. "I'll use the few minutes in this crisp fall air to clear my head of pageant thoughts and refocus on classroom business."

"Have it your way," Mr. Warren said flatly. "Let's get you home, Katie." Everyone paused to watch the pair head for the Model T, Katie moving rather too fast for someone not feeling well.

The following Tuesday afternoon, Velma rushed through the back door of the mercantile with Eugene after collecting the afternoon's egg production. She found her mother seated at the kitchen table with Mrs. Hanks and Mrs. Jones deep in conversation.

Looking up, Alice directed Velma, "Get a cookie off the cooling rack for you and Eugene, then head upstairs."

"Should I take one to Wilma and Edward?"

"Yes, yes," her mother replied sharply before turning back to the other women.

Curious, Velma took her time picking out the four cookies and putting them on a plate. Noticing this, Alice barked, "Get goin', girl."

Without further delay, Velma grabbed the plate and ordered Eugene, "Get," while pulling him along.

Hurrying upstairs with Eugene, she found her sister busily pinning the bottom of a dress hanging on the sewing mannequin. While distributing the cookies, Velma asked, "Do you know anything about what's going on downstairs, Wilma?"

"Not much," her sister replied as she took a bite. After swallowing, she went on. "I was in the kitchen when Mrs. Jones arrived saying she had some news for Mama."

"Really!" Velma said excitedly. "Then what did she say?"

"I don't know. Mama shooed me upstairs."

"Just like she did to me. Do you think she'll tell us later?"

Wilma shrugged. "I doubt it. Otherwise, she'd a let us hang around and listen."

"You're probably right," Velma said, then turned around and headed out the sewing room door.

"Hey, where are you going?" Wilma protested. "You're supposed to take over caring for the boys while I work on my sewing."

Velma ignored her sister, concentrating instead on creeping downstairs to the curtain dividing the kitchen from the mercantile. She arrived just in time to hear her mother say, "Well, it will be a cold day in hell when I..."

"Alice, don't speak such blasphemy," Grace Jones interrupted sharply.

"Sorry, Grace," a calmer Alice replied. "It's just that now after all these years and after what happened to me and mine, thanks in no small part to them, they want to make nice."

"Well, there is no time limit on seeking forgiveness, Alice," Grace replied in a reverent tone.

"Grace is right, my dear," Tessa added soothingly. "This could be a very good thing."

"Easy for you to say," Alice retorted. "They show up here after over two years without so much as a how-do-you do, after knowin' we'd been thrown off our land by that, that..."

"Careful, Alice," Grace admonished.

"That sour old man Steele. Now Ma and Pa show up sayin' they want to warn me about some cockeyed attempt to get my children, and only the boys at that."

"You think they just made that up?" Tessa asked incredulously.

Grace spoke again before Alice could answer. "That seems unlikely. Why not just come over, say they were sorry, and ask for forgiveness?"

Velma heard Mrs. Hanks snicker. "Come on, Grace. You know why. That would be like innocent sheep willingly presenting themselves for slaughter."

"I guess you're right, Tessa."

"Hey, that's not true," Alice said, then meekly added, "Well, maybe so."

"Let's get back to the details of what Edith told you," Tessa suggested.

"I'm suspicious of everything she said," Alice said with renewed vigor. "Edith Brown hates my guts."

"I'm not so sure that's the case anymore," Grace countered. "Her daughter Nancy and Velma have gotten to be friends from what I hear."

"From who?"

"Miss Fletcher for one. Katie Warren for another. And, for that matter, Velma too."

"Why didn't Velma tell me?" Alice asked, then went on before either woman could answer. "Never mind. I know why."

Velma heard Tessa and Grace grunt agreement before the reverend's wife began to share again, "There was a lot of small talk about the pageant and all, but just before she left, Edith told Alan and me to warn you, Alice, that William's folks had been to see a lawyer in Des Moines."

"Did you ask how my parents heard about this? They ain't exactly friendly with my former in-laws."

Grace nodded. "Seems the lawyer came out to talk with your parents, kind of sly like."

Alice interrupted harshly, "As if they know anything about us anymore."

Ignoring her, Grace continued, "Anyway, one thing led to another, and they learned enough to share their concerns with the Browns."

"Ha!" Alice huffed. "The only concern they might have is losin' out on something the Steeles want."

"Didn't sound that way to me, but I suppose you know better."

"You're missing the point, Alice," Tess said sharply.

"Which is?"

"That one or the other is out to get your children."

Alice laughed sarcastically. "How?"

"I don't know, but, if they're paying a slick attorney from Des Moines some of their hard-earned cash, well, you ought to be concerned."

"And remember," Grace added, "They apparently only want the boys, not Velma and Wilma."

"Extra pairs of hands on the farm," Alice snorted. "Just like old man Steele."

"Think of how that would impact all four of them." Tessa sounded mournful to Velma as she went on, "The girls feeling rejected and the boys torn away from you. Terrible."

"So, what can I do with this information?" Alice asked softly.

"Get yourself a lawyer."

"I cain't affort no lawyer. We're still just gettin' by."

The kitchen fell silent for a time before Grace said, "Let's go see Carl."

"Why?"

"Because his brother-in-law over in Perry is an attorney."

"I still can't afford to pay no attorney."

"If we appeal to Carl..."

Alice interrupted Tessa sharply, "I'm not takin' no charity."

"I'm only suggesting a consultation to find out if there is anything to worry about," Tessa clarified. "That would be a wise thing to do and not charity."

"Sounds like charity to me."

"Oh, Alice," Grace said in frustration. "Don't you remember what the Bible says about pride?"

There was a brief pause before Velma heard her mother's weak, "Yes, ma'am."

"We're talking about your children here, not to mention your future," Tessa pressed the matter.

Just then Velma heard a noise behind her and turned to see Charity Jones headed her way, bundled up against a cool afternoon. The girl didn't notice Velma's finger to her lips. "Hello, Velma."

Velma sighed, "Hi, Charity."

"Have you seen my mother?"

"She's in the kitchen with mine and Mrs. Hanks. Want a cookie?"

She led Charity through the curtain, avoiding her mother's eye. "Look who I found."

"I thought I told you to help your sister," Alice said warily. "You been snoopin' again, girl?"

"Oh, no, Mama," Velma fibbed. "The boys were asking for another cookie. I told them no, but they insisted I ask."

"Well, you were right. No more sugar for them two," her mother said, then turned to Charity. "But you can have one if you like."

"Can I, Mother?" the new arrival asked.

Grace replied as she stood. "I suppose so but just one. Then you and I need to get home and start dinner."

"Thank you, and you too, Mrs. Steele," Charity said, moving quickly to the trays of cookies.

Grace pulled on her light coat as she addressed her two friends. "I'll stop by the bank on the way and see what Carl has to say about the idea, that is, if he's available."

"I'm still not sure about this," Alice said tentatively.

"If you won't ask, then one of us will," Tess countered.

"So, you might as well agree."

After a moment, Alice nodded. "Okay."

Velma saw this as a good opportunity to cover her white lie. "What are you talking about, Mama?"

"Never you mind, girl. Now get back upstairs and give your sister a break from the boys."

"Yes, Mama," Velma said, glad for the opportunity to escape. One thing she couldn't escape was thoughts about what she had overheard.

It was several days later that a well-dressed stranger came to town and began asking questions about the Steele family. Only after he'd left, Alice learned that he was a lawyer from Des Moines. The collective opinion of Alice's friends was that the man must be representing her former in-laws.

The very next day, Carl Warren drove Alice over to Perry to visit with an attorney recommended by his brother-in-law. His name was Milo Price. Newly moved to that town from the capital city, he specialized in family law. At the meeting, Carl and the attorney did most of the talking while Alice just listened.

In the end, the consensus was that as long as Alice continued to provide for the children as she was and had the support of her friends, there should be no risk of her ex-father-in-law prevailing. As they parted, Mr. Price indicated his willingness to represent Alice if circumstances proved otherwise.

Though no formal legal action was taken initially, the grandparents did send their lawyer to see Alice several weeks later. He brought a proposal for her with the request that she take the time to consider it carefully. Though the attorney didn't provide any specifics, he suggested there would be consequences if she declined the offer.

Alice kept the document and conversation she had had to herself, waiting until the next Sunday supper at the Jones' to tell her friends. Once the children had left the table, she drew the others' attention by announcing in a hushed tone, "I've got somethin' to share."

Though Velma had not heard her mother's words, she sensed something was up. So, she again lingered just out of sight and settled in to listen. What she heard filled her with anxiety.

"You sound ominous," Grace said, receiving nods of agreement. "Come on, out with it."

"You all know about that fancy lawyer that came to town a month ago asking around about us on behalf of my ex-father-in-law?" Everyone nodded. "Well, he was back a couple of days ago. Visited me at the apartment, or at least on the back porch. I wouldn't let him inside."

"Good idea," Tess interjected.

"What did he want?" Reverend Jones got them back on topic.

"He brought a proposal." Alice pulled out a piece of paper. "Shall I read it to you?" Everyone nodded again. When finished, she added, "Mind you, he said this was just a draft, subject to, how did he say it, my additions, ah..."

Henry helped her, "Additions, deletions, or corrections."

"Right," Alice said. "That was it."

"Did you read it while he was there?" Henry asked.

"Yes."

"And you didn't tell him and his clients to get lost right then?" Tessa followed up with the obvious question.

"Thought about it, but then waved him off without so much as a good day."

"I get it. You decided to let the Steeles twist in the wind for a while," Carl Warren said with a smile. This was the first supper

Carl and Katie had attended since Agnes's passing. He and his daughter had been subdued during most of the meals. Having the diversion of the topic had helped bring Carl out of his funk. He concluded his comments by adding, "Serves them right."

"That doesn't seem very Christian," Reverend Jones said with more humor than judgment.

"Oh, that's not why I didn't answer right off," Alice quickly replied, missing Alan's tone.

"Then why?" Grace asked.

"I promised Milo Price to meet with him to discuss any developments before responding to a lawsuit or other demand."

"Makes good sense," Henry replied.

Alice gave him an appreciative smile. "Glad you agree. So, I'm goin' to send a telegram first thing tomorrow over to Perry and see if he can come over to talk."

"I've got a better idea," Carl interjected. "You can make a call to him from the bank. If he's in, you can ride over there with me as I have a meeting at our main branch. Could you be free by then?"

"When do you plan on returnin'?"

"Oh, I'll be back by three or so."

"Well, if Mr. Price is there, I guess I can make the trip if we don't dawdle." Alice turned to Tessa. "Would you be able to watch the boys and supervise the girls for a few hours?"

Mrs. Hanks laughed. "Lordy, I do it all the time."

"We, you mean," Henry said with a smile. "And Annie too. That will be no problem."

"Then it's settled," Carl said, adding, "assuming Milo is available."

"I'm still not sure why you need such a meeting. We all know what your answer will be," Grace suggested.

"Of course," Henry replied quickly before Alice had a chance to decline.

"Is he right, Alice?" Reverend Jones asked.

"Well, thanks to help from you all since we moved here, that would be the logical reply, but with the lawyer's veiled threats, well, maybe Milo..."

"*Milo*, is it?" Tessa teased, breaking the tension.

In return, Mrs. Hanks got one of Alice's famous killer looks. "I want to hear if *my lawyer* has any ideas about how to address the proposal to my advantage for the sake of the children."

Tessa's expression went from teasing to shock in a flash. "Don't tell me you'd consider any part of the arrangement. The man's trying to divide your family, for God's sake—ah, sorry reverend."

"I couldn't have said it better myself," Alan said with a smile, "but let's hear what Alice is thinking."

"I'm not sure what I'm thinkin', really," She said sheepishly. "That's what I hope to find out tomorra."

"Maybe you could get him to give you some money for the chance to see *all* the children once in a while," Grace suggested, then added an addendum, "under your supervision, of course."

"That's one possibility, I suppose," Alice replied with a frown. "Any other ideas I could run by Mr. Price?"

"Good question," Tessa said, then with a wink added, "Let's have another cup of coffee and help put a list together for Alice to share with *Milo*."

"Cut that out, Tessa Hanks," Alice said sourly as she colored.

"What am I missing here?" Henry asked.

"Nothin'," Alice barked, trying to squelch the subject. It didn't work.

"Well, Mr. Price is quite a handsome fella, if I do say so myself," Carl explained. "Our friend here had nothing but high praise for the man the whole way back from our first visit to Perry."

"Haven't you gotten several posts from him since then?" Tessa asked knowingly.

"All business, thank you very much," Alice shot back. "Now are you all going to help me make a list of things to discuss with *my attorney* or shall we call it a night?"

This drew a mixture of laughter and grunts before the group got down to the business of creating a list. Unnoticed by the adults was the presence of Velma in the shadows. Her habit of eavesdropping sometimes proved to be a curse. This latest revelation left her quite anxious and at a loss whether to share what she knew.

Declining to inform her sister, fearing an emotional outburst that would give her nosiness away, she headed for Katie and pulled her aside. "I just heard some awful news."

"What's wrong? Is someone sick?" Katie said, apparently connecting anything labeled as awful to her mother's death.

"No, it's not that," Velma replied, seeing her friend's face soften.

"Then what?"

"My bad old Grandpa Steele is trying to take the boys from Mama, from us."

"How can he do that?"

Velma shrugged. "I'm not sure. One of them lawyer types gave Mama a letter talking about taking Eugene and Edward away."

"For good?"

"I don't know. She read something about visiting with them, but I don't remember Mama saying how often."

"Why would she agree to that?" Katie said incredulously.

Velma thought for a moment. "I heard something about him, my mean old Grandpa, giving Mama some money for us girls."

"How much?"

"What difference does that make?" Velma's loud response drew the other children's attention. She gave the others a faux smile and waited for them to go back to their play before speaking again. "Sorry, Katie. I'm scared."

Katie moved in and hugged her friend. "I know. And I'm sorry for asking such a stupid question."

"It weren't stupid."

Katie's face suddenly took on a shocked expression. "Oh, goodness, Velma. If that happened, we'd both be without our brothers."

Velma hadn't thought about that. Realizing how distraught her friend had been since Freddie was sent away, her heart sank. "Oh, Katie. I take back all those awful things I've said about my brothers. I can't imagine them not being around. And Mama..." She didn't finish.

Katie held her out at arms-length. "That isn't going to happen, Velma. Your mother will never allow it."

"But you don't understand." Velma's voice trembled. "Mama said that 'torney said if she didn't agree there would be con'quences."

"Consequences?" Velma nodded. "What consequences?"

"She didn't say."

Katie sighed. "What's going to happen then?"

Velma paused to recall the conversation at the table. "Mama's going to Perry, I think tomorrow, to see her lawyer."

"Didn't she do that before?" Velma nodded again. "The one my Uncle Edgar found?"

"Yes."

"Well, that's good, isn't it?"

Velma shrugged. "I guess."

Seeing her friend's frown, Katie probed, "You don't look happy about that. Don't you think he can help?"

"I don't know one way or another about that."

"Then what is it?"

Velma thought back to comments made by the adults in the kitchen. "It's just something..." She paused. "Well, they was making fun of how Mama talked about the lawyer man."

"Fun?"

Velma bristled at the thought. "Yeah, and Mama didn't like it one bit. Neither did I."

"So, what did they say."

Velma shook her head. "It weren't nothing." Then she changed the subject, "Anyway, Mama will be meeting with him again soon, and I hope he can do something about this. It would kill Mama to lose any of us."

"Really." Katie broke into a weak smile. "You wouldn't know it by the way she talks to you guys sometimes."

Velma replied angrily, "Don't say that."

"I was just trying to get you to calm down," Katie said apologetically.

Velma's demeanor softened as she gave her friend a forgiving smile. "I'm sorry for barking. You're right. Mama can come across like we annoy her."

Katie laughed, "She can come across that way sometimes toward her friends, oh, and me too."

This finally had Velma laughing, easing her anxiety briefly and tempered her sour mood. "You're right about that." Glancing back toward the kitchen, she added, "Mama's going to be calling for us to get home."

"Well, let's grab Charity and see if we get something else to eat before then," Katie said eagerly. The two girls stood and headed across the room toward their friend, exchanging the concerns of the moment for the possibility of a last treat.

"Well, did Mr. Price ease your concerns?" Carl Warren asked Alice as they drove back from Perry to Woodward.

Alice didn't reply immediately, so he pushed the issue. "So, he *didn't* ease your mind?"

"I wasn't there to get my mind eased so much as to get advice on how to address the proposal," she said, irritated.

"And so?"

"Well, he didn't come up with any brilliant ideas, if that's what you're askin'."

"That's too bad," Carl said genuinely. Then, in a lighter tone, he asked, "You plan on seeing him again?"

"Why would I do that?" Alice replied loudly over the sound of the Model T. "I ain't made a money."

"How much is he charging you?"

"Well, actually, he didn't give me a bill," she said meekly. "I tried to get him to, but he said it was just a consultation."

"Wasn't your first visit with him a consultation too?"

"Yes," she replied curtly.

"Hum."

Carl's curious response didn't help Alice's mood. "Hum what?" she said, giving him one of her patented looks.

"Oh, nothing." Carl mused. "It's just that, in my experience, attorney's offer a single consultation free of charge. Yet you say this was another free consultation, right?"

"Like I said already, I tried to pay the man, but he refused," Alice replied indignantly.

"Oh, I see."

"See what?" Alice snapped back.

Carl attempted to extricate himself from Alice's ire. "Just that Mr. Price has a different billing method than most in his line of work."

"Well, I certainly didn't know that was the case," Alice said through a confused expression. Then she stiffened again. "Take me back."

"Back?"

"Yes, back to Mr. Price's office. I will not accept charity from him, from anyone."

Carl protested. "But I just said that he *might* use a different method." When Alice's expression remained unchanged, he shook his head. "I am not going back, Alice. I have work: we both have work waiting. If you wish, I'll let you call Mr. Price from the bank and clear this up, but I will not turn around."

"Very well, Carl," Alice huffed. "I'll accept that offer, but only if I can pay for the call."

Carl snorted, "You're the proudest, most stubborn woman I have ever met."

"I'll take that as a compliment," Alice said with the arrogance of one used to getting her way.

The look angered Carl, so he changed his commitment. "I'll let you make the call and pay for it, but only if you tell me in detail what Mr. Price said. Do we have a deal?"

Alice pondered for a moment, then nodded and said, "Deal. But it may take longer than the rest of the trip."

"Then get started. I can slow this contraption down to a walk if necessary."

"Let's see." Alice paused to think over her half-hour meeting with the attorney. "First, Mr. Price suggested it was a good thing that the Steeles had waited so long to seek legal counsel. You see, I'd told him at our first meeting about the difficult time we had that first year in Woodward."

"You mean when you got so sick?"

"Yes, he said that would have given old man Steele a good reason to seek custody."

Carl nodded agreement, then asked, "But now?"

"Price said that there was little chance what with how well we are set with greatly improved circumstances thanks to good friends. Plus, I have the means to care for all the children adequately, if not generously."

"Glad to hear he thinks so." Carl gave Alice a big smile.

Alice didn't smile back. "He is concerned, however, about how hard I'm workin' the girls."

Mr. Warren chuckled. "Does he have any idea what life for those girls would be like out on the farm?"

"I don't think so," Alice replied, adding, "but remember, he only wants the boys."

"True, but you've plenty of folks, your entire adopted family, that will vow those girls have a hard but happy existence," Carl said confidently. "And I know they would say the same. Why, look at how well they're doing in school, Velma and Katie love Miss Fletcher..." He paused seeing Alice's look, which had him asking sarcastically, "Now who is funning who?"

Alice smiled coyly. "Why, whatever do you mean, Mr. Warren?"

He sighed in surrender, then continued, "As I was saying, besides school, they have great friends and a wonderful adult support system, including yours truly, your personal chauffeur."

"I said much the same thing to Milo—I mean, Mr. Price."

"Hum."

"There you go again," Alice complained.

Regaining the romantic upper hand, Carl gave her a coy smile while saying, "So, *Milo* knows all that." Alice just nodded. "And therefore?"

"*Therefore*, Mr. Price sees no grounds for the filing of a custody suit unless circumstances change drastically."

"What would be drastic enough to change the situation?"

"Oh, if I died, failed in my parental duties, or did harm to one of the children."

Carl snorted again. "Not a chance of that unless one of your evil eyes constitutes harm." This drew a knowing smile from Alice. "I'm sure Wilma or Velma might claim that, if put on the stand."

"Then we won't let that happen, will we?" They both laughed. By then, they were approaching the outskirts of Woodward. "That would seem to cover the chances of formal legal action, but what about the proposal?"

"He said to turn it down flat."

"Why?"

"For several reasons. First, it would formalize an agreement that would require legal action to change or void. Second, it would divide the family. Third, it would give the grandparents unsupervised time with the boys, time to turn them against me. Lastly, Mr. Price just doesn't trust them."

"I'd agree with all, that especially the last point given their total absence from the children's lives for over two years. And what kind of person would take brothers away from sisters like pieces of property?" Carl's anger grew. "That's not the way real grandparenting works."

"That is very much what Mr. Price said."

"So, that's what you're going to do?"

Alice nodded then added. "Mr. Price suggested that I mollify old man Steele by suggesting something that you just pointed out."

"What's that?"

"That they start acting like good grandparents. By that, I mean the kind that don't suggest dividing a family like Solomon, or bribing a mother to accomplish just that, or requiring a signed agreement in lieu of familial love."

"Well said."

"Thank ya. I just made that up," Alice said with some pride.

"I'll say again, well done. Now just don't forget those words."

"I'll count on you to help with that," Alice said, patting Carl's hand that firmly gripped the steering wheel.

"There is one problem with that great speech," Carl pointed out. "It's not likely to mollify the man."

"You're probably right." Alice's hand dropped back in her lap. "That's why, after I've said all that to the man, I'll be suggestin' how he might get a chance to be a part of the family goin' forward."

Carl considered this for a moment as he turned onto Main Street in Woodward. "Okay. So, how would you say that?"

"I'm still workin' on that."

Carl nodded, then suggested, "You can practice that part of your speech when we see the others tonight."

"Tonight?" Alice sounded surprised.

Carl chuckled. "You don't think they're not going to be clamoring to hear what happened?"

"No doubt," Alice said as they pulled up in front of the mercantile. "Thank ya so much for the ride and your ear."

Carl smiled. "My pleasure. Will you be over to the bank after checking on things?"

"The bank?" Alice seemed confused.

Carl's smile became a laugh. "Yes, the bank where there is a phone for you to call *Milo* about his bill."

"Oh, right," Alice said blushing. "I'll do that, assuming all is well inside." She nodded toward the mercantile.

"You do that." Carl's smile remained. "Just remember we'll be closing soon."

Alice climbed down and stepped up on the sidewalk. "Well, if I don't make it today..."

Carl interrupted mockingly, "I know. There is always tomorrow." With that, he put the Model T in gear and headed for his office.

A half-hour later, Carl looked up to see Alice stride purposefully into the bank. She waited for him at the teller counter as he approached. "Hello again, Alice. To what do I owe this visit?" he joked.

Alice replied stonily, "Very funny. Now may I take you up on your offer?"

"But of course," Carl said, holding the half-swinging door.

As Alice passed him, she said in serious tone, "I sure hope this call don't cost me too much."

"A dozen cookies for the staff will do," the banker replied, leading her to his desk and waving her toward his seat. "Make yourself at home."

Carl took up the phone and, after clicking the switch-hook, waited. A moment later, he spoke into the microphone rather loudly. "Mr. Milo Price's line, please." He waited again, then said, "Hello, Jean, this is Carl Warren over in Woodward. Good afternoon to you too. Is Mr. Price available?" There was another pause then, "Good, I have a Mrs. Steele on this end who wants to speak with him. Thank you."

Carl extended the earpiece toward Alice, who shrank back as if he were handing her a snake. He chuckled. "It won't bite, Alice."

"I ain't never used one of these before."

"Just talk directly into this." He pointed to the top of the candlestick phone. "Speak firmly and distinctly. Then listen through this." He gently pushed the receiver against her short-cropped hair.

Tentatively, she complied, saying loud enough for all those in the bank to hear, "Hello, Mr. Price." She looked up at Carl. "His secretary is puttin' me through."

"Good." Carl moved away, waving for his staff to get back to work.

Alice's side of the brief conversation did not require repeating. By the end, Carl and the others nearby knew that Mr. Price would be coming to Woodward the next Sunday to settle the matter. Milo and Mrs. Steele had agreed that his bill could be handled in the form of a home-cooked meal.

One look at Carl after she hung up, and Alice's blushing face said it all. "It looks like you came to an agreement," Carl said, endeavoring to remain straight-faced. "I assume he will be joining us all for supper on Sunday. It is your turn, right?"

"Yes, it is. And I'll be cookin' everythin' since this will be my payment for his services."

Carl nodded, trying hard not to laugh. "Indeed. I wouldn't miss this meal for the world."

"What do you mean by that?"

"I mean just that."

"Why?"

"Because not only will I get some of your famous pie, but I expect this meal will be fit for a king."

Alice scowled, stood abruptly, and uttered a chillingly formal, "thank you", as she exited to hidden smiles and snickers from many in the room. What Carl had so casually predicted, however, proved more than accurate. It was the best meal he had had for a very long time.

12
NEGOTIATIONS

A few days after Sunday supper with the attorney present, Alice looked up from rolling out dough to see Edith Brown poke her head into the Hanks' kitchen. "Somethin' I can do for you?" Alice asked curtly, then followed that up with, "Mrs. Hanks ain't—isn't here right now."

"Oh, that's alright. I actually came to see you, Alice," Mrs. Brown said, smiling awkwardly.

"I'd prefer you call me Mrs. Steele."

Alice's clipped response wiped the smile from Edith's face. "Very well. Anyway, as I said, I was looking for you."

"Well, you found me," Alice continued her pattern of rudeness. "And, as you can see, I'm quite busy." With that, Alice returned to her kneading.

"Yes, of course." Edith hesitated as if questioning the wisdom of the visit. "I'll keep it brief."

"Do that."

Edith's gave her cousin a hostile look, which contrasted with her words. "Very well. I came with a message from Albert and Maude."

This stopped Alice's work as a wary look crossed her face. "Really," was all she could manage.

"They wanted me to say how impressed they were with Wilma and Velma's performance in the plays last October."

"Kind of them," Alice said with a mixture of sarcasm and relief. "Is that all?"

Edith tried another smile. "And they also wanted me to share that they thought you clearly hadn't lost your touch in the baking department."

"That's not news, Mrs. Brown," Alice said flatly. "Not very genuine either."

After a nervous chuckle, Edith agreed. "Of course. But I would think that the important part of the message was that your parents wanted me to share that with you."

"Is that so?" Alice's curtness was offset by a softening expression. "Anything else?"

"Well, yes," Edith said hesitantly.

"Then get to it." Alice was unable to hide her interest in hearing what was to come.

"They were disappointed not to get a look at the boys." Edith immediately regretted saying this as Alice's expression darkened. "Anyway, they wanted me to ask that if they came to visit again, could they see the family … "

"Stop right there," Alice interrupted. "The only family I have now is my own and the friends I've made here in Woodward. I got no use for the Skinners, even less for the Steeles."

Edith started to bristle, then checked herself. "I'm just the messenger, Alice. But I understand your feeling that way."

"Oh really?"

"Yes. And I know that Walter and I contributed to that when you first came here." She went on before Alice could reply. "And I know you haven't noticed, but we've changed our opinion."

"Well, isn't that *nice*."

Edith ignored her cousin's sarcasm. "Your Velma and my Nancy got us started. Now they are good friends."

"I'll have to talk to her about the company she's been a-keepin'." This snipe was delivered with a little venom.

Undaunted, Mrs. Brown continued. "I don't expect you to forgive Walter and me anytime soon."

"Try ever."

"Whatever you say, Alice." The use of her first name went unchallenged this time. "But please don't get between my Nancy and Velma. They have been good for each other, especially my girl."

"How so?" Alice actually seemed interested in the answer.

"Well, they are both smart and help each other do well in school. You saw how they performed together at that wonderful pageant."

"I suppose I did."

Edith smiled. "That's the way they get along most all the time. The two of them have also been working hard to help Katie Warren cope with the loss of her mother and her brother. And that rubbed off on Walter and me, then to your parents."

Alice suddenly stiffened. "You sayin', I mean, saying my Velma was talking to Ma and Pa?"

"No, no, that never happened," Edith replied, shaking her head vigorously. "Just ask her."

"I surely will," Alice replied coolly. "You got—I mean, do you have anything else to share? This dough won't wait for no one. Anyone."

"Just that your parents also wanted me to warn you again about your father-in-law."

"*Ex*-father-in-law," Alice shot back. "And I don't need no—any warning about him."

Edith nodded. "That's good to know, and here's something else good to know." She paused to get Alice's full attention. "Your parents will do anything they can to spoil old man Steele's plans."

Alice took some time to absorb this, then asked with a humorless smile. "By making a play for my children themselves?"

Edith actually looked shocked at the suggestion. "Oh, no. That's not what I meant. They just want to help."

"Next time you see them, say thanks, but I can take care of things myself."

A look between sadness and disappointment appeared on Mrs. Brown's face. "I'll do that. I'm sorry to have bothered you."

"I'll get over it."

With a sigh, Edith turned to leave, but paused as Alice added, "Don't worry."

"About what?"

"Me breaking up our daughters," Alice replied, reaching for the cinnamon and sugar. "Now, if you don't mind, I gotta, I've got to make a living."

Wearing a slight smile, Edith turned and passed back into the mercantile. She stopped at the front counter long enough to buy a loaf of Alice's bread and two cinnamon rolls before bidding Annie Andrews a good day.

As Mrs. Brown exited the store, a well-dressed man held the door open for her, then stepped up to the counter. "Good day young lady," he said to Annie pleasantly. "Is Mrs. Steele available?"

"Who should I say is asking?" Annie said in a formal tone.

"My name is Robert Cross."

"And your business?"

"I am an attorney representing Mr. John Alexander Steele."

Annie nodded curtly and began moving toward the back of the store. "Please wait here and I'll see if she's available."

A minute later, Annie returned carrying an envelope. Reaching the counter, she held it out to the attorney. "She is unable to see you, Mr. Cross, but asked me to give you this."

"Unable or unwilling?" the attorney asked with a raised brow.

"Not my business, sir," Annie said firmly. "Now, is there something else I can do for you?" She looked to the table of pastries. "Perhaps one of Mrs. Steele's famous buns."

Cross glanced in that direction, then shook his head. "No, thank you." Then holding the envelope up, he said, "There is no name on the envelope. Is this for Mr. Steele or for me?"

"Mrs. Steele said to suit yourself in that regard," Annie replied as the bell on the front door rang. This gave the young lady an excuse to break off the conversation. "Hello, Mrs. Peterson. How may I help you?"

"Oh, hello, Annie," came the cheerful reply from a heavyset older woman. "Mr. Hanks said the material I ordered was scheduled to be in a couple of days ago."

Annie turned to the attorney, who was reading the contents of the single sheet from the envelope while wearing a deep frown. "I need to step away, sir, unless you need something else from me."

Mr. Cross shook his head slowly. "No, I've got what I came for."

Annie couldn't pass up giving him a parting shot. "You don't look too happy about what you're reading."

"Oh, it means no never mind to me, but it will to John Steele to be sure, miss."

"It's Mrs. Anderson, if you please."

"Oh, sorry, ma'am," Cross tipped his hat. "I'll just be going. Thank you for your help."

"You're welcome."

As soon as he was gone, Alice, who had been watching the exchange through the curtain at the back, quickly joined Annie, who gave her a big smile. "I think he got your message. I'd love to be there when he shares the news with Mr. Steele."

"Me too," Alice said, suddenly releasing pent-up tension via a deep sigh. "But I'm sure we haven't seen the last of Mr. Cross."

Annie's expression sobered. "I sure hope this doesn't go bad for you and yours."

"Ever the optimist, hey, Annie?" Alice asked rhetorically, then changed subjects. "You better get busy sellin', I mean selling the last of those cinnamon rolls. I got, I mean I have a fresh batch coming out. In a few minutes."

Hearing this, Mrs. Peterson spoke up, "I'll take a few of them."

Grabbing a paper bag and beginning to fill it, Annie addressed Alice. "I'm curious about something, Mrs. Steele."

"Mrs. Steele?" Alice replied incredulously.

"Well, it's kind of a personal question." Annie's reply earned quizzical looks from not only Alice but Mrs. Peterson.

"I'll just pay for those and be on my way," the customer said, groping in her handbag. As the other women waited, she quickly brought out a handful of change and counted out some coins. "There, I think that's correct," she said, taking the bag of buns from Annie, who started adding up the coins.

"Right you are. Thanks, Mrs. P, and..." Annie stopped, seeing the back of the matronly woman as she hurried out of the store. With a smile, she turned back to Alice. "Ready for those fresh buns."

Alice nodded, turning to head for the kitchen, then pausing. "You had a *personal* question for me?"

"Well, yes. But you don't have to answer," Annie offered. Alice just nodded. "Well, I've noticed you've been working hard on, ah..."

"Spit it out, dearie," Alice said in a curious tone. "Remember the buns."

"Oh, right," Annie replied with a nervous chuckle. "Well, I've noticed you're working hard on improving your grammar and wondered why? Is it because of the girls? Is it because they are getting good, or ... ?"

Alice held up a hand. "I understand the question and that is indeed the reason. I cain't, *can't* have my children embarrassed by me. So, that's the reason."

"Really?"

Alice was incredulous at the question. "You don't believe me?"

"Oh, sure, I do," Annie said hastily. "It's just I thought there might be another reason."

Instead of becoming angry, Alice actually blushed. "Let's just stick with it's because of the girls shall we." Her expression suddenly turned anxious. "Do you smell somethin'? Drat. I meant—oh, never mind."

"The buns," Annie cried out as Alice headed off at a near run. In a flash she disappeared through the curtain.

A few tense moments later, Alice's muffled voice could be heard from the kitchen. "I think they're alright." And with that, the routine of the mercantile was quickly restored.

"Hello, Mr. Price," Alice practically shouted over the phone. "This is Mrs. Steele."

"Oh, hello, Alice," came the cheerful reply. "How have you been."

Alice's anxiety eased at the sound of Milo's deep bass voice. "Ah, I was doin', doing just fine until I got another letter."

"A letter?"

"Yes. It's from that attorney, Mr. Cross from Des Moines. He represents..."

Price interrupted. "John Steele, right?"

"That's right."

"That was quick," came Milo's terse reply. "I assume the letter was in response to the one I drafted for you."

"Yes, and it, well, it isn't what I'd hoped it would say."

After a pause, Price suggested, "It would likely be best if we got together to go over it. I assume the phone you are using isn't exactly in a private place."

"No. It's the one on Carl Warren's desk at the bank."

There was another pause, accompanied by the sound of shuffling papers. "I know how hard it is for you to get away from Woodward, Alice, so I'll come to you. How does Friday afternoon sound?"

"But this letter demands..."

Once again Milo interrupted. "I know, Alice. I expect it demands an immediate response. But that's just lawyer talk, trying to intimidate you into a hasty decision. Just ignore that part."

"Really?"

"Really. Now about Friday?" It was Alice's turn to delay long enough for Price to ask, "Are you still there, Alice?"

"Yes, sir."

Milo laughed into the phone. "Sir is it? I thought we were past that."

"Not when we're doin', I mean doing business."

"Of course, *Mrs. Steele*," Price's gentle mocking was lost on Alice.

She cleared her throat, then blurted out, "I can't pay you, and I won't take charity."

"Understood, Alice." Then Milo went on lightheartedly. "I thought we had an arrangement. You feed me one of your gourmet meals occasionally as payment."

"That just doesn't seem right," Alice replied. "Do you have that kind of arrangement with anyone else?"

"Well, no."

"There you have it."

Milo responded incredulously, "What's this '*it*' I supposedly have?"

"You're givin', giving me charity."

"No, I'm not," Milo protested. "Barter is a common means of payment. Why I know for a fact that Doc Joseph over your way will take a chicken as payment. Under our terms, I get a whole meal. A great deal for me."

This stymied Alice briefly, but she recovered. "How much would you normally charge for this next visit?

"Either a pot roast or fried chicken dinner," Milo quipped, then added, "Plus a whole pie if you take up too much of my time."

Alice couldn't help but laugh. "I was being serious. How much would it cost in dollars and cents?"

"My fees vary depending on how complex the case is and the financial circumstances of the client."

Alice responded hotly, "I knew it."

"Knew what?" came the incredulous reply.

"That I'm a charity case," was her indignant reply.

Milo's voice on the other end of the line rose. "Absolutely not."

"Then what do I owe you?"

"A pot roast or fried chicken dinner," Milo answered humorously this time, then added, "I am free to set my terms, and you are free to accept or reject them."

"Then I'll do just that."

The line was quiet for a moment before Milo replied in a much more serious voice, "Then I wish you well with the matter at hand. Good day, Mrs. Steele."

"Wait, wait," Alice shouted into the speaker, causing the bank to fall silent. Looking around to find all eyes on her, she went on in a much softer tone, "Okay, Mr. Price. I accept your terms."

"I'm glad to hear that, *Alice*," Milo said back in his normal, pleasant tone. "Say, why don't we make the appointment for Sunday instead? Then I can enjoy your company and the others in your circle."

"But the letter?" Alice protested.

"Can wait," Milo replied. "What do you say? I'm sure the others would love for you to do all the cooking again." Not giving her a chance to protest, he added, "Who's hosting this time anyway?"

"Ah, Henry and Tessa I think."

"Good. I'll be over Sunday afternoon."

"But I need to check with..." The line went dead before she could finish.

Alice hung up sheepishly and nodded to Carl, who had been at the teller windows keeping his distance. He ambled over trying to look like he'd heard nothing. "So, what's happening?"

"You know perfectly well." She gave him a glare, which the banker ignored. "Everyone in the place heard at least my half of the conversation."

Carl gave her a wry smile. "I fear you exaggerate, Mrs. Steele. All these folks heard was you received a troublesome letter. Do you plan on sharing its contents with your friends soon?"

"Of course," Alice said, rising. "Well, with the exception of you, maybe."

This had Carl laughing loudly, the sound echoing off the high ceiling and drawing more curious looks from his customers. Then his expression grew serious. "You do that, Alice. I've got my own problems to deal with anyway."

"Really?" Alice asked incredulously. "Like what?"

"Oh, no you don't." Carl's smile was back. "If you're going to exclude me from your trials and tribulations, you'll get nothing more out of me."

Alice shrugged and headed for the bank entrance with Carl at her side. "Okay, but I bet I can guess." When Carl said nothing, Alice continued, "Is it of the female variety?"

"Good guess," Carl replied in a whisper. "But that's not all."

Alice gave him a raised brow. "Something else?"

"Thanksgiving is coming."

"And?" Alice prodded.

"One word." Carl paused until Alice gave him an imploring gesture. "Freddie."

Alice flitted around the Hanks' kitchen, preparing platters of fried chicken with all the trimmings, refusing help. Milo sat at the table reviewing the letter from John Steele's attorney, while the others stayed out of the way while trying not to stare. Suddenly, with a touch of surprise, Price shared, "Now they want all the kids."

At that moment, Wilma and Velma came in the Hanks' back door. This time Alice's youngest daughter arrived without any knowledge of the latest letter. Given the recent past and the presence of Mr. Price, however, she immediately became alarmed. The looks on adult faces reinforced that opinion.

"What's wrong, Mama?" Velma blurted out without thinking.

"Wrong?" Alice said, looking surprised and confused. "There's nothing wrong."

At first, the young girl was relieved. Soon, however, her emotions moved on to annoyance and jealousy. If there was nothing wrong, then Mr. Price's presence was a personal call. What she had only sensed through a casual word or look now seemed obvious. For once, she wasn't enjoying having eavesdropped on the adults.

"Go get washed up, all of you," Alice ordered. Dinner will be on the table when you get back."

Further conversation on the letter was put off until after dinner and dessert. It was getting dark earlier now in early November. To Wilma's surprise and delight, Velma volunteered to take the boys home and get them in bed early, claiming the need to do homework. Katie and Charity went with their friend while Wilma went upstairs to sew.

No sooner were the children out of earshot than Tessa got back to the letter. "You were saying something about the Steeles wanting the girls now too. Is that right?"

"Yes."

"I don't understand why."

"Simple, Mrs. Hanks," Milo explained. "A judge would likely look askance at a claim the children were being neglected but then only wanting two of the four. It can also be a negotiating tool."

"I can see that," Carl Warren said. "Demand all of the children, then settle for the boys."

Milo nodded, then perused the rest of the letter in a silent room before speaking again, "It seems Mr. Steele found some help in preparing this."

"Really, how can you tell?" Henry asked.

"There's too much local information, as distorted as it may be. Old man Steele wouldn't have that much firsthand knowledge."

Alice came over, wiping her hands on her flour-coated apron. "There's a lot of hogwash in that letter, not to mention most of it is from a couple years ago."

"I didn't know that timeline," Milo replied, his expression brightening. "That is conveniently missing from this letter."

"So, that should take care of this whole matter, right?" Carl Warren asked.

"Well, it will go a long way," Milo replied. "I'll write something back to that effect and hopefully avoid the filing of a formal suit. The other claims made in the letter may make that more difficult, however."

"Who could have been the source of this information?" Tessa asked angrily.

"I hate to say it, but Edith Brown comes to mind," Mrs. Jones replied.

"Let's not stoop to their level, Grace," Reverend Jones countered, giving his wife a harsh look. "After all, that letter is filled with rumor and innuendo."

"We all know that Edith and Walter made Alice's life difficult from the day they arrived," Grace shot back, her usual meek tone replaced with an angry spark.

"That used to be the case," Alice said, her words shocking the group.

Carl was the first to recover. "What's this? A kind word for the Browns coming from you?"

"Ain't, I mean, I'm not vouching for Walter, but Edith has been a lot more cordial recently."

"That's good to hear," Alan said, giving his wife a "told you so" look.

Grace blushed. "Well, maybe I was a bit hasty."

Milo cut the inquisition short. "It could have come from any number of sources, including the Browns, and have been provided in total innocence and ignorance."

"How could that be?" Tessa asked incredulously.

"I have sent people out to gather information on cases before," Milo explained. "The people I send out don't interrogate, they converse. It is amazing what you can learn around the pickle barrel."

"Not around *our* pickle barrel," Henry said defiantly.

Milo shook his head, wearing a wry smile. "Of course not, Mr. Hanks. I was just using that metaphorically."

"Oh, right."

Milo went on quickly. "That's an assumption on my part. We'll find out the source if this ever gets to court."

This brought a deep frown to Alice's face. "If this goes to court, I'll be cookin' for you forever."

"Deal," Milo shot back, his grin broadening.

"I don't find that funny, Mr. Price," Alice said, standing abruptly and starting to clear the table.

"Sorry, Alice," Milo said, unwilling to echo her formality. "I wasn't making fun of your circumstances."

Carl stepped in trying to ease the tension. "Does Mr. Steele have the resources to push the matter?"

After considering the question for a moment, Price nodded. "Well, yes. From what I hear, he was one of the few that didn't overextend during the war. As a result, he remained quite solvent, solvent enough to buy up several other farms that were forced into foreclosure."

"I see," Carl replied, looking to Alice, whose expression had grown even darker. Then Carl had a thought. "But farm prices are still pretty depressed, right?"

"True," Milo said, then added, "but Steele turned the farms over to his own family, allowing them to share equipment and labor. Plus, he converted one property to all livestock and feeds the beasts from his other farms."

Henry uttered a soft whistle. "Smart guy."

"Evil guy," Alice shot back from the sink as Tessa and Grace brought over more dirty dishes.

"Undoubtedly true," Price said with a nod.

Reverend Jones, ever the forgiver, suggested, "Maybe Mr. Steele just wants his grandchildren in his life." Seeing the collective looks on the others' faces, he retreated. "Ah, well, it was just a thought."

Tessa beat Alice to a reply. "God love you, Alan, but sometimes you're way too Pollyanna."

"Tell me about it," Grace added.

This had the group chuckling, but only for a moment before Carl directed a question to the attorney. "So, since he can afford to drag this out in court and Alice can't, what do you suggest, Milo?"

Everyone stopped what they were doing and stared at Price who, after a long pause, shrugged. "I don't have an answer to that question. Put me in that courtroom and I'd rip their case to shreds, but..."

"I won't accept charity, so that is out," Alice interrupted, adding, "Maybe I should just pack up and head for..." She stopped unable to come up with a location.

"That would make her look quite guilty, wouldn't it, Milo?" Tessa asked.

He nodded. "They'd probably send the law after you."

"Not to mention the havoc that would wreak on you and the kids," Grace pointed out.

"You'd have to start all over," Henry added, "and you'd need help."

"The kind of help you appear to have gotten here." The attorney capped the argument.

"That still leaves the question of what Alice can, should do," Carl repeated.

The only response for a long time was the clinking of dishes and an occasional cough. Then suddenly, Tessa blurted out, "I've got it."

Henry gave his wife a wary look. "I know that look."

"What look?"

"The look you get just before uttering some kind of harebrained idea."

His wife glared at him, hands on hips. "You take that back, Henry Hanks."

The attorney objected in his best legal voice, "I think we are getting off topic. Shouldn't we hear the idea first then decide if it's harebrained?"

"Right," Reverend Jones concurred.

Henry relented. "Yes, dear, go ahead."

"Thank you," Tess said with a scowl at her husband and a nod to the others. "The answer is simple really. Alice needs to get married."

As silence descended again for what seemed an eternity, everyone's face took on a variety of expressions, including shock, disdain and one of possibility. Then Henry said in a whisper, "See, I told you it would be harebrained."

13

An Uneasy Alliance

All the Steele children were dressed in their Sunday best and sitting in the apartment's living room a week and a half after the dramatic meeting in the Hanks' kitchen. That discussion, triggered by Tessa Hanks' marriage suggestion, was proving to be monumental, though not in the way Mrs. Hanks had envisioned.

That same night, when Alice returned to the apartment with Carl Warren, who had come to get Katie, nothing was said, but Velma noticed her mother's distractedness. No amount of probing by both girls over the next few days provided any explanation. Soon their attention turned to Thanksgiving less than a week away.

The first hint that something momentous was about to happen came on the Monday before the holiday break. The information didn't come from their mother or any of the other adults, however. It came from Miss Fletcher.

She approached Velma, who was talking to Katie and Nancy Brown just inside the school's front entrance, apparently not eager to go out into a crisp November wind. "Well, it appears we all have special Thanksgivings to look forward to."

"What do you mean?" Velma said, genuinely confused. "Most of my friends will be leaving town for the holiday."

Realizing Velma had not been told, Emily sputtered out, "I guess you're right," as she blushed slightly.

"Yeah, Daddy is hauling me off on the train Wednesday morning to see Freddie," Katie added unenthusiastically, her expression showing concern.

"I wish I could go on the train with you," Nancy chimed in disappointedly. "I just got old relatives coming over, and they're such bores."

Miss Fletcher gave the now fifth-grader a warning look, which the girl missed. Then Emily added, "I'm heading back to Illinois to visit family," Emily said with a smile. "In fact, I think *I'll* be on the same train with you and your father, Katie."

Velma felt her friend stiffen. "Daddy never said."

"I don't expect he knows. I only assumed that when you said you were taking the train from Perry on Wednesday. I think there is only the one."

Nancy Brown broke in to say, "You all can ride to the station together, right?"

"I don't know about that," Emily replied while looking to Katie. "It would be up to Katie and her father."

"Oh, I'm sure that won't be a problem," Nancy said, then turned to Katie for confirmation, just in time to see her head for the door. "Katie, wait."

Katie hesitated long enough at the door to say, "I don't know. Are you two coming?" Then she was out the door.

"Wait up, Katie," Velma shouted as she headed off.

"What's the matter with her?" Nancy asked absently as she followed.

Velma caught her friend at the bottom of the steps. "That was really rude, Katie."

"So what," Katie snapped back glancing, back up the steps. "I hate her."

Nancy Brown heard this as she joined them. In shocked surprise, she asked, "You hate Miss Fletcher? I don't under..."

Velma interrupted her. "She's just joking."

"Doesn't sound like joking to me."

Recovering, Katie laughed halfheartedly, "Well, I was referring to Miss Fletcher's annoyingly constant cheerfulness. And I guess I'm anxious about seeing my brother for the first time since..." She let the sentence drop.

"Oh, I see," Nancy said, not appearing to totally understand.

Velma suddenly realized she was late getting home. "I have to go, girls. Will you come over to the mercantile later?"

"I can't," Katie said with a frown. "Daddy and I are getting stuff together for the trip tonight."

Nancy quickly suggested, "Don't forget to tell you father about Miss Fletcher needing a ride."

Scowling at the older girl, Katie replied disingenuously, "Oh, I'll be sure to do that." Then turning back to Velma, she added, "Remember, we're eating at your place tomorrow night since we won't be together for Thanksgiving."

"Oh, right," Velma said, turning to Nancy. "What about you? Can you come over this afternoon?"

Nancy shook her head. "I don't think so. Mother wants help preparing for our guests. I'll see you two tomorrow at school for lunch."

"See you in class, Katie, and at lunch, Nancy," Velma said as she took off into the stiff wind at a run, her skinny legs tossing the hem of her too-small coat from side to side.

The next Wednesday evening found the entire Steele family waiting in their living room. Alice's nerves had spread to the children even though they didn't know why. She continually paced in front of the windows, her gaze fixed outside.

Suddenly, Velma saw her mother stiffen at the sound of feet on the wooden stairs. Then Alice moved quickly to the front door, opening it before anyone could knock. There on the threshold stood Edith, Walter, and Nancy Brown.

"Hello, Alice." The tremble in Edith's voice betrayed her appearance of calm. "May we come in?"

"Well, since we've been waitin' for quite a while for your arrival, I expect so." She immediately recognized the curtness in her voice and changed her tone. "Of course, cousin. Welcome to our humble abode."

"Thank you." Edith gently shoved Nancy forward, and the girl quickly crossed the room to Velma's side.

Walter removed his hat and stepped aside, making way for the couple behind him. "I believe you know these two," he said with a timid smile.

"Hello, daughter." The gaunt woman wrapped in a thick wool shawl eased forward.

"Mother," Alice responded flatly. "Father." Her expression remained emotionless.

Walter endeavored to push Alice's parents through the door, but they hesitated until their daughter stepped aside saying, "Come on in."

Once inside, everyone stalled, making it impossible to close the door against the cold November afternoon. With a tug, Alice sent Edith toward Nancy, while commanding, "Let's get in before everyone catches their death."

Nervous chuckles accompanied the others as they moved deeper into the room. While Albert Skinner, clutching a burlap bag, and Walter moved toward chairs against the far wall, Maude stepped up to the four children seated primly on the couch, hands folded in their laps. Leaning over tentatively, she extended a hand to the eldest. "Hello, Wilma, remember me?"

Wilma only nodded, while Velma answered, "You're our Grandma Maude, the gooder grandma."

An expression of mild shock appeared on Maude's face as she looked toward her other granddaughter. Soon her face creased into a grin. "That's right, Velma. I'm your gooder grandma Maude."

There was no smile on Alice's face. "Don't be rude, child."

"Sorry, Mama." The little girl's face turned red with embarrassment. "Should I have said something different?"

"No need, child," Maude said, trying to ease her granddaughter's mind.

"I'll tell her what's necessary if you don't mind," came Alice's snarky reply.

Maude turned to give her daughter a contrite look, "Yes, of course, Alice. I do apologize."

Now Alice seemed embarrassed at her overreaction as she replied sheepishly, "No harm done. I guess. I'm a little out of sorts right now."

"Aren't we all," Maude said in a gentle tone.

As if to make up for her outburst, Alice said to Velma, "Go ahead dear, say whatever you want to Grandma Maude."

"Really?" Velma asked uncertainly.

"Yes," Alice answered anxiously, wondering what her daughter might say.

Velma thought for a moment, then quickly said, "Happy Thanksgiving." Alice restrained a sigh of relief just before her youngest daughter added, "Can we come see your farm? I miss all the animals we had at our place back when..."

"That's enough, Velma," Alice interrupted loudly, her face suffused with anger.

Though she said nothing, Maude gave her own daughter a look of disapproval edged with disappointment.

Seeing the look, Alice's attempt at justification fell short. "Well, you see, Velma is a somewhat willful girl."

"I seem to recall another little girl that was the same way," Maude said, careful to frame this remark with a half-smile. "Now will you introduce us to the boys?"

After a pause to compose herself, Alice nodded toward her oldest son. "This here is Eugene."

The boy continued staring at the floor, saying nothing until Alice ordered, "Eugene, say hello to your grandparents."

"Hello," came the nearly inaudible reply as his head came slowly up to stare at the strangers.

"My, how much you have grown," Maude said warmly to the clearly frightened boy. "Last time I saw you, you was just startin' to get around on your own feet."

"Can't stop him now." The casual response was out before Alice could stop herself. She quickly went on, saying, "He's five now and growin' like a weed. And this is Edward, now three."

Maude leaned down, causing the boy to sink deeper into the couch. "Don't be afraid, son. I won't hurt you."

"Don't make promises you might not be able to keep," Alice said, then seemed to regret her words immediately. "Oh, I'm so sorry. That just came out. Please, forget I even said it."

While Walter frowned and Albert bristled, Maude replied with a coy smile, "Said what, dear?"

This brought a brief smile to Velma's face as the tension in the room eased. "Thank you, Mother," Alice replied thankfully.

Velma was struck by how her mother's response sounded so much like her own when seeking forgiveness. She found this comforting and raised her hopes that it might be just fine having grandparents, or at least a grandma around. She didn't feel the same way at all toward the tall thin man sitting next to Mr. Brown.

"Get over here, Albert, and meet your grandchildren," Maude ordered. "Can't have them thinking you're some kind of mute grump."

"A grump-pa?" Velma suggested with a smile.

While the adults tried to decide how to respond, all the children, including the boys started giggling. Soon the room was filled with laughter.

When things had died down, Maude waved her husband over. "Come on over, grump-pa, and don't forget the gifts."

"Gifts?" the children exclaimed, more or less, as one.

Soon the boys were on the floor with grump-pa and Mr. Brown, playing with a wooden tractor and wagon Mr. Skinner had made himself. Grandma Maude sat between the girls on the couch, examining the dresses bought that morning at the mercantile. Everyone shared in the box of divinity Maude had brought for the occasion.

This was the beginning of a wonderful week of healing and bonding after many lonely years apart. When Maude and Albert returned to the farm that seemed so far away to the children, they left with happy hearts and an invitation to come for Christmas.

Unfortunately, the weather didn't cooperate, so they did not see Grandpa and Grandma Skinner until the next spring. They did, however, start seeing the Browns regularly, adding them to the monthly Sunday supper group.

14
Changing Times Changing Minds

As some kind of omen, December 1923 in mid-Iowa came in with persistent cold and gray skies. There was no snow, just rock-hard ground in the stripped and barren fields. The chill wore everyone down, physically and emotionally, under their heavy coats. A constant wind seemed to blow people in and out of Woodward as if on a whim.

For Velma, the malaise started the Sunday afternoon after Thanksgiving when Katie, her father, and Miss Fletcher drove back into town. She had been waiting for their return impatiently at the front window of the mercantile, while her mother and the others ate leftovers around the kitchen table.

When the Model-T finally passed at sunset, Velma rushed to the kitchen, "Mama, Katie's back. Can I go say hello?"

Looking at the big kitchen clock over the stove and glancing out into the gathering gloom, Alice hesitated. "It's almost dark and tomorrow's a school day."

"I know, Mama, so I'll just say hello and then head to bed." Velma was pretty sure her mother wouldn't object to such a plan.

"Be sure to bundle up then, and be gone no more than a half-hour, you hear?"

Velma already had her coat on and was buttoning it up tight as she replied, "Promise, Mama."

"Wait a minute," Tessa said. "They likely don't have any food in the house. Let me make a basket."

"Good idea," Alice said. "I'll help."

"What about Miss Fletcher?" Velma asked.

"Oh, right." Tessa grabbed a second basket, and within a few minutes, there were two petite feasts beneath checkered napkins.

"You sure you can carry all that?" her mother asked doubtfully. "It's awful cold and windy out there."

"Ah, Mama, it's only a few blocks. I'll be careful."

"Here." Tessa brought over some twine and quickly tied it around both baskets. "There. Now you're good to go."

"Thanks Mrs. H.," Velma said while putting on her scarf and hat. "I'll see you at home, Mama."

"Thirty minutes, mind you," Alice said emphatically to her daughter's back as she slammed the kitchen door, sending a chill across the room.

"That child is one bundle of joy, Alice," Grace said.

Looking over at Wilma minding the boys in a corner of the large kitchen, she replied, "All my children are joys."

This got a raised eyebrow from Henry. "Truer words were never spoken by a mother."

A strong west wind escorted Velma down the alley to the side street. She jogged right to Main, then left past the school. Another block and she arrived on the street where both the Warrens and Miss Fletcher lived. Hesitating briefly, she headed to see Katie, figuring Mr. Warren could deliver the other basket if it got too late.

Out of breath from the exertion and excitement, Velma put down the baskets and rapped on the door. After what seemed a long time and a second knock, Mr. Warren opened the door. His expression made her shiver even more than the cold weather. "Welcome home, Mr. Warren."

"Hello, Velma," he said flatly.

Hesitantly, Velma asked, "Can I see Katie? I can only stay a few minutes."

"I don't think it's a good time. I sent her straight to bed. It was a long trip and there is school tomorrow." Mr. Warren's tone and haggard look stifled any argument.

"Okay, Mr. Warren," Velma said and turned to go before remembering the baskets. She quickly bent down and grabbed it before the door closed. "Oh, this is for you and Katie, Mr. Warren. My mother and the others thought you might be hungry."

He took the basket unenthusiastically, saying weakly, "Thank them for me. I'm sure we'll make good use of it."

Velma smiled broadly. "Oh, I know you will, especially the pumpkin pie on top."

With an absent nod, he closed the door, leaving Velma out in the cold. Grabbing the other basket, she turned, and hurried next door, hoping Miss Fletcher wasn't already in bed too. Lights blazing on both floors of the old Victorian emboldened her effort.

Her knock brought an older man she had never met before to the door. Initially he gave her a stern look, reminding the girl of a scarecrow, until he smiled warmly. "Hello, young lady. What brings you to our door at this hour?"

Velma held up the basket. "My mother sent me over with this food for Miss Fletcher, knowing she just got back."

"And who's your mother?"

"Alice Steele, sir," Velma said with pride.

His eyes widened. "The baker?" Velma nodded. "Come in out of the cold, child. I'm Mr. Adams."

"Pleased to meet you sir. I'm Velma."

As she entered, the man spoke to someone out of sight in the drawing room. "Martha, we have a visitor, or rather, Miss Fletcher has a visitor."

"It's kind of late, Oscar."

While Mr. Adams snuck a peek under the checkered napkin, Velma said, "Oh, I'm just dropping this off and will be on my way real soon. I have school tomorrow."

Just then, a very tall, slender woman with gray hair pulled back in a bun, came into view. Mr. Adams introduced her. "This is Velma Steele. Her mother is that…"

"I know the name, and you know her pies quite well." Though the woman's face remained bland, the words were delivered with humor.

"Oh, there's a pumpkin pie in there," Velma blurted out. "Maybe Miss Fletcher will share."

"I certainly will," the familiar voice came from the top of the stairs. Looking up excitedly, Velma was concerned to see her teacher looking so exhausted. It seemed effortful for her to descend to join them in the foyer. "Is that for me?"

"Yes, Miss Fletcher," Velma said, holding out the basket. "Mother and the other ladies packed this one up for you. I just left another at the Warren's. Didn't get to see Katie and Mr. Warren seemed awful tired, a lot like you do." Velma realized how bad this might sound and blushed. "Sorry, Miss Fletcher, I didn't mean to..."

"It's alright, dear." Emily managed a halfhearted smile. "Your observation would be correct. I was just finishing up unpacking and heading to bed."

"Oh." Velma gave the basket a concerned look.

Miss Fletcher got the message. "But before I do, perhaps I can take this basket in the kitchen and see what's inside. That is if you don't mind, Mrs. Adams?"

"Not at all, Emily," Martha said, then turned to Velma. "Leave your things on that chair, Miss Steele, and follow me." Mrs. Adams led the way to the kitchen. "I'm sure Oscar will be eager to check out what's inside."

"What's that supposed to mean?" the man said indignantly.

"It means that Miss Fletcher better take a close inventory of her booty with you around."

Within minutes, the contents had been surveyed and stored either in the icebox or pantry, all except one big slice of pie. That was quickly devoured by Mr. Adams in front of the others without embarrassment.

"I'm sorry, everyone," Miss Fletcher suddenly said with a yawn. "I really do need some sleep. I'll have a room full of eager brains tomorrow, and I won't be worth my salt without it."

"Of course, Emily," Martha said, shooing Velma toward the front door. "It was awfully nice to meet you, Velma."

"Nice meeting you too," the little girl said while putting on her coat and scarf. "Have a good night, Miss Fletcher. I'm sure all of us will want to know about your visit back in Illinois."

"Oh, I doubt that," Emily yawned again. "Do thank your mother and the others for their kind gift. I will make good use of it."

"Likely so will Oscar," Martha said through a high-pitched cackle.

"Now cut that out, woman," Oscar barked, then opened the door for Velma. "Good night, dear. And do come back again soon."

"You forgot something," Martha said, still smiling.

"I did? What was that?"

"Come back soon with another basket."

Velma looked back, wearing her own smile only to have it fade as she watched Miss Fletcher drag herself up the steep stairs. Then the door closed, and she headed off for home at a run. What had started off with expectations of happy reunions instead had left her uneasy.

Arriving home at the apartment, Velma decided it would be a good idea for her to get a good night's sleep as well. So, she was in bed when her mother, sister, and brothers came in a short time later. Soon the others, worn out by all the holiday food and constant activity, were asleep, all except Velma.

In spite of a fitful sleep, Velma popped out of bed, did her chores, and headed to school, eager to hear from Katie about seeing Freddie. She also wanted to see how Miss Fletcher acted. She wasn't convinced that her behavior the previous evening was only from the fatigue of a long day's travel. There was a lot to learn this day.

Unfortunately, Velma was disappointed on both counts. First, Miss Fletcher was back to her old self from the moment class began, sharing amusing stories about the visit back home. Everyone was enthralled by the telling, all except Katie. She wasn't there.

Risking a scolding from her mother, Velma headed straight for the Warren house after school. She was surprised to have her friend answer the front door looking well, well enough to have gone to school in Velma's humble opinion, and she said so. "You don't look sick. What's the matter with you?"

"I just didn't want to go today," Katie replied snootily then turned and walked inside leaving the door open.

Velma hesitated. "I really can't stay, got chores to do. Besides, since you ain't sick, there's no reason for me to stay."

"Then go," came the terse reply over Katie's shoulder.

The response irritated Velma, propelling her inside as she spat out angrily, "You've got something stuck in your craw. Out with it."

"It's none of your business," Katie shot back.

"What do you mean, none of my business?" Velma snapped as she dropped her outerwear on the entry hall chair. "Ain't I your best friend?"

"Aren't I, or am I not, not ain't," Katie spit back, raising Velma's ire even more. Ignoring her friend's glare, Katie added, "I really don't want to talk about it."

Velma looked around quickly. "Are you alone?"

"Yes," Katie replied. "As you pointed out, I *ain't* sick and Daddy had to go to work. He checked in on me at noon."

"So, we're alone?"

"I already said yes."

Velma moved forward quickly and pushed Katie none too gently toward the living room. "Then I ain't, I'm not leaving until you tell me what's going on." With a last shove, Velma deposited her friend on the sofa and plopped down beside her. "Now talk."

There was a long silence, requiring another demand from Velma. "I swear, if you don't tell me, I'll drag you down to the mercantile and have my mother have a word with you."

Instead of responding angrily, Katie began to cry. Velma said nothing more, just waited for the tears to stop. Then she encouraged her friend to talk with a nod and smile. "You can tell me, Katie. We have no secrets, remember."

"I, I suppose so." Katie sniffled. "It's just the whole holiday was, was awful for me."

"Why?"

Katie took a deep breath. "Because of Freddie and, and..." She hesitated.

"And what?"

"Not what. Who," Katie replied, then blurted out, "Miss Fletcher."

"Miss Fletcher?" Velma asked incredulously. "But she just rode on the train with you."

"Going and coming," Katie said harshly.

"I don't understand how that could have..."

Katie interrupted, "She and Daddy made eyes at each other the whole time. At least, until I got mad just before we got off the train in Perry last night."

"Oh," was all Velma could manage. Her thoughts went back to the last night of the pageant when she'd overheard Mr. Warren and Miss Fletcher on the porch. Now it seemed the commitment that night not to pursue a relationship was coming apart.

Velma was brought back to the present when Katie added, "And when they thought I was asleep, I saw them..." Again, the girl stopped.

"Kiss?" Velma blurted out reflexively.

"Yes," Katie confirmed the supposition, then gave her friend a curious look. "How did you know?"

"I didn't know. Just a good guess." The fib satisfied her friend.

"And Mother not gone even a year." Katie's sadness had evolved to anger. "How could he, how could they do that to me? And with Freddie still..."

Velma was growing frustrated by Katie's tendency to leave her sentences hanging but pressed ahead. "That's right. You started by saying something about your brother. How was he?"

Even before Katie responded, Velma knew it wasn't good news. "He hadn't changed a bit. In fact, I think he might have been worse."

"Oh, no."

"Oh, yes," Katie said emphatically. "When we arrived, he was confined to his room. The headmaster outlined a series of rules he'd broken since arriving. I wasn't at that meeting, but when Daddy came out, I couldn't tell if he was more angry or disappointed."

"I'm so sorry, Katie," Velma said, taking her friend's hand.

Katie squeezed hard as she continued. "That wasn't the worst of it. When we got to see Freddie, he said cruel things to father and ignored me. Our Thanksgiving was spent staring across the table at a restaurant in silence. It was like my brother was a total stranger."

"So, the whole weekend was a waste?"

"More or less, though Daddy tried to save it by taking me into downtown Chicago."

"Chicago!" Velma couldn't restrain her excitement. "I can't imagine that not being fun."

"Well, it wasn't," Katie replied hotly. "Even though we did eat at a fancy place and went to a play."

"Which one?" Velma immediately wished she hadn't asked as Katie gave her an evil eye. "Never mind. I'm sorry I asked."

"That's okay," Katie said, her anger turned to sadness. "Nothing worked. We went back to where Freddie's school was on Saturday, but he wouldn't see us. Where we stayed was right across from the school. While Daddy stared out the window, I cried myself to sleep. I kept crying while Daddy kept staring out the window."

"How awful."

"Then on the way back, Miss Fletcher boarded the train at her stop in Illinois, and I watched as she consoled Daddy."

"She didn't pay you any mind?"

"Oh, she tried, but I'd have none of it. Instead, I threw a hissy fit around Des Moines, said I hated them both, and how dare they act that way with my mother barely cold in the ground."

"You didn't," Velma cried in disbelief.

"I sure did," Katie said defiantly. Then she suddenly blushed. "After that I got so embarrassed that I couldn't face either of them. So, I stayed home today."

Suddenly thinking of her own feelings about her mother and Mr. Price, Velma understood exactly what had motivated her friend. "I don't blame you at all. I just wish I had the gumption to say things like that to my mother."

"You mean about that attorney fellow?"

"Yes. We, you and I don't need no stranger in our lives."

"Agreed," Katie's said as her expression turned worried. "Regardless, I have to face Daddy tonight and Miss Fletcher tomorrow."

"Well, Miss Fletcher sure didn't act like anything was wrong today," Velma said, trying to give her friend a glimmer of hope,

"That's good to know." Katie didn't sound convinced. Then she gave her friend a weak smile. "It might be easier with Daddy if you were here."

Katie's words reminded Velma that she should have been at the mercantile helping her mother at that moment. "Oh, shoot. I got to run, Katie. I'm likely in trouble already." She jumped up and headed for the front door with her friend in pursuit.

"I guess that means I'll be on my own tonight."

Velma threw on her coat and dashed out the door, yelling, "Yes, but I'll be there for you tomorrow at school."

"I'm counting on it."

Covering the distance to the mercantile quickly, Velma feared the worst. Her concern was well-founded. Bursting through the back door into the Hanks' kitchen, she was greeted by a very stern look and angry question, "Where have you been, little lady?"

"I'm sorry, Mama, but Katie Warren wasn't at school today, and I went by to see how she was."

At hearing this, Alice's anger abated. "How did you find her?"

"She wasn't sick, more sad and angry I'd say."

"Well then get in here and help me finish rolling out this dough while you tell me more."

So, Velma explained about Freddie. She didn't go into the issue of Mr. Warren and Miss Fletcher, however, since she had similar feelings about her mother and Mr. Price.

When finished, Alice asked, "I can see why that would make her sad, but why angry?"

Velma wasn't prepared for the question, so fumbled around for an answer settling on, "She's still angry about all this coming because her mother died. You know, she thinks it isn't fair."

"Not much in life is fair. She'll just have to get over it," Alice said without emotion. "Her father will see to that. Speaking of Mr. Warren, didn't you see him and Katie last night when you dropped off the basket?"

"Just Mr. Warren, Katie was already in bed," Velma said, hoping her mother would move on to a safer subject. She didn't.

"How was he?"

"Tired and upset like Katie."

After a beat, Mrs. Steele asked, "You saw Miss Fletcher last night and today. How was she?"

"Well, she was exhausted last night too but back to her old self as school, more or less."

Something in Velma's response or tone had Alice asking, as she slipped another tray of rolls into the oven, "More or less. What does that mean?"

"Oh, nothing." Velma sensed her weak response had not put the topic to rest, so she quickly and mistakenly added, "Honest."

"Honest, you say?" Her daughter nodded vigorously, while returning to the dough she was now kneading with a vengeance. Alice began to ask something else, but instead settled for, "Well, let's get the rest of these in the oven so you can relieve your sister with the boys."

"Yes, Mama," Velma said, attacking the dough, glad to let the subject drop.

Over the course of the evening, during dinner, finishing evening chores, and doing homework, Velma had a hard time concentrating. Her mind kept going over her conversation with Katie, especially the part about her father and Miss Fletcher.

The little girl was conflicted by what she felt about the situation. Katie was like another sister, in many ways closer than Wilma. Velma recalled how important Katie had been to her from the first time they met. The time they had spent together since Agnes Warren died had cemented their relationship.

On the other hand, Miss Fletcher had become as important to Velma in her own way. She was a wonderful, kind, and generous person who made learning a joy. In many ways, she reminded Velma of Katie's mother, always helpful and welcoming to everyone.

Then there was Mr. Warren. She didn't know him very well, but thought him a good man, though terribly sad since the tragic loss of his wife. Then his children both had breakdowns, plunging him deeper into despair. Thankfully, at least Katie had come out of hers. Freddie seemed to be continuing to head in the wrong direction.

With sleep eluding her, Velma suddenly recalled it was the time of the pageant when Mr. Warren began to recover with Miss Fletcher's help. Thanks to that breakthrough, a good man was now helping Velma's mother combat John Steele's effort to take her children. Unfortunately, Mr. Warren's emergence from his malaise had triggered Katie's regression.

Velma could not deny that Katie's father and Miss Fletcher seemed good for each other. They worked well together on the pageant, enjoyed being together, and supported each other in emergent and emotional times. But Katie still clung to the memory of her mother. There was no room in her heart or reason in her head to let Miss Fletcher in, at least anytime soon.

The situation created a dilemma for the not-yet-eight-year-old, mature beyond her years. She didn't want to take sides or upset two of the most important people in her life. She finally decided that short of a brilliant idea, the solution to this problem would only come with the passage of time.

The same could be said for the other matter filling her head. The image of Mr. Price and Mama sitting at the Hanks' kitchen table reminded her that she didn't like that budding relationship either. Velma saw even less of a chance of influencing that, however, given her mother's powerful nature and stern will.

A very sleepy Velma hurried off to school the next day, worried whether she would find Katie had fulfilled her promise.

She rushed in the schoolhouse and was relieved to see Katie placing her coat, hat, and scarf in her cubby. "Oh, I'm so glad to see you're here."

"I said I would be," Katie snipped, her displeasure apparent on her face.

Velma gave her friend a hug, saying, "Of course. I was just, just excited to see you. Maybe things can get back to normal."

"What's that?" Katie asked rhetorically.

"Well, getting ready for Christmas for one," Velma replied. "I'll fill you in on what Miss Fletcher told us yesterday, about the holiday program she's planning."

Katie shrugged. "You don't need to do that. I'll catch up. It was only one day. Now hurry it up. It's cold out here."

"Right," Velma said, quickly putting her things in the space next to her friend. They headed for class where, thankfully, there seemed to be a truce between Katie and Miss Fletcher, at least temporarily. By the end of the day, everyone was immersed in lessons, as well as excited about the program they would present to their family and the townsfolk. The challenge was trying to top the success of the fall pageant.

While Velma was totally engaged in the planning, Katie remained on the fringe initially. Slowly, however, she got caught up in the activity, showing signs of her old self. What didn't change was the coolness between Katie and Miss Fletcher.

Christmas came in a rush. The holiday program at the school, though well done, didn't seem to inspire the audience like the fall pageant had. The children didn't notice the subdued reaction, however, being too excited by thoughts of presents under the tree.

The adults were feeling a growing concern for the local economy. Farm foreclosures, though down from a few years earlier, still continued at an alarming rate. This had a ripple effect on the surrounding communities. Woodward was no exception. Almost every week one or more families was coming or going. Most who came had no work, only family or friends to give them shelter.

Conversation at the table during the annual Christmas Eve dinner at the Jones' home, was filled with worry. Everyone was feeling the impact. Sales were off at the mercantile, including Alice's baking trade as well as her laundry and sewing business. She had taken on several extra housekeeping jobs as a result.

"We've lost a few customers too," Carl Warren said. "That's a sure sign of a deepening downturn."

While the smaller children occupied themselves with cookies, candy, and games, Velma and Wilma listened to the conversation with growing interest. Being working girls at such a young age, the Steele sisters had watched their mother's business shrinking at a time of year when it should have been robust.

Charity soon joined them to see what their friends were so interested in hearing. Katie hung back, however, since Miss Fletcher had been invited to attend the celebration against her wishes. Soon curiosity overtook her, and she joined the others as her father continued, "Now there's the closing of the mines."

"How many have closed?" Henry asked.

"I'm not sure," Carl replied. "The largest was at Buxton, and I know there were some along the chain of mines all the way up to Boone. Some of the mines remain open on a reduced schedule."

"So, there were layoffs there too?" Grace Jones said with a tremor in her voice.

"Yes," was Carl's terse response.

Katie turned and whispered to Velma, "I wonder if Daniel is one of them."

Before Velma could reply, her mother asked, "Is that why we've seen some strangers in town?"

"You mean from the farms or the mines?"

"I mean those colored folks I've been seeing around town."

Her mother's words startled Velma. She hadn't paid any attention to any strangers in town, negro or white. A black man had worked the last harvest at the farm before her father died. He'd made the girls laugh and entertained them playing his harmonica. It was at that time Velma first heard Alice use the term "colored."

There was no malice in her mother's use of the word. In fact, Velma recalled the man receiving high praise from her parents for his hard work. "He weren't lazy like some of the white boys" was an expression her mother had used more than once at the time.

Emily Fletcher's response brought Velma's attention back to the present conversation. "Yes. There are at least two negro families moving here from Buxton after the New Year. Several children will be joining our school."

"And what will they be doing?" Alice asked, her tone cool.

"I'm not sure," Emily responded, "but they seemed fine folk ready to join our community."

"Well, my experience has been they are a hard-working lot. William and I were always glad to see them among our harvesting crew. But what is there for them, heck, for anyone new to do around here these days?" Alice asked skeptically. "There ain't, I mean aren't any mines around here."

Tessa echoed Alice's concern. "I agree. This is not exactly a thriving metropolis right now."

"I don't know of many other negroes around here either," Emily added.

"There's Able Cotton," Reverend Jones pointed out, referring to the only black member of his congregation and the custodian for the church. "You wouldn't know him, Miss Fletcher, being Presbyterian and all."

Grace added, "He's widowed. Like Tessa and Henry here, his children moved away."

"I think one of the families coming has the name Cotton," Emily said with some enthusiasm. "That would be a good thing, right?"

"Well, at least it would mean the family would have a roof over their heads," Carl Warren answered.

"Whatever the case, we'll have to do our part to make them welcome," Alan stated flatly.

Emily gave him a surprised look. "Should that be a problem?"

"Well, for most Iowans, it won't be, but there is still prejudice around."

"True." Henry said with a frown. "We still got a few veterans of that war still kicking. Some still seeing coloreds as slaves."

Velma was confused by Mr. Hanks' comment for a moment. Then she realized the reference was to the Civil War, something they had been recently studying in class. It was a bit shocking to her that there were still people around who thought colored people were slaves.

"Or at least second-class citizens," Tessa added.

"I though most of those folks still lived in the south," Alice said.

"Lot of moving around since 1865. We have a real mix of people in Woodward these days," Carl offered. "Besides, it's human nature to be wary of strangers, no matter the color of their skin."

"Especially because of their skin color," Tessa said then added, "You tend to stand out in a crowd, at least initially."

"True," said Alice, "but my concern ain't about the coloreds' skin color. It's what they are going to find for work."

"And if the work they find is at the expense of someone already here, well..." Henry left his conclusion unstated.

After an interlude of silence, Reverend Jones suggested, "We need to make sure that these new members of the community, any new members of the community, are welcomed and we do our part to keep the peace. Agreed?"

"Agreed," everyone at the table said in unison.

Then Alice turned to the older children arrayed around the edge of the table. "You hear that girls?" They all nodded. "That means you too."

"That's right," Emily added to that thought. "Come January, you can set an example for the other students in the way we treat the new arrivals who will be different from us."

Grace picked up on the theme, "And by welcoming your new classmates, you will surely help others in the community to embrace them as well."

"From your lips to God's ears, dear," Reverend Jones said, bringing the discussion to a somber close.

The approach of New Year's 1924 carried with it much of the same feeling that had marked previous New Years. Though not filled with the same anxiety, fear, and ultimate sorrow surrounding the illness and death of Agnes Warren, it dawned with an air of foreboding, nonetheless.

Two days after Christmas, many in the town observed the arrival of the two negro families. Able Cotton, having borrowed old Nelly from the local farm and the Steeles' old wagon, accompanied his son and daughter-in-law through Woodward to his small home. This new family of five would surely fill the space to the breaking point.

Then an older black couple, Melva and Otis Johnson, arrived late that same day. They moved into a space above the Delmonico restaurant. Mr. Johnson had apparently gotten a position at the nearby sanitorium, while his wife immediately began to look for housekeeping jobs. Alice saw this as a threat, having just taken on more of this work to supplement dwindling sales of her baked goods.

Early on a Monday in late January, there was a knock at the Hanks' kitchen door where Alice stood alone up to her elbows in flour. With her arms held high, she walked to the door, peering out to see a black woman shivering in the cold. With an unhappy snort, Alice threw open the door, depositing flour on the knob and floor.

She stepped back, saying harshly, "Now look what you've gone and made me do."

This froze the woman in the doorway. With a jerk of her head toward the inside, Alice barked, "Well, no real damage is done. Get in here before we both catch our death."

"Thank ya ma'am," the woman said, quickly entering and shutting the door firmly, generating a cloud of flour in the process.

Alice frowned at the mess. "As you can see, I'm a little busy at the moment. So, I'd be obliged if you'd state your business. You here to see the Hanks? 'Cause if that's the case, you came to the wrong door. They're both up front."

"No, ma'am," the black woman said shyly, "My name is Melva Johnson."

"Yes, I kind of figured that," Alice replied curtly. "I've seen you around town looking for work. Have you found any?" There was a touch of smugness in the question.

Melva shook her head but wore a gentle smile, "No. Seems there's a popular woman in town who got the house cleanin' business pretty well sewed up, at least what there is of it."

Alice smiled back a bit sheepishly saying, "Well, I got a head start on you. And you got that right about not being many customers in this economy."

"Well, it's been my experience that head starts don't mean much if you can't finish. But it's clear you got them folks' loyalty."

"Thanks be to God for that," Alice replied, moving to the sink and ringing out a cloth to clean up the trail of flour across the floor.

"Let me get that, ma'am," Melva said, extending her hand, "since I be the one that caused that."

After hesitating briefly, Alice said, "Oh, you needn't bother."

"No bother, ma'am. I's got plenty of time on my hands."

Unable to contain a smile at hearing that, Alice handed over the cloth. "Much obliged, Mrs. Johnson."

"Oh, please call me Mel," the woman replied, dropping to her knees and beginning to mop. "Besides, it's good to be doin' somethin'."

Alice went back to her pie making as she asked, "Was housekeeping your work in Buxton?"

"Well, sorta," Melva replied while concentrating on the floor. "I worked for one of the mine owners up until the mine closed. Couldn't find another job there and what with Otis losin' his place at the mine's infirmary, well, we had to move. Didn't want to, but..." She let the obvious conclusion drop.

"I know all about that sort of thing," Alice replied sympathetically.

"Oh?" Melva replied inquisitively.

Alice explained briefly. "I lost my husband unexpectedly three years ago and had to leave our farm and move here. It weren't, I mean wasn't easy."

"Children?"

"Four."

"Gracious me!" Melva said, resting back on her knees. "How old?"

"Then or now?"

Melva thought for a moment, "Then."

"Seven, five, two and a half, and four months."

"Gracious me."

This brought a laugh from Alice, "You're repeating yourself."

Melva struggled to her feet, checking to see if she'd completed the task. Then she observed, "I was feelin' sorry for myself when I came here this mornin'. But after hearin' that, well, I guess me and Otis don't have it so bad."

"My late husband, William, used to say no matter how good or bad you have it, someone else's story can always top your own." She chuckled. "Come to think of it, Henry Hanks often says the same thing. Now give me that rag," Alice said, then asked, "Coffee? We always have a pot on the stove."

"Well, if it's not a bother."

"It won't be if you get it yourself."

Melva chuckled, "Glad to. How about you? I see your cup is near empty."

"Thank you. Cups are in the cupboard on the right of the stove."

Once she had completed the task, Melva found a seat at the table facing Alice and took a sip while gripping the warm mug. "I don't know which I'm enjoyin' more, the taste of the coffee or the warmth of the cup."

"Being in this hot kitchen baking most of the day, I don't notice the cold," Alice said, putting a pie in the oven and taking a tray of cookies out. "It will be quite a shock going out in it a bit later."

Melva nodded. "I can't remember it bein' this cold in Buxton. I guess movin' up north here made a big difference."

"Up north?" Alice cackled, "What are we, maybe 70 miles north?"

Melva smiled broadly, "About that. I was just funnin' ya."

"I figured," Alice replied as she transferred the cookies to the cooling rack. As her smile faded, she asked, "So, what about your family?"

The expression that crossed the black woman's face had Alice regretting her question. So she quickly added, "That's really none of my business, Mrs. Johnson."

"Mel, remember?"

"Alright, but only if you call me Alice."

"Agreed." This exchange eased the tension of the moment. Then Melva answered the question in a few short words. "Our two children died of the flu in nineteen. Too late for me to have more."

Alice was stunned. After a long silence she said softly, "You just proved that old saying. I am so sorry."

"Thank you, ma'am, Alice," Melva whispered back. Then the two fell silent again, the thump, thump, thump of Alice's kneading the only sound.

It was Alice who broke the spell by asking, "So, what brought you here this morning?"

"I just thought we ought to meet and..." she paused, "and so I could let you know I'm not tryin' to take your livelihood away."

"I appreciate hearing that, but you can't promise that what with needing work yourself. Why, just last week I lost a laundry client because they closed the restaurant. A steady customer too."

Melva frowned. "I'm sorry to hear that for a lot of reasons. You see, I was also hopin' to pick your brain about where to find work."

"Am I right that Mr. Johnson had work?"

"Yes, but he isn't makin' near as much up at the center north of town."

"What's he doing there?"

"He's just an aide," Melva explained, a touch of anger in her voice. "He ran the infirmary at the mine you see. I only took on work in Buxton to keep from goin' crazy as his pay was good. Now…" She trailed off, drowning the truth in another sip of coffee.

Alice pondered what she'd heard as she began rolling out another piecrust. "So, I can surely see why you need work."

"We have a little savings, but that won't last long." Melva replied. "Otis is a proud man who'd gotten used to takin' care a me. So, he's not keen on me havin' to go back to work."

"Not facing reality, right?"

"Stubborn as a mule." The two women laughed at this.

"Never had that problem with my William. Working the farm was more than we could both handle some days. He'd have been happy to have several wives working full time if it were legal." Both women laughed heartily again.

As their laughter faded, Alice said, "Well, this conversation isn't leading to any help for you."

"But I'm surely enjoyin' it, Alice," Melva replied.

Just then the curtain leading to the mercantile parted, and Tessa Hanks came in with the nearly two-year-old Lizzy Anderson on her hip. "Whoa. I swear this child's putting on a pound a month these..." She stopped, seeing Melva sitting at the kitchen table. "Oh, sorry. Am I interrupting something here?"

"Oh, no, ma'am," Mrs. Johnson said, leaping to her feet.

Alice waved her back down with a floured hand, "Sit, Mel. No need to worry about this one. I guess you two haven't met yet."

"No. I haven't had the pleasure," Tessa said while unceremoniously dumping the toddler in the black woman's arms. "Here."

The surprised look on Melva's face quickly dissolved into a grateful smile, "Oh, what a lovely child."

"Try holding her for a while and see if you think that," then adding, as she awkwardly found Melva's free hand, "I'm Tessa Hanks, owner of half this place. My husband Henry owns the other half. And who might you be?"

"I'm Mrs. Johnson, Melva Johnson," the woman replied, struggling to get Lizzy better situated. "My husband and I..."

Tessa interrupted, "Just moved to town. I know. Well, welcome to the not so bustling village of Woodward."

"That's what we were just talking about," said Alice, joining the conversation. "Mel here is in need of work but..."

Tessa interrupted again, "There isn't any to find, right?"

Mrs. Johnson nodded forlornly. "I'd settle for shoveling snow if we had any."

"I don't know which I like less, bitter cold or knee-deep snow," Tessa said, heading for the coffee pot. "Anyway, you can always come here to bemoan not having work. The pot's always on."

"Alice told me that. About the pot always bein' on, not that I could come by anytime."

"Well, you can," Tessa said, joining her at the table, cup in hand. "Just be prepared to mind a child or two."

Alice felt the need to explain. "My youngest is upstairs napping, I hope. That's Edward. His brother, Eugene, is supposed to be watching him if he isn't sleeping too."

"It must be hard to manage your work and the boys at the same time," Mel suggested.

"Well, I get help from Tessa and Annie Anderson who clerks here," Alice replied.

Tessa glanced at the kitchen clock as she added, "For a while longer that is. Annie's well along on her way to number two. I expect she'll be in here momentarily. Can't stay on her feet very long these days. Lovely young thing. Remember when we were young like that, Alice?"

"Vaguely," Alice retorted, "Now hush up and help this nice colored lady find work."

Tessa frowned at Mel while asking, "You aren't having trouble finding something because of that?"

"Being colored?" Seeing Tess nod, Mel shook her head. "No. I don't think so. We ain't been here but a few days, but everyone's been welcomin'."

"Iowans are that way," Mrs. Hanks stated proudly. "Real accepting."

Alice modified the praise. "Well, except for those German folks that just arrived."

"Because of the war and all," Tessa said in agreement.

"Don't help that they hardly speak any English," Alice pointed out.

"What brought them here?" Mel asked.

Tessa shrugged, "I suppose the same reason that brought you, the possibility of work."

"At the expense of some of the local farmers," Alice said resentfully. "I hear they managed to buy a piece a land out west of town, God only knows how."

"The old Tomlin place, I think," Tessa added. "They seem nice enough. Don't cause any problems."

"Except for pushing one of our neighbors off the land." Alice's voice carried even more displeasure.

Tessa stopped Alice's complaining quickly when she said, "It was foreclosure, not those Germans, that threw the Tomlins off that land. If you want to be mad at someone, take it out on Carl Warren's bank."

While Alice sulked back to her baking, Tessa turned back to Mel, asking, "Now what skills do you have Mrs. Johnson?"

"Please call me Mel," she requested with a broad smile.

"Okay, Mel. Tell us what you can do."

"Well, I spent a lot of years being a maid or housekeeper for folk in Buxton. So, I's can cook, clean, do laundry, and mend."

"In other words, everything I can do." Alice sounded defensive. "I suppose you can bake up a storm too."

"Well, I don't do bad," Mel said. Seeming to recognize she was in dangerous territory, Melva quickly added, "But I've already heard you're the best in town."

"In the state," Tessa said with enthusiasm. "Why, she's even managed to make me a decent baker."

"Well, without baking, my family would likely be starving." Alice said flatly.

Melva quickly tried to ease Alice's mind. "I can't compete with the best, so you have no worries there. Maybe if you get real busy and need some help..."

Alice didn't let her finish, "Not likely, Mel, but thanks for the offer."

"Say," Tessa said suddenly, "That reminds me, have you ever done any store selling?"

Melva frowned as she replied, "No, ma'am. Afraid not, but I'm a quick learner. Why do you ask?"

"Well, Annie's going to be off soon, at least a few weeks with the baby due in January. Plus we'll be doing inventory, part of which Annie couldn't handle because of the exertion. So, we'll likely need someone at least part time. It won't be a lot of hours or pay much, but..."

"I'll take it," Melva cried.

Tessa held up a hand, "Hold on a minute. I'll have to talk to Henry about this, and you should probably spend a little time in the store to see how it goes."

"Of course," Melva said, "I apologize if I'm rushing you. I just really need the work."

"Understood. I'll talk to Henry when he gets back from wherever he's off to. Can never keep track of the man," Tessa concluded with a smile.

Alice brought over the coffee pot, pouring them all a refill. "Well, that's a start," she said, joining the others.

"You're sitting down?" Tessa said with humor. "This woman hardly ever sits down," she added to Melva, "just to eat and sleep, but then sleeping doesn't count as sitting does it?"

Alice went on ignoring Tessa's teasing, "Tell me more about your mending skills."

"Well, I make all my own clothes as well as for my husband."

"Hum," Alice mumbled as she thought for a moment. "Well, right now I've got a reasonably good dress-making business but often get request to mend things. I can only take on so much and limit it to simple things that my daughters, Wilma and Velma can do. At their ages, that isn't much, especially with only one machine."

"But I have my own!" Melva blurted out. "The last family I worked for gave it to me as a parting gift. It's old but works fine."

Alice replied warily, "Well, that's good to know. But as I was saying, I've been turning down some of this type of work because it was too complicated for the girls and would require a machine. So, let me give that some consideration. Why don't you come back tomorrow afternoon late and we'll see what you can do?"

"Wonderful," Melva said with glee. "Should I bring the machine?"

Alice shook her head, "Let's not get ahead of ourselves. You can show me what you can do on my machine."

"I'll warn you, she's a hard taskmaster, Mel," Tessa said, only half teasing.

"That's fine. I'm the same way."

Tessa stood and reached for the baby, noticing for the first time that Lizzy was sound asleep. "Looks like you could put nanny on your list of skills as well."

"That might have been a good option if times were better," Alice said, wearing a regretful expression.

"Can't hurt to check around," Melva said. "Thanks for the idea."

As Tessa headed through the curtain, she said, "By the time you come tomorrow, I'll have talked to Henry and can give you a firmer answer."

"Thank you, thank you, both," Melva said, choking up with emotion. "You have been so kind and welcoming."

"We got to be in these times, Mel," Alice pointed out. "It doesn't look like things are going to get any easier soon."

15
Turn Again

On the last Sunday of 1923, Able Cotton and his newly arrived family stood beside Reverend Jones in front of a congregation that included Emily Fletcher for the first time. She had already been presented as a guest by Alice, who referred to her as "the fine teacher of my Velma."

Now it was time for the main event as the pastor began, "I am delighted to welcome a new family into our church community. Able Cotton here should be no stranger to any of us. He's been the heart and soul of this church for years."

Able dropped his head in embarrassment and whispered, "Ah, reverend."

Ignoring the weak protest, Alan continued in a more serious tone, "In these hard and unpredictable times, there is nothing more important in our lives than God and family. In his house today, we are in the presence of all three—God, the Cottons, and the extended family: this church."

This produced an amen or two along with polite applause before the pastor turned to Able. "Will you do the introductions?"

With an uncomfortable nod, Able cleared his throat and began, "This here is my oldest boy, Isaiah." He turned to Reverend Jones. "After the prophet."

"I kind a figured that out, Able," Alan said with a grin.

Mr. Cotton smiled sheepishly then quickly turned back and went on. "Next to him is his lovely wife, Caroline Mae. Then we have my oldest grandson. I'm proud to say his name is Able too. He's eight and already nearly as tall as me. Lily is next; she's five."

"Six, Grandpa," the little girl interrupted in an exasperated tone.

"Oh, that's right. You just turned six."

Lily shook her head. "I've been six for a long time now. Since October."

Able gave the congregation a shrug. "A little strong-willed wouldn't you say?"

This brought peals of laughter throughout the room. Once it died down, Able reached down and picked up his last grandchild. "This be Amelia, Amy for short. She's named after my late wife and is three." He turned to Lily. "That's right, isn't it?" This got a firm nod in reply and generated more laughter. "And that's all us Cottons."

Then Reverend Jones took the floor again, "Let's give them all a welcoming round of applause." This lasted for quite some time.

"Please join them in the fellowship hall after the closing prayer and get to know them. Now, let us pray."

After the benediction, everyone headed to the basement where tables overflowed with leftover Christmas treats. As the

Steele family had done years earlier, the Cottons stood next to the pastor as everyone passed by to meet and greet.

When it was their turn, Alice approached tentatively holding each of the boy's hands, "Hello Mr. and Mrs. Cotton. We're the Steeles." She quickly introduced the children, gave the Cottons a guarded, "welcome," then tried to move on so the others in line could have a turn, but her children didn't move.

While Edward and Eugene hovered around little Amelia hiding behind her mother's skirt, Velma boldly approach young Able. "I'm in the third grade. What about you?"

"Don't know," was the boy's blunt reply. Velma sensed he wasn't being rude. His expression was more one of embarrassment.

His mother put an arm on his shoulder while addressing Velma, "Miss Fletcher says he'll likely be in your grade. We had no school last year, you see. The teacher moved away and no one new came. I've been trying to teach him ever since."

"Why not?"

"Come along, child," Alice said from a few feet away. "Other folk are waiting."

"Okay, Mama," Velma replied but hesitated another moment. "See you in class tomorrow then." The only reply she got was a timid nod.

After grabbing a cookie, Velma found Katie standing with Nancy and Charity. "What do you think of the Cottons?"

"Can't say one way or the other," Nancy said. "The only colored person I've talked to before was old Mr. Cotton and that was no more than a hello. I do like his smile, though, and his son's is just like it."

"They look sad to me," Charity said.

"Frightened to me," Katie suggested.

Glancing back over to the family, she could see all of what her friends were saying written on their faces, all except the elder Mr. Cotton. This brought back memories. She turned back, saying, "I can understand why. I felt the same way when I was standing up there years back."

"Well, at least you looked like the rest of us." Katie replied without humor.

Somewhat sheepishly, Nancy Brown pointed out that, "They don't have to put up with people bad-mouthing them like, well, like my folks did to you all."

"I wouldn't be so sure about that." This comment from Charity had the others looking for an explanation. "I just heard my parents talking last night, kind of mysterious-like, that there were more than a few in town that weren't pleased to see the Cottons arrive."

"'Cause they're colored?" Katie prodded.

Charity shrugged. "I'm not sure, maybe. My father said some were worried about there being enough work to go around. And..." She hesitated.

"And what?" Velma urged Charity to finish.

"And that more coloreds might be coming just adding to the surplus of workers."

"Your father specifically mentioned, what was it, Boxtown?" Velma asked curiously.

"It's Buxton," Charity corrected, then explained, "That was a company town, a good-ways from here, where most of the miners were negroes."

"Oh, I see."

Nancy changed the subject. "That Able boy sure is big for his age. You think he's in your grade?"

"I asked, but he didn't know," Velma offered. "Seemed that town didn't have school 'cause the teacher moved away. His mother's been teaching him though."

"Well, Miss Fletcher will sort all that out I'm sure," Nancy proclaimed.

A disturbance across the room drew the group's attention. They saw six-year-old Lily give Eugene a hearty shove, sending him to the floor. Then the little girl stood over him with fire in her eyes yelling something unintelligible. Eugene began to cry.

Alice rushed over and there was an exchange, first between mothers and their children, then between the women. Alice and Caroline Mae talked softly, while Eugene continued to whimper, and Lily scowled. After another minute, the mothers parted with their children in tow and mortified looks on their faces.

In neutral corners, each had a whispered conversation with the combatants. This scolding generated more tears from the boy and a recalcitrant look from the girl. Then it was over. Caroline Mae returned to her husband's side with a firm grip on Lily. Alice took Eugene to the nursery room and left him with the attendant before joining the Hanks, Carl, and Emily Fletcher.

Velma watched as her mother spoke rapidly to her friends. When she'd finished, the group began to smile and snicker. At first Alice gave them one of her famous stares, but soon relented and also broke into a grin.

Most in the room had hardly noticed the fuss, but it captivated the circle of girls across the room. "I'm going to go find out what all that was about," the always curious Velma said. "Anyone coming with me?"

"I think I'll get some punch," Charity said.

Nancy thought that was a good idea while Katie hesitated. "What about you?" Velma asked, beginning to drift toward the adults.

"No thanks," was Katie's cool reply. "I think I'll head home."

Velma was surprised at this response until she glanced across the room and saw Katie's father whispering into Miss Fletcher's ear. The teacher was obviously both amused by his comment and comfortable with the proximity of the delivery. "Oh, I see," Velma said, taking her friend's arm. "I'll see if I can go with you, okay?"

With Katie's nod of approval, Velma headed to her mother's side. "Mama, may I go over to Katie's for a while before Sunday dinner?"

"She wants to go home?" Carl asked in surprise. "Why didn't she come to ask?"

"I don't really know, sir," Velma replied, looking over at Katie and feeling caught in the middle. "You want me to go get her?"

Carl looked to Emily, then shook his head. "No, I guess that's not really necessary."

"And what exactly will you be doing?" Alice asked warily.

Velma knew she couldn't share the real reason, so she thought quickly, "Well, it's the last day before school starts, and she wants to, ah, to study some. I could use the work too. It has been over two weeks since school got out, you see."

"That is impressive," Emily Fletcher said with admiration in her voice.

Carl Warren didn't look convinced. "We won't be here that much longer," he started, then looked to Emily, "but I guess that's a pretty good reason." He turned to Alice. "What do you say?"

"Well, if it's okay with Mr. Warren, it's okay with me. And if you promise not to get your Sunday best dirty, you can wear it over there, but be home no later than noon."

"Mama," Velma protested.

After a pause, Alice relented just a bit, "Okay, one o'clock."

"Thank you, Mama," the girl said, turning to dash back to her friend.

"Wait," Carl Warren said sharply. When Velma stopped, he went on, "Send Katie to come over. I forgot to tell her something."

"Okay."

A moment later, Katie and Velma arrived together in front of the group. "Yes, Daddy," Katie said, looking directly at him while ignoring her teacher.

"I forgot to tell you that Miss Fletcher will be joining us for Sunday supper." Carl's look and voice broached no argument.

The look on Katie's face delivered her hostility to this news without the necessity of words. "Come on, Velma."

"Ouch," Velma croaked reflexively as Katie grabbed her arm hard and pulled her toward the exit. At the top of the stairs, she broke free and said, "hey, you're hurting me."

Katie said nothing, just grabbed her belongings from the narthex and headed out the large double doors without waiting. Velma considered staying behind, but only for a moment. By the time she got her own things on and headed after her friend, Katie was moving at a run, nearly a block away, her coat flapping wide open.

Running against the cold seemed a good idea to Velma. By the time the two girls reached the Warren home, Katie had slowed to a brisk walk, allowing Velma to catch up. When she did, her friend was sobbing between gulps for air.

Once inside the chilly house, Katie flung her coat, hat, and scarf on the floor and headed to the kitchen. Velma struggled to get her hands to work on coat buttons as she yelled, "Are you trying to catch your death?"

"Maybe," came the terse response. "A lot Daddy would care. He could be with Miss Fletcher, and I'd be with Mother."

By this time, Velma had hung their collective belongings on the coat rack near the front door and was scurrying down the hall, trying to think of an appropriate response. Entering the room, she saw Katie, head down on the kitchen table, sobbing even more intensely than before, if that were possible.

"Oh, Katie," was all Velma could manage as she sat down, draping an arm around her shoulders.

They remained this way for what seemed like forever to Velma until Katie seemed to be cried out. Then her tone turned from sadness to anger. "I hate them both."

"Oh, you don't mean that," Velma protested.

"The hell I don't," Katie fired back, stunning her friend with the use of such language, especially on the Sabbath.

"Katie, don't talk like that. It's Sunday. We just came from church," Velma said, taking her arm from around Katie.

This had her friend looking up ruefully. "Sorry, Velma. About the language, not the rest."

"I still don't believe you mean that," Velma persisted, as she moved to the other side of the table and faced her friend. "I know this has to be a real hard time for you what with it being just a year ago when your mother got sick," Her words took away Katie's anger, replacing it with yet more tears. "Sorry, Katie."

"That's alright." Katie's mumbled response was lost in her sobs.

"No, it wasn't," Velma replied, "but I believe what I said." She waited for a further response but got none. "Anyway, I'm just saying you don't know what *you're* saying."

Katie lifted her head from the table, her face wracked with pain. "Maybe I don't, but I know what I feel. I feel alone and abandoned."

"You have me."

"But not my Daddy or brother, or," she paused, choking back yet more tears, then added, "my mother." These last words came out as an anguished wail.

Velma dropped to a chair without responding. It was several more minutes before either girl spoke. "Do you want me to leave?" Velma finally asked.

Katie's head shot up. "Oh, no. Please stay. I promise to stop crying."

"And saying stupid things?" Velma asked, daring to smile.

Though Katie didn't laugh, she didn't lash out either. "I promise. Let's get something to nibble and head into the living room." Rising to see what could be found, she added, "Daddy set up logs for a fire this morning. We can start it and get warmer."

"That would be good," Velma said, noticing for the first time how cold she still was even inside the house. "I hope the whole winter isn't this bad."

Katie opened the icebox, paused, then shut the door. "Looks like what's in there is for Sunday supper with *Miss Fletcher*." Some of the anger was back.

"That's all right. I had plenty of goodies at church. Didn't you?"

Katie shrugged. "I suppose so. You want a glass of milk?

"Sure."

A short time later, the girls were settled in front of a roaring fire, snug under a shared throw. Katie's tears and anger had been replaced with melancholy and silence. Not wanting to risk reopening the floodgates or reigniting the rage, Velma said nothing for a long time. When she did speak, it was about another topic.

"What do you make of the Cotton children?"

Katie was startled by the sudden break in the silence. "Oh, what?"

"The Cotton family. What do you think of them?"

After some thought, Katie said, "Well, that Lily is a handful. Whoever gets her in class will have trouble with her."

"For sure." Velma tossed off her portion of the throw. "Whew. That fire's got me hot already. Anyway, the boy, little Able sure was quiet just like his father."

"Really?" Katie said absently. "I didn't notice."

"Yup," Velma reaffirmed. "I don't think I saw Isaiah Cotton talking to anyone for very long. As for his wife, what was her name?"

"Ah, Caroline something, I think," Katie offered.

"Right. Caroline Mae," Velma said cheerfully. "Anyway, she sure liked to talk and had a great smile. I liked her a lot."

"Ah-huh." Katie was only half listening. "I didn't notice."

"You were too busy watching Miss Fletcher with your father." Velma immediately regretted her words when she saw Katie's evil look.

"That's not true!" Katie practically screamed, giving her friend a not-so-gentle shove. "You take that back!"

Velma started to do just that, then stopped. She was suddenly angry. "No, I won't. That was exactly what you were doing and why you ran out of church like the devil was on your tail."

"Maybe you should just go home," Katie fired back as she stood abruptly.

Velma didn't move. "No. I don't think so."

"This is my house," Katie said, reaching down and yanking Velma onto her feet.

Jerking free, Velma flopped back down on the sofa. "I think I'll wait for your father to see what he has to say."

"You will not."

"Will too."

"Will not."

Just then the front door opened, "Hey, hey, what's going on, girls?" came the concerned voice of Carl Warren. Still in his topcoat, he and Emily Fletcher appeared at the entrance of the living room. Suddenly the only sound was the crackling of the fire.

Velma jumped to her feet now eager to leave. "Oh, I was just going, Mr. Warren."

She had no chance to move, however, as Katie's father spoke sharply. "Stay put, Miss Steele." As far as she could recall, Velma had never heard him refer to her as *Miss Steele*.

"Yes, sir," she said, abruptly sitting back down.

Turning to Katie, Mr. Warren asked. "Now what's this all about?"

Before his daughter could respond, Emily interjected, "I should go, Carl."

"No," Mr. Warren said in a softer tone. "I have an idea what this is all about, and, if I'm right, it involves you. So, please stay. This needs to be brought out in the open once and for all." He then waved Miss Fletcher to a nearby chair.

As she reluctantly took the proffered seat, Carl turned back to Katie saying, "Now, why were you and Velma yelling at each other?"

She said nothing, so her father continued, "Alright, let me guess. You two were fighting over something to do with Miss Fletcher and me. Am I close?" Though Katie's expression revealed nothing, Velma's spoke volumes. "Seems I should be asking Velma. Shall I?"

"No," Katie replied sharply. Once started, she could not stop or measure her words. "I don't like it that you and my teacher are going around making eyes at each other." She paused long enough to take a ragged breath and glare in Miss Fletcher's direction.

"Mother is barely in the ground, and you two are making fools of yourself and embarrassing me. Between her and Freddie, you have no time for me. I'm still hurting, but as far as you know or care, I might as well be buried too. I hate her, I hate you."

"Now listen here, young lady," Carl barked.

Emily interrupted him before he could continue. "Don't be too harsh on her."

It was Katie's turn to interrupt. "I don't want or need you to defend me."

"Very well," Emily said softly, then added, "but I wanted to share that I think much of what you say is right and to apologize."

"Like that will change anything."

"Right again." Emily's voice remained calm. "But I needed to say it, just like you need to get your feelings and the anger out."

This seemed to take the air out of Katie who, when more words wouldn't come, fell back on tears. Velma watched Miss Fletcher start to rise, seeming intent on comforting the girl. Instead, Carl put a hand out to stop her and went himself.

Putting his arm around her shoulder, he spoke gently, "I understand too, Katie. This thing, my feelings for Miss Fletcher were not expected, planned, or intended to hurt you. In fact, the two of us have worked hard not to let this happen."

Velma, of course, knew what he said was true, based on what she'd overheard a few months earlier. Clearly those efforts to avoid the obvious and deep attraction had failed, however. Now she watched three of the most important people in her life struggle with that reality. It was heartbreaking in the moment.

"This is not the way I had envisioned today going," Carl said, then sighed deeply. "but it is the hand I've been dealt. So, here goes."

"I think I should go now," Velma said, but didn't stand.

"Me too," Emily echoed the suggestion.

"No," Carl said, firmly but without rancor. "I think it will be good for us all to work through this together, best friends included. That way, Katie will have someone to talk with going forward."

Velma was not sure how true that was, but she didn't challenge Mr. Warren's logic. Instead, she just nodded and waited for Miss Fletcher to mount an argument. None came. Though it appeared for a moment that Katie might make a break for it, in the end, she stayed put.

"Good," Carl Warren said, then fell silent, seeming to search for a place to start. Having made a decision, he began, "First, let me say that Miss Fletcher has no blame in this."

"That's not true, Carl," Emily protested, "I don't want Katie to think otherwise."

"I don't agree," Carl said over his shoulder, then addressed Katie again, "You need to know that I pressed the issue, but Emily would have none of it."

"Yeah, I can see that," his daughter replied sarcastically.

This had Carl changing direction. "Okay, let me start again. I would like to tell you a story about your mother and me. May I?"

This caught Katie off guard, blunting her anger for a moment. Curiosity got the better of her temper and she nodded.

"Thank you," her father replied, then took a deep breath, "I don't think you ever knew your mother was engaged to another man when we met."

Katie looked stunned. "No. Really?" she asked in a doubtful tome.

"Yes. That's the truth. It was someone she'd known for years, but within a month after we met, she had fallen in love with me."

"You stole her from him?" Katie replied in disbelief. "How could you?"

"I didn't," Carl shot back. "I didn't even know how she felt until after she broke the engagement."

"How could that be?"

"You know that your mother worked before we married?" Katie nodded. "Well, she was a teller at the bank when I came in as the assistant manager long ago. We hit it off as friends, at least I thought it was just a friendship. From the first day, I was told of her engagement and that was that."

Katie's mood had mellowed as she asked, "So, what happened?"

"Well, as I've already said, I concentrated on my work and then started a relationship with another woman."

Hearing this, Velma couldn't contain her own curiosity. "Who?"

"No one in this room would know her," Carl said, glancing at Velma while smiling weakly. "She moved to Des Moines years ago. It was never very serious, but Agnes apparently didn't know that."

"Mother got jealous?" Katie asked incredulously.

Carl shrugged, "I won't flatter myself with that thought. Whatever the reason, I learned a few weeks afterwards that your mother had broken off the engagement."

"So, that's when you got together?" Velma asked, apparently having taken over the mock interrogation from Katie.

Mr. Warren shook his head. "No. Not for quite a while."

"But why?" It was Velma's turn to be incredulous.

The question had Carl chuckling. "Because I was a fool, too focused on my new job and not paying attention. It took one of the other tellers, old Mrs. Abbott, to point out the error of my ways. Once I fell, I fell hard."

"Like you've done with Miss Fletcher?" The words were out of her mouth before Velma could stop them. Turning crimson, the little girl covered her mouth and looked anxiously at Katie, whose expression had not changed.

"Why did you say that?" Emily, who looked shocked, demanded.

Velma hesitated then began apologetically, "Oh, Miss Fletcher, I'm sorry. But you see, I heard you and Mr. Warren talking awhile back."

"What?" Carl interrupted. "I don't understand. Where was this? When?"

"It was out there," Velma waved toward the front of the house, "late on the night I slept here during the pageant."

"And what did you hear?" From the look on Emily's face as she asked, Velma was sure her teacher already knew the answer.

"You two were kind of arguing," Velma replied quickly as her gaze alternated between the two adults. "You were telling Mr. Warren it was too early and that you should not go on for Katie's sake. You didn't agree, Mr. Warren."

"Too early for what?" The sharp tone of Katie's question made Velma jump. "What shouldn't go on?" she added vehemently.

Haltingly, Velma stuttered out her reply. "I don't remember exactly. It had to do with your mother dying, and, well, Miss Fletcher said something about not seeing each other anymore, or something like that."

"You were *seeing* her?" Katie asked her father with venom in her voice.

Carl didn't answer her. Instead, he addressed Velma in a harsh tone, "And how did you happen to hear all this, young lady?"

"I was standing inside the front door, and..."

"You were what?" Carl interrupted angrily. "Why on earth were you there at that hour?"

"I, I couldn't sleep what with the excitement and all." Velma's voice was shaking now. "Then I heard voices and got curious."

"Nosy, you mean," Mr. Warren snapped.

"Carl," Emily said sternly.

This had Mr. Warren easing back in his chair uttering a sigh. "Sorry, Velma. Please go on."

"That's all," Velma replied, hoping to bring the unpleasant exchange to an end.

Katie wouldn't let that happen. "So, what was going on between you two?"

"Nothing," came Carl's quick reply.

"Nothing?" She looked disbelievingly to Miss Fletcher as she spoke.

Emily cleared her throat. "That's not exactly true."

"I thought so," Katie said, folding her arms across her chest and glariing out the front window.

Emily ignored the girl and continued. "Nothing had happened before that night except conversations about our growing feelings for each other."

"That's why I wanted to share the story about your mother and me," Carl interjected pleadingly. "I fell in love with Agnes back then and that's a love that will never die. But by the grace of God, I had room in my heart to fall again."

"So, now it's God's fault." Somehow Katie's hot retort struck Velma as funny. Her snicker drew hostile looks around the room.

"Sorry," she said, then giggled again.

"Stop that," Katie shouted.

Velma stood abruptly, saying, "Ah, I think now would be a good time for me to..."

"Sit down," Carl ordered. "You've created part of this, this..."

"Mess?" Velma suggested.

This time it was Mr. Warren's turn to snort a laugh.

"Daddy!" Katie cried.

"Sorry, dear," he said, sighing deeply and regaining control.

Emily cleared her throat again and pressed ahead, "I will not lie to you."

"Anymore?" Katie asked.

"We never lied to you, Katie," Emily clarified, "We just didn't tell you about our feelings for each other."

"Until now. Happy New Year," Katie added sarcastically.

"That's right," Carl said his own anger returning. "We're telling you now."

Emily stepped in again. "Other than waiting, perhaps waiting too long, to share this with you, your father and I have done nothing to be ashamed of, to embarrass you, or be disrespectful of your mother's memory."

"So you say."

"Think what you will, but that is the last I will say on that subject," Emily concluded in a calm but cool tone.

"I believe you, Miss Fletcher." Once again, Velma regretted her words before they had died in the room.

"Who asked you?" Katie said through clenched teeth.

Velma's head dropped as she apologized, "Sorry, Katie. It's just that..." she stopped.

"Just what?" Katie asked annoyedly.

After looking at everyone and wondering if she should go on, Velma relented. "It's just that you aren't seeing things too clearly."

"What?" Katie shot back defensively.

"Look, you asked me to say what I meant. Did you mean it?"

After a long pause, Katie nodded, saying, "I suppose so."

"Well, it came to me awhile back that you and I were in the same situation. You saw your father and Miss Fletcher getting close after your mother died. And my Mama and that attorney, Mr. Price have been making eyes at each other too."

This generated smiles on Emily and Carl's faces while Katie just glared at her friend. Ignoring everyone, Velma carried on, "Anyway, I suddenly realized being upset over my situation was a lot worse than yours."

Katie started to speak, but Velma forged ahead, "Naturally, you were more upset about your father, and I was more upset about my mother. You were missing your mother and I was missing my Papa. Why, I even felt guilty having fun again. You too, I bet. It was like being unfaithful.

"That's why we see what your father and my mother have been up to in the same way. And that's *all* we can see about *our situation, our parent*. But when it comes to your situation from a distance, I can see other things."

Katie could not restrain herself, "You're not making any sense."

"I know. It's just hard to find the words. I guess what I mean is we aren't really seeing, we're just feeling."

"Meaning?"

"Well, when I look at your father and Miss Fletcher, I see a lot of good things." Velma's eyes shifted to the adults. "Up until this happened, Katie, you loved Miss Fletcher, couldn't wait to learn from her. You loved your father and wanted him to get over his sorrow. Now look at you. What changed?"

"Well..." was all Katie could manage before Velma answered for her.

"What changed is two people you love have found each other. And since then, has your father been happier, something you wanted for him?'

"Ah, I guess so."

"You know so," Velma said insistently, then rushed on. "But what about Miss Fletcher? Does she seem happier?" She didn't wait for a reply. "I'll tell you that answer is no because she feels guilty about how you feel."

"I never said anything."

"You didn't have to," Emily said softly.

Velma nodded in appreciation of the confirmation, then tried to conclude her speech. "Not being quite as emotional about *your* situation, I can *see* some things more than just *feel* everything when it comes to your situation. I wish I could do the same with mine."

"Why, that is very insightful, Velma," Emily said while looking to Katie, who suddenly found something in the corner of the room interesting.

"Indeed. Well said," Carl echoed Miss Fletcher's opinion.

The room was silent for a while before Velma decided she wasn't quite finished. "Can I ask you a couple questions, Katie?"

Receiving a shrug, she took it as permission, Velma asked, "Are you afraid of losing your father if he and Miss Fletcher get married?"

Katie bristled, "Married?"

Velma could not suppress a giggle, "What else would we be talking about? So, answer my question."

"I don't know, maybe."

Velma turned to the adults. "What do you say to that?"

"That would never happen." Carl responded passionately.

"I was willing to let our relationship go for that very reason," Emily said, fighting back tears.

Velma turned back to Katie. "Do you believe them?" After another shrug, Velma asked, "Do you think your mother would want your father to be sad for the rest of his life?"

"I don't know. I guess not."

"Well, then," Velma said with finality. "Maybe you're now seeing a bit more than just feeling. Seeing what I've seen for some time but was afraid to say. Your father and Miss Fletcher are good for each other and for you. Why, if I didn't have Mama, I'd want her to be mine."

With that Velma stood. "Now I am definitely going." She headed for the front door, followed by Mr. Warren and Miss Fletcher. "I'm sorry if I said too much," she offered while puting on her coat.

"Nonsense," Miss Fletcher replied, handing the girl her scarf. "You may have saved the day."

Carl Warren hung back awkwardly. "Sorry I was so hard on you. I was just surprised..."

"Oh, that's all right," Velma saved him continued embarrassment. "I don't blame you a bit. My mother, Miss Fletcher too, can tell you that's my worst habit, being nosy that is."

"Well, in this case, that might have been a good thing," Mr. Warren said, giving her a playful pat on the top of her stocking cap.

"I hope Katie gets over being mad at us all soon. I can't imagine not being with her."

"Oh, I'm pretty sure it won't last," Emily said confidently.

"Not when she has you and me to be upset with," Carl said in a whisper.

Emily gave the man a gentle poke in the ribs in response, then turned to Velma. "Now go enjoy the rest of your last day of vacation. See you in class tomorrow."

"Good luck with *her*," Velma nodded toward the living room, "and please be nice to her, to each other."

"We got a lot out this morning," Emily said, looking somewhat relieved, "but we better get back in there and build on that."

Velma watched as Mr. Warren's expression turned gloomy. "Yes indeed. That will likely be much easier than what will come with Freddie."

They all understood how difficult that would be, given the boy's already troubled state. "One thing at a time, Carl."

"Indeed," Carl said, smiling weakly as he opened the door. "And don't worry, Velma. You two will be together again in no time."

"I hope you're right," she said, stepping out into the bitter cold, "and Happy New Year."

Velma shivered while scurrying for home, unsure whether the chill was from the cutting wind or what had just transpired, hoping her words had been helpful. Now if only she could practice some of what she had been preaching when it came to her own mother.

Back at the apartment, she was relieved to find her mother in the kitchen baking, as usual, this time for the New Year's gathering at the Jones'. Velma went to her room, changed into work clothes, and joined the family in the toasty, warm kitchen to help.

Looking at the clock on the kitchen wall, Alice nodded approvingly, "Ah, good. You're actually home a bit early." Her smile faded as she read Velma's face. "Is everything alright, girl?"

"Oh, yeah, sure."

This terse reply earned a raised brow and further inquiry. "Come on, girl. Out with it."

Velma didn't want to say anything, especially in front of her sister. Thankfully, Eugene spoke up just then, "I need to go."

"Me tooph," the three-year-old Edward said.

Sensing her younger daughter's hesitancy to share, Alice spoke to Wilma. "Please take your brothers to the outhouse."

"Ah, Mama," the familiar protest came. "It's really cold and..."

That's as far as she got. "Just do as I say, girl, and I suggest you take the opportunity yourself seeing as it's *so* cold."

"But it will take forever to get them ready."

"Nonsense. Just throw their coats on and run. That way they won't dawdle."

Shortly the three headed out the front door. When it closed, Alice turned to Velma, giving her a hard glare, "Now out with it and be quick about it."

Just as Wilma and the boys returned, Velma finished sharing what had happened at the Warren's. Alice's tongue spent a good deal of time clucking during the telling. "Well, I knew that was all going to come to a head soon. I guess now was as good a time as any."

Velma asked in surprise, "You knew about Mr. Warren and Miss Fletcher?"

"Lordy, girl, you would have to be blind not to, blind or a child," Alice said mockingly.

"Well, I hope what I said didn't do any harm."

It was Alice's turn to be surprised. "You said something? You didn't say that just now."

"I just hit the important stuff, Mama. There wasn't time for more."

Just then Wilma and the boys came into the room, "It's getting colder if that's possible," the oldest said.

"My bottom stuck to the seat," Eugene added with some odd sense of pride.

"Me tooph," Edward cried.

"No, it didn't," Wilma said.

"No fun, no fun," Edward chanted.

This had everyone laughing and allowed Velma to escape sharing any details of what she'd said at the Warren house. Several times, Alice asked for more, only to be interrupted by the children or chores. Then, bedtime arrived, puting off the subject for good, or so Velma hoped.

16
More Signs of Hard Times

As school resumed, the promised new students joined Miss Fletcher's class. One was Able Cotton. She immediately assigned him to Katie and Velma's team, something that seemed to please them more than him. In spite of his apathy, the group welcomed him warmly in the time before class started.

Just as the bell rang, the classroom door flew open. As one, Velma and Katie turned to see who had created this last-minute disruption. Their mouths fell open at the sight of the lanky Daniel Waters.

"Oh, my goodness," Katie shouted, causing Miss Fletcher to whirl around.

After a moment's pause to collect herself, the teacher smiled broadly. "Welcome back, Mr. Waters. I'd almost given up on you."

"Sorry, Miss Fletcher," Daniel said, his face bright red. "It's just that..."

Miss Fletcher held up her hand to stop him. "No need to explain. You should be up in Mrs. Rogers' eighth grade room on the third floor.'

"Oh, I didn't know."

"Just step across the main hall to the office, and someone will sign you in and show the way."

Daniel nodded. "Thank you, Miss Fletcher." Before turning to go, he gave Katie and Velma a smile and wink. Then he was gone.

It wasn't until lunch that the two girls and others that had known Daniel could corner him. "What are you doing back here?" Katie got off the first and most relevant question as the group converged in a corner of the cafeteria.

"Back to finish my last year."

Velma gave him a big hug. "That's great news." Seeing a curious Able next to her, Velma added, "This here is another new student, Able Cotton. He's in third grade with Katie and me."

"Glad to meet ya, friend," Daniel said, extending his hand. Able took it tentatively, while remaining silent. His only response was a nod.

From behind Daniel, Nancy Brown asked the next obvious question, "But what about your job at the mine?"

Daniel looked down, "I lost it because I was the low man on the totem pole. I wasn't the only one to be let go either."

"That happened to my father." It took a moment for the group to recognize the comment had come from Able.

"So, that's why your family is here?" Velma asked.

Able nodded but added no details, so Daniel went on, "Bottom line is my pay was helping keep my family above water."

"So, you moved back here *because?*" Katie asked in confusion.

Daniel smiled. "I know. Woodward isn't exactly a boom town."

"That's an understatement," Charity replied.

"Well, first, I'm the only one in the family that moved back. The mine manager told me about a job with a new freight line out of Des Moines that was starting deliveries up in this area. Thanks to the man's recommendation—I guess he thought I was a good worker—I got the job. How lucky was that?" He asked with a broad grin.

"I didn't know there was a new business in town," Charity Jones said, then asked, "any of you hear about that?"

As heads shook, Able Cotton spoke for a second time. "My father runs the office."

Everyone stared at him in surprise. "Well, I'll be darned," Daniel exclaimed, "My boss is your pa?"

"I guess so," Able replied, considering a smile briefly, but settling for a nod.

"That's wonderful," Velma said. "But if you're the only one who moved back, where are you staying?"

"I just got in yesterday, so that has to be a priority," Daniel replied. "Mr. Cotton said I could bunk in the back of the new freight office; it used to be that big old farm implement store on Main. I can't stay there for long, have to find a place quick-like. It better be cheap though. I'm open to suggestions."

"What are you looking for?" Charity inquired.

Daniel smiled, "I don't need nothin' but a room and a bed." Then he added, "maybe with food included. But I won't have much to spare. I'll mail whatever extra I make back to my folks in Boone."

"Golly, won't you miss your family?" Charity asked, giving the handsome young man a sorrowful look.

Daniel nodded weakly saying, "Sure, but it ain't that far to Boone. I'll get back there whenever I can. If I'm lucky, Able here's father will send me that way from time to time." He glanced at the boy, giving him a hopeful look. Able didn't react.

"Well, we all can ask around about a place to stay, starting with our own families," Nancy Brown suggested.

Velma chuckled. "I don't think I should ask my Mama, seeing as we're busting at the seams in our apartment already. I can sure help with the looking though."

There was a total agreement among the group, which had Daniel looking humbled. "Gee, thanks everyone."

The bell called everyone back to class. The distraction of Able's arrival and Daniel's return had everyone in a good mood. In spite of the circumstances that brought them, it was good to have students joining, rather than leaving, school.

When Velma and Wilma arrived at the mercantile that afternoon, they were full of chatter about events of the day. Wilma got in the first licks. "I heard Lily Cotton was quite a handful for Mrs. Jacobs. She talked constantly and bad-mouthed the teacher. She spent one whole hour standing in the corner, facing the wall."

Alice clicked her tongue on the top of her mouth, making a sound of displeasure, then said, "how did you get any learning done?"

"Oh, we managed," Wilma replied, then added, "But there's more."

Alice and Velma waited impatiently while Wilma finished her glass of milk before continuing, "We got another new girl in class. Her name is Gretchen, and..." She paused for effect, "her folks just came over from Germany."

"Must be from the family out at the old Tomlin farm," Alice speculated. "I heard a family had moved in there. Rumor had it they were foreign. They have a last name?"

Wilma thought for a moment. "I think it's Swartz, Schultz, something like that."

"What was she like?" Velma asked, eager for more.

"Well, she could barely speak any English and was very shy. She is old enough to be in an upper grade, maybe 12 or 13, but since she couldn't communicate good, Mrs. Jacobs put her in my class. And guess what."

"Out with it, girl," Alice barked, "we don't have all day."

Wilma shot her mother an angry look but did as she was told. "Mrs. Jacobs knows how to speak German."

At hearing this, Alice issued an amused snort, "Land-a-Goshen, child, there are a ton of folks with German roots around here. We even have some German blood." At this both girls' eyes grew wide. Alice nodded and went on, "So, it doesn't surprise me that Mrs. Jacobs speaks the language."

"But the Germans were the enemy in the war," Wilma said with a sneer. "They killed some of our soldiers."

"We killed a lot of theirs too," Alice said flatly.

Velma abruptly asked, "Do you know anyone from here who died?"

"No." Her mother's abrupt tone had her younger daughter wondering if that was true. She chose not to press the matter, however.

Alice headed for the kitchen while saying, "Best we put all that behind us. After all, now we're all on the same side fighting this cruel economy. Hard work is what will get people through. Speaking of which, we all have work to do."

As she followed her mother, Wilma said, "I do feel sorry for her though."

Alice gave her oldest a hard look. "Maybe so, but there's nothin' much you can do about it. So mind your own business I say."

"But aren't we supposed to love our neighbor," Velma said innocently.

Alice was caught up short. "Well, yes. That's what the good book says, but loving and associating are two different things," Alice retorted.

Velma looked confused. "So, it's alright for us to welcome and be friends with the Cottons and Johnsons who are colored, but ignore white folk who talk funny?"

"It's not that simple. You're too young to understand," Alice said dismissively. "For now, both of you mind what I say, understood?"

"Yes, Mama," the girls replied as one.

"Good," Alice said, with a firm nod to end the discussion. To ensure that was the case, she asked Velma, "And what about your first day back?"

"Oh, it was a wonderful day, Mama," Velma said with a broad smile.

Alice pressed for more. "Did Katie Warren do all right?"

"Oh, she did good."

"Really?" Alice was clearly unconvinced. "After what you told me yesterday..."

Wilma interrupted, "What did you tell Mama? What happened with Katie?"

"Never you mind, girl," Alice said sharply before Velma could reply. "Go find the boys. I think they are with Annie up front. Then to your sewing or homework."

"Ah, Mama."

"Git!"

Once Wilma was out of earshot, Alice said, "now tell me about how Katie and Miss Fletcher got along."

"Honest, Mama," Velma stood firm, "you would never have known anything bad had happened."

"Uh huh," Alice grunted doubtfully, then she remembered something else. "You never told me what you said at the Warren's yesterday. Mind you, girl, saying nothing would have been the right thing to do."

"I know, Mama," Velma said, dropping her eyes.

"Well, don't let me hold you back now."

With that, Velma did the best she could to recall her words. She concluded with, "And I just told Katie I thought Mr. Warren and Miss Fletcher were good for each other, and..."

Her pause had Alice prodding, "And what? Finish girl."

"And, I said if I didn't have you, I'd be happy to have Miss Fletcher as a mother."

Alice was speechless for a moment, her face slack. Recovering, she said sternly, "Well you *do* have me, thank you very much." Velma cringed as her mother added, "But Miss Fletcher would—will make a very good stepmother."

"You think so?" Velma said with relief.

"Wouldn't have said so if I didn't mean it."

Velma smiled, then realized exactly what her mother had said. "You said 'will', Mama. Do you really think..."

Alice broke in, "That's up to God, but I'm pretty sure how this is going to turn out."

"Wonderful!" Velma practically shouted.

Alice gave her youngest daughter a rare warm look while adding, "And, Velma, what you said, though inappropriate to have said at all, well, those were good words. You're quite..." She paused, searching for the right word.

"Nosy?"

Alice's laugh surprised Velma. "That too. I was thinking more along the lines of perceptive."

"What does per, per-petive mean?'

"You can look it up in the dictionary upstairs where you're going right now to help with the boys."

"Yes, Mama." Velma turned and headed for the curtain leading into the store, then turned back. "So, you're not mad at me?"

The corners of Alice's mouth turned up again. "Only a little, nosy one." Then she added, "More important, has Katie forgiven you?"

"I think so." Then she turned again, only to whirl around like a top. "Oh, I forgot the other news."

"What other news?"

She smiled broadly. "Two new boys came to school."

"Two?" Alice asked incredulously.

"One was Able Cotton."

Alice nodded, "I assumed as much. And the other?"

"Daniel Waters is back," Velma said excitedly.

"Daniel?" Alice said with real surprise. "I thought he was working at a mine up Boone way."

"He got laid off."

"So, his family's back?'

Velma shook her head. "Just him. Oh, and he has no place to stay right now."

"Does he even have a job?"

Velma's smile was back. "Yes, and guess what? He'll be working for little Able Cotton's father."

"Isaac? Doin' what?"

"Hauling freight."

Alice pondered all this for a moment. "You are surely a wealth of information today, girl."

"I guess so, Mama," Velma agreed, then remembered, "and one thing more. Daniel's classmates are helping to find a place for him to live."

"That's nice of you all."

Velma nodded, basking in her mother's praise. "So, will you ask around too?"

"Of course. Now git upstairs before Wilma starts whining again."

"I hear you found a place," Nancy Brown said to Daniel a few days later. This was the first day that his work schedule allowed him time to attend class.

"He did?" Velma asked, pleasantly surprised.

Daniel nodded. "But it's only temporary."

Overhearing this, young Able Cotton said, "My grandpa arranged it."

"He sure did, along with Reverend Jones and his wife," Daniel said with a smile, "I'm stayin' in the basement of the church, provided I keep it neat."

"Well, I guess we can stop our looking," Velma said with relief.

Daniel's smile remained as he reiterated, "Like I said, this is just temporary until I can afford a room of my own, assuming business picks up that is. So, don't stop looking."

"You aren't having as much luck getting to class as you have been at getting a place to stay," Charity Jones pointed out.

Daniel nodded forlornly. "That's for sure. I don't know if this is going to work." Just then Miss Fletcher entered the room. "If you'll excuse me," Daniel said while moving in the teacher's direction. "I want to talk with Miss Fletcher before class starts."

His friends watched Daniel and Miss Fletcher hold a brief conversation until the bell rang. As he passed her desk, Velma whispered, "what did she say?"

"That we'd talk more at the end of the day," he whispered in reply.

Soon the classroom's focus turned to the day's lessons. Before the students realized it, lunchtime had arrived. A bitter January day kept them all inside, so everyone headed for the overcrowded gym that served as the lunchroom.

Once Velma and friends had found a table and opened ther lunchboxes, she asked them, "You all are coming to our apartment on Wednesday for my birthday party, right?" Everyone's head nodded excitedly.

"What about Wilma and the boys?" Katie asked, wearing a concerned look.

"They'll be at the mercantile doing some of *my* chores as a birthday gift. So, you can head over to our place right after school gets out."

"What's your mother making for us—I mean you," Nancy said with a snicker.

Velma gave the group a big smile, "She's making that cake she makes for me every year."

Nancy considered this for a moment, then said, "I didn't come to the party last year, so I wouldn't know what kind of cake it was."

"I didn't have a party last year since Mrs. Warren..." Velma stopped abruptly and turned to her best friend, "Sorry, Katie."

Katie gave her a forgiving shrug, then spoke to Nancy, "If it's the same one Mrs. Steele served when Velma turned six, it will be devil's food with thick white frosting."

"Yum," Charity said, licking her lips. "What else?"

Velma laughed, "You do like to eat, missy."

"When it comes to something your mother makes, you are absolutely right," Charity replied with enthusiasm. "What else will she have?"

"I don't know. We'll all be surprised when we get there I guess."

"Surprised about what?" Daniel Waters' deepening voice startled the group as he approached their table.

"Just a girl thing," Charity said through a suddenly shy smile. Having just turned thirteen, she had started to show interest in the older boys. The arrival of the now seventeen-year-old had definitely drawn her attention this day.

"That sounds mysterious," Daniel said mischievously.

"I'm having a birthday party with all my girlfriends, that's all," Velma explained.

Daniel just nodded and turned to leave before Velma stopped him by asking, "What did you find out from Miss Fletcher?"

"She thinks me attending class in fits and starts isn't going to work."

A look of despair appeared on Charity's face. "So, you won't be coming to school anymore."

"Afraid not," Daniel replied, not seeming to be disappointed, however, as he added, "but Miss Fletcher offered to tutor me in preparation for the necessary test to graduate."

Everyone chattered excitedly at once before Nancy said, "The two of you are already awfully busy. How will you both manage that?"

"Well, she figures, I wasn't that far off graduatin' when I left. I had mastered some subjects pretty well, but others I ain't so good at."

"Like English," Charity interrupted, giving Daniel a disapproving look while the others chuckled.

"Correct," he replied with a friendly wink. "So, I've promised to spend every spare minute doin', I mean doing homework she'll be giving me and meeting once a week until she thinks I'm ready."

"How long will that take?" Katie asked.

"If I'm lucky, I'll take the test with the rest of the current eighth-graders next May or June."

Charity stepped over to Daniel and gave him a gentle hug. "That's great. And if I can help in any way, just ask."

"The same goes for the rest of us, Daniel," Velma said.

He snorted, "I think I'm beyond what a seven-year-old can teach me."

"I'll be eight in two days, smarty-pants," she shot back defiantly, "and I bet I can still teach you a thing or two about history, and..."

"I'm just joking, Velma." Daniel cut her off holding up his hands defensively. "I know there is a lot that you all can and will do, if you get the chance."

Then Nancy raised a good question, "When you pass, what then?"

"Not sure," Daniel answered. "I haven't gotten that far. For now, the goal is to get that certificate and make some money at the same time."

"That's a lot to chew." Charity sounded impressed.

"I know, but I gotta do it, me and my family need the money," Daniel sounded a bit desperate. "Plus, I've seen the hard life of farming and mining. I don't want to go back into a hole or push a horse around a field no more—I mean, anymore."

"So, hauling freight will be better?" Nancy asked without sarcasm.

"It has to be," Daniel answered, then continued, "but that's not what I expect to do the rest of my life."

"What then?" Charity asked.

"Who knows with the way things are going." Daniel replied. "For now, it's a darn sight better than being unemployed. Which reminds me, I better get back to work."

"Goodbye, Daniel," Charity said, nearly swooning as the other girls giggled. Her sudden glare stopped that and prevented the possibility of further teasing.

"Don't be a stranger," Velma said to ease the tension.

Daniel replied over his shoulder a bit too loudly for her liking, "Count on it, and happy birthday, *little one*." He missed seeing her tongue stuck out in reply.

A harsh, nearly snowless winter followed, lasting deep into a spring that spawned the usual array of tornados across the state. A couple hit near Woodward, bringing back terrifying memories for Velma. Fortunately, no one had died, but property damage had been significant.

All during this time, a steady stream of people flowed in and out of Woodward. More left than came, headed primarily to bigger cities. As a result, Woodward's business community continued a slow, but steady, downward spiral. By summer, two more long-standing businesses had shuttered their doors.

There were exceptions to this norm, however, one being the new freight line. Combining reliability with rock-bottom pricing, it soon became the carrier of choice. The effort this required took a toll on both Isaiah Cotton and Daniel Waters. For the boss, the cost was mainly in lost family time. For Daniel it was long hours for a meager paycheck, leaving little time to study. Still the two, like so many others, did what it took to survive.

Compounding the problem for the community at large was a poor harvest. This was the result of a dry planting season, followed by a wet fall. Though crop prices rose, that was not enough to offset the low yields. As a result, farm foreclosures continued.

While Alice and her adult friends worried constantly about these developments, Wilma and Velma enjoyed a year full of learning and adventure. At the end of the school year, the two went off for two weeks at the Skinner farm. There, after nearly three years, they had the chance to once again experience farm life, though the focus was much more on having fun than doing chores.

With the girls gone, Alice's mother came to help with the boys. During the two weeks, the women worked to rebuild their relationship while baking and chasing Eugene and Edward. The women often remarked at the end of the day how much they missed the girls' help with the boys, who always seemed to be in some kind of trouble.

When her husband David's hours were cut in March, Annie Anderson returned to work part-time, bringing toddler Lizzy and month-old Timmy with her. This had Tessa complaining that young'uns were taking over the place. Indeed, when Eugene and Edward joined the others, her observation seemed spot on.

With Annie's return, Melva Johnson's clerking duties shrank. This loss of income was a strain for her and Otis. Thankfully, over the course of the year, Melva's fledgling mending business coupled with overflow sewing from Alice, helped to see them through. In the process, the Johnsons had become a welcomed fixture in the community.

For over five years, Woodward and Dallas County had seen little respite from worry and sacrifice. This constant strain invariably led to conflicts, some of them quite intense. Just when tensions would reach the boiling point, however, something usually happened to bring the community together. Such was the case on Christmas Eve, 1924.

"Are you about ready?" Alice impatiently called out to Wilma, as she and Velma waited. The boys were already at the Anderson's for the night so the rest of the Steeles could enjoy a peaceful Church service. It was going to be a very cold walk on this bitter cold night, which promised a hard winter to come. The almanac said so.

School break had started that afternoon. Once home, everyone pitched in to finish baking the night's abundance of treats. Some were earmarked for the church, with the rest going to the Jones' house for the traditional Christmas Eve gathering of close friends.

Velma was excited that Katie and Carl Warren would be coming for the first time in two years. Miss Fletcher would not, however. Though Katie was growing more comfortable with the relationship between her father and the teacher, it was still too early to make the leap to the tradition started by Agnes Warren before she passed.

Katie had promised to come by to help carry the bounty of baked goodies. So, it was no surprise when hasty footsteps could be heard on the stairs, followed by a heavy knock on the door.

With a start, Velma headed that way saying, "It must be really cold outside for Katie to pound like that." As she threw open the door and began to admonish her friend, "You don't have to knock the door ... " She didn't finish.

Standing next to Katie was a wide-eyed blond in her early teens, shivering uncontrollably. Without a word, Katie shoved the girl through the door. After a moment's hesitation, Velma slammed the door against the cold.

"I found Gretchen at the bottom of your stairs looking about half dead."

"Who?" Alice asked incredulously.

"Gretchen?" Wilma said in surprise as she entered the livingroom. "What is she doing here?"

"I don't know," Katie replied as all eyes stared at the girl.

She was wearing a threadbare coat over an equally worn summer cotton dress. With no boots, no scarf, and no gloves to fend off the bitter cold, it was no wonder she was shaking uncontrollably. Her skin appeared to be an eerie shade of blue.

Alice stood quickly and moved to Gretchen's side. "What is it girl?" When she didn't reply, she added, "Cat got your tongue?"

"Gretchen doesn't speak much English," Wilma did the answering. "This is the new girl I told you about when school started, Gretchen Schultz, the German." Then in a guilty tone, she added, "I kinda made friends with her." Hurrying on, she added, "I know you said not to, but ... "

"Never you mind that," Alice cut her off. "Hand me that throw on the back of the couch and, Velma, get her some water, oh, and if the coffee is still warm, bring some of that too."

A moment later, Gretchen was on the couch wrapped in the blanket. Only then did she speak, repeating in a quivering voice, "bitte helfen sie, bitte helfen sie," as her shaking grew stronger.

"Don't just stand there," Alice said to the room, get another blanket. Wilma immediately headed down the hall.

Then with a sudden reassuring smile Alice seldom showed her daughters, she calmly asked the girl, "Help, you need help?"

As if reminded of her purpose, Gretchen leaped to her feet nearly knocking the glass from Velma's hand, "Ja, ja." Then, with intensity, she added, "yes, I mean ... help."

"Now we're gettin' someplace," Alice said with a nod. "Are you hurt?"

After processing the word, Gretchen shook her head. "Nein."

"That means no," Katie offered.

Alice frowned. "I know that much."

Wilma arrived with a blanket from her bed, handing it to her mother. As Alice took it, she asked her oldest in a judgmental tone, "Bein' her *friend* and all, have you learned some of her language?"

"Oh, no, mama."

"Wilma?" Alice said, sending her daughter one of her famous looks.

"Well, maybe a little."

"Then sit down here and help me sort this out."

It seemed to Velma that it took hours to get the story haltingly from Gretchen. Her father had fallen from the loft in their barn. Somehow his wife and daughter had gotten him into the house. Then she had walked nearly two miles in the bitter cold for help.

"What does *schafen* mean?" Alice asked Wilma, "She keeps saying that."

She shrugged then, concentrating and in a stilted tone, said, "Ah, was bedeutet schafen?"

Gretchen shook her head, "Nein, no. It is *schlafen*. I am sorry. He, how you say, sleep."

"Your father is asleep?"

"Ja."

Alice was up in a flash, "Wilma, you stay here with Gretchen and keep her warm and drinking plenty of liquids. Katie, you head out to see if Doc Joseph is home. If he isn't, head to the church and tell Mr. Hanks what's happened."

"What are you going to do, Mama?" Wilma asked anxiously.

"We're gonna help them, right?" Velma said, already heading for the coat rack.

"Right," Alice replied emphatically. "While I gather some other stuff together ... "

Velma interrupted as she headed to the door, "While I get old Nelly hitched up."

"Right again," Alice said, headed for the kitchen. "I'll be right behind you."

At the barn, Alice found Nelly harnessed and Velma throwing wood from the stack next to the Hanks' barn into the back. "I thought they might need some on a night like tonight."

"Always thinkin', Velma," Alice's compliment warmed her daughter's heart while sweat rolled down her face in spite of the bitter cold. Minutes later, they were ready to leave. Unfortunately, no other adults joined them. So the two climbed aboard, covered up with blankets and headed off.

Though still not six o'clock, the cold was so intense that the steam from Nelly's heavy labor nearly obscured the road. Thankfully, the Schultz farm was just off the main road, easy to find. Careful not to overtax the horse in the cold, it took a good while to cover the two miles. As they approached the nearly dark house, the front door flew open.

A woman emerged, waving frantically, a mixture of relief and worry etched on her face. Smiling reassuredly and ignoring what she was saying in German, Alice grabbed an armload and went inside. Velma scooped up what was left and quickly followed.

Once across the threshold, the nearly nine-year-old suddenly stopped. Staring into the living room, dark except for a gas lantern, she saw the figure of a man lying inert on a couch.

"Papa," she whispered reflexively, suddenly transported back in time.

"Don't just stand there girl," Alice said in a hoarse whisper. "Can't you see the fire is down to embers?"

"Yes, Mama," Velma said and, pushing aside the memory, dashed to the hearth. Finding no wood in the bucket, she rushed back out the front door and grabbed some of the wood she'd brought.

Soon the fire was coaxed back to life. As it intensified, Velma could now see her mother helping Mrs. Schultz tend to her husband. She heard her mother call the wife, Gertrude and the man Otto. Gertrude was gently covering Otto with another blanket, then put a cold cloth on his head. Meanwhile, Alice rebandaged a wound on the man's arm.

Throwing another log on the fire, Velma headed outside. She unloaded the rest of the wood, then unharnessed Nelly and led her to an empty stall in the Schultz's barn. Thankfully there was a pile of fresh hay waiting to reward the loyal animal. Closing the double doors carefully to cut the cold, she ran back to the house across the rock-hard yard.

The blazing fire now had the chill in retreat. With a sigh, Velma fell into an old stuffed chair in a corner, suddenly exhausted from all the tension, excitement, and exertion in the debilitating cold. Slowly warmed by the roaring fire, she drifted off, only to awaken with a start from a nightmare about that cold night years earlier.

Across the living room, Velma saw Alice and Gertrude sprawled in two side chairs, looking just as exhausted as she. A quick glance toward the sofa eased her sudden anxiety. Unlike her father, it seemed Otto Schultz would survive.

Then looking back to her mother, who for once was not in perpetual motion, she was struck by how courageous and capable Mama was in almost every situation. It also struck Velma that, in spite of what she perceived to be a bit of lingering prejudice, her mother had not hesitated to help the Schultz family, perfect strangers. It made her smile.

The warmth in the room began to lull her back to sleep, until suddenly the front door burst open and what seemed like half of Woodward arrived. With a mixture of German and English filling the house, the place was alive with light and hope.

Dr. Joseph checked Otto over and declared he would fully recover. Grace Jones, Melva Johnson and others set out food from the Christmas Eve potluck, while Otis and Henry fed livestock in the barn. And Daniel Waters took over fireplace duty, while Charity Jones listened attentively to Velma sharing details of the night's events.

Very early Christmas morning, Alice and Velma left in their wagon driven by Henry Hanks. While Alice sat at his side, Velma lay in the back under a down comforter loaned to her by Mrs. Schultz. Alice had promised Gertrude they would return it with Gretchen later that day. This had her smiling broadly and wishing all *Frohe Weihnachten!*

Tessa was waiting when the two arrived at the apartment. The Johnsons had swung by to tell Gretchen her father would be fine. Gleefully, she had fallen into bed with Wilma, exhausted. Without a word, Velma headed to her room, hardly noticing the presents under the Christmas tree. Alice was too tired to protest this kindness from the community and just hugged Mrs. Hanks long and hard before she left.

In the silent apartment, snug under Mrs. Schultz's comforter, Velma's thoughts turned to her mother's unyielding courage and steadfastness always. Tonight was no exception. She wanted to be like that, have the courage to face whatever the future brought.

As the last bit of excitement faded, Velma wondered if she'd dream again about her Papa's death. Suddenly Velma realized that, even though she had been terrified at the time, she'd done what needed to be done. And this night she had acted with some of the same courage born four years earlier. With that thought, Velma drifted off thinking this would be a Christmas to remember, a special kind of gift.

The End

ACKNOWLEDGMENTS

First and foremost, I must acknowledge my late mother, Velma Gooding, who spent many an hour with her youngest sharing endless stories of life across her century plus of life. Her memory was amazing.

Dixie and Russell Boyles, an inspiring couple who shared with me their vast knowledge of local Iowa history. They served the Woodward community through the 1970s and 1980s publishing the local newspaper *The Woodward Enterprise*.

Thanks to Myrna Griffith, the Woodward Library Director, who connected me with so many members of the community, and also read the early draft of the book to help ensure historical accuracy.

Woodward Councilwoman Mary Bustad, who loves her Iowa community, and took a close look at the manuscript at a key moment in its development.

To Onnie Vandusen, who grew up in a neighboring state at about the same time frame as my mom and read the book in its early drafts and encouraged my efforts.

Tracy Lyn, who lovingly worked with the image of my mom and created a dynamic cover, a true tribute to her story and spirit.

Audrey Mapes and Katya Mason, whose dedicated and meticulous attention to detail polished the work, making it shine.

Colleen Sheehan, for the elegant layout that compliments the words making for a satisfying read.

Creative Center of America—Robin Blakely, Melanie Geiss and Garrett Stroginis—who have nurtured, encouraged, and loved me through this book and more.

And for my dearest Sarah, a wife that tolerates living with a writer with patience, grace, and humor.

The sweet aroma of Alice Steele's cinnamon rolls is one of the most comforting reminders of the community's traditional values.

Visit
WWW.GLGOODING.COM/CINNAMON

Iowa ... It's simply the Heartland. Find out more about Woodward, Iowa, where this story began.

Visit
WWW.GLGOODING.COM/IOWA

G. L. GOODING

American novelist G. L. Gooding is the author of four compelling novels.

Met with glowing industry reviews, *Fresh Snow on Bedford Falls* is the award-winning historical mystery that picks up where the classic film "It's a Wonderful Life" ends. Available in paperback, e-book, and a separate large-print edition, the novel shares new layers of suspense, history, revelation, and redemption as a determined bank examiner pursues the truth about George Bailey, Mr. Potter, and the money that Uncle Billy failed to deposit that fateful day.

Gooding's second book, *Yellum*, shines the spotlight on the challenging life of an orphaned donkey with the divine purpose to carry the pregnant Mary to Bethlehem for the birth of the Christ child.

Murder in Minnesota, launches the Wandering Woodie Mystery series about a young veteran who returns home from the Vietnam War in the early 1970s and takes the road trip of a lifetime with his ragtag group of friends.

Where Courage Began kicks off the series based on the life of the author's mother and shines light on Depression-era life for a widow and her young children in Woodward, Iowa.

Author G. L. Gooding and wife, Sarah, live in Chagrin Falls, Ohio.

VELMA'S STORY CONTINUES.

In Book Two: *The Road to Resilience*, Velma finds the arduous experiences of her early years essential to overcoming the unexpected events that are yet to come.

It's Christmas Day, 1924, and young Velma is still breathless from the excitement of the previous night. The events of that Christmas Eve brought her a feeling of warm satisfaction, knowing that the small town she loved had rallied around outsiders in their moment of real need. Still, the future for the Steele family and others in the community, continued to require great fortitude, courage, and most of all, resilience.

Follow Velma's continuing journey, one filled with family, friends, and challenges, old and new. Experience her transitions from child to woman as the Great Depression breaks like a wave across the country, and the clouds of yet another war gather.

READ CHAPTER ONE OF THE ROAD TO RESILIENCE NOW AT:

WWW.GLGOODING.COM/READ-MORE

Made in the USA
Monee, IL
23 August 2021